THE GIRL AT
COBHURST

FRANK R. STOCKTON

1st WORLD
LIBRARY
Literary Society

The Girl at Cobhurst

Frank Richard Stockton

© 1st World Library, 2007
PO Box 2211
Fairfield, IA 52556
www.1stworldlibrary.com
First Edition

LCCN: 2007901788

Softcover ISBN: 978-1-4218-4256-1
Hardcover ISBN: 978-1-4218-4158-8
eBook ISBN: 978-1-4218-4354-4

Purchase *"The Girl at Cobhurst"*
as a traditional bound book at:
www.1stWorldLibrary.com/purchase.asp?ISBN=978-1-4218-4256-1

1st World Library is a literary, educational organization
dedicated to:

- Creating a free internet library of downloadable ebooks

  - Hosting writing competitions and offering book
    publishing scholarships.

Interested in more 1st World Library books?
contact: literacy@1stworldlibrary.com
Check us out at: www.1stworldlibrary.com

1st World Library Literary Society

Giving Back to the World

"If you want to work on the core problem, it's early school literacy."

- James Barksdale, former CEO of Netscape

"No skill is more crucial to the future of a child, or to a democratic and prosperous society, than literacy."

- Los Angeles Times

Literacy... means far more than learning how to read and write... The aim is to transmit... knowledge and promote social participation."

- UNESCO

"Literacy is not a luxury, it is a right and a responsibility. If our world is to meet the challenges of the twenty-first century we must harness the energy and creativity of all our citizens."

- President Bill Clinton

"Parents should be encouraged to read to their children, and teachers should be equipped with all available techniques for teaching literacy, so the varying needs and capacities of individual kids can be taken into account."

- Hugh Mackay

CONTENTS

CHAPTER I

DR. TOLBRIDGE

It was about the middle of a March afternoon when Dr. Tolbridge, giving his horse and buggy into the charge of his stable boy, entered the warm hall of his house. His wife was delighted to see him; he had not been at home since noon of the preceding day.

"Yes," said he, as he took off his gloves and overcoat, "the Pardell boy is better, but I found him in a desperate condition."

"I knew that," said Mrs. Tolbridge, "when you told me in your note that you would be obliged to stay with him all night."

The doctor now walked into his study, changed his overcoat for a well-worn smoking-jacket, and seated himself in an easy chair before the fire. His wife sat by him.

"Thank you," he said, in answer to her inquiries, "but I do not want anything to eat. After I had gone my round this morning I went back to the Pardells, and had my dinner there. The boy is doing very well. No, I was not up all night. I had some hours' sleep on the big sofa."

"Which doesn't count for much," said his wife.

"It counts for some hours," he replied, "and Mrs. Pardell did not sleep at all."

Dr. Tolbridge, a man of moderate height, and compactly built, with some touches of gray in his full, short beard, and all the light of youth in his blue eyes, had been for years the leading physician in and about Thorbury. He lived on the outskirts of the little town, but the lines of his practice extended in every direction into the surrounding country.

The doctor's wife was younger than he was; she had a high opinion of him, and had learned to diagnose him, mentally, morally, and physically, with considerable correctness. It may be asserted, in fact, that the doctor seldom made a diagnosis of a patient as exact as those she made of him. But then it must be remembered that she had only one person to exert her skill upon, while he had many.

The Tolbridge house was one of the best in the town, but the family was small. There was but one child, a boy of fourteen, who was now away at school. The doctor had readjusted the logs upon the andirons, and was just putting the tongs in their place when a maidservant came in.

"There's a boy here, sir," she said, "from Miss Panney. She's sent for you in a hurry."

In the same instant the doctor and his wife turned in their chairs and fixed their eyes upon the servant, but there was nothing remarkable about her; she had delivered her message and stood waiting. The doctor's fists were clenched and there was a glitter in his eye. He seemed on the point of saying something in a loud voice, but he changed his mind, and quietly said, "Tell the boy to come here," and turned back to the fire. Then, when the girl had gone, he struck his fist upon his knee and ejaculated, "Confound Miss Panney!"

"Harry!" exclaimed his wife, "you should not speak of your patients in that way, but I agree with you perfectly;" and then, addressing the boy, who had just entered, and who stood by the door, "Do you mean to say that there is anything serious the matter with Miss Panney?" she said severely. "Does she really want to see the doctor immediately?"

"That's what they told me, ma'am," said the boy, looking about him at the books and the furniture. "They told me that she was took bad, and that I must come here first to tell the doctor to come right away, and if he wasn't at home to leave that message."

"How did you come?" asked Mrs. Tolbridge; "on horseback?"

"No, ma'am; with a wagon."

"You could have come a great deal quicker without the wagon," said she.

"Oh, yes, but then I've got to stop at the store going back."

"That will do," said Mrs. Tolbridge; "you can go now and attend to your other business."

The doctor was quietly looking into the fire, and as his wife turned to him he gave a little snort.

"I was just beginning to get up enough energy," he remarked, "to think of putting on my slippers."

"Well, put them on," said she, in a very decided tone.

"No," replied the doctor, "that will not do; of course I must go to her."

"You mustn't do anything of the kind!" exclaimed Mrs. Tolbridge, her eyes sparkling. "How many times by night and by day has that woman called you away on a fool's errand? It is likely as not that there is nothing more the matter with her than there is with me. She has no right to worry the life out of you in this way. She ought to have gone to heaven long ago."

"You shouldn't talk of my patients in that way, Kitty," said the doctor; "and in the opinion of a good many of her neighbors the old lady is not bound for heaven."

"I don't care where she is going, but one thing is certain: you are not going to her this afternoon. You are not fit for it."

"You must remember, Kitty," said the doctor, "that Miss Panney is an old lady, and though she may sound many a false alarm, the true alarm is to be expected, and I would much prefer to go by daylight than to wait until after supper. The roads are bad, the air is raw, and she would keep me nobody knows how late. I want to go to bed early to-night."

"And that is what you are going to do," said Mrs. Tolbridge.

He looked at her inquiringly. "Harry," said she, "you have been up nearly all night. You have been working the greater part of this day, and I do not intend to let you drive three miles to be nearly talked to death by Racilia Panney. No, you needn't shake your head in that way; she is not to be neglected. I shall go myself and see what is the matter with her, and if it is really anything serious, I can then let you know. I do not believe she would have sent for you at all, if she had not known the wagon was going to town."

"But, my dear," said the doctor, "you cannot—"

"Yes, I can," interrupted his wife. "I want some fresh air and shall enjoy the drive, and Buckskin has done nothing for two days. I shall take the cart, Tom can get up behind, and I can go there in less than half an hour."

"But if there really is anything the matter—" said the doctor.

"It's just as likely as not," interrupted his wife, "that what she wants is somebody to talk to, and that a minister or a lawyer or a stranger from foreign parts would do just as well as you. And now put on your slippers, push the sofa up to the fire, and take your nap, and I'll go and see how the case really stands."

The doctor smiled. "I have no more to say," said he. "There are angels who bless us by coming, and there are angels who bless us by going. You belong to both classes. But don't stay too long."

"In any case I shall be back before dark," she said, and with a kiss on his forehead she left him.

Dr. Tolbridge looked into the fire and considered.

"Ought I to let her go?" he asked himself. This question, mingled with various thoughts and recollections of former experiences with Miss Panney, occupied the doctor's mind until he heard the swift rolling of the dog-cart wheels as they passed his window. Then he arose, put on his slippers, drew up the soft cushioned sofa, and lay down for a nap.

In about half an hour he was aroused by the announcement that Miss Bannister had called to see him.

Long practice in that sort of thing made him wake in an instant, and the young lady who was ushered into the study had no idea that she had disturbed the nap of a tired man. She was a very pretty girl, handsomely dressed; she had large blue eyes, and a very gentle and sweet expression, tinged, however, by an anxious sadness.

"Who is sick, Miss Dora?" asked the doctor, quickly, as he shook hands with her.

She did not seem to understand him. "Nobody," she said. "That is, I have come to see you about myself."

"Oh," said he, "pray take a seat. I imagined from your face," he continued, with a smile, "that some one of your family was in desperate need of a doctor."

"No," said she, "it is I. For a long time I have thought of consulting you, and to-day I felt I must come."

"And what is the matter?" he asked.

"Doctor," said she, a tear forcing itself into each of her beautiful eyes, "I believe I am losing my mind."

"Indeed," said the doctor; "and how is your general health?"

"Oh, that's all right," answered Miss Dora. "I do not think there is the least thing the matter with me that way. It is all my mind. It has been failing me for a good while."

"How?" he asked. "What are the symptoms?"

"Oh, there are ever so many of them," she said; "I can't think of them all. I have lost all interest in everything in this world. You remember how much interest I used to take in things?"

"Indeed I do," said he.

"The world is getting to be all a blank to me," she said; "everything is blank."

"Your meals?" he asked.

"No," she said. "Of course I must eat to live."

"And sleep?"

"Oh, I sleep well enough. Indeed, I wish I could sleep all the time, so that I could not know how the world—at least its pleasures and affections—are passing away from me. All this is dreadful, doctor, when you come to think of it. I have thought and thought and thought about it, until it has become perfectly plain to me that I am losing my mind."

Dr. Tolbridge looked into the fire.

"Well," said he, presently, "I am glad to hear it."

Miss Dora sprang to her feet.

"Oh, sit down," said he, "and let me explain myself. My advice is, if you lose your mind, don't mind the loss. It really will do you good. That sounds hard and cruel, doesn't it? But wait a bit. It often happens that the minds of young people are like their first teeth—what are called milk teeth, you know. These minds and these teeth do very well for a time, but after a while they become unable to perform the services which will be demanded of them, and they are shed, or at least they ought to be. Sometimes, of course, they have to be extracted."

"Nonsense, doctor," said the young lady, smiling in spite of herself, "you cannot extract a mind."

"Well, perhaps not exactly that," he answered, "but we can help it to be absorbed and to disappear, and so make a way for the strong, vigorous mind of maturity, which is certain to succeed it. All this has happened and is happening to you, Miss Dora. You have lost your milk mind, and the sooner it is gone the better. You will be delighted with the one that succeeds it. Now then, can you give me an idea about how angry you are?"

"I am not angry at all," she replied, "but I feel humiliated. You think my mental sufferings are all fanciful."

"Oh, no," said the doctor; "to continue the dental simile, they are the last aches of your youthful mentality, forced to make way for the intellect of a woman."

Miss Bannister looked out of the window for a few moments.

"Doctor," she then said, "I do not believe there is any one else who knows me, who would tell me that I have the mind of a child."

"Oh, no," replied Dr. Tolbridge, "for it is not likely that there is any one else to whom you have made the fact known."

There was a quick flush on the face of Miss Dora, and a flash in her blue eyes, and she reached out her hand toward her muff which lay on the table beside her, but she changed her purpose and drew back her hand. The doctor looked at her with a smile.

"You were just on the point of jumping up and leaving the room without a word, weren't you?"

"Yes, I was," said she, "and I have a great mind to do it now, but first I must—"

"Miss Dora," said the doctor, "I am delighted. Actually you are cutting your new mind. Before you can realize the fact, you will have it all full-formed and ready for use. Let me see; this is the ninth of March; bad roads; bad weather; no walking; no driving; nothing inspiriting; disagreeable in doors and out. I think the full change will occur within three weeks. By the end of this month, you will not only have forgotten that your milk mind has troubled you, but that the world was ever blank, and that your joys and affections were ever on the point of passing away from you. You will then be the brave-hearted, bright-spirited woman that Nature intended you to be, after she had passed you through some of the preliminary stages."

The flush on the face of Miss Dora gradually passed away as she listened to this speech.

She rose. "Doctor," said she, "I like that better than what you have been saying. Anyway, I shall not be angry, and I shall wait three weeks and see what happens, and if everything is all wrong then, the responsibility will rest on you."

"Very good," said he, "I agree to the terms. It is a bargain."

Now Miss Dora seemed troubled again. She took up her muff, put it down, drew her furs about her, then let them fall again,

Frank Richard Stockton

and finally turned toward the physician, who had also risen.

"Doctor," she said, "I don't want you to put this visit in the family bill. I wish to—to attend to it myself. How much should I pay you?" and she took out her little pocketbook.

Dr. Tolbridge put his hands behind him.

"This case is out of my usual line of practice," he said, "and my ordinary schedule of fees does not apply to it. For advice such as I have given you I never charge money. I take nothing but cats."

"What!" exclaimed Miss Dora; "what on earth do you mean?"

"I mean cats," he replied, "or rather kittens. I am very fond of kittens, and at present we have not one in the house. So, if you have a kitten—"

"Dr. Tolbridge," cried Miss Dora, her eyes sparkling, "do you really mean that? Would you truly like to have an Angora kitten?"

"That is exactly the breed I want," he answered.

"Why, I have five," she said; "they are only four days old, and perfect beauties. I shall be charmed to give you one, and I will pick out the very prettiest for you. As soon as it is old enough, I will bring it to you, already named, and with a ribbon on its neck. What color would you like the ribbon to be?"

"For Angoras, blue," he said; "I shall be so glad to have a kitten like that; but remember that you must not bring it to me until its eyes are opened, and it has—"

"Doctor," interrupted Miss Dora, raising her forefinger, "you were just on the point of saying, 'and has shed its milk mind.' Now I am going away before you make me angry again."

When his patient had gone, Dr. Tolbridge put another log on the fire, shook up the cushions of the sofa, and lay down to continue his nap.

CHAPTER II

MISS PANNEY

The Witton family, distant relatives of Miss Panney, with whom she had lived for many years, resided on a farm in the hilly country above Thorbury, and when Mrs. Tolbridge had rattled through the town, she found the country road very rough and bad—hard and bumpy in some places, and soft and muddy in others; but Buckskin was in fine spirits and pulled her bravely on.

When she reached the Witton house she left the horse in charge of the boy, and opening the hall door, went directly up to Miss Panney's room. Knocking, she waited some little time for an answer, and then was told, in a clear, high voice, to come in. The room was large and well lighted. Against one of the walls stood a high-posted bed with a canopy, and on one of the pillows of the bed appeared the head of an elderly woman, the skin darkened and wrinkled by time, the nose aquiline, and the black eyes very sharp and quick of movement. This head was surrounded by the frills of a freshly laundered night-cap, and the smooth white coverlid was drawn up close under its chin.

"Upon my word," exclaimed the person in the bed, "is that you, Mrs. Tolbridge? I thought it was the doctor."

"I don't wonder at that, Miss Panney," said Mrs. Tolbridge. "At times we have very much the same sort of knock."

"But where is the doctor?" asked the old lady.

"I hope he is at home and asleep," was the reply. "He has been working very hard lately, and was up the greater part of last night. He was coming here when he received your message, but I told him he should not do it; I would come myself, and if I found it absolutely necessary that you should see him, I would let him know. And now what is the trouble, Miss Panney?"

Miss Panney fixed her eyes steadfastly upon her visitor, who had taken a seat by the bedside.

"Catherine Tolbridge," said she, "do you know what will happen to you, if you don't look out? You'll lose that man."

"Lose him!" exclaimed the other.

"Yes, just that," replied the old lady; "I have seen it over and over again. Down they drop, right in the middle of their harness. And the stouter and sturdier they are, the worse it is for them; they think they can do anything, and they do it. I'll back a skinny doctor against a burly one, any day. He knows there are things he can't do. He doesn't try, and he keeps afloat."

"That is exactly what I am trying to do," said the doctor's wife, "and if those are your opinions, Miss Panney, don't you think that the doctor's patients ought to have a regard for his health, and that they ought not to make him come to them in all sorts of weather, and at all hours of the day, unless there is some-thing serious the matter with them? Now I don't believe there is anything serious the matter with you today."

"There is always something serious the matter with a person of my age," said Miss Panney, "and as for Dr. Tolbridge's visits to me doing him any harm, it is all stuff and nonsense. They do him good; they rest him; they brighten him up. He's never livelier than when he is with me. He doesn't have to hang over me all the night, giving me this and that, to keep the breath in my body, when he ought to be taking the rest that he needs more than any of us."

Mrs. Tolbridge laughed. "No, indeed," said she, "he never has to do anything of that kind for you. I believe you are the healthiest patient he has."

"That may be," said the other, "and it is much to his credit, and to mine, too. I know when I want a doctor. I don't send for him when I am in the last stages of anything. But we won't talk anything more about that. I want to know all about your husband. Do you think he is really out of health?"

"No," said Mrs. Tolbridge, "he is simply overworked, and needs rest. Just the sort of rest I hope he is getting this afternoon."

"Nonsense," said Miss Panney; "rest is well enough, but you must give him more than that if you do not want to see him break down. You must give him good victuals. Rest, without the best of food, amounts to little in his case."

"Truly, Miss Panney!" exclaimed her visitor, "I think I give my husband as good living as any one in Thorbury has or can expect."

"Humph!" said the old lady. "He may have all that, and yet be starving before your eyes. There isn't a man, woman, or child, in or about Thorbury, who really lives well—excepting, perhaps, myself."

Mrs. Tolbridge smiled. "I think you do manage to live very well, Miss Panney."

"Yes," said the other, "and I'd like to manage to have my friends live well, too. By the way, did you ever make rum-flake for the doctor when he comes in tired and faint?"

"I never heard of it," replied the other.

"I thought as much," said Miss Panney. "Well, you take the whites of two eggs and beat them up, and while you are beating you sprinkle rum over the egg, from a pepper caster, which you ought to keep clean to use for this and nothing else. Then you should sift in sugar according to taste, and when you have put a dry macaroon, which has been soaking in rum all this time, in the bottom of a glass saucer, you pile the flake over it, and it's ready for him, except that sometimes you put in,—let me see!—a little orange juice, I think, but I've got the recipe there in my scrap-book, and I can find it in a minute." So saying, the old lady threw aside the coverlid, and jumped to the floor with the activity of a cat.

Mrs. Tolbridge burst out laughing.

"I declare, Miss Panney!" she exclaimed, "you have your dress on."

"What of that?" said the old lady, opening a drawer. "A warm dress is a good thing to wear, at least I have always found it so."

"But not with a night-cap," said the other.

"That depends on circumstances," said Miss Panney, turning over the pages of a large scrap-book.

"And shoes," continued Mrs. Tolbridge, laughing again.

"Shoes," cried Miss Panney, pushing out one foot, and looking at it. "Well, truly, that was an oversight; but here is the recipe;" and without the aid of spectacles, she began to read. "It's exactly as I told you," she said presently, "except that some people use sponge cake instead of macaroons. The orange juice depends on individual taste. Shall I write that out for you, or will you remember it?"

Frank Richard Stockton

"Oh, I can remember it," said the other; "but tell me, Miss Panney—"

"Well, then," said the old lady, "make it for him, and see how he likes it. There is one thing, Mrs. Tolbridge, that you should never forget, and that is that the doctor is not only your husband, but the mainstay of the community."

"Oh, I know that, and accept the responsibility; but you must tell me why you are in bed with all your clothes on. I believe that you did not expect the doctor so soon, and when you heard my knock, you clapped on your night-cap and jumped into bed."

"Catherine," quietly remarked the old lady, "there is nothing so discouraging to a doctor as to find a person who has sent for him out of bed. If the patient is up and about, she mystifies him; he is apt to make mistakes; he loses interest; he wonders if she couldn't come to him, instead of his having to go to her; but when he finds the ailing person in bed, the case is natural and straightforward; he feels at home, and knows how to go to work. If you believe in a doctor, you ought to make him believe in you. And if you are in bed, he will believe in you, and if you are out of it, he is apt not to. More than that, Mrs. Tolbridge, there is no greater compliment that you can pay to a physician you have sent for, than to have him find you in bed."

The doctor's wife laughed. She thought, but she did not say so, that probably this old lady had paid her husband a great many compliments.

"Well, Miss Panney," she said, rising, "what report shall I make?"

The old lady took off her night-cap, and replaced it with her ordinary headgear of lace and ribbons.

"Have you heard anything," she asked, "of the young man who

is coming to Cobhurst?"

"No," said Mrs. Tolbridge, "nothing at all."

"Well," continued Miss Panney, "I think the doctor knows something about him through old Butterwood. I have an idea that I know something about him myself, but I wanted to talk to the doctor about him. Of course this is a mere secondary matter. My back has been troubling me a good deal lately, but as the doctor is so pushed, I won't ask him to come here on purpose to see me. If he's in the neighborhood, I shall be very glad to have him call. For the present, I shall try some of the old liniments. Dear knows, I have enough of them, dating back for years and years."

"But it will not do to make any mistakes, Miss Panney. Those old prescriptions might not suit you now."

"Don't trouble yourself in the least about that," said the old lady, lifting her hand impressively; "medicine never injures me. Not a drop of it do I ever take inside of me, prescription or no prescription. But I don't mind putting things on the outside of me—of course, I mean in reason, for there are outside applications that would ruin the constitution of a jack-screw."

There were very few people in the neighborhood of Thorbury who were older than Miss Panney, and very few of any age who were as alert in both mind and body. She had been born in this region; had left it in her youth, and had returned about thirty years ago, when she had taken up her abode with the Wittons, who at that time were a newly married couple. They were now middle-aged people, but Miss Panney still lived with them, and seemed to be much the very same old lady as she was when she arrived. She was a woman who kept a good deal to herself, having many resources for her active mind. With many people who were not acquainted with her socially but knew all about her, she had the reputation of being wicked. The principal reason for this belief was the well-known fact that she always took her breakfast in bed. This was considered to be a French habit, and the French were looked upon as infidels. Moreover, she never went to church, and when questioned upon this subject, had been known to answer that she could not listen with patience to a sermon, for she had never heard one without thinking that she could preach on that subject a great deal better than the man in the pulpit.

In spite of this fact, however, the rector of the Episcopal church of Thorbury and the Methodist minister were both great friends of Miss Panney, and although she did not come to hear them, they liked very much to go to hear her. Mr. Hampton, the Methodist, would talk to her about flower-gardening and the by-gone people and ways of the region, while Mr. Ames, the rector, who was a young man, did not hesitate to assert that he frequently got very good hints for passages in his sermons, from remarks made by Miss Panney about things that were going on in the religious and social world.

But although Miss Panney took pleasure in the company of clergymen and physicians, she boldly asserted that she liked lawyers better.

"In the law," she would say, "you find things fixed and settled. A law is a law, the same for everybody, and no matter how much people may wrangle and dispute about it, it is there, and you can read it for yourself. But the practice of medicine has to be shifted to suit individual cases, and the practice of theology is shifted to suit individual creeds, and you can't put your finger on steady principles as you can in law. When I put my finger down, I like to be sure what is under it."

Miss Panney had other reasons for liking lawyers, for her first real friend had been her legal guardian, old Mr. Bannister of Thorbury. She was one of the few people of the place who remembered this old gentleman, and she had often told how shocked and pained she had been when summoned from boarding-school to attend his funeral, and how she had been impressed by the idea that the preparations for this important event consisted mainly in beating up eggs, stemming raisins, baking cakes and pies, and making all sorts of provision for the sumptuous entertainment of the people who should be drawn together by the death of the principal citizen of the town. To her mind it would have been more appropriate had the company been fed on bread and water.

Thomas Bannister, who succeeded to his father's business, had been Miss Panney's legal friend and counsellor for many years. But he, too, was dead, and the office had now devolved on Herbert Bannister, the grandson of the old gentleman, and the brother of Miss Dora.

Herbert and Miss Panney were very good friends, but not yet cronies. He was still under thirty, and there were many events of the past of which he knew but little, and about which he could not wholly sympathize with her. But she believed that years would ripen him, and that the time would come when she would get along as well with him as she had with his father and grandfather.

She was not supposed to be a rich woman, and she had not been much engaged in suits at law, but it was surprising how much legal business Miss Panney had, as well as business of many other kinds.

When Mrs. Tolbridge had left her, the old lady put away her scrap-book, and prepared to go downstairs.

"It is a great pity," she said to herself, "that one of the bodily ailments which is bound to show itself in the family in the course of the spring, should not have turned up to-day. I want very much to talk to the doctor about the young man at Cobhurst, and I cannot drive about the country in such weather as this."

CHAPTER III

BROTHER AND SISTER

There were other people in and around Thorbury, who very much wanted to know something about the young man at Cobhurst, but this desire was interfered with by the fact that the young man was not yet at Cobhurst, and did not seem to be in a hurry to get there.

Cobhurst was the name of an estate a mile or so from the Witton farm, whose wide fields had lain for a half a dozen years untilled, and whose fine old mansion had been, for nearly a year, uninhabited. Its former owner, Matthias Butterwood, a bachelor, and during the greater part of his life, a man who took great pride in his farm, his stock, and his fruit trees, had been afflicted in his later years with various kinds of rheumatism, and had been led to wander about to different climates and different kinds of hot springs for the sake of physical betterment.

When at home in these latter days, old Butterwood had been content to have his garden cultivated, for he could still hobble about and look at that, and had left his fields to take care of themselves, until he should be well enough to be his own farmer, as he had always been. But old age, coming to the aid of his other complaints, had carried him off a few months before this story begins.

The only person now living at Cobhurst was a colored man

named Mike, who inhabited the gardener's house and held the office of care-taker of the place.

Whenever Mike now came to town with his old wagon and horse, or when he was met on the road, he found people more and more inquisitive about the new owner of Cobhurst. Mike was not altogether a negro, having a good deal of Irish blood in his veins, and this conjunction of the two races in his individuality had had the effect upon his speech of destroying all tendency to negro dialect or Irish brogue, so that, in fact, he spoke like ordinary white people of his grade in life. The effect upon his character, however, had been somewhat different, and while the vivacity of the African and that of the Hibernian, in a degree, had neutralized each other, making him at times almost as phlegmatic as the traditional Dutchman, he would sometimes exhibit the peculiarities of a Sambo, and sometimes those of a Paddy.

Mike could give no satisfaction to his questioners; he knew nothing of the newcomer, except that he had received a postal card, directed to the man in charge of Cobhurst, and which stated that Mr. Haverley would arrive there on the fourth of April.

"More'n that," Mike would say, "I don't know nothin'. Whether he's old or young, and what family he's got, I can't tell ye. All I know is, that he don't seem in no hurry to see his place, an' he must be a reg'lar city man, or he'd know that winter's the time to come to work a farm in the spring of the year."

Other people, however, knew more about Mr. Haverley than Mike did, and Miss Panney could have informed any one that he was a young man, unmarried, and a second nephew to old Butterwood. She had faith that Dr. Tolbridge could give her some additional points, provided she could get an opportunity of properly questioning him.

Meanwhile the days passed on; the roads about Thorbury

dried up and grew better; in low, sheltered places, the grass showed a greenish hue; the willows turned yellow, and people began to ponder over the catalogues of seed merchants. At last, it was the third of April, and on that day, in a large bright room of a New York boarding-house, kneeling in front of an open trunk, were Mr. Ralph Haverley and his sister Miriam.

Presently Miriam, whose years had not yet reached fifteen, vigorously pushed a pair of slippers into an unoccupied crevice in the trunk, and then, drawing back, seated herself on a stool.

"The delightful thing about this packing is," she said, "that it will never have to be done again. I am not going to any school, or any country place to board; you are not going to a hotel, not to any house kept by other people; our things do not have to be packed separately; we can put them in anywhere where they will fit; we are both going to the same place; we are going home, and there we shall stay."

"Always?" asked her brother, looking up with a smile.

"Always," answered Miriam. "When one gets a home, one stays there. At least I do."

"And you will not even go away to school?" he asked.

"By no means," said his sister, looking at him with much earnestness. "I have been to school ever since I was six years old,—nearly nine years,—and I positively declare that that is long enough for any girl. Others stay later, but then they do not begin so soon. As to finishing my education, as they call it, I shall do that at home. What a happy thought! It makes me want to skip. And you are to be my teacher, Ralph. I am sure you know everything that I shall need to know."

Ralph laughed.

"I suppose you will examine me to see what I do know," he said, as he folded a heavy overcoat and laid it in the trunk.

Miriam sprang up and began to collect more of her effects.

"We shall see about that," she said, and then, suddenly stopping, she turned toward her brother. "There is one thing, Ralph, about which I need not examine you at all, and that is goodness of heart. If you had not had a very good heart indeed, you would not have waited and waited and waited—fairly pinching yourself, I expect—till I could get away from school and we could both go together and look at our new home in the very same instant."

Ralph Haverley was a brown-haired, bright-eyed young fellow under thirty. He had been educated for a profession, but the death of his parents, before he reached his majority, made it necessary for him to go to work at something by which he could immediately earn money enough to support not only himself, but his little sister. At his father's death, which occurred a month or two after that of his mother, young Haverley found that the family resources, which had never been great, had almost entirely disappeared. He could barely scrape together enough money to send Miriam to a boarding-school and to keep himself alive until he could get work. He had spent a great part of his boyhood in the country. His tastes and disposition inclined him to an out-door life, and, had he been able, he would have gone to the West, and established himself upon a ranch. But this was impossible; he must do the work that was nearest at hand, and as soon as he found it, he set himself at it with a will.

For eight long years he had struggled and labored; changing his occupation several times, but always living in the city; always making his home in a boardinghouse or a hotel. His pluck and energy had had its reward, and for the past three years he had held a responsible and well-paid position in a mercantile house. But his life and his work had for him nothing but a passing interest; he had no sympathy with bonded warehouses, invoices, and ledgers. All he could look forward to was a higher position, a larger salary, and, when Miriam should graduate, a little home somewhere where she could keep house for him. In his dreams of this home, he would sometimes place it in the suburbs, where Sundays and holidays spent in country air would compensate for hasty breakfasts, early morning trains, and late ones in the afternoon. But when he reflected that it would not do to leave his young sister alone all day in a thinly settled, rural place, at the mercy of tramps, he was forced to the conclusion that the thing for them to do was to live in a city apartment. But there was nothing in either of these outlooks to create fervent longings in the soul of Ralph Haverley.

For some legal reason, probably connected with the fact that old Butterwood died at a health resort in Arkansas, Haverley did not learn until late in the winter that his mother's uncle had left to him the estate of Cobhurst. The reason for this bequest, as stated in the will, was the old man's belief that the said Ralph Haverley was the only one of his blood relations who seemed to be getting on in the world, and to him he left the house, farm, and all the personal property he might find therein and thereon, but not one cent of money. Where the testator's money was bestowed, Ralph did not know, for he did not see the will.

When Ralph heard of his good fortune, his true life seemed to open before him; his Butterwood blood boiled in his veins. He did not hesitate a moment as to his course, for he was of the opinion that if a healthy young man could not make a living out of a good farm he did not deserve to live at all. He gave immediate notice of his intention to abandon mercantile life, and set himself to work by day and by night to wind up his business affairs, so that he might be free by the beginning of April. It was this work which helped him to control his desire to run off and take a look at Cobhurst without waiting for his sister.

Of the place which was to be their home, Miriam knew absolutely nothing, but Ralph had heard his mother talk about her visits to her uncle, and, in his mind, the name Cobhurst had always called up visions of wide halls and lofty chambers, broad piazzas, sunny slopes and lawns, green meadows, and avenues bordered with tall trees—a grand estate in fact, with woods full of nuts, streams where a boy could fish, and horses that he might ride. Had these ideas existed in Miriam's mind, the brother and sister would have visited Cobhurst the day after he brought her the letter from the lawyer; but her conceptions of the place were vague and without form, except when she associated it with the homes of girls she had visited. But as none of these suited her very well, she preferred to fall back upon chaotic anticipation.

"When I think of Cobhurst," she wrote to her brother, "I smell marigolds, and think of rather poor blackberries that you pick from bushes. Please do not put in your letters anything that you know about it, for I would rather see everything for myself."

CHAPTER IV

THE HOME

It was late in the afternoon when Ralph and Miriam Haverley alighted at the station at Thorbury. Miss Dora Bannister, who had come down to see a friend off, noticed the two standing on the platform. She did not know who they were, but she thought the one to be a very handsome young man, and the other a nice-looking girl who seemed to be all eyes.

"What a queer-looking colored man!" said Miriam. "He looks mashed on top."

The person alluded to was getting down from a wagon drawn by a mournful horse, and now approached the platform.

"Is you Mr. Hav'ley, sir?" he said, touching his hat. "Thought so; I'm the man in charge o' yer place. Got any baggage, sir?"

On being informed that the travellers had brought three trunks with them, and that some boxes would be expected on the morrow, Mike, who with his worn felt hat pressed flat upon his head, might give one the idea of a bottle with the cork driven in, stood for a moment in thought.

"I can take one trunk," he said, "the one ye will want the most tonight, and ye'd better have the others hauled over tomorrow with the boxes. Ye can both go in the wagon, if ye like. The seat can be pushed back, and I can sit on the trunk myself, or ye can hire a kerridge."

"Of course we will take a cab," said Ralph. "How far is it to Cobhurst?"

"Well, some says three miles, and some says four. It depends a good deal on the roads. They're pretty good today."

Having engaged the services of a country cabman, who declared that he had known Cobhurst ever since he was born, and having arranged for the transfer of their goods the next day, the Haverleys rattled out of the town.

"Now," said Miriam, "we are truly going home, and I do not remember ever doing that before. And, Ralph," she continued, after gazing right and left from the cab windows, "one of the first things we ought to do is to get a new man to take charge of the place. That person isn't fit. I never saw such slouchy clothes."

Ralph laughed. "I am the man who is to have charge of the place," he said. "What do you think of my clothes?"

Miriam gave a little pull at his hair for reply. "And there is another thing," she continued. "If that is our horse and wagon, don't you really think that we ought to sell them? They are awful."

"Don't be in a hurry," said Ralph. "We shall soon find out whether we own the horse or not. He may belong to the man. He's not a bad one, either. See, he is passing us now with that big trunk in the wagon."

"Passing us!" exclaimed Miriam. "Almost any horse could do that. Did you ever see such an old poke as we have, and such a bouncy, jolting rattletrap of a carriage? It squeaks all over."

"Alas," said Ralph, "I am thinking of something worse than jolts or squeaks. I am hungry, and I am sure you must be, and

I don't see what we are going to do about supper. I am afraid I am not a very good manager, yet. I had an idea that Cobhurst was not so far from the station, and that we could go over and look at the house, and come back to a hotel and stay there for the night; but now I see it will be dark before we get there, and we shall not feel like turning round and going directly back. Perhaps it would be better to turn now."

"Turn back, when we are going to our home!" cried Miriam. "How can you think of such a thing, Ralph? And you needn't suppose that neither of us is a good manager. I am housekeeper now, and I did not forget that we shall need our supper. I have it all there in my bag, and I shall cook it as soon as we reach the house. Of course I knew that we could not expect anything to eat in a place with only a man to take care of it."

"What in the world have you?" asked Ralph, much amused.

"I have four breakfast rolls," she said, "six mutton chops, a package of ground coffee, another of tea, a pound of sugar, and a good big piece of gingerbread. I am sorry I couldn't bring any butter, but I was afraid that might melt in a warm car, and run over everything. As for milk, we shall have to make up our minds to do without that for one meal. I got up early this morning, and went out and bought all these things."

Ralph was on the point of saying, "What are we going to have for breakfast?" But he would not trouble his sister's mind with any such suggestions.

"You are a good little housewife," said he; "I wish we were there, and sitting down at the table—if there is any table."

"I have thought it all out," said Miriam, "if it is one of those large farm-houses, with a big kitchen, where the family eat and spend their evening, we shall eat there, too, this once. You shall build a fire, and I'll have the coffee made in no time. There must be a coffee-pot, or a tin cup, or something to boil in. The chops can be broiled over the coals."

"On what?" asked Ralph.

"You can get a pointed stick and toast them, if there is no other way, sir. And you need not make fun of my supper; the chops are very nice ones, and I have wrapped them up in oiled silk, so that they will not grease the other things."

"Oh, don't talk any more about them," exclaimed Ralph. "It makes me too dreadfully hungry."

"If it is a cottage," remarked Miriam, looking reflectively out of the window, "I cannot get it out of mind that there will be all sorts of kitchen things hanging around the old-fashioned fireplace. That would be very nice and convenient, but—"

"You hope it is not a cottage?" said her brother.

"Well," answered Miriam, presently, "home is home, and I made up my mind to be perfectly satisfied with it whatever kind of house it may be. It seems to me that a real home ought to be like parents and relations; we've got them, and we can't change them, and we never think of such a thing. We love them quite as they are. But I cannot help hoping, just a little, that it is not a cottage. The only ones I have ever been in smelt so much of soapsuds."

It was now quite dark, and the road appeared to be growing rougher. Every now and then they jolted over a big stone, or sunk into a deep rut. Ralph let down the front window.

"Are we nearly there?" he asked of the driver.

"Yes, sir," said the man; "we are on the place now."

"You don't mean," exclaimed Miriam, "that this is our road!"

"It's a good deal washed just here," said the man, "by the heavy rains."

Presently the road became smoother and in a few minutes the carriage stopped.

"I am trembling all over," said Miriam, "with thinking of being at home, and with not an idea of what it is like."

In a moment they were standing on a broad flagstone. Although it was dark, they could see the outline of the house before them.

"Ralph," whispered Miriam, drawing close to her brother, "it is not a cottage." Without waiting for a reply she went on: "Ralph," she said, her hands trembling as they held his arm, "it is lordly."

"I had some sort of an idea like that myself," he answered; "but, my dear, don't you think it will be well to keep this man until we go inside and see what sort of accommodations we shall find? Perhaps we may be obliged to go back to the town."

Miriam immediately began to ascend the broad steps of the piazza.

"Come on, Ralph," she said, "and please don't talk like that."

Her brother laughed, paid the driver and dismissed him.

"Now, little girl," he cried, "we have burned our ships, and must take what we shall find."

"Oh, Ralph," cried Miriam, "I couldn't have gone back. If there are floors to the rooms, they will do to sleep on for to-night."

At this moment a wide front door opened, revealing a colored woman holding a lamp.

"Good evenin'," said she; "walk in."

When Ralph and Miriam had entered, the woman looked out the open door.

"Is you all?" she asked.

"Oh, yes," said Ralph.

The woman hesitated a moment, looked out again, and then closed the door.

"Would you like to go to your rooms afore supper?" she asked.

The brother and sister were so absorbed in gazing about them, that they did not hear the question. The lamp, still in the woman's hand, gave a poor and vacillating light, but they could see a wide, long hall, tall doors opening on each side, some high-backed chairs, and other dark-colored furniture.

"Yer rooms is ready," continued the woman; "ye can take yer pick of them. Supper'll be on the table the minute ye come down. Ye'd better take this lamp, sir, and thar's another one in the upper hall. I expect ye two is brother and sister. Ye're alike as two pins of different sizes."

"You're right," said Ralph, holding up the lamp, and looking about him; "but please tell me, where are the stairs?"

"Oh, yer open that glass door right in front of ye," said the woman. "I'd go with yer, but I smell somethin' bilin' over now."

Opening the glass door, they saw before them a narrow staircase in two flights.

"Stairs shut up in a room of their own," said Ralph, as they ascended. "Did you ever see anything like this before?"

"I never saw anything like anything before," said Miriam, in a low, reverent voice.

On the floor above they found another wide hall, and four or five open doors.

"There is your lamp," said Ralph to his sister; "take the first room you come to, and to-morrow we will pick and choose."

"Who would have thought," said Miriam, "that a woman—"

"Don't let us think or talk of her now," interrupted her brother. "To hurry down to supper is our present business."

When the two went downstairs, they found the colored woman standing by an open door in the rear of the hall.

"Supper's ready, sir," said she, and they entered the dining-room.

It was a large and rather sparely furnished room, but Miriam and Ralph took no note of anything except the table, which stood in the middle of the floor, lighted by a hanging lamp. It was a large table and arranged for eight people with chairs at every place. The woman gave a little laugh, as she said:—

"I reckon you all may think this is a pretty big table for two people, an' one not growed up, but you see I didn't know nothin' about the size of the family, an' Mike he didn't know nothin' either. I'm Phoebe, Mike's wife, an' I ain't got nothin' in the world to do with this house, for mostly I go out to service in the town, but I'm here now; and of course we didn't want you all to come an' find nothin' to eat, an' no beds made, an' as you didn't write no orders, sir, we had just to do the best we could accordin' to our own lights. I reckoned there would be the gem'en and his wife, an' perhaps two growed-up sons, though Mike, he was doubtful about the growed-up sons, especially as to thar bein' two of them. Then I reckoned thar'd be a darter, just about your age, Miss, an' then there'd be two younger chillen, one a boy an' one a girl, an' a gov'ness for these two. Of course I didn't know whether the gov'ness was in the habit of eatin' at your table or not, but I reckoned that this time, comin' so late, you'd all eat at the same table, an' I put a plate an' a cheer for her. An' Mike went ter town, an' got groc'ries an' things enough for to-night and tomorrow, an' as everything was ready I just left everything as it was. I reckoned you wouldn't want ter wait until I'd sot the whole table over again."

"By no means," cried Ralph, and down they sat, Ralph at one end of the long table, and Miriam at the other. It was a good supper; beefsteak, an omelet, hot rolls, fried potatoes, coffee, tea, preserved fruit, and all on the scale suited to a family of eight.

When Phoebe had retired to the kitchen, presumably for additional supplies, Miriam stretched her arms over the table.

"Think of it, Ralph," she said, "this is our supper. The first meal we ever truly owned."

They had not been long at the table when they were startled by the loud ringing of the door-bell.

"'Pon my word," ejaculated Phoebe, "it's a long time since that bell's been rung," and getting down a plate of hotter biscuit, with which she had been offering temptations, she left the room. Presently she returned, ushering in Dr. Tolbridge.

Briefly introducing himself, the doctor welcomed the brother and sister to the neighborhood of Thorbury, and apologized for the extreme promptness of his call.

"I heard you had arrived," he said, "from a hackman I met on the road, and having made a visit near by I thought I would look in on you. It might be days before I should again have a chance. But don't let me disturb your supper; I beg that you will sit down again."

"And I beg you, sir," said Ralph, "to sit down with us."

Frank Richard Stockton

"Well," said the doctor, smiling, "I am hungry, and my own supper-time is passed. You seem to have plenty of room for a guest."

"Oh, yes, indeed, sir," said Miriam, who had already taken a fancy to the doctor's genial face. "Phoebe thought we were a large family, and you can take the seat of one of the grown-up sons, or the daughter's chair, or the place that was intended for either the little boy or little girl, or perhaps you would like the governess' seat."

At this Phoebe turned her face to the wall and giggled.

"A fine imagination," said the doctor, "and what is better, a bountiful meal. Please consider me, for the present, the smallest boy, who might naturally be supposed to have the biggest appetite."

"It would have been funnier," said Miriam, gravely, "if you had been the governess."

The supper was a lively one; the three appetites were excellent; the doctor was in his jolliest mood, and Ralph and Miriam were delighted with him. On his part, he could not help looking upon it in the light of a joke—an agreeable one, however—that these two young people, one of them a mere child, should constitute the new Cobhurst family. He had known that the property had gone to an unmarried man who was in business, and had not thought of his coming here to live.

"And now," said the doctor, as they rose from the table, "I must go. My wife will call on you very soon, and in the meantime, what is there that I can do for you?"

"I think," answered Miriam, looking about her to see that Phoebe was not in the room, "that it would be very nice if you could get us a new man. We like the woman well enough, but the man is awful."

The doctor looked at her, astonished.

"Do you mean Mike?" he asked, "the faithful Mike, who has been in charge here ever since Mr. Butterwood took to travelling about for the good of his rheumatisms? Why, my dear young lady, the whole country looks upon Mike as a pattern man-of-all-work. He may be getting a little cranky and independent in his notions, for he has been pretty much his own master for years, but I am sure you could find no one to take his place who would be more trustworthy or so generally useful."

Ralph was about to explain that it was only the appearance of the man to which his sister objected, but she spoke for herself.

"Of course, we oughtn't always to judge people by their looks," she said, "but in my thoughts about our home, I never connected it with such a very shabby person. But then, if he is an old family servant, he may be the very kind of a man the place needs."

"Oh, I advise you to stick to Mike, by all means," said the doctor, "and to Phoebe, too, if she will stay with you. But I think she prefers the town to this somewhat secluded place."

"A good omen," said Ralph, as he closed the door after the doctor. "As a neighbor, I believe that man is at the head of his class, and I am very glad that he happened to be the first one who came to see us."

"Well," said Miriam, "we haven't seen the others yet, and I am glad that we don't know whether this doctor is homeopathic or allopathic, so that we can get started in liking him before we know whether we approve of his medicines or not."

"Upon my word," cried Ralph, "I never knew that you had opinions about the different medical schools. Did they teach you that sort of thing at Mrs. Stone's?"

"I suppose I can have opinions without having them taught to me, can't I?" she answered. "I saw a lot of sickness among the girls, and I am homeopathic."

"Stuff," exclaimed Ralph, "I don't believe you ever took any medicine in your life."

"I have not taken much," answered Miriam, "but I have taken enough to settle it in my mind that I am never going to take any more of the same sort."

"And they were not little sugar pills?"

"No, indeed they were not," said Miriam, very decidedly.

"I've made a fire in the parlor," said Phoebe, coming in, "if you all want to sit there afore you go to bed."

"I don't want to sit anywhere," cried Miriam, "and I am crazy to get a peep out of doors. Come on, Ralph, just for a minute."

Ralph followed her out on the piazza.

"It's awfully dark," said Miriam, "but if we walk carefully, I think we can get far enough away from the house to look up at it, and find out a little what it looks like."

They groped their way across the driveway, and on to the grass beyond.

"We can see a good deal of it against the sky!" exclaimed Miriam. "What tall pillars! It looks like a Greek temple in front. And from what I can make out, it's pretty much all front."

"I suppose it is a regular old-fashioned house," said her brother, "with a Grecian portico front, and perhaps another at the back. But you must come in now, for you have on neither hat nor wrap." And he took her by the hand.

"It isn't cold," said Miriam, "and oh, Ralph, look up at the stars. Those are our stars, every one of them."

Ralph laughed, as he led her into the house.

"Yes, indeed," she insisted, "we own all the way down, and all the way up."

"Now then," said Miriam, when they had closed the door behind them, "how shall we explore the house? Shall we each take a lamp, or will candles be better?"

"Little girl!" exclaimed her brother, "I had no idea that you were such a bunch of watch springs. It is nearly nine o'clock, and after the day's work that you have done, it is time you were in bed. House exploring can be done to-morrow."

"Yes, indeed, Miss," said Phoebe, who stood by, anxious to shut up the house and retire to her own domicile, "and I will go up into your room with you and show you about things."

Half an hour after this, Miriam came out of her bedroom, holding a bit of lighted candle in her hand. She was dressed, with the exception of her shoes. Softly she advanced to the foot of the stairs which led to the floor above.

"They are partly my stairs," she said to herself, as she paused for a moment at the bottom of the step. "Ralph told me that he considered the place as much mine as his, and I have a right to go up. I cannot go to sleep without seeing what is up here. I never imagined such a third floor as this one."

In less than a minute, Miriam was slowly creeping along the next floor of the house, which was indeed an odd one. For it was nothing more than a gallery, broader at the ends than the sides, with a railed open space, through which one could look down to the floor below. Some of the doors were open and she peeped into the rooms, but saw nothing which induced her to enter them. Having made the circuit of the gallery, she reached a narrow staircase which wound still higher upward.

"I must go up," she said; "I cannot help it."

Arrived at the top of these stairs, Miriam held up her candle and looked about her. She was in a great, wide, magnificent, glorious garret! Her soul swelled. To own such a garret was almost too much joy! It was the realization of a thousand dreams.

Slowly advancing, she beheld fascinations on every side. Here were old trunks, doubtless filled with family antiquities; there was a door fastened with a chain and a padlock—there must be a key to that, or the lock could be broken; in the dim light at the other end of the garret, she could see what appeared to be a piled-up collection of boxes, chests, cases, little and big, and all sorts of old-fashioned articles of use and ornament, doubtless every one of them a treasure. A long musket, its stock upon the floor, reclined against a little trunk covered with horse-hair, from under the lid of which protruded the ends of some dusty folded papers.

"Oh, how I wish Ralph were here, and that we had a lamp. I could spend the night here, looking at everything; but I can't do it now with this little candle end."

At her feet was a wooden box, the lid of which was evidently unfastened, for it lay at an angle across the top.

"I will look into this one box," she said, "and then I will go down."

She knelt down, and with the candle in her right hand, pushed aside the lid with her left. From the box there grinned at her a human skull, surrounded by its bones. She started back.

"Uncle Butterwood," she gasped and tried to rise, but her strength and senses left her, and she fell over unconscious, upon the floor. The candle dropped from her hand, and, fortunately, went out.

Frank Richard Stockton

CHAPTER V

PANNEYOPATHY

About ten o'clock the next morning, Mike, in his little wagon, rattled up to the door of Dr. Tolbridge.

The doctor was not at home, but his wife came out.

"That young girl!" she exclaimed. "Why, what can be the matter with her?"

"I dunno, ma'am," answered Mike. "Phoebe told me just as the wagon got there with the boxes an' trunks, an' nobody but me to help the man upstairs with 'em, an' said I must get away to the doctor's jes' as fast as I could drive. She said somethin' about her sleepin' in the garret and ketchin' cold, but she wouldn't let me stop to ax no questions. She said the doctor was wanted straight off."

"I am very sorry," said Mrs. Tolbridge, "that he is not here, but he said he was going to stop and see Miss Panney. I can't tell you any other place to which he was going. If you drive back by the Witton road, you may find him, or, if he has not yet arrived, it might be well to wait for him."

Arrived at the Witton house, Mike saw Miss Panney, wrapped in a heavy shawl and wearing a hood, taking her morning exercise on the piazza.

"They want the doctor already!" she exclaimed in answer to Mike's inquiries. "Who could have thought that? And he left here nearly half an hour ago. His wife will send him when he gets home, but there is no knowing when that will be. However, she must have somebody to attend to her. Mike, I will go myself. I will go with you in your wagon. Wait one minute."

Into the house popped Miss Panney, and in a very short time returned, carrying with her an umbrella and a large reticule made of brown plush, and adorned with her monogram in yellow. One of the Witton girls came with her, and assisted her to the seat, by the side of Mike.

"Now then," said she, "get along as fast as you can. I shall not mind the jolts."

"Phoebe," said Miss Panney, as she entered the Cobhurst door, "it's a long time since I have seen you, and I have not been in this house for eight years. I hope you will be able to tell me something about this sudden sickness, for Mike is as stupid as a stone post, and knows nothing at all."

"Now, Miss Panney," said Phoebe, speaking very earnestly, but in a low voice, "I can't say that I can really give you the true head and tail of it, for it's mighty hard to find out what did happen to that young gal. All I know is that she didn't come down to breakfast, and that Mr. Haverley went up to her room hisself, and he knocked and he knocked, and then he pushed the door open and went in, and, bless my soul, Miss Panney, she wasn't there. Then he hollered, and me and him, we sarched and sarched the house. He went up into the garret by hisself, for you may be sure I wouldn't go there, but he was just wild, and didn't care where he went, and there he found her dead asleep on the floor, and a livin' skeleton a sittin' watchin' her."

"Nonsense!" exclaimed Miss Panney; "he never told you that."

"That's the pint of what I got out of him, and you know, Miss Panney, that that garret's hanted."

Miss Panney wasted no words in attempting to disprove this assertion.

"He found her asleep on the floor?" said she.

"Yes, Miss Panney," answered Phoebe, "dead asleep, or more likely, to my mind, in a dead faint, among all the drafts and chills of that garret, and in her stockin' feet. She had tuk up a candle with her, but I'spect the skeleton blowed it out. And now she's got an awful cold, so she can scarcely breathe, and a fever hot enough to roast an egg."

At this moment Ralph appeared in the hall. The visitor immediately went up to him.

"Mr. Haverley, I suppose. I am Miss Panney. I am a neighbor, and I came to see if I could do anything for your sister before the doctor arrives. I am a good nurse, and know all about sicknesses;" and she explained why she had come and the doctor had not.

When Miriam turned her head and saw the black eyes of Miss Panney gazing down upon her, she pushed herself back in the bed, and exclaimed,—

"Are you his wife?"

"No, indeed," said Miss Panney, "I wouldn't marry him for a thousand pounds. I am your nurse. I am going to give you something nice to make you feel better. Put your hand in mine. There, that will do. Keep yourself covered up, even if you are a little warm, and I will come back presently with the nicest kind of a cup of tea."

"It's a cold and a fever," she said to Ralph, outside the chamber door. "The commonest thing in the world. But I'll make her a hot drink that will do her more good than anything else that could be given her, and when the doctor comes, he'll tell you so. He knows me, and what I can do for sick people. I brought everything that's needed in my bag, and I am going down to the kitchen myself. But how in the world did she come to stay on the garret floor all night? She couldn't have been in a swoon all that time."

"No," answered Ralph; "she told me she came to her senses, she didn't know when, but that everything was pitch dark about her, and feeling dreadfully tired and weak, she put her head down on her arm, and tried to think why she was lying on such a hard floor, and then she must have dropped into the heavy sleep in which I found her. She was tired out with her journey and the excitement. Do you think she is in danger, Miss Panney?"

"Don't believe it," said the old lady. "She looks strong, and these young things get well before you know it."

"Now, my young lady," said Miss Panney, as she stood by Miriam's bedside, with a steaming bowl, "you may drink the whole of this, but you mustn't ask me for any more, and then you may go to sleep, and to-morrow morning you can get up and skip around and see what sort of a place Cobhurst is by daylight."

"I can't wait until to-morrow for that," said Miriam, "and is that tea or medicine?"

"It's both, my dear; sit up and drink it off."

Miriam still eyed the bowl. "Is it homeopathic or allopathic?" she asked.

"Neither the one or the other," was the discreet reply; "it is Panneyopathic, and just the thing for a girl who wants to get out of bed as soon as she can."

Frank Richard Stockton

Miriam looked full into the bright black eyes, and then took the bowl, and drank every drop of the contents.

"Thank you," she said. "It is perfectly horrid, but I must get up."

"Now you take a good long nap, and then I hope you will feel quite able to go down and begin to keep house for your brother."

"The first thing to do," said Miriam, as Miss Panney carefully adjusted the bedclothes about her shoulders, "is to see what sort a house we have got, and then I will know how I am to keep it."

When her young patient had dropped asleep, Miss Panney went downstairs. In the lower hall she found Ralph walking up and down.

"There is no earthly need of your worrying yourself about your sister. I am sure the doctor would say she is in no danger at all," said the old lady. "And now, if you don't mind, I would like very much to go up into the garret and see what frightened your sister."

"It was apparently a box of human bones," he said, "but I barely glanced at it. You are perfectly welcome to go up and examine."

It was a quarter of an hour before Miss Panney came down from the garret, laughing.

"I studied anatomy on those bones," she said. "Every one of them is marked in ink with its name. I had forgotten all about them. Mathias' brother Reuben was a scientific man, and he used the skeleton. That is, he studied all sorts of things, though he never did anything worth notice. I took a look round the garret," she continued, "and I tell you, sir, that if you care anything for family relics and records, you have them to your heart's content. I expect there are things up there that have not been touched for fifty years."

"I should suppose," said Ralph, "that the servants of the house would have had some curiosity about such objects, if no one else had."

Miss Panney laughed.

"There hasn't been a servant in that garret for many a long year," said she. "You evidently don't know that this house is considered haunted, particularly the garret; and I suppose that box of bones had a good deal to do with the notion."

"Well," said Ralph, "no doubt the ghosts have been a great protection to our family treasures."

"And to your whole house," said the old lady; "watch-dogs would be nothing to them."

Miss Panney and Ralph ate dinner together. The old lady would not leave until the doctor had come; and the conversation was an education to young Haverley in regard to the Butterwood family and the Thorbury neighborhood. At the conclusion of the meal, Phoebe came into the room.

"I went upstairs to see how she was gettin' on, sir," she said; "an' she was awake, an' she made me get a pencil an' paper out of her bag, an' she sent you this note."

On a half-sheet of note-paper, he read the following: "Dear Ralph, I went upstairs and looked at the third floor and a good deal of the garret, without you being with me. I really want to be perfectly fair, and so you must not stop altogether from looking at things until I am able to go with you. I think good things to look at by yourself would be stables and barnyards, and the lower part of barns. Please do not go into haylofts, nor into the chicken-yard, if there is one. You might keep your eyes on the ground until you get to these places and then look up. If there are horses and cows, don't tell me anything about them when you see me. Don't tell me anything. I think I shall be well to-morrow, perhaps to-night. Miriam."

Ralph laughed heartily, and read the note aloud.

"I should say," said Miss Panney, "that that girl has a good deal more conscience than fever. She ought to have slept longer, but as she is awake I will go up and take a look at her; while you can blindfold yourself, if you like, and go out to the barns."

The doctor did not arrive until late in the afternoon, and it was nearly half an hour after he had gone up to his patient before he reported to Ralph.

"She is all right," said he, "but I am not."

The young man looked puzzled.

"By which I mean," continued the other, "that Miss Panney's concoction and the girl's vigorous young nature have thrown off the effects of her nap in the haunted garret, and that I am an allopathist, whereas I ought to be a homeopathist. The young lady and I have had a long conversation on that subject and others. I find that she is a Nonconformist."

"What?" asked Ralph.

"I use the word in its political and social, as well as its religious meaning. That is a sister worth taking care of, sir. Lock her up in her room, if she inclines to any more midnight wanderings."

"And now, having finished with the young patient," said Miss Panney, who was waiting with her bonnet and shawl on, "you can take up an old one, and I will get you to drive me home on your way back to Thorbury."

The doctor had been very much interested in Miriam, and

talked about her to Miss Panney as he drove her to the Witton house, which, by the way, was a mile and a half out of his direct road. The old lady listened with interest, but did not wish to listen very much; she wished to talk of Ralph.

"I like him," she said; "he has pluck. I have had a good deal of talk with him, and he told me frankly that he could not afford to put money into the place and farm it as it ought to be farmed. But he was born a country man, and he has the heart of a country man; and he is going to see if he can make a living out of it for himself and his sister."

"Which may result," said the doctor, "in his becoming a mere farm laborer and putting an end to his sister's education."

"Nonsense!" exclaimed the old lady. "Young fellows—college men—go out on ranches in the West and do that sort of thing, and it lowers them in nobody's estimation. Let young Haverley call his farm a ranch and rough it. It would be the same thing. I've backed him up strongly. It's a manly choice of a manly life. As for his sister, she has been so long at school that it will do her more good to stop than to go on."

"It will be hard scratching," said the doctor, "to get a living out of Cobhurst, and I hope these young people will not come to grief while they are making the experiment."

Miss Panney smiled without looking at her companion.

"Don't be afraid of that," she said presently; "I have pretty good reason to think that he will get on well enough."

That evening Miriam sat up in bed with a shawl about her shoulders and discoursed to her brother.

"Now, Ralph," said she, "you must have seen a lot of things about our place, because, when I came to think of it, it was plain enough that you couldn't help it. I am crazy to see what you saw, but you mustn't tell me anything except what I ask you. Please be particular about that."

"Go on," said Ralph. "You shall not have a word more or less than you want."

"Well, then, is your bed comfortable?"

"Perfectly," he answered.

"And have you pillows enough?"

"More than I want," said Ralph.

"And are the doors and windows all fastened and locked downstairs?"

He laughed. "You needn't bother yourself about that sort of thing. I will attend to the locking up."

She slightly knitted her brows in reflection. "Now then, Ralph," said she, "I am coming to it, and mind, not a word more than I ask for. Have we any horses?"

"We have," he replied.

"How many?"

"Four."

Miriam clasped her hands and looked at her brother with sparkling eyes.

"Oh!" she exclaimed, "four horses!"

"Two of them," he began, but she stopped him in an instant.

"Don't tell me another thing," she cried; "I don't want to know what color they are, or anything about them. To-morrow I shall see them for myself. Oh, Ralph, isn't it perfectly wonderful that we should have four horses? I can't stand anything more just now, so please kiss me good-night."

About an hour afterwards Ralph was awakened by a knock at his door.

"Who is there?" he cried.

The door opened a very little way.

"Ralph," said Miriam, through the crack, "is there one of our horses which can be ridden by a lady?"

Ralph's first impulse was to throw a pillow at the door, but he remembered that sisters were different from fellows at school.

"Can't say anything about that until we try," said he; "and now, Miriam, please go to bed and to sleep."

Miriam shut the door and went away, but in her dreams she rode a prancing charger into Miss Stone's schoolyard, and afterwards drove all the girls in a tally-ho.

CHAPTER VI

MRS. TOLBRIDGE'S CALLERS

The next day was a very fine one, and as the roads were now good, and the air mild, Miss Panney thought it was quite time that she should begin to go about and see her friends without depending on the vehicles of other people, so she ordered her little phaeton and her old roan mare, and drove herself to Thorbury to see Mrs. Tolbridge.

"The doctor tells me," said that good lady, "that you take great interest in those young people at Cobhurst."

"Indeed I do," said Miss Panney, sitting up as straight in her easy chair as if it had been a wooden bench with no back; "I have been thinking about him all the morning. He ought to be married."

Mrs. Tolbridge laughed.

"Dear me, Miss Panney," said she, "it is too soon to begin thinking of a wife for the poor fellow. He has not had time to feel himself at home."

"My motto is that it is never too soon to begin, but we won't talk about that. Kitty, you are the worst matchmaker I ever saw."

"I think I made a pretty good match for myself," said

the other.

"No, you didn't. The doctor made that, and I helped. You had nothing to do with the preliminary work, which is really the most important."

Mrs. Tolbridge smiled. "I am sure I am very much obliged," she said.

"You ought to be. And now while we are on the subject, let me ask you: Have you a new cook?"

"I have," replied the other, "but she is worse than the last one."

Miss Panney rose to her feet, and walked across the room.

"Kitty Tolbridge!" she exclaimed, "this is too bad. You're trifling with the greatest treasure a woman can have on this earth—the life of a good husband."

"But what am I to do?" asked Mrs. Tolbridge. "I have tried everywhere, and I can get no one better."

"Everywhere," repeated Miss Panney. "You mean everywhere in Thorbury. You oughtn't to expect to get a decent cook in this little town. You should go to the city and get one. What you want is to keep the doctor well, no matter what it costs. He doesn't look well, and I don't see how he can be well, on the kind of cooking you can get in Thorbury."

Mrs. Tolbridge flushed a little.

"I am sure," she said, "that Thorbury people, for generations and generations, have lived on Thorbury cooking, and they have been just as healthy as any other people."

"Ah, Kitty, Kitty!" exclaimed the old lady, "you forget how things have changed. In times gone by the ladies of the household superintended all the cooking, and did a good deal of it besides; and they brought something into the kitchen that seldom gets into it now, and that is brains. A cook with a complete set of brains might be pretty hard to get, and would cost a good deal of money. But it is your duty, Kitty, to get as good a one as you can. If she has only a tea-cup full of brains, it will be better than none at all. Don't mind the cost. If you have to do it, spend more on cooking, and less on raw material."

This was all Miss Panney had to say on the subject, and shortly she departed.

After brief stops at the post-office and one or two shops, she drove to the abode of the Bannisters. Miss Panney tied her roan to the hitching-post by the sidewalk, and went up the smooth gravel path to the handsome old house, which she had so often visited, to confer on her own affairs and those of the world at large with the father and the grandfather of the present Bannister, attorney-at-law.

She and the house were all that were left of those old days. Even the widow was the second wife, who had come into the family while Miss Panney was away from Thorbury.

Mrs. Bannister was not at home, but Miss Dora was, and that entirely satisfied the visitor. When the blooming daughter of the house came hurrying into the parlor, Miss Panney, who had previously raised two of the window shades, gazed at her earnestly as she saluted her, and nodded her head approvingly. Then the two sat down to talk.

They talked of several things, and very soon of the Cobhurst people.

"Oh, have you seen them?" exclaimed Dora. "I have, but only for a minute at the station, and then I didn't know who they were, though I was told afterward. They seemed to be very nice."

"They are," said Miss Panney. "The girl is bright, and young Mr. Haverley is an exceedingly agreeable gentleman, just the sort of man who should be the owner of Cobhurst. He is handsome, well educated, and spirited. I saw a good deal of him, for I spent the best part of yesterday there. I should say that your brother would find him a most congenial neighbor. There are so few young men hereabout who are worth anything."

"That is true," replied Dora, with a degree of earnestness, "and I know Herbert will be delighted. I am sure he would call if he were here, but he is away, and doesn't expect to be back for a week."

It crossed Miss Panney's mind that a week's delay in a matter of this sort would not be considered a breach of courtesy, but she did not say so.

"It would be friendly if Mrs. Bannister and you were to call on the sister, before long," she remarked.

"Of course we will do it," said Dora, with animation. "I should think a young lady would be dreadfully lonely in that great house, at least at first, and perhaps we can do something for her."

Although Miss Panney had seen Miriam only in bed, she had a strong conviction that she was not yet a young lady, but this, like the other reflection, was not put into words.

It was not noon when Miss Panney left the Bannister house, and the mind of Miss Dora, which had been renewing itself within her with all the vigor and freshness which Dr. Tolbridge had predicted, was at a loss how to occupy itself until dinner-time, which, with the Bannisters and most of the gentlefolk of Thorbury, was at two o'clock.

Dora put on her prettiest hat and her wrap and went out. She wanted to call on somebody and to talk, and suddenly it struck

Frank Richard Stockton

her that she would go and inquire about the kitten she had given Dr. Tolbridge, and carry it a fresh ribbon. She bought the ribbon, and found Mrs. Tolbridge and the kitten at home.

When the ornament had been properly adjusted, Miss Dora put the kitten upon the floor and remarked: "Now there is some comfort in doing a thing like that for Dr. Tolbridge, because he will be sure to notice it. There are some gentlemen who hardly ever notice things you do for them. Herbert is often that way."

"Yes, my dear," said Mrs. Tolbridge, who had turned toward a desk at which she had been writing. "The doctor is a man I can recommend, and I hope you may get a husband as good as he is. And by the way, if you ever do get such a one, I also hope you will be able to find some one who will cook his meals properly. I find that I cannot do that in Thorbury, and I am going to try to get one in the city. I am now writing an advertisement which I shall put into several of the papers, and day after to-morrow I shall go down to see the people who answer."

"Oh, that will be fun," cried Dora; "I wish I could go with you."

"And why not?"

"Why not, indeed?" replied the young lady, and the matter was immediately arranged.

"And while we are talking about servants," said Dora, whose ebullient mind now found a chance to bring in the subject which was most prominent within it, "I should think that the new people at Cobhurst would find it troublesome to get the right sort of service."

"Perhaps so," replied Mrs. Tolbridge, "although I have a fancy they are going to have a very independent household, at least for a time. It is a great pity that the young girl was taken sick just as she entered into her new home."

"Sick!" exclaimed Dora; "I never heard of that."

"Oh, it wasn't anything serious," said the other, her thoughts turning to the advertisement, which she wished to get into the post-office before dinner, "and I have no doubt she is quite well now, but still it was a pity."

"Indeed it was!" exclaimed Dora, in tones of the most earnest sympathy and commiseration. "It was the greatest kind of a pity, and I think I really ought to call on her very soon." And in this mood she went home to dinner.

Frank Richard Stockton

CHAPTER VII

DORA BANNISTER TAKES TIME
AND A MARE BY THE FORELOCK

Very early that afternoon Miss Dora Bannister was driven to Cobhurst to call upon the young lady who had been taken sick, and who ought not to be neglected by the ladies of Thorbury. Dora had asked her stepmother to accompany her, but as that good lady seldom made calls, and disliked long drives, and could not see why it was at all necessary for her to go, Dora went alone.

When the open carriage with its pair of handsome grays had bumped over the rough entrance to the Cobhurst estate, and had drawn up to the front of the house, Miss Dora skipped lightly out, and rang the door-bell. She rang twice, and as no one came, and as the front door was wide open, she stepped inside to see if she could find any one. She had never been in that great wide hall before, and she was delighted with it, although it appeared to be in some disorder. Two boxes and a trunk were still standing where they had been placed when they were brought from the station. She looked through the open door of the parlor, but there was no one there, and then she knocked on the door of a closed room.

No answer came, and she went to the back door of the long hall and looked out, but not a soul could she see. This was discouraging, but she was not a girl who would willingly turn back, after having set out on an errand of mercy. There was a door which seemed to lead to the basement, and on this she knocked, but to no purpose.

"This is an awfully funny house," she said to herself. "If I could see any stairs, I might go up a little way and call. Surely there must be somebody alive somewhere." Then the thought suddenly came into her mind that perhaps want of life in the particular person she had come to see might be the reason of this dreadful stillness and desertion, and without a moment's hesitation she stepped out of the back door into the open air. She could not stay in that house another second until she knew. Surely there must be some one on the place who could tell her what had happened.

Approaching the gardener's house, she met Phoebe just coming out of the door.

"Bless my soul!" exclaimed the woman of color. "Is that you, Miss Dora? Mike hollered to me that a kirridge had come, and I was a-hurryin' up to the house to see who it was."

"I came to call on Miss Haverley," said Dora. "How is she, Phoebe, and can I see her?"

"Oh, she's well enough, and you can see her if you can find her; but to save my soul, Miss Dora, I couldn't tell you where she is at this minute. You never did in all your life see anybody like that Miss Miriam is. Why, true as I speak, the very sparrers in the trees isn't as wild as she is. From sunrise this morning she has been on the steady go. You'd think, to see her, that the hens and the cows and the colts and even the old apple trees was all silver and gold and diamonds in her eyes, she takes on so about 'em. I can't keep up with her, I can't. The last time I see her, she was goin' into the barn, and I reckon she's thar yit, huntin' hens' nests. If you like, I'll go look for her, Miss Dora."

Phoebe had often worked for the Bannister family, and Dora knew her to be one of the slowest movers among mankind;

besides, the idea of calling upon a young lady who was engaged in looking for hens' nests in a barn was an exceedingly attractive one. It had not been long since Dora had taken much delight in that sort of thing herself.

"You needn't trouble yourself, Phoebe," she said; "I will walk over to the barn. I would a great deal rather do that than wait in the house. If I don't see her there, I will come back and leave our cards."

"You might as well do that," said Phoebe, laughing, "for if she isn't thar, she's as like as not at the other end of the farm in the field where the colts is."

The Cobhurst barn was an unusual, and, indeed, a remarkable structure. It was not as old as the house, although it had been built many years ago by Mathias Butterwood, in a fashion to suit his own ideas of what a barn should be.

It was an enormous structure, a great deal larger than the house, and built of stone. It stood against a high bluff, and there was an entrance on the level to the vast lower story, planned to accommodate Mr. Butterwood's herd of fine cattle. A little higher up, a wide causeway, supported by an arch, led into the second story, devoted to horses and all kinds of vehicles, and still higher, almost on a level with the house, there was a road, walled on each side, by which the loaded haywagons could be driven in upon the great third floor of the barn.

When Dora Bannister reached this barn, having followed a path which led to the lower story, she looked in at an open door, and received the impression of vast extent, emptiness, and the scent of hay. She entered, looking about from side to side. At the opposite end of the great room, was an open door through which the sun shone, and as she approached it, she heard a voice and the cracking of cornstalks outside.

Standing in the doorway, she looked out, and saw a large

barnyard, the ground near the door covered with fresh straw which seemed to have been recently strewn there. The yard beyond was a neglected and bad-looking expanse, into which no young lady would be likely to penetrate, and from which Dora would have turned away instantly, had she not seen, crossing it, a young man and a horse.

The young man was leading the horse by its forelock, and was walking in a sidewise fashion, with his back toward Dora. The horse, a rough-looking creature, seemed reluctant to approach the barn, and its leader frequently spoke to it encouragingly, and patted its neck, as he moved on.

This young man was tall and broad-shouldered. He wore a light soft hat, which well suited his somewhat curling brown hair. A corduroy suit and high top boots, in which he strode fearlessly through the debris and dirt of the yard, gave him, in Dora's eyes, a manly air, and she longed for him to turn his face toward her, that she might speak to him, and ask him where she would be apt to find his sister—for of course this must be Mr. Haverley.

But he did not turn; instead of that he now backed himself toward the stable door, pulling the horse after him. Dora was pleased to stand and look at him; his movements struck her as athletic and graceful. He was now so near that she felt she ought to make her presence known. She stepped out upon the fresh straw, intending to move a little out of his way and then accost him, but he spoke first.

"Good," he said; "don't you want to take hold of this mare by the forelock, as I am doing, and keep her here until I get a halter?" And as he spoke he turned toward Miss Bannister.

His face was a handsome one, fully equal in quality to his height, his shoulders, and his grace of movement. His blue eyes opened wide at the sight of the young lady in gray hat and ostrich plumes, fashionable driving costume edged with fur, for the spring air was yet cool, and bright silk parasol, for the

Frank Richard Stockton

spring sun was beginning to be warm. With almost a stammer, he said:—

"I beg your pardon, I thought it was my sister I heard behind me."

"Oh, it doesn't matter in the least," said Dora, with a charming smile; "I am Miss Bannister. I live in Thorbury, and I came to call on your sister. Phoebe told me she thought she was out here, and so I came to look for her myself. A barn is so charming to me, especially a great one like this, that I would rather make a call in it than in the house."

"I will go and look for her," said Ralph. "She cannot be far away." And then he glanced at the horse, as if he were in doubt what to do with it at this juncture.

"Oh, let me hold your horse," cried Dora, putting down the parasol by the side of the barn and approaching; "I mean while you go and get its halter. I am ever so fond of horses, and like to hold them and feed them and pet them. Is this one gentle?"

"I don't know much about her," said Ralph, laughing, "for we have just taken possession of the place, and are only beginning to find out what animals we own, and what they are like. This old mare seems gentle enough, though rather obstinate. I have just brought her in out of the fields, where she has been grazing ever since the season opened."

"She looks like a very good horse, indeed," said Dora, patting the tangled hair on the creature's neck.

"I brought her in," said Ralph, "thinking I might rub her down, and get her into proper trim for use. My sister is much disappointed to find that out of our four horses, two are unbroken colts, and one is in constant use by the man. I think if I can give her a drive, even if it is behind a jogging old mare, it will set up her spirits again."

"You must let me hold her," said Dora, "while you get the halter, and then you can tie her, while we go and look for your sister. Don't think of such a thing as letting her go, after all your trouble in catching her."

"If I could get her into these stables," said Ralph, "I might shut her in, but I don't think that I shall be able to pull her through that doorway in this fashion."

Without further ado, Miss Dora put out her right hand, in its neatly fitting kid glove, and took hold of the mare's forelock, just above Ralph's hand. The young man demurred an instant, and then, laughing, ran into the stable to find a halter. His ownership of everything was so fresh that he forgot that the lower part of the barn was occupied by the cow stables—which the old mare did not wish to enter, or even approach. He hurriedly rummaged here and there among the stalls, finding nothing but some chains and rope's ends fastened to the mangers, but in his hasty search he could not help thinking how extremely ingenuous and neighborly was that handsome girl outside.

Dora held firmly the forelock of the mare, and patted the good animal's head with the other hand; but, strange to say, the animal did not like being held by the young lady, and gradually she backed, first toward the side of the barn, and then out toward the open yard. Dora attempted to restrain her, but in spite of all her efforts was obliged to follow the retrogressive animal.

"It's my gloves she doesn't like," she said to herself; "I know some horses can't bear the smell of kid, but I can't take them off now, and I will not let go. I wish he would hurry with the halter."

Little by little poor Dora was pulled forward, until she reached a spot which was at the very end of the clean straw, and yet not very far from the wall of the barn. Here she vigorously endeavored to make a stand, for if she went another step

Frank Richard Stockton

forward her dainty boots would sink into mud and dirt.

"Whoa!" she called out to the mare; "whoa, now!"

At the sound of these words, plainly uttered in trouble, Ralph, who happened to be in a stall next to the barn wall looking over some ropes, glanced through a little window about four feet from the ground, and saw Miss Bannister very close to him, tottering on the edge of the straw, and just about to let go of the mare, or step into the mire. Before he could shape words to tell her to release her dangerous hold, or make up his mind to rush around to the door to go to her assistance, she saw him, and throwing out her left hand in his direction, she exclaimed:—

"Oh, hold me, please."

Instantly Ralph put out his long arm, and caught her by the hand.

"Thank you," said Miss Dora. "In another moment she would have pulled me into the dirt. Perhaps now I can make her walk up on the clean straw. Come, come," she continued persuasively to the mare, which, however, obstinately declined to advance.

"Let go of her, I beg of you, Miss Bannister," cried Ralph. "It will hurt you to be pulled on two sides in this way."

Dora was a strong young girl, and so far the pulling had not hurt her at all. In fact, she liked it, at least on one side.

"Oh, I couldn't think of letting her go," she replied, "after all the trouble you have had in catching her. The gate is open, and in a minute she would be out in the field again. If she will only make a few steps forward, I am sure I can hold her until you come out. If you would draw me in a little bit, Mr. Haverley, perhaps she would follow."

Ralph did not in the least object to hold the smoothly gloved little hand in his own, but he was really afraid that the girl would be hurt, if she persisted in this attempt to make a halter of herself. If he released his hold, he was sure she would be jerked face forward into the mire, or at least be obliged to step into it; and as for the mare, it was plain to be seen that she did not intend to come any nearer the shed. He therefore doubled his entreaties that she would let the beast go, as it made no difference whether she ran into the fields or not. He could easily catch her again, or the man could.

"I don't want to let her go," said Dora. "Your sister would have a pretty opinion of me when she is ready to take her drive, and finds that I have let her horse run away; and, besides, I don't like to give up things. Do you like to give up things? I am sure you don't, for I saw you bringing this horse into the yard, and you were very determined about it. If I let her go, all your determination and trouble will have been for nothing. I should not like that. Come, come, you obstinate creature, just two steps forward. I have some lumps of sugar in my pocket which I keep to give to our horses, but of course I can't get it with both my hands occupied. I wish I had thought of the sugar. By the way, the sugar is not in my pocket; after all, it is in this little bag on my belt; I don't suppose you could reach it."

Ralph stretched out his other hand, but he could not reach the little leather bag with its silver clasp. If he could have jumped out of the window, he would have done so without hesitation, but the aperture was not large enough. He could not help being amused by the dilemma in which he was placed by this young lady's inflexibility. He did not know a girl, his sister not excepted, whom, under the circumstances, he would not have left to the consequences of what he would have called her obstinacy. But there was something about Dora—some sort of a lump of sugar—which prevented him from letting go of her hand.

"I never saw a horse," said she, "nor, indeed, any sort of a living thing, which was so unwilling to come to me. You are very good to hold me so strongly, and I am sure I don't mind waiting a little longer, until some one comes by."

"There is no one to come by," exclaimed Ralph, "and I most earnestly beg of you—"

At this moment the horse began to back; Miss Dora's fingers nervously clasped themselves about Ralph's hand, which pressed hers more closely and vigorously than before. There was a strong pull, a little jerk, and the forelock of the mare slipped out of Miss Dora's hand.

"There!" she cried; "that is exactly what I knew would happen. The wicked creature has galloped out of the gate."

The young lady now made a step or two nearer the barn, Ralph still holding her hand, as if to assist her to a better footing.

She did not need the assistance at all, but she looked up gratefully, as Ralph loosened his grasp, and she gently withdrew her hand.

"Thank you ever so much," she said. "If it had not been for you, I do not know where I should have been pulled to; but it is too bad that the horse got off, after all."

"Don't mention it," said Ralph. "I'll have her again in no time," and then he ran outside to join her.

"Now, sir," said she, and giving him no time to make any proposition, "I should like very much to find your sister, and see her, for at least a few moments before I go. Do you think she is anywhere in this glorious old barn? Phoebe told me she was."

"Is this a girl or a woman?" thought Ralph to himself. The charming and fashionable costume would have settled this question in the mind of a lady, but Ralph felt a little puzzled. But be the case what it might, it would be charming to go with her through the barn or anywhere else. As they walked over the lower floor of the edifice toward the stairway in the corner, Dora remarked:—

"How happy your cows ought to be, Mr. Haverley, to have such a wide, cool place as this to live in. What kind of cows have you?"

"Indeed, I don't know," said Ralph, laughing. "I haven't had time to make their acquaintance. I have seen them, only from a distance. They are but a very small herd, and I am sure there are no fancy breeds among them."

"Do you know," said Dora, as they went up the broad steps, sprinkled with straw and hayseed, "that what are called common cows are often really better than Alderneys, or Ayrshires, and those sorts? And this is the second story! How splendid and vast! What do you have here?"

"On the right are the horse stables," said Ralph, "and in those stalls there should be a row of prancing chargers and ambling steeds; and on the great empty floor, which you see over here, there should be the carriages,—the coupe, the family carriage, the light wagon, the pony phaeton, the top buggy, and all the other vehicles which people in the country need. But, alas! you only see that old hay-wagon, which I am sure would fall to pieces if horses attempted to pull it, and that affair with two big wheels and a top. I think they call it a gig, and I believe old Mr. Butterwood used to drive about in it."

"Indeed he did," said Dora. "I remember seeing him when I was a little girl. It must be very comfortable. I should think your sister and you would enjoy driving in that. In a gig, you know, you can go anywhere—into wood-roads, and all sorts of places where you couldn't turn around with anything with four wheels. And how nice it is that it has a top. I've heard it said that Mr. Butterwood would always have everything comfortable for himself. Perhaps your sister is in some of these smaller rooms. What are they?"

"Oh, harness rooms, and I know not what," answered Ralph, and then he called out:—

"Miriam!" His voice was of a full, rich tone, and it was echoed from the bare walls and floors.

"If my sister is in the barn at all," said Ralph, "I think she must be on the floor above this, for there is the hay, and the hens' nests, if there are any—"

"Oh, let us go up there," said Dora; "that is just where we ought to find her."

There was not the least affectation in Dora's delight, as she stood on the wide upper floor of the barn. Its great haymows rose on either side, not piled to the roof as before, but with enough hay left over from former years to fill the air with that delightful scent of mingled cleanliness and sweetness which belongs to haylofts. At the back was a wide open door with a bar across it, out of which she saw a far-stretching landscape, rich with varied colors of spring, and through a small side door at the other end of the floor, which there was level with the ground, came a hen, clucking to a brood of black-eyed, downy little chicks, which she was bringing in for the night to the spacious home she had chosen for them.

Whether or not Dora would have enjoyed all this as much had she been alone is a point not necessary to settle, but she was a true country girl, and had loved chickens, barns, and hay from her babyhood up. She stepped quickly to the open door, and she and Ralph leaned upon the bar and looked out upon the beautiful scene.

"How charming it will be," she said, "for your sister to come here and sit with her reading or sewing. She can look out and see you, almost wherever you happen to be on your farm."

"I don't believe Miriam will be content to sit still and watch anybody," replied Ralph. "I wonder where she can be;" and twice he called her, once directing his voice up toward the haymows and once out into the open air. Dora still leaned on the bar and looked out.

"It would be nice if we could see her walking somewhere in the fields," she said, and she and Ralph both swept the landscape with their eyes, but they saw nothing like a moving girl in shade or sunshine.

Miss Bannister was not in the least embarrassed, as she stood here with this young man whom she had met such a little time before. She did not altogether feel that she was alone with him. The thought that any moment the young man's sister might make one of the party, produced a sensation not wholly unlike that of knowing she was already there.

The view of the far-off hills with the shadows across their sides and their forest-covered tops glistening in the sunshine was very attractive, and there was a blossomy perfume in the outside air which mingled charmingly with the hay-scents from within; but Dora felt that it would not do to protract her pleasure in these things, especially as she noticed signs of a slight uneasiness on the face of her companion. Probably he wanted to go and look for his sister, so they walked slowly over the floor of the great hayloft, and out of the little door where the hen and chickens had come in, and Ralph accompanied the young lady to her carriage.

"I am sure I shall find Thomas and the horses fast asleep," said she, "for I have made a long call, or, at least, have tried to make one, and you must tell your sister that my stay proves how much I wanted to see her. I hope she will call on me the first time she comes to Thorbury."

"Oh, I shall drive her over on purpose," said Ralph, and, with a smile, Miss Bannister declared that would be charming.

Frank Richard Stockton

When the carriage had rolled upon the smooth road outside of Cobhurst, Miss Dora drew off her left glove and looked at her wrist. "Dear me!" said she to herself, "I thought he would have squeezed those buttons entirely through my skin, but I wouldn't have said a word for anything. I wonder what sort of a girl his sister is. If she resembles him, I know I shall like her."

CHAPTER VIII

MRS. TOLBRIDGE'S REPORT IS NOT ACCEPTED

A few days after Miss Bannister's call at Cobhurst, it was returned by Ralph and Miriam, who drove to Thorbury with the brown mare and the gig. To their disappointment, they found that the young lady was not at home, and the communicative maid informed them that she had gone to the city to help Mrs. Tolbridge to get a new cook.

They went home by the way of the Witton house, and there they found Miss Panney at home. The old lady was very much interested in Miriam, whom she had not before seen out of bed. She scrutinized the girl from hat to boots.

"What do you want me to call you, my dear?" she asked. "Don't you honestly think you are too young to be called Miss Haverley?"

"I think it would be very well if you were to call me Miriam," said the other, who was of the opinion that Miss Panney was old enough to call any woman by her Christian name.

The conversation was maintained almost entirely by the old lady and Ralph, for Miriam was silent and very solemn. Once she broke in with a question:—

"What kind of a person is Miss Bannister?" she asked. Miss Panney gave a short laugh.

"Oh, she is a charming person," she answered, "pretty, good-humored, well educated, excellent taste in dress and almost everything, and very lively and pleasant to talk to. I am very fond of her."

"I am afraid," said Miriam, "that she is too old and too fine for me," and turning to a photograph album she began to study the family portraits.

"Your sister's ideas are rather girlish as yet," said Miss Panney, "but housekeeping at Cobhurst will change all that;" and then she went on with her remarks concerning the Haverley and Butterwood families, a subject upon which Ralph was not nearly so well informed as she was.

When the brother and sister had driven away, Miss Panney reflected that the visit had given her two pieces of information. One was that the Haverley girl was a good deal younger than she had thought her, and the other was that Mrs. Tolbridge was really trying to get a new cook. The first point she did not consider with satisfaction.

"It is a pity," she thought, "that Dora and his sister are not likely to be friends. That would help wonderfully. This school-girl, probably jealous of the superiority of grown-up young ladies, may be very much in the way. I am sorry the case is not different."

In regard to the other point the old lady was very well satisfied, and determined to go soon to see what success Mrs. Tolbridge had had.

About the middle of the next forenoon, Miss Panney tied her horse in front of the Tolbridge house and entered unceremoniously, as she was in the habit of doing. She found the doctor's wife standing by the back-parlor window looking out on the garden. When the old lady had seated herself she immediately proceeded to business.

"Well, Kitty," said she, "what sort of a time did you have yesterday?"

"A very discouraging and disagreeable one," said Mrs. Tolbridge. "I might just as well have stayed at home."

"You don't mean to say," asked Miss Panney, "that nobody answered your advertisement?"

"When I reached the rooms of the Non-Resident Club, where the applicants were to call—"

"That's the first time," interrupted Miss Panney, "that I ever heard that that Club was of the slightest use."

"It wasn't of any use this time," said the other; "for although I found several women there who came before the hour appointed, and at least a dozen came in the course of the morning, not one of them would do at all. I was just now looking out at our asparagus bed, and wondering if any of those beautiful heads would ever be cooked properly. The woman in our kitchen knows that she is to depart, and she is in a terribly bad temper, and this she puts into her cooking. The doctor is almost out of temper himself. He says that he has pretty good teeth, but that he cannot bite spite."

Miss Panney now appeared to be getting out of temper.

"I must say, Kitty," she said, in a tone of irritation, "that I do not understand how it was that out of the score or more of applicants, you could not find a better cook than the good-for-nothing creature you have now. What was the matter with them?"

"Everything, it seemed to me," answered Mrs. Tolbridge. "Now here is Dora. She was with me yesterday, and you can ask her about the women we saw."

Miss Panney attached no value whatever to the opinions, in

regard to domestic service, of the young lady who had just entered the room, and she asked her no questions. Miss Bannister, however, did not seem in the least slighted, and sat down to join the chat.

"I suppose," said Miss Panney, sarcastically, "that you tried to find that woman that the doctor used to say he wanted: a woman who had committed some great crime, who could find no relief from her thoughts but in constant work, work, work."

Mrs. Tolbridge smiled.

"No, I did not look for her; nor did I try to find the person who was of a chilly disposition and very susceptible to draughts. We used to want one of that sort, but she should be a waitress. But, seriously, there were objections to every one of them. Religion was a great obstacle. The churches of Thorbury are not designed for the consciences of city servants. There was no Lutheran Church for the Swedes; and the fact that the Catholic Church was a mile from our house, with no street-cars, settled the question for most of them. The truth is, none of them wanted to come into the country, unless they could get near Newport or some other suitable summer resort."

"But there was that funny old body in a shawl," said Dora, "who made no objections to churches, or anything else in fact, as soon as she found out your husband wasn't in trade."

"True," replied Mrs. Tolbridge; "she didn't object, but she was objectionable."

Miss Panney was beginning to fasten her wrap about her. She had heard quite enough, but still she deigned to snap out:—

"What was the matter with her?"

"Oh, she was entirely out of the question," said the lady of the house. "In the first place, she was the widow of a French chef, or somebody of that sort, and has a wonderful opinion of her abilities. She understands all kinds of cooking,—plain or fancy."

"And even butter," said Dora; "she said she knew all about that."

"Yes; and she understood how butcher's meat should be cut, and the choosing of poultry, and I know not what else besides."

"And only asked," cried Dora, laughing, "if your husband was in trade; and when she heard that he was a professional man, was perfectly willing to come."

Miss Panney turned toward Mrs. Tolbridge, sat up very straight in her chair, and glared.

"Was not this the very woman you were looking for? Why didn't you take her?"

"Take her!" repeated Mrs. Tolbridge, with some irritation. "What could I do with a woman like that? She would want enormous wages. She would have to have kitchen maids, and I know not whom, besides, to wait on her; and as for our plain style of living, she could not be expected to stand that. She would be entirely out of place in a house like this."

"Her looks were enough to settle her case," said Dora. "You never saw such an old witch; she would frighten the horses."

"Kitty Tolbridge," said Miss Panney, severely, "did you ask that woman if she wanted high wages, if she required kitchen maids, if she would be satisfied to cook for your family?"

"No, I didn't," said the other; "I knew it was of no use. It was plain to see that she would not do at all."

"Did you get her address?"

"Yes," said Dora; "she gave me a card as we were going out, and insisted on my taking it. It is in my bag at home."

Miss Panney was silent for a moment, and was evidently endeavoring to cool her feelings so as to speak without indignation.

"Kitty Tolbridge," she said presently, "I think you have deliberately turned your back on one of the greatest opportunities ever offered to a woman with a valuable husband. There are husbands who have no value, and who might as well be hurried to their graves by indigestion as in any other way, but the doctor is not one of these. Now, whatever you know of that woman proves her to be the very person who should be in your kitchen at this moment; and whatever you have said against her is all the result of your imagination. If I were in your place, I would take the next train for the city; and before I closed my eyes this night, I would know whether or not such a prize as that were in my reach. I say prize because I never heard of such a chance being offered to a doctor's wife in a country town. Now what are you going to do about it, Kitty? If your regard for your husband's physical condition is not sufficient to make you look on this matter as I do, think of his soul. If you don't believe that true religion and good cooking go hand in hand, wait a year and then see what sort of a husband you will have."

Mrs. Tolbridge felt that she ought to resent this speech, that she ought to be, at least, a little angry; but when she was a small girl, Miss Panney was an old woman who sometimes used to scold her. She had not minded the scoldings very much then, and she could not bring herself to mind this scolding very much now. Occasionally she had scolded Miss Panney, and the old lady had never been angry.

"I shall not go to the city," she said, with a smile; "but I will write, and ask all the questions. Then our consciences will be easier."

Miss Panney rose to her feet.

"Do it, I beg of you," she said, "and do it this morning. And now, Dora, if you walked here, I will drive you home in my phaeton, for you ought to send that address to Mrs. Tolbridge without delay."

As the old roan jogged away from the doctor's house, Miss Panney remarked to her companion, "I needn't have hurried you off so soon, Dora, for it is three hours before the next mail will leave; but I did want Mrs. Tolbridge to sit down at once and write that letter without being interrupted by anything which you might have come to tell her. Of course, the sooner you send her the address, the better."

"The boy shall take it to her as soon as I get home," said Dora.

She very much disliked scoldings, and had not now a word to say against the old body who would frighten the horses. Desirous of turning the conversation in another direction without seeming to force it, "It seems to me," she said, "that Mr. and Miss Haverley ought to have somebody better to cook for them than old Phoebe. I have always looked upon her as a sort of a charwoman, working about from house to house, doing anything that people hired her to do."

"That's just what those Haverleys want," said Miss Panney. "At present, everything is charwork at their place, and as to their food, I don't suppose they think much about it, so that they get enough. At their age they can eat anything."

"How old is Miss Haverley?" asked Dora.

"Miss Haverley!" repeated Miss Panney, "she's nothing but a girl, with her hair down her back and her skirts a foot from the ground. I call her a child."

A shadow came over the soul of Miss Bannister.

Frank Richard Stockton

Would it be possible, she thought, to maintain, with a girl who did not yet put up her hair or wear long skirts, the intimacy she had hoped to maintain with Mr. Haverley's sister?

Very much the same idea was in the mind of Miss Panney, but she thought it well to speak encouragingly. "I wish, for her brother's sake, the girl were older," said she: "but housekeeping will help to mature her much more quickly than if she had remained at school. And as for school," she added, "it strikes me it would be a good thing for her to go back there—after awhile."

Dora thought this a good opinion, but before she could say anything on the subject, she lifted her eyes, and beheld Ralph Haverley walking down the street toward them. He was striding along at a fine pace, and looked as if he enjoyed it.

"I declare," ejaculated Miss Bannister, "here he is himself. We shall meet him."

"He? who?" and Miss Panney looked from side to side of the road, and the moment she saw the young man, she smiled.

It pleased her that Dora should speak of him as "he," showing that the brother was in her mind when they had been talking of the sister.

Miss Panney drew up to the sidewalk, and Ralph stopped.

He was greatly pleased with the cordial greeting he received from the two ladies. These Thorbury people were certainly very sociable and kind-hearted. The sunlight was on Dora's soul now, and it sparkled in her eyes.

"It was my other hand that I gave you when I met you before," she said, with a charming smile.

"Yes," said Ralph, also with a smile, "and I think I held it an uncommonly long time."

"Indeed you did," said Dora; and they both laughed.

Miss Panney listened in surprise.

"You two seem to know each other better than I supposed," she said. "When did you become acquainted?"

"We have met but once before," replied Dora, "but that was rather a peculiar meeting." And then she told the story of her call at Cobhurst, and of the mare's forelock, and the old lady was delighted with the narration. She had never planned a match which had begun so auspiciously. These young people must be truly congenial, for already a spirit of comradeship seemed to have sprung up between them. But of course that sort of thing could not be kept up to the desirable point without the assistance of the sister. In some way or other, that girl must be managed. Miss Panney determined to give her mind to it.

With Ralph standing close by the side of the phaeton, the reins lying loose on the back of the drowsy roan, and Dora leaning forward from her seat, so as to speak better with the young man, the interview was one of considerable length, and no one seemed to think it necessary that it should be brought to a close. Ralph had come to attend to some business in the town, and had preferred to walk rather than drive the brown mare.

"Did you ever catch that delightfully obstinate creature?" cried Dora. "And did you give your sister a drive in the gig?"

"Oh, yes," said Ralph, "I easily caught her again, and I curried and polished her up myself, and trimmed her mane and tail and fetlocks, and since she has been having good meals of oats, you can hardly imagine what a sleek-looking beast she has become. We drove her into Thorbury when Miriam returned your call. I am sorry you were not at home, so that you might have seen what a change had come over Mrs. Browning."

Dora looked inquiringly.

Frank Richard Stockton

"That is the name that Miriam has given to the mare."

Dora laughed.

"If Mrs. Browning is one of your sister's favorite poets," she said, "that will be a bond between us, for I like her poems better than I do her husband's, at least I understand them better. I wonder if your sister will ever ask me to take a drive with her in the gig? I could show her so many pretty places."

"Indeed she will," said Ralph; "but you mustn't think we are going to confine ourselves to that sedate conveyance and the old mare. The colts are old enough to be broken, and when they are ready to drive we shall have a spanking team."

"That will be splendid," exclaimed Dora. "I cannot imagine anything more inspiriting than driving with a pair of freshly broken horses."

Miss Panney gave a little sniff.

"That sort of thing," she said, "sometimes exalts one's spirit so high that it is never again burdened by the body; but all horses have to be broken, and people continue to live."

She smiled as she thought that the pair of young colts which she had taken in hand seemed to give promise of driving together most beautifully. But it would not do to stop here all the morning, and as there was no sign that Dora would tire of asking questions or Ralph of answering them, the old lady gathered up the reins.

"You mustn't be surprised, Mr. Haverley," she said, "if the ladies of Thorbury come a good deal to Cobhurst. We have more time than the gentlemen, and we all want to get well acquainted with your sister, and help her in every way that we can. Miss Bannister is going to drive over very soon and stop for me on the way, so that we shall call on her together."

When the young man had bowed and departed, and the old roan was jogging on, Dora leaned back in the phaeton and said to herself, that, without knowing it, Miss Panney was an angel. When they should go together to Cobhurst, the old lady would be sure to spend her time talking to the girl.

CHAPTER IX

JOHN WESLEY AND LORENZO DOW
AT LUNCHEON

Two days after her lecture to Mrs. Tolbridge, Miss Panney was again in Thorbury, and, having finished the shopping which brought her there, she determined to go to see the doctor's wife, and find out if that lady had acted on the advice given her. She had known Mrs. Tolbridge nearly all that lady's life, and had always suspected in her a tendency to neglect advice which she did not like, after the adviser was out of the way. She did not wish to be over-inquisitive, but she intended, in some quiet way, to find out whether or not the letter about which she had spoken so strongly had been written. If it had not, she would take time to make up her mind what she should do. Kitty Tolbridge and she had scolded each other often enough, and had had many differences, but they had never yet seriously quarrelled. Miss Panney did not intend to quarrel now, but if she found things as she feared they were, she intended to interfere in a way that might make Kitty uncomfortable, and perhaps produce the same effect on herself and the doctor; but let that be as it might, she assured herself there were some things that ought to be done, no matter who felt badly about it.

She found the doctor's wife in a state of annoyance and disquiet, and was greatly surprised to be told that this condition had been caused by a note which had just been brought to her from her husband, stating that he had been called away to a distant patient, and would not be able to come home to luncheon.

"My dear Kitty!" exclaimed Miss Panney, "I should have thought you were thoroughly used to that sort of thing. I supposed a country doctor would miss his mid-day meal about half the time."

"And so he does," said Mrs. Tolbridge; "but I was particularly anxious that he should lunch at home to-day, and he promised me that he would."

"Well," said the old lady, "you will have to bear up under it as well as you can, and I hope they will give him something to eat wherever he is going."

Mrs. Tolbridge seemed occupied, and did not answer.

"Miss Panney," she said suddenly, "will you stay and take lunch with me? I should like it ever so much."

"Are you going to have strawberries?" asked Miss Panney.

Mrs. Tolbridge hesitated a little, and then replied, "Yes, we shall have them."

"Very well, then, I'll stay. The Witton strawberries are small and sour this year; and I haven't tasted a good one yet."

During the half hour which intervened before luncheon was announced, Miss Panney discovered nothing regarding the matter which brought her there. She would ask no questions, for it was Kitty Tolbridge's duty to introduce the subject, and she would give her a chance; but if she did not do it in a reasonable time, Miss Panney would not only ask questions, but state her opinion.

When she sat down at the pretty round table, arranged for two persons, Miss Panney was surprised at the scanty supply of

Frank Richard Stockton

eatables. There was the tea-tray, bread and butter, and some radishes. Her soul rose in anger.

"Slops and fruit," she said to herself. "She isn't worthy to have any sort of a husband, much less such a one as she has."

There was a vase of flowers in the centre of the table; but although Miss Panney liked flowers, at meal-times she preferred good honest food.

"Shall I give you a cup of tea?" asked her hostess.

The old lady did not care for tea, but as she considered that she could not eat strawberries on an empty stomach, she took some, and was just about to cast a critical eye on the bread, when a maid entered, bearing a dish containing two little square pieces of fish, covered with a greenish white sauce, and decorated with bits of water-cress.

As soon as Miss Panney's eyes fell upon this dish, she understood the situation—Mrs. Tolbridge had actually fallen back upon Kipper. Kipper was a caterer in Thorbury, and a good one. He was patronized by the citizens on extraordinary festive occasions, but depended for his custom principally upon certain families who came to the village for a few months in the summer, and who did not care to trouble themselves with much domestic machinery.

"Kipper, indeed," thought the old lady; "that is the last peg. A caterer's tid-bit for a hard-working man. If she would have her fish cooked properly in her own house, she could give him six times as much for half the money. And positively," she continued, in inward speech, as the maid presented the bread and butter, "Kipper's biscuit! I suppose she is going to let him provide her with everything, just as he does for those rich people on Maple Avenue."

The fish was very good, and Miss Panney ate every morsel of it, but made no remark concerning it. Instead of speaking of food, she talked of the doings of the Methodist congregation in Thorbury, who were planning to build a new church, far more expensive than she believed they could afford. She was engaged in berating Mr. Hampton, the minister, who, she declared, was actually encouraging his flock in their proposed extravagance, when the maid gave her a clean plate, and handed her a dish of sweetbread, tastefully garnished with clover blossoms and leaves. Miss Panney stopped talking, gazed at the dish for a minute, and then helped herself to a goodly portion of its contents.

"Feathers," she said to herself; "no more than froth and feathers to a man who has been working hard half a day, and as to the extravagance of such flimsy victuals—" She could keep quiet no longer, she was obliged to speak out, and she burst into a tirade against people who called themselves pious, and yet, wilfully shutting their eyes, were about to plunge into wicked wastefulness. She ate as she talked, however, and she had brought up John Wesley, and was about to give her notion of what he would have had to say about a fancy church for a Thorbury congregation, when the plates were again changed, and a dainty dish of sirloin steak, with mushrooms, and thin slices of delicately browned potatoes, was put before her.

"Well!" inwardly ejaculated the old lady, "something substantial at last. But what money this meal must have cost!"

As she cut into the thick, juicy piece of steak, which had been broiled until it was cooked enough, and not a minute more, Miss Panney's mind dropped from the consideration of congregational finances into that of domestic calculation. She knew Kipper's charges; she knew everybody's charges.

"That dish of fish," she said to herself, "was not less than sixty cents; the sweetbreads cost a dollar, if they cost a cent; this sirloin, with mushrooms, was seventy-five cents; that, with the French biscuit, is two dollars and a half for a family lunch for two people."

Miss Panney did not let her steak get cold, for she could talk and eat at the same time, and the founder of Methodism never delivered so scorching a tirade against pomp and show in professors of religion as she gave forth in his name.

Mrs. Tolbridge had been very quiet during the course of the meal, but she was now constrained to declare that she had nothing to do with the plans for the new Methodist church, and, in fact, she knew very little about them.

"Some things concern all of us," retorted Miss Panney. "Suppose Bishop White, when he was ordained and came back to this country, had found a little village—"

Her remarks were stopped by a dish of salad. The young and tender leaves of lettuce were half concealed by a mayonnaise dressing.

"This makes three dollars," thought Miss Panney, as she helped herself, "for Kipper never makes any difference, even if you send your own lettuce to be dressed." And then she went on talking about Bishop White, and what he would have thought of a little cathedral in every country town.

"But the Methodists do not have cathedrals," said Mrs. Tolbridge.

"Which makes it all the worse when they try to build their meeting-houses to look like them," replied the old lady.

It was a long time since Miss Panney had tasted any mayonnaise dressing as good as this. But she remembered that the strawberries were to come, and did not help herself again to salad.

"If one of the old Methodist circuit-riders," she said, "after toiling over miles of weary road in the rain or scorching sun, and preaching sometimes in a log meeting-house, sometimes in a barn, and often in a private house, should suddenly come upon—"

The imaginary progress of the circuit-rider was brought to a stop by the arrival of the last course of the luncheon. From a pretty glass dish uprose a wondrous structure. Within an encircling wall of delicate, candied tracery was heaped a little mound of creamy frost, the sides of great strawberries showing here and there among the veins and specks of crimson juice.

Miss Panney raised her eyes from this creation to the face of her hostess.

"Kitty," said she, "is this the doctor's birthday?"

"No," answered Mrs. Tolbridge, with a smile; "he was born in January."

"Yours then, perhaps?"

Mrs. Tolbridge shook her head.

"A dollar and a half," thought the old lady, "and perhaps more. Five dollars at the very least for the meal. If the doctor makes that much between meals, day in and day out, she ought to be thankful."

The dainty concoction to which the blazing-eyed old lady now applied herself was something she had never before tasted, and she became of the opinion that Kipper would not get up a dish of that sort, and so much of it, for less than two dollars.

"There was a Methodist preacher," she said, spoonful after spoonful of the cold and fruity concoction melting in her mouth as she spoke, "a regular apostle of the poor, named Lorenzo Dow. How I would like to have him here. He was a man who would let people know in trumpet tones, by day and by night, what he thought of wicked, wasteful prodigality, no matter how pleasant it might be, how easy it might be, or how proper in people who could afford it. Is there to be anything more, Kitty Tolbridge?"

The doctor's wife could not restrain a little laugh.

"No," she said, "there is to be nothing more, unless you will take a little tea."

Miss Panney pushed back her chair and looked at her hostess. "Tea after a meal like that! I should think not. If you had had champagne during the luncheon, and coffee afterwards, I shouldn't have been surprised."

"I did not order coffee," said Mrs. Tolbridge, "because we don't take it in the middle of the day, but—"

"You ordered quite enough," said her visitor, severely; "and I will say this for Kipper, that he never got up a better meal, although—"

"Kipper!" interrupted Mrs. Tolbridge. "Kipper had nothing to do with this luncheon. It was prepared by my new cook. It is the first meal she has given us, and I am so sorry the doctor could not be here to eat it."

Miss Panney rose from her chair, and gazed earnestly at Mrs. Tolbridge.

"What cook?" she asked, in her deepest tones.

"Jane La Fleur," was the reply; "the woman you urged me to write to. I sent the letter that afternoon. Yesterday she came to see me, and I engaged her. And while we were at breakfast this morning, she arrived with her boxes, and went to work."

"And she cooked that meal? She herself made all those things?"

"Yes," said Mrs. Tolbridge, "she even churned the butter and made the biscuit. She says she is going to do a great deal better than this when she gets things in order."

"Better than this!" ejaculated Miss Panney. "Do you mean to say, Kitty Tolbridge, that this sort of thing is going to happen three times a day? What have you done? What sort of a creature is she? Tell me all about it this very minute."

Mrs. Tolbridge led the way to the parlor, and the two sat down.

"Now," said the doctor's wife, "suppose you finish what you were saying about the Methodist church, then—"

Miss Panney stamped her foot.

"Don't mention them!" she cried. "Let them build tower on tower, spire on spire, crypts, picture galleries, altars, confessionals, if they like. Tell me about your new cook."

"It will take a long time to tell you all about her, at least all she told me," said Mrs. Tolbridge, "for she talked to me more than an hour this morning, working away all the time. Her name is Jane La Fleur, but she does not wish any one to call her Jane. She would like the family to use her last name, and the servants can do the same, or call her 'madam.' She is the widow of two chefs, one a Florentine, named Tolati, and the other a Frenchman, La Fleur. She acted as 'second' to each of these, and in that way has thoroughly learned the art of Italian cooking, as well as the French methods. She herself is English, and she has told me about some of the great families she and her husbands lived with."

"Kitty," said Miss Panney, "I should think she was trying to impose upon you with a made-up story; but after that luncheon I will believe anything she says about her opportunities. How in the world did you get such a woman to come to you?"

"Oh, the whole business of engaging her was very simple," answered Mrs. Tolbridge. "Her last husband left her some money, and she came to this country on a visit to relatives, but she loved her art so much, she said—"

Frank Richard Stockton

"Did she call it art?" asked Miss Panney.

"Yes, she did—that she felt she must cook, and she lived for some time with a family named Drane, in Pennsylvania, with whom the doctor used to be acquainted. She had a letter from them which fully satisfied me. On her part she said she would be content with the salary I paid my last cook."

"Did she call it salary?" exclaimed the old lady.

"That was the word she used," answered Mrs. Tolbridge, "and as I said before, the only question she asked was whether or not my husband was in trade."

"What did that matter?" asked the other.

"It seemed to matter a great deal. She said she had never yet lived with a tradesman, and never intended to. She was with Mrs. Drane, the widow of a college professor, for several months, and when the family found they could no longer afford to keep a servant who could do nothing but cook, La Fleur returned to her relatives, and looked for another position; but not until I came, she said, had any one applied who was not in trade."

"She must be an odd creature," said Miss Panney.

"She is odder than odd," was the answer. At this moment the maid came in and told Mrs. Tolbridge that the madam cook wanted to see her. The lady of the house excused herself, and in a few minutes returned, smiling.

"She wished to tell me," 'said she, "before my visitor left, that the name of the 'sweet' which she gave us at luncheon is *la promesse*, being merely a promise of what she is going to do, when she gets about her everything she wants."

"Kitty Tolbridge," said Miss Panney, solemnly, "whatever happens, don't mind that woman's oddity. Keep your mind on her cooking, and don't consider anything else. She is an angel, and she belongs to the very smallest class of angels that visit human beings. You may find, by the dozen, philanthropists, kind friends, helpers and counsellors, the most loving and generous; but a cook like that in a Thorbury family is as rare as—as—as—I can't think of anything so rare. I came here, Kitty, to find out if you had written to that woman, and now to discover that the whole matter has been settled in two days, and that the doors of Paradise have been opened to Dr. Tolbridge—for you know, Kitty, that the Garden of Eden was truly Paradise until they began to eat the wrong things—I feel as if I had been assisting at a miracle."

Frank Richard Stockton

CHAPTER X

A SILK GOWN AND A BOTTLE

It was toward the end of June that Miss Dora Bannister returned from a fortnight's visit to some friends at the seashore, and she had been home a very little while, when she became convinced that her most important duty was to go to see that young girl at Cobhurst. It seemed very strange that so long a time had passed since the arrival of the Haverleys into the neighborhood, and she had never yet seen his sister. In Miss Bannister's mind there was a central point, about which clustered everything connected with Cobhurst: that point was a young man, and the house was his house, and the fields were his fields, and the girl was his sister.

It so happened, the very next day, that Herbert Bannister found it necessary to visit a lady client, who lived about four miles beyond Cobhurst, and when Dora heard this she was delighted. Her brother should take her as far as Cobhurst with him; they should start early enough to give him time to stop and call on Ralph Haverley, which he most certainly ought to do, and then he could go on and attend to his business, leaving her at Cobhurst. Even if neither the brother nor the sister were at home, she would not mind being left at that charming old place. She would take a book with her, for there were so many shady spots where she could sit and read until Herbert came back.

Herbert Bannister, whose mind was devoted to business and

the happiness of his sister, was well pleased with this arrangement, and about three o'clock in the afternoon the buggy containing the two stopped in front of the Cobhurst portico.

The front door was open, and they could see through the hall and the open back door into the garden beyond.

Dora laughed as she said, "This is just what happened when I came here before,—everything wide open, as though there were no flies nor dogs nor strangers."

Herbert got out and rang the bell: he rang it twice, but no one came. Dora beckoned him to her.

"It is of no use," she said; "that also happened when I came before. They don't live in the house, at least in the daytime. But Herbert, there is a man."

At this moment, the negro Mike was seen at a little distance, hurrying along with a tin pitcher in his hand. Herbert advanced, and called to him, and Mike, with his pitcher, approached.

"The boss," he said, in response to their inquiries, "is down in the big meadow, helpin' me get in the hay. We tried to git extry help, but everybody's busy this time o' year, an' he an' me has got to step along pretty sharp to git that hay in before it rains. No, Miss, I dunno where the young lady is. She was down in the hay-field this mornin', rakin', but I 'spects she is doin' some sort of housework jes' now, or perhaps she's in the garden. I'd go an' look her up, but beggin' your pardon, I ain't got one minute to spare, the boss is waitin' for me now," and, touching his shabby old hat, Mike departed.

"What shall we do?" asked Herbert, standing by the buggy.

"I think," said Dora, slowly and decisively, as if she had fully considered the matter, "that you may as well go on, for I don't suppose it would do to disturb Mr. Haverley now. I know that when people are making hay, they can't stop for anything."

"You are right," said her brother, with a smile; "hay-making the will of a rich man on his death-bed; it must be done promptly, if it is done at all. I shall go on, of course, and you will go with me?"

"No, indeed," said Dora, preparing to get down from the buggy; "I would not want to wait for you in that tiresome old horse-hair parlor of the Dudleys. I should ever so much rather sit here, by myself, until you come back. But of course I shall see her before long. Isn't it funny, Herbert? I had to look for her when I came here before, and I suppose I shall always have to look for her whenever I come."

Her brother admitted that it was funny, and accepting her arrangement, he drove away. Dora rang the bell, and stepped into the hall. "I will wait here a little while," she said to herself, "then I will go to Phoebe's house, and ask her where she is. If she does not know, I do not in the least mind walking over to the hay-field, and calling to Mr. Haverley. It would not take him three minutes to come and tell me where I would better go to look for his sister."

At this Miss Bannister smiled a little. She would be really glad to know if Mr. Haverley would be willing to leave that important hay, and make everything wait until he came to speak to her. As she stood, she looked about her; on a table by the wall lay a straw hat trimmed with flowers, and a pair of long gloves, a good deal soiled and worn. Dora's eyes passed carelessly over these, and rested on another pair of gloves, larger and heavier.

"He hasn't driven much, yet," she said to herself, "for they look almost new. I wonder when he will break his colts. Then, I suppose, he will drive a good deal."

Dora was a girl who noticed things, and turning to the other side of the hall, she saw a larger table, and on it lay a powder-horn and a shot-flask, while in the angle of the table and the wall there stood a double-barrelled fowling-piece. This sight made her eyes sparkle; he must like to hunt and shoot. That pleased her very much. Herbert never cared for those things, but she thought a young man should be fond of guns and dogs and horses, and although she had never thought of it before, she now considered it a manly thing to be able to go out into the hay-field and work, if it happened to be necessary.

She went to the back door, and stood, looking out. There was nobody stirring about Phoebe's house, and she asked herself if it would be worth while to go over to it. Perhaps it might be as well to stroll toward the hay-field. She knew where the great meadow was, because she had looked over it when she had stood at the wide barn window with Mr. Haverley. He had pointed out a good many things to her, and she remembered them all.

But she did not go to the hay-field. Just as she was about to step out upon the back porch, she heard a door open behind her, and turning, saw, emerging from the closed apartment which contained the staircase, a strange figure. The head was that of a young girl about fourteen, with large, astonished blue eyes, and light brown hair hanging in a long plait down her back, while her form was attired in a plum-colored silk gown, very much worn, torn in some places, with several great stains in the front of the skirt, and a long and tattered train. The shoulders were ever so much too wide, the waist was ever so much too big, and the long sleeves were turned back and rolled up. In her hand the figure held a large glass bottle, from the mouth of which hung a short rubber tube, ending in a bulbous mouth-piece.

Dora could not suppress a start and an expression of surprise, but she knew this must be Miriam Haverley, and advanced toward her. In a moment she had recovered her self-possession sufficiently to introduce herself and explain the situation. Miriam took the bottle in her left hand, and held out her right to Dora.

"I have been expecting you would call," she said, "but I had no idea you were here now. The door-bell is in the basement, and I have been upstairs, trying to get dough off my hands. I have been making bread, and I had no idea it was so troublesome to get your hands clean afterwards; but I expect my dough is stickier than it ought to be, and after that I was busy getting myself ready to go out and feed a calf. Will you walk into the parlor?"

"Oh, no," cried Dora, "let me go with you to feed the calf; I shall like that ever so much better."

"It can wait just as well as not," said Miriam; "we can sit in the hall, if you like," and she moved toward an old-fashioned sofa which stood against the wall; as she did so, she stepped on the front of her voluminous silk gown, and came near falling.

"The horrid old thing!" she exclaimed; "I am always tripping over it," and as she glanced at Dora the two girls broke into a laugh. "I expect you think I look like a perfect guy," she said, as they seated themselves, "and so I do, but you see the calf is not much more than a week old, and its mother has entirely deserted it, and kicks and horns at it if it comes near her. It got to be so weak it could scarcely stand up, and I have adopted it, and feed it out of this bottle. The first time I did it I nearly ruined the dress I had on, and so I went to the garret and got this old gown, which covers me up very well, though it looks dreadfully, and is awfully awkward."

"To whom did it belong?" asked Dora. "It is made in such a queer way,—not like really old-fashioned things."

"I am sure I don't know to whom it belonged," said Miriam. "There are all sorts of things in our garret,—except things that are good for some particular purpose,—and this old gown was the best I could find to cover me up. It looks funny, but then the whole of it is funny,—calf-feeding and all."

"Why do you have to make your own bread?" asked Dora.

"Don't Phoebe do that?"

"Oh, Phoebe isn't here now. She went away nearly a week ago, and I do all the work. I went to Thorbury and engaged a woman to come here; but, as that was three days ago and she has not come yet, I think she must have changed her mind."

"But why did Phoebe leave you?" exclaimed Miss Bannister. "She ought to be ashamed of herself, to leave you without any one to help you."

"Well," replied Miriam "she said she wasn't regularly employed, anyway, and there were plenty of cooks in the town that I could get, and that she was obliged to go. You see, the colored church in Thorbury has just got a new minister, and he has to board somewhere; and as soon as Phoebe heard that, she made up her mind to take a house and board him; and she did it before anybody else could get the chance. Mike, her husband, who works for us, talked to her and we talked to her, but it wasn't of any use. I think she considers it one of the greatest honors in the world to board a minister. Mike does not believe in that sort of business, but he says that Phoebe has always been in the habit of doing what she wants to, and he is getting used to it."

"But it is impossible for you to do all the work," said Dora.

"Oh, well," replied Miriam, "some of it doesn't get done, and some of it I am helped with. Mike does ever so much; he makes the fires, and carries the heavy things, and sometimes even cooks. My brother Ralph helps, too, when there is anything he can do, which is not often; but just now they are so busy with their hay that it is harder upon me than it was before. We have had soda biscuit and all that sort of thing, but I saw that Ralph was getting tired of them; and to-day I thought I would try and make some real bread,—though how it is going to turn out, I don't know."

"Come, let us go out and feed the calf," said Dora; "I really want to see how you do it. I have come to make you a good long call, you must know;" and then she explained how her brother had left her, while he went on to attend to his business.

At this Miriam was much relieved. She had been thinking that perhaps she would better go upstairs and take off that ridiculous silk dress, and entertain her visitor properly during the rest of her call; but if Miss Bannister was going to stay a good while, and if there was no coachman outside to see her and her train, there was no reason why she should not go and feed the calf, and then come back and put herself into the proper trim for the reception of visitors. It seemed strange to her, but she was positively sure that she would not have felt so much at ease with this handsomely dressed young lady, if she herself had been attired in her best clothes; but now they had met without its being possible for either Miss Bannister or herself to make any comparisons of attire. The old, draggled silk gown did not count one way or the other. It was simply a covering to keep one's clothes clean when one fed a calf. When they should return to the house, and she took off her old gown, she and her visitor would be better acquainted, and their comparative opinions of each other would not depend so much on clothes. Miriam was accustomed to making philoso-phical reflections concerning her relations with the rest of the world; and in regard to these relations she was at times very sensitive.

CHAPTER XI

TWO GIRLS AND A CALF

Having gone to the kitchen to fill the bottle with milk, which she had set to warm, Miriam accompanied her guest to the barn. As she walked by the side of Dora, with the bottle in one hand and the other holding up her voluminous silk robe, it was well for her peace of mind that no stately coachman sat upon a box and looked at her.

In a corner of the lower floor of the barn they found the calf, lying upon a bed of hay, and covered by a large piece of mosquito netting, which Miriam had fastened above and around him. Dora laughed as she saw this.

"It isn't every calf," she said, "that sleeps so luxuriously."

"The flies worried the poor thing dreadfully," said Miriam, "but I take it off when I feed it."

She proceeded to remove the netting, but she had scarcely done so, when she gave an exclamation that was almost a scream.

"Oh, dear, oh, dear!" she cried; "I believe it is dead," and down she sat upon the floor close to the calf, which lay motionless, with its head and neck extended. Down also sat Dora. She did not need to consider the hay-strewn floor and her clothes; for although she wore a very tasteful and becoming costume, it

Frank Richard Stockton

was one she had selected with reference to barn explorations, field strolls, and anything rural and dusty which any one else might be doing, or might propose. No one could tell what dusty and delightful occupation might turn up during an afternoon at Cobhurst.

"Its eye does look as if it were dead," she exclaimed. "What a pity!"

"Oh, you can't tell by that eye," said Miriam, over whose cheeks a few tears were now running. "Dr. Tolbridge says it has infantile ophthalmia in that eye, but that as soon as it gets strong enough, he can cure it. We must turn up its other eye."

She took the little creature's head in her lap, with the practicable eye uppermost. This slowly rolled in its socket, as she bent over it.

"There is life in it yet," she cried; "give me the bottle." The calf slowly rolled its eye to the position from which it had just moved, and declined to consider food.

"Oh, it must drink; we must make it drink," said Miriam. "If I open its mouth, will you put in the end of that tube? If it gets a taste of the milk, it may want more. We must not let it die. But you must be careful," she continued. "That bottle leaks all round the cork. Spread part of my skirt over you."

Dora followed this advice, for she had not considered a milk-stained lap among the contingent circumstances of the afternoon. Holding the bottle over the listless animal, she managed to get some drops on its tongue.

"Now," said Miriam, "we will put that in its mouth, and shut its jaws, and perhaps it may begin to suck. It will be perfectly dreadful if it dies."

The two girls sat close together, their eyes fixed upon the apparently lifeless head of the bovine infant.

"See!" cried Miriam, presently, "its throat moves; I believe it is sucking the milk."

Dora leaned over and gazed. It was indeed true; the calf was beginning to take an interest in food. The interest increased; the girls could see the milk slowly diminishing in the bottle. Before long the creature gave its head a little wobble. Miriam was delighted.

"That is the way it always does, when its appetite is good. We must let it drink every drop, if it will."

There they sat on the hard, hay-strewn floor, one entirely, and the other almost entirely covered with purple silk, their eyes fixed upon the bottle and the feeding calf. After a time the latter declined to take any more milk, and raised its head from Miriam's lap.

"There," she cried; "see, it can hold up its own head. I expect it was only faint from want of food. After this I will feed it oftener. It was the bread-making that made me forget it this time."

"Let us wait a minute," said Dora, who was now taking an earnest and womanly interest in the welfare of this weakling. "Perhaps after a while it may want some more." And so they continued to sit. Every motion of the calf's head, and every effort it made to bend its legs, or change its position, sent sparkles of delight into Miriam's eyes, and brightened Dora's beautiful face with sympathetic smiles.

Dora had taken up the bottle, and was about to give the calf an opportunity to continue its repast, when suddenly she stopped and sat motionless. Outside the barn, approaching footsteps could be plainly heard. They were heavy, apparently those of a man. Dora dropped the bottle, letting it roll unheeded upon the floor; then pushing Miriam's skirt from her lap, she sprang to her feet, and stepped backwards and away from the little group so quickly, that she nearly stumbled over some inequalities in the floor. Miriam looked up in astonishment.

"You needn't be frightened," she said. "How red you are! I suppose it is only Ralph."

"I was afraid it was," said Dora, in a low voice, as she shook out her skirts. "I wouldn't have had him see me that way for anything."

Now Miriam was angry. There was nothing to be ashamed of, that she could see, and it was certainly very rude in Miss Bannister to drop her bottle, and nearly push her over in her haste to get away from her and her poor calf.

The person who had been approaching the barn now entered, but it was not Ralph Haverley. It was a shorter and a stouter young man, with side whiskers.

"Why, Herbert!" exclaimed Dora, in a tone of surprise and disappointment, "have you got back already?"

Her brother smiled. "I haven't got back," he said, "for I haven't been anywhere yet. I had not gone a mile before one of the springs of the buggy broke, and it keeled over so far that I came near tumbling out. It happened at a place where there were no houses near, so I drew the buggy to the roadside, took out the horse, and led him back. I heard voices in here, and I came in. I must go and look for Mr. Haverley, and ask him to lend me a vehicle in which we may return home."

Dora stood annoyed; she did not want to return home; at least, not so soon. She had calculated on Herbert making a long stay with Mrs. Dudley.

"I suppose so," she replied, in an injured tone; "but before we say anything else, Herbert, let me introduce you to Miss Haverley."

She turned, but in the corner to which she directed her eyes, she saw only a calf; there was no young person in silk attire. The moment that Miriam perceived that the man who came in was not her brother, but the brother of some one else, her face had crimsoned, she had pushed away the unfortunate calf, and, springing to her feet, had darted into the shadows of an adjoining stall. From this, before Dora had recovered from her surprise at not seeing her, Miriam emerged in the costume of a neatly dressed school-girl, with her skirts just reaching to the tops of her boots. It had been an easy matter to slip off that expansive silk gown. She advanced with the air of defensive gravity with which she generally greeted strangers, and made the acquaintance of Mr. Bannister.

"I am sure," she said, when she had heard what had happened, "that my brother will be very glad to lend you the gig. That is the only thing we have at present which runs properly."

"A gig will do very well, indeed," said Mr. Bannister. "We could not want anything better than that; although," he continued, "I am not sure that my harness will suit a two-wheeled vehicle."

"Oh, we have gig harness," said Miriam, "and we will lend you a horse, too, if you like."

Dora now thought it was time to say something. She was irritated because Herbert had returned so soon, and because he was going to take her away before she was ready to go; and although she would have been delighted to have a drive in the Cobhurst gig, provided the proper person drove her, she did not at all wish to return to Thorbury in that ridiculous old vehicle with Herbert. In the one case, she could imagine a delightful excursion in she knew not what romantic by-roads and shaded lanes; but in the other, she saw only the jogging old gig, and all the neighbors asking what had happened to them.

"I think," she said, "it will be well to see Mr. Haverley as soon as possible. Perhaps he knows of a blacksmith's shop, where the buggy can be mended."

Herbert smiled. "Repairs of that sort," he said, "require a good deal of time. If we waited for the buggy to be put in travelling condition, we would certainly have to stay here all night, and probably the greater part of tomorrow."

In the sudden emotions which had caused her to act almost exactly as Dora had acted, Miriam had entirely forgotten her resentment toward her companion.

"Why can't you stay?" she asked. "We have plenty of room, you know."

The man of business shook his head.

"Thank you very much," he replied, "but I must be in my office this evening. I think I shall be obliged to borrow your gig. I will walk over to the field—"

"Oh, you need not take the trouble to do that," said Miriam. "They are way over there at the end of the meadow beyond the hill. The gig is here in the barn, and I can lend it to you just as well as he can."

"You are very kind," said Herbert, "and I will accept your amendment. It will be the better plan, because if I saw your brother, I should certainly interfere with his work. He might insist upon coming to help me, which is not at all necessary. Where can I find the gig, Miss Haverley?"

Miriam led her visitors to the second floor.

"There it is," she said, "but of course you must have the harness belonging to it, for your buggy harness will not hold up the shafts properly. It is in the harness room, but I do not know which it is. There is a lot of harness there, but it is mostly old and worn out."

"I will go and look," said Herbert. "I think it is only part of it that I shall need."

During this conversation Dora had said nothing. Now as she stood by the old gig, toppling forward with its shafts resting upon the floor, she thought she had never seen such a horrible, antediluvian old trap in her life. Nothing could add so much to her disappointment in going so soon, as going in that thing. If there had been anything to say which might prevent her brother from carrying out his intention, she would have said it, but so far there had been nothing.

She followed the others into the harness room, and as her eyes glanced around the walls, they rested upon a saddle hanging on its peg. Instantly she thought of something to say.

"Herbert," she remarked, not too earnestly, "I think we shall be putting our friends to a great inconvenience by borrowing the gig. You will never be able to find the right harness and put it on so that there will not be an accident on the road, and Mr. Haverley or the man will have to be sent for. And, besides, there will be the trouble of getting the gig back again. Now, don't you think it will be a great deal better for you to put that saddle on the horse, and ride him home, and then send the carriage for me? That would be very simple, and no trouble at all."

Mr. Bannister turned his admiring eyes upon his sister.

"I declare, Dora," he said, "that is a good practical suggestion. If Miss Haverley will allow me, I will borrow the saddle and the bridle and ride home; I shall like that."

"Of course you are welcome to the saddle, if you wish it," said Miriam; "but you need not send for your sister. Why can't she stay with me to-night? I think it would be splendid to have a girl spend the night with me. Perhaps I oughtn't to call you a girl, Miss Bannister."

Frank Richard Stockton

Dora's eyes sparkled. "But I am a girl, just as you are," she exclaimed, "and I should be delighted to stay. You are very good to propose it. Herbert is an awfully slow rider (I believe he always walks his horse), and I am sure it would be after dark before the carriage would get here."

"Do let her stay," cried Miriam, seizing Dora's arm, as if they had been old friends; "I shall be so glad to have her."

Mr. Bannister laughed.

"It is not for me to say what Dora shall do," he replied. "You two must decide that, and if I go home to report our safety, it will be all right. It is now too late for me to go to Mrs. Dudley's, especially as I ride so slowly; but I will drive there to-morrow, and stop for Dora on my return."

"Settled!" cried Miriam; and Dora gazed at her with radiant face. It was delightful to be able to bestow such pleasure.

In two minutes Mr. Bannister had brought in his horse. In the next minute all three of the party were busy unbuckling his harness; in ten minutes more it had been taken off, the saddle and bridle substituted, and Mr. Bannister was riding to Thorbury.

Dora of the sparkling eyes drew close to Miriam.

"Would you mind my kissing you?" she asked.

There was nothing in the warm young soul of the other girl which in the least objected to this token of a new-born friendship.

As Dora and Miriam, each with an arm around the waist of the other, walked out of the barn and passed the lower story, the calf, who had been the main instrument in bringing about the cordial relations between the two, raised his head and gazed at them with his good eye. Then perceiving that they had forgotten him, and were going away without even arranging his mosquito net for the night, he slowly turned his clouded visual organ in their direction, and composed himself to rest.

Frank Richard Stockton

CHAPTER XII

TO EAT WITH THE FAMILY

As the two girls entered the house, Miriam clapped her hands.

"What a surprise this will be for Ralph!" she exclaimed. "He hasn't the slightest idea that you are here, or that anybody is going to spend the night with us. If Mike said anything about you and your brother,—which I doubt, for he is awfully anxious to get in that hay,—Ralph thought, of course, that you were both gone long ago."

The situation suited Dora's fancy admirably.

"Let us make it a regular surprise," she said. "I am going to help you to get supper, and to do whatever you have to do. Suppose you don't tell your brother that I am here, and let him find it out by degrees. Don't you think that will be fun?"

"Indeed it will," cried the other; "and if you don't mind helping a little about the cooking, I think that will be fun too. Perhaps you can tell me some things I don't know."

"Let us begin," exclaimed Dora, "for everything ought to be ready before he comes in. Can you lend me a big apron?"

"I have only one," said Miriam, "and it is not very big; I intended to make some more, but I haven't had time. But you needn't do anything, you know. You can just give me advice and keep me company."

"Oh, I want to do things. I want to work," cried Dora; "it would be cruel to keep me from the fun of helping you get supper. Haven't you something I can slip on instead of this dress? It is not very fine, but I don't want to spatter or burn it."

"None of my clothes are long enough for you," said Miriam; "but perhaps I might find something in the garret. There are all sorts of clothes up there. If you choose, we can go up and look."

In the next minute the two girls were in the great garret, kneeling in front of a trunk, in which Miriam had found the silk robe, which now lay tumbled up in a corner of a stall in the cow-stable. Article after article of female attire was drawn out and tossed on the floor. Dora was delighted; she was fond of old-fashioned things, and here were clothes of various eras. Some colonial, perhaps, and none that had been worn since these two girls had come into the world. There was a calico dress with large pink figures in it which caught Dora's eye; she sprang to her feet, shook it out, and held it up before her.

"This will do," she said. "The length is all right, and it does not matter about the rest of the fit."

"Of course not," said Miriam; "and now let us go down. We need not wait to put the rest of the things back."

As Dora was about to go, her eyes fell on an old-fashioned pink sunbonnet.

"If you don't mind," she said, "I will take that, too. I shall be awfully awkward, and I don't want to get cinders or flour in my hair."

When Dora had arrayed herself in the calico dress with pink flowers, she stood for a moment before the large mirror in

Frank Richard Stockton

Miriam's room. The dress was very short as to waist, and very perpendicular as to skirt, and the sleeves were puffy at the elbows and tight about the wrists, but pink was a color that became her, the quaint cut of the gown was well suited to her blooming face, and altogether she was pleased with the picture in the glass. As for the sunbonnet, that was simply hideous, but it could be taken off when she chose, and the wearing of it would help her very much in making herself known to Mr. Ralph Haverley.

For half an hour the girls worked bravely in the kitchen. Dora had some knowledge of the principles of cookery, though her practice had been small, and Miriam possessed an undaunted courage in culinary enterprises. However, they planned nothing difficult, and got on very well. Dora made up some of Miriam's dough into little rolls.

"I wish I could make these as the Tolbridges' new cook makes them. They say that every morning she sends in a plate of breakfast rolls, each one a different shape, and some of them ever so pretty."

"I don't suppose they taste any better for that," remarked Miriam.

"Perhaps not," said the other, "but I like to see things to eat look pretty." And she did her best to shape the little rolls into such forms that they might please the eye of Mr. Ralph as well as satisfy his palate.

Miriam went up to the dining-room to arrange the table. While doing this she saw Ralph approaching from the barn. In the kitchen, below, Dora, glancing out of the window, also saw him coming, and pulling her sunbonnet well forward, she applied herself more earnestly to her work. Ralph came in, tired and warm, and threw himself down on a long horse-hair sofa in the hall.

"Heigh ho, Miriam," he cried; "hay-making is a jolly thing, all the world over, but I have had enough of it for to-day. How are you getting on, little one? Don't put yourself to too much trouble about my supper. Only give me enough of whatever you have; that is all I ask."

"Ralph," said Miriam, standing gravely by him, "I did not have to get supper all by myself; there is a new girl in the kitchen."

"Good," cried Ralph; "I am very glad to hear that. When did she come?"

"This afternoon," said Miriam, "and she is cooking supper now. But, Ralph," she continued, "there is hardly any wood in the kitchen. We have—she has used up nearly all that was brought in this morning."

"Well," said Ralph, "there is plenty of it cut, in the woodhouse."

"But, Ralph," said Miriam, "I don't like to ask her to go after the wood, herself, and some is needed now."

"Mike is just as busy as he can be down at the barn," said her brother, "and I cannot call him now. If you show her the woodhouse, she can get what she wants with very little trouble, and Mike will bring in a lot of it to-night."

"But, Ralph," persisted his sister, "I don't want to ask her to stop her cooking and go out and get wood. It does not look like good management, for one thing, and for other reasons I do not want to do it. Don't you think you could bring her some wood? Just a little basketful of short sticks will do."

Ralph sat up and knitted his brows. "Miriam," said he, "if your new cook is the right sort of a woman, she ought to be able to help herself in emergencies of this kind, with the woodhouse not a dozen yards from the kitchen. But as she is a stranger to the place, and I don't want to discourage anybody who comes to help you, I will get some wood for her, but I must say that it does not look very well for the lord of the manor to be carrying fuel to the cook."

"It isn't the lord of the manor," cried Miriam; "it is the head hay-maker, and when you dress yourself for supper, she will never think of you as the man who brought in the wood."

Dora, from the kitchen window, saw Ralph go out to the woodhouse, and she saw him returning with an arm-load of small sticks. Then she turned her back to the kitchen door, and bent her head over a beefsteak she was preparing for the gridiron.

Ralph came in with the wood, and put it down by the side of the great stove. As he glanced at the slight form in the pink gown, it struck him that this woman would not be equal to the hard work which would be sometimes necessary here.

"I suppose this wood will be as much as you will want for the present," he said, as he turned toward the door, "and the man will fill this box to-night, but if you need any more before he does so, there is the woodhouse just across the yard, where you can easily get a few sticks."

Dora half turned herself in the direction of the woodhouse, and murmured, "Yes, sir."

"Miriam," said Ralph, as he went into the dining-room, where his sister was putting the knives and forks upon the supper table, "do you think that woman is strong enough to wash, iron, and do all the things that Phoebe used to do when she was here? How old is she?"

"I don't know, exactly," answered Miriam, going to a cupboard for some glasses; "and as to rough work, I can't tell what she can do, until she tries."

When Ralph had made his toilet and come downstairs, attired in a very becoming summer suit, his sister complimented him.

"Hay-making makes you ever so much handsomer," she said; "you look as if you had been on a yachting cruise. There is one thing I forgot to say to you, but I do not suppose it will make any difference, as we are real country people now: our new cook is accustomed to eating at the table with the family."

Ralph's face flushed. "Upon my word!" he exclaimed, staring at his sister. "Well," he continued, "I don't care what she is accustomed to, but she cannot eat at our table. I may carry wood for cooks, but I do not eat with them."

"But, Ralph," said Miriam, "you ought to consider the circumstances. She is not a common Irishwoman, or German. She is an American, and has always taken her meals with the family in which she lived. I could not ask her to eat in the kitchen. You know, Mike takes his meals there since Phoebe has gone. Indeed, Ralph, I cannot expect her to do a thing that she has never done in her life, before. Do you really think you would mind it? You work with Mike in the field, and you don't mind that, and this girl is very respectable, I assure you."

Ralph stood silent. He had supposed his sister, young as she was, knew more of the world than to make an arrangement with a servant which would put her, in many respects, on an equality with themselves. He was very much annoyed, but he would not be angry with Miriam, if he could help it, nor would he put her in the embarrassing position of revoking the agreement with this American woman, probably a farmer's daughter, and, in her own opinion, as good as anybody. But, although he might yield at present, he determined to take the important matter of engaging domestic servants into his own hands. His sister had not yet the necessary judgment for that sort of thing.

"Miriam," said he, "for how long have you engaged this woman?"

"Nothing at all has been said about time," she answered.

Frank Richard Stockton

"Very well, then," said he, "she can come to the table to-night and to-morrow morning, for, I suppose, if I object, she will go off and leave you again without anybody, but to-morrow she must be told that she cannot eat with us; and if she does not like that, she must leave, and I will go to the city and get you a proper servant. The hay is in now, and there is no more important work to which I could give a day. Now do not be angry, little one, because I object to your domestic arrangements. We all have to make mistakes, you know, when we begin."

"Thank you, Ralph," said Miriam. "I really am ever so much obliged to you," and going up to her brother, she lifted her face to his. Ralph stooped to kiss her, but suddenly stopped.

"Who, in the name of common sense, is that!" he exclaimed. The sound of wheels was plainly heard upon the driveway, and turning, they saw a buggy stop at the door.

"It is Dr. Tolbridge!" cried Miriam.

Through the open front door Ralph saw that it was the doctor, preparing to alight.

"Miriam," said he, quickly, "we must ask the doctor to stay to supper, and if he does, that cook must not come to the table. It will not do at all, as you can see for yourself. We cannot ask our friends and neighbors to sit down with servants."

"I will see," said Miriam. "I think that can be made all right," and they both went to the door to meet their visitor.

The doctor shook hands with them most cordially.

"Glad to see you both so ruddy; Cobhurst air must agree with you. And now, before we say anything else, let me ask you a question: Have you had your supper?"

"No," answered Ralph, "and I hope you have not."

"Your hopes are realized. I have not, and if you do not mind letting me sup with you, I will do it."

The brother and sister, who both liked the hearty doctor, assured him that they would be delighted to have him stay.

"The reason of my extending an invitation to myself is this: I have been making a visit in the country, where I was detained much longer than I expected, and as I drove homeward, I said to myself, 'Good sir, you are hungry, and where are you going to get your evening meal? You cannot reach home until long after the dinner hour, and moreover you have a patient beyond Cobhurst, whom you ought to see this evening. It would be a great pity to drive all the way to Thorbury, and then back again, to-night. Now there are those young Cobhurst people, who, you know, have supper at the end of the day, instead of dinner, like the regular farmers that they are, and as you want to see them, anyway, and find out how they are getting on, it will be well to stop there, and ten to one, you will find that they have not yet sat down to the table.'"

"A most excellent conclusion," said Ralph, "and I will call Mike, and have him take your horse."

Having left the doctor in the charge of her brother, Miriam hurried downstairs to apprise Dora of the state of affairs.

"I am sorry," she said, "but we will have to give up the trick we were going to play on Ralph, for Dr. Tolbridge has come, and will stay to supper, and so, while you go upstairs and put on your own dress, I will finish getting these things ready. I will see Ralph before we sit down, and tell him all about it."

Dora made no movement toward the stairs.

"I knew it was the doctor," she said, "for I went out and looked around the corner of the house, and saw his horse. But I do not see why we should give up our trick. Let us play it on the doctor as well as on your brother."

Miriam stood silent a few moments.

"I do not know how that would do," she said. "That is a very different thing. And besides, I do not believe Ralph would let you come to the table. You ought to have seen how angry he was when I told him the new cook must eat with us."

"Oh, that was splendid!" cried Dora. "I will not come to the table. That will make it all the funnier when we tell him. I can eat my supper anywhere, and I will go upstairs and wait on you, which will be better sport than sitting down at the table with you."

"But I do not like that," said Miriam. "I will not have you go without your supper until we have finished."

"My dear Miriam!" exclaimed Dora, "what is a supper in comparison with such a jolly bit of fun as this? Let me go on as the new cook. And now we must hurry and get these things on the table. It will make things a great deal easier for me, if they can eat before it is time to light the lamps."

When Miriam went to call the gentlemen to supper, the doctor said to her:—

"Your brother has told me that you have a new servant, and that she is so preposterous as to wish to take her meals with you, but that he does not intend to allow it. Now, I say to you, as I said to him, that if she expected to sit at the table before I came, she must do it now. I am used to that sort of thing, and do not mind it a bit. In the families of the farmers about here, with whom I often take a meal, it is the custom for the daughter of the family to cook, to wait on the table, and then sit down with whomever may be there, kings or cobblers. I beg that you will not let my coming make trouble in your household."

Miriam looked at her brother.

"All right," said Ralph, with a smile, "if the doctor does not mind, I shall not. And now, do let us have something to eat."

CHAPTER XIII

DORA'S NEW MIND

When Ralph Haverley made up his mind to agree to anything, he did it with his whole soul, and if he had had any previous prejudices against it, he dismissed them; so as he sat at supper with the doctor and his sister he was very much amused at being waited upon by a woman in a pink sunbonnet. That she should wear such a head-covering in the house was funny enough in itself, but the rest of her dress was also extremely odd, and she kept the front of her dark projecting bonnet turned downward or away, as if she had never served gentlemen before, and was very much overpowered by bashfulness. But for all that she waited very well, and with a light quickness of movement unusual in a servant.

"I am afraid, doctor," said Miriam, when the pink figure had gone downstairs to replenish the plate of rolls, "that you will miss your dinner. I have heard that you have a most wonderful cook."

"She is indeed a mistress of her art," replied the doctor; "but you do very well here, I am sure. That new cook of yours beats Phoebe utterly. I know Phoebe's cooking."

"But you must not give her all the credit," exclaimed Miriam; "I made that bread, although she shaped it into rolls. And I helped with the beefsteak, the potatoes, and the coffee."

"Which latter," said Ralph, "is as strong as if six or seven women had made it, although it is very good."

The meal went on until the two hungry men were satisfied, Miriam being so absorbed in Dora's skilful management of herself that she scarcely thought about eating. There was a place for the woman in pink, if she chose to take it, but she evidently did not wish to sit down. Whenever she was not occupied in waiting upon those at the table, she bethought herself of some errand in the kitchen.

"Well," said Ralph, "those rolls are made up so prettily, and look so tempting, that I wish I had not finished my supper."

"You are right," said the doctor, "they are aesthetic enough for La Fleur," and then pushing back his chair a little, he looked steadfastly, with a slight smile on his face, at the figure, with bowed sunbonnet, which was standing on the other side of the table.

"Well, young woman," he said, "how is your mind by this time?"

For a moment there was silence, and then from out of the sunbonnet there came, clearly and distinctly, the words:—

"That is very well. How is your kitten?"

At this interchange of remarks, Ralph sat up straight in his chair, amazement in his countenance, while Miriam, ready to burst into a roar of laughter, waited convulsively to see what would happen next. Turning suddenly toward Ralph, Dora tore off her sunbonnet and dashed it to the floor. Standing there with her dishevelled hair, her flushed cheeks, her sparkling eyes and her quaint gown, Ralph thought her the most beautiful creature he had ever gazed upon.

"How do you do, Mr. Haverley?" said Dora, advancing and extending her hand; "I know you are not willing to eat with

Frank Richard Stockton

cooks, but I do not believe you will object to shaking hands with one, now and then."

Ralph arose, and took her hand, but she gave him no opportunity to say anything.

"Your sister and I got up this little bit of deception for you, Mr. Haverley," she continued, "and we intended to carry it on a good deal further, but that gentleman has spoiled it all, and I want you to know that I stopped here to see your sister, and finding she had not a soul to help her, I would not leave her in such a plight, and we had a royal good time, getting the supper, and were going to do ever so many more things—I should like to know, doctor, how you knew me. I am sure I did not look a bit like myself."

"You did not look like yourself, but you walked like yourself," replied Dr. Tolbridge. "I watched you when you first tried to toddle alone, and I have seen you nearly every day since, and I know your way of stepping about as well as I know anything. But I must really apologize for having spoiled the fun. I discovered you, Dora, before we had half finished supper, but I thought the trick was being played on me alone. I had no idea that Mr. Haverley thought you were the new cook."

"I certainly did think so," cried Ralph, "and what is more, I intended to discharge you to-morrow morning."

There was a lively time for a few minutes, after which Dora explained what had been said about her mind and a kitten.

"He was just twitting me with having once changed my mind—every one does that," she said; "and then I gave him a kitten. That is all. And now, before I change my dress, I will go and get some wood for the kitchen fire. I think you said, Mr. Haverley, that the woodhouse was not far away."

"Wood!" cried Ralph; "don't you think of it!"

Miriam burst into a laugh.

"Oh, you ought to have heard the lord of the manor declare that he would not carry fuel for the cook," she cried.

Ralph joined in the laugh that rose against him, but insisted that Dora should not change her dress.

"You could not wear anything more becoming," he said, "and you do not know how much I want to treat the new cook as one of the family."

"I will wear whatever the lord of the manor chooses," said Dora, demurely, and was about to make reference to his concluding remark, but checked herself.

When the two girls joined the gentlemen on the porch, which they did with much promptness, having delegated the greater part of their household duties to Mike, who could take a hand at almost any kind of work, Dr. Tolbridge announced that he must proceed to visit his patient.

"Are you coming back this way, doctor?" asked Dora. "Because if you are, would it be too much trouble for you to look for our buggy on the side of the road, and to bring back the cushions and the whip with you? Herbert may think that in this part of the country the people are so honest that they would not steal anything out of a deserted buggy, but I do not believe it is safe to put too much trust in people."

"A fine, practicable mind," said the doctor; "cuts clean and sharp. I will bring the cushions and the whip, if they have not been stolen before I reach them. And now I will go to the barn and get my horse. We need not disturb the industrious Mike."

"If you are going to the barn, doctor," cried Miriam, seizing her hat, "I will go with you and put the mosquito net over my calf, which I entirely forgot to do. Perhaps, if it is light enough, you will look at its eye."

The doctor laughed, and the two went off together, leaving Dora and Ralph on the piazza.

Dora could not help thinking of herself as a very lucky girl. When she had started that afternoon to make a little visit at Cobhurst, she had had no imaginable reason to suppose that in the course of a very few hours she would be sitting alone with Mr. Haverley in the early moonlight, without even his sister with them. She had expected to see Ralph and to have a chat with him, but she had counted on Miriam's presence as a matter of course; so this tete-a-tete in the quiet beauty of the night was as delightful as it was unanticipated. More than that, it was an opportunity that ought not to be disregarded.

The new mind of Miss Dora Bannister was clear and quick in its perceptions, and prompt and independent in action. It not only showed what she wanted, but indicated pretty clearly how she might get it. Since she had been making use of this fresh intellect, she had been impressed very strongly by the belief that in the matter of matrimonial alliance, a girl should not neglect her interest by depending too much upon the option of other people. Her own right of option she looked upon as a sacred right, and one that it was her duty to herself to exercise, and that promptly. She had just come from the seaside, where she had met some earnest young men, one or two of whom she expected to see shortly at Thorbury. Also Mr. Ames, their young rector, was a very persevering person, and a great friend of her brother.

Of course it behooved her to act with tact, but for all that she must be prompt. It was easy to see that Ralph Haverley could not be expected to go very soon into the society of Thorbury, to visit ladies there, and as she wanted him to learn to know her as rapidly as possible, she resolved to give him every opportunity.

Miriam was gone a long time, because when she reached the barn, the calf was not to be found where she had left it, and she had been obliged to go for Mike and a lantern. After anxious search the little fellow had been found reclining under an apple tree, having gained sufficient strength from the ministrations of its fair attendants to go through the open stable door and to find out what sort of a world it had been born into. It required time to get the truant back, secure it in its stall, and make all the arrangements for its comfort which Miriam thought necessary. Therefore, before she returned to the piazza, Miss Bannister and Ralph had had a long conversation, in which the latter had learned a great deal about the disposition and tastes of his fair companion, and had been much interested in what he learned.

CHAPTER XIV

GOOD-NIGHT

When the three young people had been sitting for half an hour on the wide piazza of Cobhurst, enjoying the moonlight effects and waiting for the return of Dr. Tolbridge, Miriam, who was reclining in a steamer chair, ceased making remarks, but very soon after she became silent she was heard again, not speaking, however, but breathing audibly and with great regularity. Ralph and Dora turned toward her and smiled.

"Poor little thing," said the latter in a low voice; "she must be tired out."

"Yes," said Ralph, also speaking in an undertone, "she was up very early this morning, and has been at some sort of work ever since. I do not intend that this shall happen again. You must excuse her, Miss Bannister,—she is a girl yet, you know."

"And a sweet one, too," said Dora, "with a perfect right to go to sleep if she chooses. I should be ashamed of myself if I felt in the least degree offended. Do not let us disturb her until the doctor comes; the nap will do her good."

"Suppose, then," said Ralph, "that we take a little turn in the moonlight. Then we need not trouble ourselves to lower our voices."

"That will be very well," said Dora, "but I am afraid she may take cold, although the night air is so soft. I think I saw a lap robe on a table in the hall; I will spread that over her."

Ralph whispered that he would get the robe, but motioning him back, and having tiptoed into the hall and back again, Dora laid the light covering over the sleeping girl so gently that the regular breathing was not in the least interrupted. Then they both went quietly down the steps, and out upon the lawn.

"She is such a dear girl," said Dora, as they slowly moved away, "and although we only met to-day, I am really growing very fond of her, and I like her the better because there is still so much of the child left in her. Do not you like her the better for that, Mr. Haverley?"

Ralph did agree most heartily, and it made him happy to agree on any subject with a girl who was even more beautiful by moonlight than by day; who was so kind, and tended to his sister, and whose generous disposition could overlook little breaches of etiquette when there was reason to do so.

As they walked backward and forward, not very far away from the piazza, and sometimes stopping to admire bits of the silver-tinted landscape, Dora, with most interesting deftness, gave Ralph further opportunity of knowing her. With his sister as a suggesting subject, she talked about herself; she told him how she, too, had lost her parents early in life, and had been obliged to be a very independent girl, for her stepmother, although just as good as she could be, was not a person on whom she could rely very much. As for her brother, the dearest man on earth, she had always felt that she was more capable of taking care of him, at least in all matters in home life, than he of her.

"But I have been very happy," she went on to say, "for I am so fond of country life, and everything that belongs to it, that the more I have to do with it, the better I like it, and I really begrudge the time that I spend in the city. You do not know with what pleasure I look forward to helping Miriam get breakfast to-morrow morning. I consider it a positive lark. By the way, Mr. Haverley, do you like rolled omelets?"

Ralph declared that he liked everything that was good, and had no doubt that rolled omelets were delicious.

"Then I shall make some," said Dora, "for I know how to do it. And I think you said, Mr. Haverley, that the coffee to-night was too strong."

"A little so, perhaps," said Ralph, "but it was excellent."

"Oh, it shall be better in the morning. I am sure it will be well for one of us to do one thing, and the other another. I will make the coffee."

"You are wonderfully kind to do anything at all," said Ralph, and as he spoke he heard the clock in the house strike ten. It was agreeable in the highest degree to walk in the moonlight with this charming girl, but he felt that it was getting late; it was long past Miriam's bedtime, and he wondered why the doctor did not come.

Dora perceived the perturbations of his mind; she knew that he thought it was time for the little party to break up, but did not like to suggest it. She knew that the natural and proper thing for her to do was to wake up Miriam, and that the two should bid Ralph good-night, and leave him to sit up and wait for the doctor as long as he felt himself called upon to do so, but she was perfectly contented with the present circumstances, and did not wish to change them just yet. It was a pleasure to her to walk by this tall, broad-shouldered young fellow, who was so handsome and so strong, and in so many ways the sort of man she liked, and to let him know, not so much by her words, as by the incited action of his own intelligence, that she was fond of the things he was fond of, and that she loved the life he led.

As they still walked and talked, the thought came to Dora, and it was a very pleasing one, that she might act another part with this young gentleman; she had played the cook, now for a while she could play the mistress, and she knew she could do it so gently and so wisely that he would like it without perceiving it. She turned away her face for a moment; she felt that her pleasure in acting the part of mistress of Cobhurst, even for a little time, was flushing it.

"Suppose," she said, "we walk down to the road, and if we see or hear the doctor coming, we can wait there and save him the trouble of driving in."

They went out of the Cobhurst gateway, but along the moon-lighted highway they saw no approaching spot, nor could they hear the sounds of wheels.

"I really think, Mr. Haverley," said Dora, turning toward the house, "that I ought to go and arouse Miriam, and then we will retire. It is a positive shame to keep her out of her bed any longer."

This suggestion much relieved Ralph, and they walked rapidly to the porch, but when they reached it they found an empty steamer chair and no Miriam anywhere. They looked at each other in much surprise, and entering the house they looked in several of the rooms on the lower floor. Ralph was about to call out for his sister, but Dora quickly touched him on the arm.

"Hush," she said, smiling, "do not call her. Do you see that lap robe on the table? I will tell you exactly what has happened; while we were down at the road she awoke, at least enough to know that she ought to go to bed, and I really believe that she was not sufficiently awake to remember that I am here, and that she simply got up, brought the robe in with her, and went to her room. Isn't it funny?"

Ralph was quite sure that Dora's deductions were correct, for when Miriam happened to drop asleep in a chair in the evening, it was her habit, when aroused, to get up and go to bed, too sleepy to think about anything else; but he did not think it was funny now. He was mortified that Miss Bannister should have been treated with such apparent disrespect, and he began to apologize for his sister.

"Now, please stop, Mr. Haverley," interrupted Dora. "I am so glad to have her act so freely and unconventionally with me, as if we had always been friends. It makes me feel almost as if we had known each other always, and it does not make the slightest difference to me. Miriam wanted to give me another room, but I implored her to let me sleep with her in that splendid high-posted bedstead, and so all that I have to do is to slip up to her room, and, if I can possibly help it, I shall not waken her. In the morning I do not believe she will remember a thing about having gone to bed without me. So good-night, Mr. Haverley. I am going to be up very early, and you shall see what a breakfast the new cook will give you. I will light this candle, for no doubt poor Miriam has put out her lamp, if she did not depend entirely on the moonlight. By the way, Mr. Haverley," she said, turning toward him, "is there anything I can do to help you in shutting up the house? You know I am maid of all work as well as cook. Perhaps I should go down and see if the kitchen fire is safe."

"Oh, no, no!" exclaimed Ralph; "I attend to all those things,— at least, when we have no servant."

"But doesn't Miriam help you?" asked Dora, taking up the candle which she had lighted.

"No," said he; "Miriam generally bids me good-night and goes upstairs an hour before I do."

"Very well," said Dora; "I will say only one more thing, and that is that if I were the lord of the manor, who had been working in the hay-field all day, I would not sit up very long, waiting for a wandering doctor."

Ralph laughed, and as she approached the door of the stairway, he opened it for her.

"Suppose," she said, stopping for a moment in the doorway, and shielding the flame of the candle from a current of air with a little hand that was so beautifully lighted that for a moment it attracted Ralph's eyes from its owner's face, "you wait here for a minute, and I will go up and see if she is really safe in her own room. I am sure you will be better satisfied if you know that."

Ralph looked his thanks, and softly, but quickly, she went up the stairs. At a little landing she stopped.

"Do you know," she whispered, looking back, with the candle throwing her head and hair into the prettiest lights and shadows, "I think this stairway is lovely;" and then she went on and disappeared.

In a few minutes she leaned over the upper part of the banisters and softly spoke to him.

"She is sleeping as sweetly and as quietly as the dearest of angels. I do not believe I shall disturb her in the least. Good-night, Mr. Haverley." And with her face thrown into a new light,—this time by the hall lamp below,—she smiled ever so sweetly, and then drew back her head. In half a minute it reappeared. She was right; he was still looking up.

"I forgot to say," she whispered, "that all the windows in Miriam's room are open. Do you think she was too sleepy to notice that, or is she accustomed to so much night air?"

"I really do not know," said Ralph, in reply.

"Very well, then," said Dora; "I will attend to all that in my own way. Good-night again, Mr. Haverley;" and with a little nod and a smile, she withdrew her face from his view.

If she had come back within the next minute, she would have found him still looking up. She felt quite sure of this, but she could think of no good reason for another reappearance.

Ralph lighted a pipe and sat down on the piazza. He looked steadily in front of him, but he saw no grass, no trees, no moonlighted landscape, no sky of summer night. He saw only the face of a young girl, leaning over and looking down at him from the top of a stairway. It was the face of a girl who was so gentle, so thoughtful for others, so quick to perceive, so quick to do; who was so fond of his sister, and so beautiful. He sat and thought of the wondrous good fortune that had brought this girl beneath his roof, and had given him these charming hours with her.

And when his pipe was out, he arose, declared to himself that, no matter what the doctor might think of it, he would not wait another minute for him, and went to bed,—his mind very busy with the anticipation of the charming hours which were to come on the morrow.

CHAPTER XV

MISS PANNEY IS AROUSED TO HELP AND HINDER

When Dr. Tolbridge returned from the visit to the patient who lived beyond Cobhurst, he did not drive into the latter place, for seeing Mike by the gate near the barn, he gave the cushions and whip to him and went on.

As it was yet early in the evening, and bright moonlight, he concluded to go around by the Wittons'. It was not far out of his way, and he wanted to see Miss Panney. What he wanted to say to the old lady was not exactly evident to his own mind, but in a general way he wished her to know that Dora was at Cobhurst.

Dora was a great favorite with the doctor. He had known her all her life, and considered that he knew, not only her good points, of which there were many, but also those that were not altogether desirable, and, of which, he believed, there were few. One of the latter was her disposition to sometimes do as she pleased, without reference to tradition or ordinary custom. He had seen her acting the part of cook, disguised by a pink sunbonnet and an old-fashioned calico gown. And what pranks she and the Haverleys—two estimable young people, but also lively and independent—might play, no one could tell. The duration of Dora's visit would depend on her brother Herbert, and he was a man of business, whose time was not at all at his own disposal, and so, the doctor thought, it would not be a bad thing if Miss Panney would call at Cobhurst the next day,

Frank Richard Stockton

and see what those three youngsters were about.

The Wittons had gone to bed, but Miss Panney was in the parlor, reading. "Early to bed and early to rise," was not one of her rules.

"Well, really!" she exclaimed, as she rose to greet her visitor, "this is amazing. How many years has it been since you came to see me without being sent for?"

"I do not keep account of years," said the doctor, "and if I choose to stop in and have a chat with you, I shall do it without reference to precedent. This is a purely social call, and I shall not even ask you how you are."

"I beg you will not," said the old lady, "and that will give me a good reason for sending for you when you ought to be informed on that point."

"This is not my first social call this evening," said he. "I took supper at Cobhurst, where Dora Bannister waited on the table."

"What do you mean?" exclaimed Miss Panney, and then the doctor told his tale. As the old lady listened, her spirits rose higher and higher. What extraordinary good luck! She had never planned a match that moved with such smoothness, such celerity, such astonishing directness as this. She did not look upon Dora's disregard of tradition and ordinary custom as an undesirable point in her character. She liked that sort of thing. It was one of the points in her own character.

"I wish I could have seen her!" she exclaimed. "She must have been charming."

"Don't you think there is danger that she may be too charming?" the doctor asked.

"No, I don't," promptly answered Miss Panney.

The doctor looked at her in some surprise.

"We should remember," said he, "that Dora is a girl of wealth; that one-third of the Bannister estate belongs to her, besides the sixty thousand dollars that came to her from her mother."

"That does not hurt her," said Miss Panney.

"And Ralph Haverley was a poor young man when he came here, and Cobhurst will probably make him a good deal poorer."

"I do not doubt it," said Miss Panney.

"Do you believe," said the doctor, after a moment's pause, "that it is wise or right in a girl like Dora Bannister, accustomed to fine living, good society, and an atmosphere of opulence, to allow a poor man like Ralph Haverley to fall in love with her? And he will do it, just as sure as the world turns round."

"Well, let him do it," replied the old lady. "I did not intend to give my opinion on this subject, because, as you know, I am not fond of obtruding my ideas into other people's affairs, but I will say, now, that Dora Bannister will have to travel a long distance before she finds a better man for a husband than Ralph Haverley, or a better estate on which to spend her money than Cobhurst. I believe that money that is made in a neighborhood like this ought to be spent here, and Thomas Bannister's money could not be better spent than in making Cobhurst the fine estate it used to be. I do not believe in a girl like Dora going off and marrying some city fellow, and perhaps spending the rest of her life at the watering-places and Paris. I want her here; don't you?"

"I certainly do, but you forget Mr. Ames."

"I do, and I intend to forget him," she replied, "and so does Dora."

The doctor shook his head. "I do not like it," he said; "young Haverley may be all very well,—I have a high opinion of him, already, but he is not the man for Dora. If he had any money at all, it would be different, but he has not. Now she would not be content to live at Cobhurst as it is, and he ought not to be content to have her do everything to make it what she would have it."

"Doctor," said Miss Panney, "if there is anything about all this in your medicine books, perhaps you know more than I do, and you can go on and talk; but you know there is not, and you know, too, that I was a very sensible middle-aged woman when you were toddling around in frocks and running against people. I believe you are trying to run against somebody now. Who is it?"

"Well," said the doctor, "if it is anybody, it is young Haverley."

Miss Panney smiled. "You may think so," she said, "but I want you to know that you are also running against me, and I say to you, confidentially, and with as much trust in you as I used to have that you would not tell who it was who spread your bread with forbidden jam, that I have planned a match between these two; and if they marry, I intend to make pecuniary matters more nearly even between them, than they are now."

The doctor looked at her earnestly.

"Do you suppose," said he, "that he would take money from you?"

"What I should do for him," she answered, "could not be prevented by him or any one else."

"But there is no reason," urged the other.

The old lady smiled, took off her glasses, wiped them with her handkerchief, and put them on again.

"There is so little in medicine books," she said. "His grandfather was my cousin."

"The one—?" asked the startled doctor.

"Yes, that very one," she answered quickly; "but he does not know it, and now we will drop the subject. I will try to get to Cobhurst to-morrow before Dora leaves, and I will see if I cannot help matters along a little."

The doctor laughed. "I was going to ask you to interfere with matters."

"Well, don't," she said. "And now tell me about your cook. Is she as good as ever?"

"As good?" said the doctor. "She is better. The more she learns about our tastes, the more perfectly she gratifies them. Mrs. Tolbridge and I look upon her as a household blessing, for she gives us three perfect meals a day, and would give us more if we wanted them; the butcher reverences her, for she knows more about meat and how to cut it than he does. Our man and our maid either tremble at her nod or regard her with the deepest affection, for I am told that they spend a great deal of their time helping her, when they should be attending to their own duties. She has, in fact, become so necessary to our domestic felicity, and I may say, to our health, that I do not know what will become of us if we lose her."

"Is there any chance of that?" eagerly asked the old lady.

"I fear there is," was the answer.

Miss Panney sprang to her feet, her eyes flashing.

"Now look here, Dr. Tolbridge," she said, "don't tell me that that woman is going to leave you because she wants higher wages and you will not pay them. I beg you to remember that I got you that woman. I saw she was what you needed, and I worked matters so that she came to you. She has proved to be everything that I expected. You are looking better now than I have seen you look for five years. You have been eating food that you like, and food that agrees with you, and a chance to do that comes to very few people in your circumstances. There is no way in which you could spend your money better than—"

The doctor raised his hand deprecatingly.

"There is no question of money," he said. "She has not asked for higher wages, and if she had, I should pay anything in reason. The trouble is more serious. You may remember that when she first came to this country, she lived with the Dranes, and she left them because they could no longer afford to employ her. She has the greatest regard for that family, and has lately heard that they are becoming poorer and poorer. There are only two of them,—mother and daughter,—and on account of some sort of unwise investment they are getting into a pretty bad way. I used to know Captain Drane, and was slightly acquainted with his family. I heard of their misfortune through a friend in Pennsylvania, and as I knew that La Fleur took such an interest in the family, I mentioned it to her. The result was disastrous; she has been in a doleful mood ever since, and yesterday assured Mrs. Tolbridge that if it should prove that Mrs. Drane and her daughter, who had been so good to her, had become so poor that they could not afford to employ a servant, she must leave us and go to them. She would ask no wages and would take no denial. She would stay with them and serve them for the love she bore them, as long as they needed her. I know she is in earnest, for she immediately wrote to Mrs. Drane, and asked me to put the letter in the post-office; and, by the way, she writes a great deal better hand than I do."

Miss Panney, who had reseated herself, gazed earnestly at the floor.

"Doctor," she said, "this is very serious. I have not yet met La

Fleur, but I very much want to. I am convinced that she is a woman of character, and when she says she intends to do a thing, she will do it. That is, unless somebody else of character, and of pretty strong character too, gets in her way. I do not know what advice to give you just now, but she must not leave you. That must be considered as settled. I am coming to your house to-morrow afternoon, and please ask Mrs. Tolbridge to be at home. We shall then see what is to be done."

"There is nothing to be done," said the doctor, rising. "We cannot improve the circumstances of the Dranes, and we cannot prevent La Fleur from going to them if her feelings prompt her to do it."

"Stuff!" said the old lady. "There is always something to be done. The trouble is, there is not always some one to do it; but, fortunately for some of my friends, I am alive yet."

CHAPTER XVI

"KEEP HER TO HELP YOU"

It was about ten o'clock the next morning when Miss Panney drove over to Cobhurst in her phaeton. She did not go up to the house, but tied her roan mare behind a clump of locust trees and bushes, where the animal might stand in peace and shade. Then she walked around the house, and hearing the clatter of crockery in the basement, she looked down through a kitchen window, and saw Mike washing the breakfast dishes.

Going on toward the back of the house, she heard voices and laughter over in the garden. Behind a tangled mass of rasp-berries, she saw a pink sunbonnet and a straw hat with daisies in it. She knew, then, that Dora and Miriam were picking berries, and then her eyes and ears began to search for Ralph.

She went up on the back piazza and looked over toward the barn, which appeared to be closed, and around and about the house, but saw nothing of the young man. But she would wait; it was scarcely likely that he was at work in the fields by himself. He would probably appear soon, and, if possible, she wanted to speak to him before she saw any one else. She went into the house, and took a seat in the hall, where, through a narrow window by the side of the door, she had a good view of the garden and the grounds at the back, and could also command the front entrance of the house.

Miss Panney had been seated but a very few minutes when the

two girls emerged from the bosky intricacies of the garden.

"Upon my word!" exclaimed the old lady, "she has got on Judith Pacewalk's teaberry gown. I could never forget that!"

At this moment there was a clatter of hoofs and a rattle of wheels, and a brown horse, drawing a very loose-jointed wagon, with Ralph Haverley, in a broad hat and light tennis jacket, driving, dashed up to the back door and stopped with a jerk.

"Back so soon!" cried Miriam. "See what a lot of raspberries we have picked. I will take them into the house, and then come out and get the things you have brought."

As Miriam went around toward the kitchen, Ralph sprang to the ground, and Dora approached him. Miss Panney could see her face under the sunbonnet. It was suffused with the light of a smiling, beaming welcome.

"You did go quickly, didn't you?" she said. "You must be a good driver."

"I didn't want to lose any time," answered Ralph, "and I made Mrs. Browning step along lively. As it was, I was afraid that your brother might arrive before I got back and that I might find you were gone."

"It was a pity," said Dora, "that you troubled yourself to hurry back. You may have wanted to do other things in Thorbury, and if Herbert missed seeing you to-day he would have plenty of other opportunities."

Ralph laughed. "I should like to meet your brother," he said, "but I am bound to say that I was thinking more of the new cook. I did not want her to leave before I got back."

Dora raised her sunbonnet toward him. Miriam's steps were heard approaching.

"You might have felt sure," she said, "that she would not have gone without seeing you again. You have been so kind and good to her that she would not think of doing that." Then, as Miriam was very near, she approached the wagon. "Did you get the snowflake flour, as I told you?" she asked. "Yes, I see you did, and I am glad you listened to my advice, and bought only a bag of it, for you know you may not like it."

"If it is the flour you use, I know we shall like it," said Ralph; "but still I am bound to follow your advice."

"You would better follow me, now," said Miriam, who had taken some parcels from the wagon, "and bring that bag into the pantry. I do not like Mike to come into our part of the house with his boots."

Ralph shouldered the bag, and Dora stepped up to him.

"I will stay with the horse until you come out again," she said, not speaking very loudly.

Miss Panney, who had heard all that had been said, smiled, and her black eyes twinkled. "Truly," she said to herself, "for so short an acquaintance, this is getting on wonderfully."

Miriam, her arms full of parcels, and her mind full of house-hold economy, walked rapidly by Miss Panney without seeing her at all, and, entering the dining-room, passed through it into the pantry. But when Ralph appeared in the open doorway, the old lady rose and confronted him, her finger on her lip.

"I have just popped in to make a little call on your sister," she whispered; "but I saw she was pretty well loaded as she passed, and I did not wish to embarrass her—I do not mind embarra-ssing you. Don't put down the bag, I beg. I shall step into the drawing-room, and you can say I am there. By the way, who is that young woman standing by the horse?"

"It is Miss Bannister," answered Ralph, his face unreasonably flushing as he spoke. "She is visiting Miriam and helping her."

When Miss Panney wished to influence a person in favor of or against another person, she was accustomed to go about the business in a very circumspect way, and to accommodate the matter and the manner of her remarks to the disposition of the person addressed, and to the occasion. She wished very much to influence Ralph in favor of Miss Bannister, and if she had had the opportunity of a conversation with him, she knew she could have done this in a very easy and natural way. But there was no time for conversation now, and she might not again have the chance of seeing him alone, so she adopted a very different course, and with as much readiness and quickness as Daniel Boone would have put a rifle-ball into the head of an Indian the moment he saw it protrude from behind a tree, so did Miss Panney concentrate all she had to say into one shot, and deliver it quickly.

"Help Miriam, eh?" she whispered; "take my advice, my boy, and keep her to help you." And without another word she proceeded to the drawing-room, where she seated herself in the most comfortable chair.

Ralph stood still a minute with the bag on his shoulder. He scarcely understood what had been said to him, but the words had been so well aimed and sent with such force that before he reached Miriam and the pantry his mind was illumined by the shining apparition of Dora as his partner and helpmate. Two minutes before there had been no such apparition. It is true that his mind had been filled with misty, cloudlike sensations, entirely new to it, but the words of the old lady had now condensed them into form.

When Miriam was informed of the visitor in the drawing-room, she frowned a little, and made up a queer face, and then, taking off her long apron, went to perform her duty as lady of the house.

Ralph returned to Dora, and as he looked at the girl who was patting the neck of the brown mare, she seemed to have changed, not because she was different from what she had been a few minutes before, but because he looked upon her differently. As he approached, every word that she had spoken to him that day crowded into his memory. The last thing she had said was that she would wait until he returned to her, and here she was, waiting. When he spoke, his manner had lost the free-heartedness of a little while before; there was a slight diffidence in it.

Hearing that Miss Panney was in the house, Dora turned her bonnet downward, and she also frowned a little.

"Why should that old person come in this very morning?" she thought.

But in an instant the front of the bonnet was raised toward Ralph, and upon the young face under it there was not a shadow of dissatisfaction.

"Of course I must go in and see her," she said, and then, speaking as if Ralph were one on whom she had always been accustomed to rely for counsel, "do you think I need go upstairs and change my dress? If this is good enough for you and Miriam, isn't it good enough for Miss Panney?"

As Ralph gazed into the blue eyes that were raised to his, it was impossible for him to think of anything for which their owner was not good enough. This impression upon him was so strong that he said, with blurting awkwardness, that she looked charming as she was, and needed not the slightest change. The value of this impulsive remark was fully appreciated by Dora, but she gave no sign of it, and simply said that if he were suited, she was.

They were moving toward the house when Dora suddenly laid her hand upon his arm.

"You have forgotten the horse, Mr. Ralph," she said.

The touch and the name by which she called him for the first time made the young man forget, for an instant, everything in the world, but the girl who had touched and spoken.

"Have you anything to tie her with? Oh, yes, there is a chain on that post."

As Ralph turned the horse toward the hitching-post, Dora ran before him, and stood ready with the chain in her hand.

"Oh, no," she said, as he motioned to take it from her, "let me hook it on her bridle. Don't you want to let me help you at all?"

As side by side Dora and Ralph entered the drawing-room, Miss Panney declared in her soul that they looked like an engaged couple, coming to ask for her blessing. And when Dora saluted her with a kiss, and, drawing up a stool, took a seat at her feet, the old lady gave her her blessing, though not audibly.

As Miss Panney was in a high good humor, she wanted everybody else to be so, and in a few minutes even the sedate Miriam was chatting freely and pleasantly.

"And so that graceless Phoebe has left you," said the old lady; "to board the minister, indeed! I will see that minister, and give him a text for a sermon. But you cannot keep up this sort of thing, my young friends; not even with Dora's help." And she stroked the soft hair of Miss Bannister, from which the sunbonnet had been removed.

"I will see Mike before I go, and send him for Molly Tooney. Molly is a good enough woman, and if I send for her, she will come to you until you have suited yourselves with servants. And now, my dear child, where did you find that gay dress? Upstairs in some old trunk, I suppose. Stand over there and let me look at you. It is a good forty years since I have seen that gown. Do you know to whom it used to belong? But of course you do not. It was Judith Pacewalk's teaberry gown."

"And who was Judith Pacewalk?" asked Dora; "and why was it teaberry? It is not teaberry color."

"No," said Miss Panney; "the color had nothing to do with it, but I must say it has kept very well. Let me see," taking out her watch, "it is not yet eleven o'clock, and if you young people have time enough, I will tell you the story of that gown. What does the master say?"

Ralph declared that they must have the story, and that time must not be considered.

CHAPTER XVII

JUDITH PACEWALK'S TEABERRY GOWN

"Judith Pacewalk," said Miss Panney, "was Matthias Butter-wood's cousin. Before Matthias got rich and built this house, he lived with his Aunt Pacewalk on her farm. That was over at Pascalville, about thirty miles from here. He superintended the farm, and Judith and he were very good friends, although he never showed any signs of caring anything for her except in the way of a cousin; but she cared for him. There was no doubt about that. I lived in Pascalville, then, and used to be a great deal at their house, and it was as plain as daylight to me that Judith was in love with her cousin, although she was such a quiet girl that few people suspected it, and I know he did not.

"The Pacewalks were poor, and always had been; and it could not be expected that a man like Matthias Butterwood could stay long on that little farm. He had a sharp business head, and was a money-maker, and as soon as he was able he bought a farm of his own, and this is the farm; but there was no house on it then, except the little one that Mike now lives in. But Matthias had grand ideas about an estate, and in the course of five years he built this house and the great barn, and made a fine estate of it.

"When this was going on, he still lived with his Aunt Pacewalk. He did not want to go to his own house until every-thing was finished and ready. Of course, everybody supposed he would take a wife there, but he never said anything about

Frank Richard Stockton

that, and gave a sniff when the subject was mentioned. During the summer in which Cobhurst was finished—he named the place himself—he told his aunt that in the fall he was going there to live, and that he wanted her and Judith to come there and make him a visit of a month. He said he intended to have his relations visit him by turns, and that was the sort of family he would have. Now it struck me that if Judith went there and played her cards properly, she could stay there as mistress. Although she was a girl very much given to keeping her own counsel, I knew very well that she had something of the same idea.

"As I said before, the Pacewalks were poor, and although they lived well enough, money was scarce with them, and it was seldom that they were able to spend any of it for clothes. But about this time Judith came to me—I was visiting them at the time—and talked a little about herself, which was uncommon. She said that if she went to Matthias' fine new house, and sat at the head of his table,—and of course that would be her place there, as it was at her mother's table,—she thought that she ought to dress better than she did. 'I do not mean,' she said, 'that I want any fine clothes for company; but I ought to have something neat and proper for everyday wear, and I want you to help me to think of some way to buy it.' So we talked the matter over, and came to the conclusion that the best way to do was to try to gather teaberries enough to pay for the material for a chintz gown.

"In those days—I don't know how it is now—Pascalville was the greatest place for teaberries. They used them as a flavor for candy, ice-cream, puddings, cakes, and I don't know what else. They made summer drinks of it, and it was used as a perfume for home-made hair-washes and tooth-powder. So Judith and I and a girl named Dorcas Stone, who was a friend of ours, went to work gathering teaberries in the woods. We worked early and late, and got enough to trade off at the store for the ten yards of chintz with which that gown is made.

"As for the making of it, Judith and I did all that ourselves.

Dorcas Stone might be willing enough to go with us to pick berries, but when she found what was to be bought with them, she drew out of the business. She was not a girl who was particularly sharp about seeing things herself, or keeping people from seeing through her; but she wanted to marry Matthias Butterwood, and when she found Judith was to have a new gown she would have nothing to do with it, which was a pity, for she was a very fine sewer, especially as to gathers.

"We cut the gown from some patterns we got from a magazine; I fitted it, and we both sewed. When it was done, and Judith tried it on, it was very pretty and becoming, and she looked better in it than in the gown she wore when she went to a party. When we had seen that everything was all right, Judith took off the dress, folded it up, and put it away in a drawer. 'Now,' said she, 'I shall not wear that until I go to Cobhurst.'"

"Well, as everybody knows, houses are never finished at the time they are expected to be, and that was the way with this house, and as Matthias would not go into it until everything was quite ready, the moving was put off and put off until it began to be cold weather, and then he said he would not go into it until spring, for it would be uncomfortable to live in the new house in the winter.

"I was very sorry for this, for I thought that the sooner Judith got here the better her chance would be for staying here the rest of her life. Judith did not say much, but I am sure she was sorry too, and Matthias seemed a little out of spirits, as if he were getting a little tired of living with the Pacewalks, and wanted to be in his own house. I think he began to feel more like seeing people, and I know he visited the Stones a good deal.

"One day when I was at the Pacewalks' and we were sitting alone, he looked at me and my clothes, and then he said, 'I wish Judith cared more for clothes than she does. I do not mean getting herself up for high days and holidays, but her everyday clothes. I like a woman to wear neat and becoming things all the time.' 'I am sure,' I said, 'Judith's clothes are always very neat!'"

"'If you mean clean,' he said, 'I will agree to that, but when the color is all washed out of a thing, or it is faded in streaks like that blue gown she wears, the wearing of it day after day is bound to make a person think that a young woman does not care how she looks to her own family, and I do not like young women not to care how they look to their families, especially when calico is only twelve cents a yard, and needles and thread cost almost nothing.' 'Matthias,' said I, 'I expect you have been to see Dorcas Stone, and are comparing her clothes with Judith's. Now, Dorcas' father is a well-to-do man, and Judith hasn't any father, and she does the best she can with the clothes she has.' 'It is not money I am talking about,' he said, 'it is disposition. If a young woman wants to look well in her own family, she will find some way to do it. At any rate, she could let it be seen that she is not satisfied to look like a dowdy.' And then he went away."

"This was the first time that Matthias had ever spoken to me about Judith, and I knew just as well as if he had told me that it was Dorcas Stone's clothes that had got him into that way of thinking.

"More than that, I knew he would never have taken the trouble to say that much about Judith if he had not been taking more interest in her than he ever had before. He was a practical, businesslike man, and I believed then, and I believe now, that he was looking for some one to be mistress of Cobhurst, and if Judith had suited his ideas of what such a woman ought to be, he would have preferred her to any one else. I think that was about as far as he was likely to go in such matters at that time, though of course if he had gotten a loving wife, he might have become a loving husband, for Matthias was a good fellow at bottom, though rather hard on top.

"When he had gone, I went straight upstairs to Judith, and

said to her, if she knew what was good for her, she would get out that teaberry gown and put it on for supper, and wear it regularly at meals and at all times when it would be suitable as a house gown. 'I shall do nothing of the sort,' she said; 'I got it to wear when I go to Cobhurst, and I shall keep it until then. If I put it on now, it will be a poor-looking thing by spring.' I told her that was all nonsense, and she could wear that and get another in the spring, but she shook her head and was not to be moved. Now, I would have been glad enough to give her the stuff to make a new gown, but I had hinted at that sort of thing before, and did not intend to do it again, for she was a good deal prouder than she was poor. Nor could I think of telling her what Matthias had said, for not only was she very sensitive, and would have been hurt that he should have talked to me in that way about her, but she would not have consented to dress herself on purpose to please a man's fancy.

"I could not do anything more then, but I have always been a matchmaker, and I did not give up this match. I did everything I could to make Judith look well in the eyes of Matthias, and I said everything I could to make his eyes look favorably on her, but it was all of no use. Judith went to a Christmas party, and she wore a purple silk gown that had belonged to her mother. It was rather large for her, and a good deal heavier than anything she had been accustomed to wear, and she got very warm in the crowded room, and coming home in a sleigh, she caught cold, and died in less than a month.

"So you see, my dears, Judith Pacewalk never wore her teaberry gown, in which, I believe, she would have been mistress of Cobhurst. When her mother died, not long afterward, everything they owned went to Matthias and his brother Reuben. The Pacewalk farm was sold, and all the personal property of both brothers, including that disastrous box of bones, was brought here, where it is yet, I suppose; and so, my good young people, I imagine you will not wonder that I was surprised to see that pink gown again, having helped, as I did, with every seam, pleat, and gather of it. If you will look at it closely, you will see that there is good work on it, for Judith

Frank Richard Stockton

and I knew how to use our needles a good deal better than most ladies do nowadays."

Miriam now spoke with much promptness.

"I am ever so glad to hear that story, Miss Panney," she said, "and as that teaberry gown should have been worn by the mistress of Cobhurst, I intend to wear it myself, every day, as long as it lasts, and if it does not fit me, I can alter it."

Whether this remark, which was delivered with considerable spirit, was occasioned by the young girl's natural pride, or whether a little jealousy had been aroused by the evident satisfaction with which the old lady gazed at Dora, arrayed in this significant garment, Miss Panney could not know, but she took instant alarm. Nothing could be more fatal to her plans than to see the sister opposed to them. She had been delighted at the intimacy that had evidently sprung up between her and Dora, but she knew very well that if this sedate school-girl should resent any interference with her prerogatives, the intimacy would be in danger.

Miss Panney had no doubt that Dora and Ralph were on the right road, and would do very well if left to themselves, but she scarcely believed that the young man was yet sufficiently in love to brave the opposition of his sister, which would be all the more wild and unreasonable because she was yet a girl, and in a position of which she was very proud.

For Dora and Ralph to marry, Dora and Miriam should be the best of friends, so that both brother and sister should desire the alliance, and in furtherance of this happy result, Miss Panney determined to take Dora away with her. She had been at Cobhurst long enough to produce a desirable impression upon Ralph, and if she stayed longer, there was no knowing what might happen between her and Miriam. Dora, as well as the other, was high-spirited and young, and it was as likely as not that as she showed an inclination to continue to wear the teaberry gown, there would be a storm in which matrimonial schemes would be washed out of sight.

"Dora," said Miss Panney, "I am now going to drive to Thorbury, and it will be a great deal better for you to go with me than to wait for your brother, for it may be very late in the day before he can come for you. And more than that, it is ten to one that by this time he has forgotten all about you, especially if his office is full of clients. So please get yourself ready as soon as possible. And, Miriam, if you will come over to see me some morning, and bring that teaberry gown with you, I will alter it to fit you, and arrange it so that you can do the sewing yourself. It is very appropriate that the little lady of the house should wear that gown."

Into the minds of Dora and Miss Panney there came, simultaneously, this idea: that no matter how much or how often Miriam might wear that gown, she would not be the first one whom it had figuratively invested with the prerogatives of the mistress of Cobhurst.

Miss Bannister, who well knew her brother's habits, agreed to the old lady's suggestion, and it was well she did so, for when she got home, Herbert declared that he had been puzzling his mind to devise a plan for sending for his sister and the broken buggy on the same afternoon. As for going himself, it was impossible.

When Dora came downstairs arrayed in her proper costume, Ralph thought her a great deal prettier than when she wore the pink chintz. Miss Panney thought so, too, and she managed to leave them together, while she went with Miriam to get pen and paper with which to write a note to Molly Tooney.

"Molly cannot read," said the old lady, "but if Mike will take that to her, she will come to you and stay as long as you like," and then she went on to talk about the woman until she thought that Ralph and Dora had had about five minutes together, which she considered enough.

"You must both come and see me," cried Miss Bannister, as, leaning from the phaeton, she stretched out her hand to Miriam.

"Indeed we shall do so," said Ralph, and as his sister relinquished the hand of the visitor he took it himself.

Miss Panney was not one of those drivers who start off with a jerk. Had she been such a one, Miss Bannister might have been pulled against the side of the phaeton, for the grasp was cordial.

CHAPTER XVIII

BLARNEY FLUFF

About three o'clock that afternoon, La Fleur, Mrs. Tolbridge's cook, sat in the middle of her very pleasant kitchen, composing the dinner. Had she been the chef of a princely mansion, she could not have given the subject more earnest nor intelligent consideration. It is true the materials at hand were not those from which a dinner for princes would have been prepared. But what she had was sufficient for the occasion, and this repast for a country gentleman in moderate circumstances and his wife was planned with conscientiousness as well as skill. From the first she had known very well that it would be fatal to her pretensions to prepare for the Tolbridges an expensive and luxurious meal, but she had determined that they should never sit down to any but a good one.

Her soup had been determined upon and was off her mind, and she had prepared that morning, from some residuary viands, which would have been wasted had she not used them in this way, the little entree which was to follow. Her filet, which the butcher had that morning declared he never separated from the contiguous portions for any one, but had very soon afterward cut out for her, lay in the refrigerator, awaiting her pleasure and convenience. The vegetables had been chosen, and her thoughts were now intent upon a "sweet" which should harmonize with the other courses.

On a chair, by the door opening into the garden, sat George, the doctor's man, who was coachman, groom, and gardener, and who, having picked a basket of peas, had been requested to shell them. By an open window, Amanda, the chambermaid, was extracting the stones from a little dish of olives.

George was working rapidly and a little impatiently.

"Madam," said he, "do you want all these peas shelled?"

La Fleur turned and looked at him with a pleasant smile.

"I want enough to surround my filet, but whether you shell enough for us to have any, depends entirely on your good will, George."

"Of course I'll shell as many as you want," said he, "but I've got a lot to do this afternoon. There is the phaeton to be washed, that I don't want the doctor to come home and find muddy yet; and I ought to have done it this morning, madam, when I was walking about the garden with you, a tellin' you what I had and a hearin' what I ought to have."

"I was so glad to have you go with me, and show me everything," said La Fleur, "because I do not yet exactly understand American gardens. It is such a nice garden, too, and you do not know how pleased I was, after you left me and I was coming to the house, to see that fine bed of aubergines. When will any of them be ripe, do you think, George?"

The man looked up in surprise.

"There is nothing of that sort in my garden," said he. "I never heard of them."

"Oh, yes, you have," said La Fleur, "you call them egg-plants. You see, I am learning your American names for things. And now, Amanda, if you have finished the olives I'll get you to make a fine powder of those things which I have put into the mortar. Thump and grind them well with the pestle; they are to make the stuffing for the olives."

"But, madam, what is to become of the sewing Mrs. Tolbridge wants me to do? I have only hemmed two of the dozen napkins she gave me to do day before yesterday."

"Now, Amanda," said La Fleur, "you ought to know very well, that without a meal on the table, napkins are of no use. You might have the meals without napkins, but it wouldn't work the other way. And I am sure those napkins are not to be used for a week, or perhaps several weeks, and this dinner must be eaten to-day. So you can see for yourself—"

At this moment there was a knock at the inner door of the kitchen.

"Who can that be!" exclaimed La Fleur. "Come in."

The door opened, and Miss Panney entered the kitchen. La Fleur rose from her seat, and for a moment the two elderly women stood and looked at each other.

"And this is La Fleur," said Miss Panney; "Mrs. Tolbridge has been talking about you, and I asked her to let me come in and see you. I want to speak to you for a few minutes, and I will sit down here. Don't you stand up."

La Fleur liked people to come and talk to her, provided they were the right sort of people, and came in the right way. Miss Panney's salutation pleased her; she had a respect for people who showed a proper recognition of differences of position. If Miss Panney had been brought into the kitchen by Mrs. Tolbridge and in a manner introduced to La Fleur, the latter would have regarded her as something of an equal, and would not have respected her. Had the old lady accosted her in a supercilious manner, La Fleur would have disliked her, even if she had supposed she were a person to be respected. But Miss Panney had filled all the requirements necessary for the cook's favorable opinion. In the few words she had spoken, she had shown that she was a friend of the mistress of the house; that she had heard interesting things of the cook, and therefore wished to see her; that she knew this cook was a woman of sense, who understood what was befitting to her position, and would therefore stand when talking to a lady, and, moreover, in consequence of the fact that this cook was superior to her class, she would waive the privileges of her class, and request the cook to sit, while talking to her. To have waived this privilege without first indicating that she knew La Fleur would acknowledge her possession of it, would have been damaging to Miss Panney.

Upon the features of La Fleur, which were inclined to be bulbous, there now appeared a smile, which was very different from that with which she encouraged and soothed her conscripted assistants. It was a smile that showed that she was pleasurably honored, and it was accompanied by a slight bow and a downward glance. Then turning to the man and the maid, she told them in a low voice that they might go, a permission of which they instantly availed themselves.

Miss Panney now sat down, and La Fleur, pushing her chair a little away from the table, availed herself of the permission to do likewise.

"I have eaten some of your cooking, La Fleur," said Miss Panney, "and I liked it so much that I wished to ask you something about it. For one thing, where did you get that recipe for that delicious ice, flavored with raspberry?"

The cook smiled with a new smile—one of genuine pleasure.

"To make that ice," she answered, "one must have more than a recipe: one must be educated. Tolati, my first husband, invented that ice, and no chef in Europe could make it but himself. But he taught me, and I make it for Dr. and Mrs. Tolbridge. It has a quality of cream, though there is no cream in it."

"I never tasted anything of the kind so good," said Miss Panney, "and I am a judge, for I have lived long and eaten meals prepared by the best cooks."

"French, perhaps," said La Fleur.

"Oh, yes," was the reply, "and those of other nations. I have travelled."

"I could see that," said La Fleur, "by your appreciation of my work. French cooking is the best in the world, and if you have an English cook to do it, then there is nothing more to be desired. It is like the French china, with the English designs, which they make now. I once visited their works, and was very proud of my countrymen."

"The conceited old body," thought Miss Panney; but she said, "Very true, very true. It is delightful to me to think that my friends here have a cook who can prepare meals which are truly fit, not only to nourish the body without doing it any harm, but to gratify the most intelligent taste. I have noticed, La Fleur, that there is always something about your dishes that pleases the eye as well as the palate. When we say that cooking is thoroughly wholesome, delicious, and artistic, we can say no more."

"You do me proud," said La Fleur, "and I hope, madam, that you may eat many a meal of my cooking. I want to say this, too: I could not cook for Dr. and Mrs. Tolbridge as I do, if I did not feel that they appreciate my work. I know they do, and so I am encouraged to do my best."

"Not only does the doctor appreciate you," said Miss Panney, "but his health depends upon you. He is a man who is peculiarly sensitive to bad cooking. I have known him all his life, and known him well. He was getting in a bad way, La Fleur, when you came here, and you are already making a new man of him."

"I like to hear that," said La Fleur. "I have a high opinion of Dr. Tolbridge. I know what he is and what he needs. I often sit up late at night, thinking of things that will be good for him, and which he will like. We all work here: every one of the household is industrious, but the doctor and I are the only ones who must work with our brains. The others simply work with their bodies and hands."

Miss Panney fixed her black eyes on the bulbous-faced cook.

"The word conceit," she thought, "is imbecile in this case."

"I am glad you are both so well able to do it," she said aloud. "And you like it here? The place suits you?"

"Oh, yes, madam," replied La Fleur; "it suits me very well. It is not what I am accustomed to, but I gave up all that of my own accord. Life in great houses has its advantages and its pleasures, and its ambitions, too; but I am getting on in years, and I am tired of the worry and bustle of large households. I came to this country to visit my relatives, and to rest and enjoy myself; but I soon found that I could not live without cooking. You might as well expect Dr. Tolbridge to live without reading."

"That is very true, La Fleur," said Miss Panney; "and it seems to me that you are in the very home where you can spend the rest of your days most profitably to others, and most happily to yourself. And yet I hear that you are considering the possibility of not staying here."

"Yes," answered La Fleur, "I am considering that; but it is not because I am dissatisfied with anything here. It is altogether a different question. I am very much attached to the family I first lived with in this country. They are in trouble now, and I think they may need me. If they do, I shall go to them. I have quite settled all that in my mind. I am now waiting for an answer to a letter I have written to Mrs. Drane."

"La Fleur," said Miss Panney, "if you leave Dr. Tolbridge, I think it will be a great mistake; and, although I do not want to hurt your feelings, I feel bound to say that it will be almost a crime."

The cook's face assumed an expression of firmness.

"All that may be," she said, "but it makes no difference. If they need me, I shall go to them."

"But cannot somebody else be found to go to them? You are not as necessary there as you are here, nor so highly prized. They let you go of their own accord."

"No one else will go to them for nothing," said La Fleur, "and I shall do that."

Miss Panney sat with her brows knit.

"If the Dranes have become poor," she said presently, "it is natural that you should want to help them; but it may not be at all necessary that you should go to them. In fact, by doing that, you might embarrass them very much. There are only two of them, I believe,—mother and daughter. Do they do anything to support themselves?"

"Miss Cicely is trying to get a situation as teacher. If she can do that, she can support her mother. At present they are doing nothing, and I fear have nothing to live on. I know my going to them would not embarrass them. I can help them in ways you do not think of."

"La Fleur," said Miss Panney, "your feelings are highly honorable to you, but you are not going about this business in the right way. I have heard of the Drane family, and know what sort of people they are. They would not have you work for them for nothing, and perhaps buy with your own money the food you cook. What should be done is to help them to help themselves. If Miss Drane wishes a position as teacher, one should be got for her."

"That is out of my line," said La Fleur, shaking her head, "out of my line. I can cook for them, but I can't help them to be teachers."

"But perhaps I can, and I am going to try. What you have told me encourages me very much. To get a position as teacher for Miss Drane ought to be easy enough. To get Dr. Tolbridge a cook who could take your place would be impossible."

La Fleur smiled. "I believe that," she said.

"Now what I do is for the sake of the doctor," continued Miss Panney. "I do not know the Dranes personally, but I have no objection to benefit them if I can. But for the sake of a friend whom I have known all his days, I wish to keep you in this kitchen. I am not afraid to say this to you, because I know you are not a person who would take advantage of the opinion in which you are held, to make demands upon the family which they could not satisfy."

"You need not say anything about that, madam," replied La Fleur. "Nobody can tell me anything about my work and value which I did not know before, and as for my salary, I fixed that myself, and there shall be no change."

Miss Panney rose. "La Fleur," she said, "I am very glad I came here to talk to you. I did not suppose that I should meet with such a sensible woman, and I shall ask a favor of you; please do not take any steps in this matter without consulting me. I am going to work immediately to see what I can do for Miss Drane, and if I succeed it will be far better for her and her mother than if you went to them. Don't you see that?"

"Yes," said La Fleur, "that is reasonable enough, but I must admit that I should like to see them."

Miss Panney ignored the latter remark.

"Now do not forget, La Fleur," she said, "to send me word

when you get a letter, and then I may write to Miss Drane, but I shall go to work for her immediately. And now I will leave you to go on with your dinner. I shall dine here to-day, and I shall enjoy the meal so much better because I know the chef who prepared it."

La Fleur resumed her seat and the consideration of her "sweet."

"She is a wheedling old body," she said to herself, "but I suppose I ought to give her something extra for that speech."

The next morning Mrs. Tolbridge came into the kitchen. "La Fleur," said she, "what is the name of that delicious dessert you gave us last night?"

The cook sighed. "She will always call the 'sweet' a dessert," she thought; and then she answered, "That was Blarney Fluff, ma'am, with sauce Irlandaise."

Mrs. Tolbridge laughed. "Whatever is its name," she said, "we all thought it was the sweetest and softest, most delightful thing of the kind we had ever tasted. Miss Panney was particularly pleased with it."

"I hoped she would be," said La Fleur.

CHAPTER XIX

MISS PANNEY IS "TOOK SUDDEN"

"I have spoken to Mr. Ames about it," said Dr. Tolbridge to Miss Panney, as two days later they were sitting together in his office, "and we are both agreed that teachers in Thorbury are like the vines on the gable ends of our church; they are needed there, but they do not flourish. You see, so many of our people send their children away to school, that is, when they are really old enough to learn anything."

"I would do it too, if I had children," said the old lady; "but this is a matter which rises above the ordinary points of view. I do not believe that you look at it properly, for if you did you would not sit there and talk so coolly. Do you appreciate the fact that if Miss Drane does not soon get something to do, you will be living on soggy, half-baked bread, greasy fried meat, water-soaked vegetables, and muddy coffee, and every one of your higher sentiments will be merged in dyspepsia?"

The doctor smiled. "I did not suppose it would be as bad as that," he said; "but if what you say is true, let us skip about instantly, and do something."

"That is the sort of action that I am trying to goad you into," said the old lady.

"Oh, I will do what I can," said the doctor, "but I really think there is nothing to be done here, and at this season. People do not want teachers in summer, and I see no promise of a later demand of this sort in Thorbury. We must try elsewhere."

"Not yet," said the other. "I shall not give up Thorbury yet. It is easier for us to work for Miss Drane here than anywhere else, because we are here, and we are not anywhere else. Moreover, she will like to come here, for then she will not be among strangers; so please let us exhaust Thorbury before thinking of any other place."

"Very good," said the doctor, leaning back in his chair, "and now let us exhaust Thorbury as fast as we can, before a patient comes in. I am expecting one."

"If she comes, she can wait," said Miss Panney. "You have a case here which is acute and alarming, and cannot be trifled with."

"How do you know I expect a 'she'?" asked the doctor.

"If it had been a man, he would have been here and gone," said Miss Panney.

Miss Panney knew as well as any one that immediate employment as a teacher could be rarely obtained in summer, and for this reason she wished to confine her efforts to the immediate neighborhood, where personal persuasion and influence might be brought into action. Moreover, she had said to herself, "If we cannot get any teaching for the girl, we must get her something else to do, for the present. But whatever is to be done must be done here and now, or the old woman will be off before we know it."

She sat for a few moments with her brows knitted in thought. Suddenly she exclaimed, "Is it Susan Clopsey you expect? Very well, then, I will make an exception in her favor. She is just coming in at the gate, and I would not interfere with your practice on her for anything. She has got money and a spinal column, and as long as they both last she is more to be depended on than government bonds. If her troubles ever get into her legs, and I have reason to believe they will, you can afford to hire a little maid for your cook. Old Daniel Clopsey, her grandfather, died at ninety-five, and he had then the same doctorable rheumatism that he had at fifty. I have something to think over, and I will come in again when she is gone."

"Depart, O mercenary being!" exclaimed the doctor, "before you abase my thoughts from sulphate of quinia to filthy lucre."

"Lucre is never filthy until you lose it," said the old lady as she went out on the back piazza, and closed the door behind her.

About twenty minutes later she burst into the doctor's office. "Mercy on us!" she exclaimed, "are you here yet, Susan Clopsey? I must see you, doctor; but don't you go, Susan. I won't keep him more than two minutes."

"Oh, don't mind me," cried Miss Clopsey, a parched maiden of twoscore. "I can wait just as well as not. Where is the pain, Miss Panney? Were you took sudden?"

"Like the pop of a jackbox. Come, doctor, I must see you in the parlor."

"Can I do anything?" asked Miss Clopsey, rising. "How dreadful! Shall I go for hot water?"

"Oh, don't be alarmed," said Miss Panney, hurrying the amazed doctor out of the room; "it is chronic. He will be back in no time."

Miss Clopsey, left alone in the office, sank back in her chair.

"Chronic by jerks," she sighed; "there can be few things worse than that; and at her age, too!"

"What can be the matter?" asked the doctor, as the two stood in the parlor.

"It is an idea," said Miss Panney; "you cannot think with what violence it seized me. Doctor, what became of that book you wrote on the 'Diagnosis of Sympathy'?"

The doctor opened his eyes in astonishment.

"Nothing has become of it. It has been in my desk for two years. I have not had time even to copy it."

"And of course your writing could not be trusted to a printer. Now what you should do is this: employ that Drane girl to copy your manuscript. She can do it here, and if she comes to a word she cannot make out, she can ask you. That will keep her going until autumn, and by that time we can get her some scholars."

"Miss Panney," said the doctor, "are you going crazy? I cannot afford charity on that scale."

"Charity!" repeated the old lady, sarcastically. "A pretty word to use. By that sort of charity you give yourself one of the greatest of earthly blessings, in the shape of La Fleur, and you get out a book which will certainly be a benefit to the world, and will, I believe, bring you fame and profit. And you are frightened by the paltry sum that will be necessary to pay the board of the girl and her mother for perhaps two months. Now do not condemn this plan until you have had time to consider it. Go back to your Clopsey; I am going to find Mrs. Tolbridge and talk to her."

CHAPTER XX

THE TEABERRY GOWN IS TOO LARGE

When Dora Bannister had gone away in Miss Panney's phaeton, Miriam walked gravely into the house, followed by her brother.

"Now," said she, "I must go to work in earnest."

"Work!" exclaimed Ralph. "I think you have been working a good deal harder than you ought to work, and certainly a good deal harder than I intend you to work. As soon as he has had his dinner, Mike shall take the wagon, and go after the woman Miss Panney told us of."

"Of course I have been working," said Miriam, "but while Dora Bannister was here, what we did was not like straight-forward work; it all seemed to mean something that was not just plain housekeeping. For one thing, the dough I intended to bake into bread was nearly all used up in making those rolls that Dora worked up into such pretty shapes; and now, if the new woman comes, I shall not have another chance to try my hand at making bread until she leaves us, for I am not going to do anything of the sort with a servant watching me. And there are all those raspberries we picked this morning. I am sure I do not know what to do with them, for there are ever so many more than we shall want to eat with cream. What was it, Ralph, that you said you liked, made of raspberries?"

Ralph looked a little puzzled.

"I think," he said, "it must have been something of the tart order. What did I tell you?"

"You did not tell me anything," said Miriam, "and I do not believe that tarts are ever made of raspberries. Dora Bannister said she wanted to cook something for you that you told her you liked, but as you have forgotten what it was, I suppose it does not make much difference now."

Ralph had said so many things to Dora that he could not remember what remark he had made about cooked raspberries; but it delighted him to think that, whatever it was, Dora had wished to make it for him.

After dinner Miriam went up to her room, where upon the bed lay Judith Pacewalk's teaberry gown. She took off her own school-girl dress, and put on the pink gown. It was the first time she had ever worn the clothes of a woman. When she had attired herself in the silken robe which had been so fatal to the fortunes and life of Judith Pacewalk, it had been slipped on in masquerade fashion, debased from its high position to a mere protection from spilt milk. Miriam had thought of the purple silk when Miss Panney was telling her story, and had said to herself that if the stall in the cow-stable had been ever so much darker and dirtier, and if the milk stains had been more and bigger, the career of that robe would have ended all the more justly.

The teaberry gown was too long for Miriam, and too large in every way. She knew that for herself; but hearing Ralph's footsteps outside, she had a longing to know what he would say on the subject, so, holding up her skirt to keep herself from tripping, she ran downstairs and called him into the big hall.

"How do you like me in the teaberry gown?" she asked.

Without a thought of any figurative significance connected

with the dress, Ralph only saw that it was as unsuitable to his sister as it had been well suited to Dora.

"You will have to grow a good deal bigger and older before you are able to fill that gown, my little one," he said.

"That is not the way I do things," said Miriam, severely. "I shall make the gown fit me."

Ralph was about to say that it would be a pity to cut down and alter that picturesque piece of old-fashioned attire into an ordinary garment, and that it would be well to keep it as a family relic, or to give it away to some one who could wear it as it was, but Miriam's manner assured him that she was extremely sensitive on the subject of this gown, and he considered it wise to offer no further opinion about it. So he went about his affairs, and Miriam, having resumed her ordinary dress, went out with her cook-book to a bench under a tree on the lawn. She never stayed in the house when it was possible to be out of doors.

"I wish I could find out," she said to herself, "what Dora Bannister intended to make for Ralph out of raspberries. Whatever it is, I know I can make it just as well, and I want to do it all myself before the new cook comes. It could not have been jam," she said, as she turned over the leaves; "for Ralph does not care much for jam, and he would not have told her he liked that. And then there is jelly; but it must take a long time to make jelly, and I do not believe she would undertake to give him that for dinner, made from raspberries picked this morning. Besides, I cannot imagine Ralph saying he wanted jelly for his dinner. Well, well!" she exclaimed aloud, as she stopped to read a recipe, "they do make tarts out of raspberries! That must have been it, for Ralph is desperately fond of every kind of pastry. I will go into the house this minute, and make him some raspberry tarts. We shall have them for supper, even if they give him the nightmare. I am not going to have him say again that he wished the new cook, as he kept calling Dora Bannister, had stayed a little longer."

Alas! at dinner time Ralph had been guilty of that indiscretion. Without exactly knowing it, he had missed in the meal a certain very pleasant element, which had been put into the supper and breakfast by Dora's desire to gratify his especial tastes. While he missed their visitor in many other ways, he alluded to her premature departure only in connection with their domestic affairs.

But so far as Miriam was concerned, he could have done nothing worse than this. To have heard her brother say that Dora Bannister was the most lovely girl he had ever seen, and that he was filled with grief at losing the delights of her society, might have been disagreeable to her, or it might not. But to have him even in the lightest way intimate that her house-keeping was preferable to that of his own sister nettled her self-esteem.

"I will show him," she said, "that he is mistaken."

In the pleasant coolness of the great barn, Ralph stretched himself on a pile of new-made hay to think. He was a farmer, and he intended to try to be a good farmer, and he knew that good farmers, during working hours, do not lie down on piles of hay to think. But notwithstanding that, in this hay-scented solitude, looking out of the great door upon the quiet land-scape with the white clouds floating over it, he thought of Dora. He had been thinking of her in all sorts of irregular and disjointed ways ever since he had risen in the morning; but now he wished to think definitely, and lay down here for that purpose. One cannot think definitely and single-mindedly when engaged in farm work, especially if he sometimes finds himself a little awkward at said work and is bothered by it.

Whenever he could do it, Ralph Haverley liked to get things clear and straightforward in his mind. He had applied this rule to all matters of his former business, and he now applied it to the affairs of his present estate. But how much more important was it to apply the rules to Dora Bannister! Nothing had ever put his mind into a condition less clear and straightforward than the visit of that young lady. The main point to be decided upon was: what should he do about seeing her again? He was filled by an all-pervading desire to do that; but how should he set about it? The simplest plan would be to go and see her; but if he did so, he knew he ought to take his sister with him, and he had no reason to believe that Miriam would be in any hurry to return Miss Bannister's visit. If he had been acquainted with the brother, the case would have been different, but that gentleman had not yet called upon him.

Having thought some time on this subject, Ralph sat upright, and rearranged his reflections.

"Why is it," he said to himself, "that I am so anxious to see her again, and to see her as soon as possible?"

To the solution of this question, Ralph applied the full force of his intellectual powers. The conclusion that came to him after about six seconds of deliberation was not well defined, but it indicated that if almost any young man had had in his house— actually living with him and taking part in his household affairs—an unusually handsome young woman, who, not only by her appearance, but by her gentle and thoughtful desire to adapt herself to the tastes and circumstances of himself and his sister, seemed to belong in the place into which she had so suddenly dropped, that young man would naturally want to see that young woman just as soon as he could. This would be so in any similar case, and there was no use in trying to find out why it was so in this case.

He rose to his feet, and at that moment he heard Miriam calling to him.

"Ralph," she said, running into the barn, "I have been looking all over for you. The new woman cannot come to-day."

"I do not see why you should appear so delighted about it," said Ralph; "I am very sorry to hear it."

"And I am not," replied Miriam. "There are some things I want to do before she comes, and I am very glad to have the chance. Mike brought back word from her that if you send the wagon in the cool of the morning, she will come over with her trunk."

"You are a funny girl," said Ralph, "to be actually pleased at the prospect of cooking and doing housework a little longer." And as he said that, he congratulated himself that his sister had not had the chance of thinking him a funny fellow for lying stretched on the hay when he ought to have been at work.

Miriam was now in good spirits again. She walked to the great open window, and, leaning on the bar, looked out.

"What a lovely air," she said, and then she turned to her brother. "It is nice to have visitors, and to have plenty of people to do your work, but it is a hundred times jollier for just us two to be here by ourselves. Don't you think so, Ralph?" And, without waiting for her brother's answer, she went on. "You see, we can do whatever we please. We can be as free as anything—as free as cats. Here, puss, puss," she called to the gray barn cat in the yard below. "No, she will not even look at me. Cats are the freest creatures in the world; they will not come to you if they do not want to. If you call your dog, he feels that he has to come to you. Ralph, do you know I think it is the most absurd thing in the world that in a place like this we should have no dog."

"I have been waiting for somebody to give me one," said Ralph, taking up a pitchfork and preparing to throw some hay into the stable below.

"That will be the nicest way of getting one," said Miriam, as she came and stood by him, and watched him thrust the hay into the yawning hole. "We do not want a dog that people are willing to sell. We want one that is the friend of the family, and which the owners are obliged to part with because they are going to Europe, or something of that sort. Such a dog we should prize. Don't you think so, Ralph?"

"Yes," said he, and went on taking up forkloads of hay and thrusting them into the hole. He was wondering if this were a good time to tell Miriam that that very morning Dora Bannister had been talking about there being no dog at Cobhurst, and had asked him if he would like to have one; for if he would, she had a very handsome black setter, which had been given to her when it was a little puppy, and of which she was very fond, but which had now grown too big and lively to be cooped up in the yard of their house. He had said that he would be charmed to have the dog, and had intended to tell Miriam about it, but now a most excellent opportunity had come to do so, he hesitated. Miriam's soul did not seem to incline toward their late visitor, and perhaps she might not care for a gift from her. It might be better to wait awhile. Then there came a happy thought to Ralph; here was a good reason for going to see Dora. It would be no more than polite to take an interest in the animal which had been offered him, and even if he did not immediately bring it to Cobhurst, he could go and look at it. Miriam now returned to the house, leaving her brother pondering over the question whether or not the next morning would be too soon to go and look at the dog.

The sun had set, and Ralph, having finished his day's work, and having helped his sister as much as she and Mike would let him, sat on the piazza, gazing between the tall pillars upon the evening landscape, and still trying to decide whether or not it would be out of the way to go the next morning to Dora Bannister. The evening light grew less and less, and Ralph's healthy instincts drew his mind from thoughts of Dora to thoughts of supper. It certainly was very late for the evening meal, but he would not worry Miriam with any signs of impatience. That would be unkind indeed, when she was slaving away in the kitchen, while he sat here enjoying the evening coolness.

In a few minutes he heard his sister's step in the hall, and then a sob. He had scarcely time to turn, when Miriam ran out, and threw herself down on the wide seat beside him. Her face, as he could see it in the dim light, was one of despair, and as sob after sob broke from her, tears ran down her cheeks. Tenderly he put his arm around her and urged her to tell him what had happened.

"Oh, Ralph," she sobbed, "it is very hard, but I know it is true. I have been just filled with vanity and pride, and after all I am nothing like as good as she is, nor as good as anybody, and the best I can do is to go back to school."

"What is the matter?" exclaimed Ralph. "You poor little thing, how came you to be so troubled?"

Miriam gave a long sigh and dropped her head on her brother's shoulder.

"Oh, Ralph," she said, "they are six inches high."

"What are?" cried Ralph, in great amazement.

"The tarts," she said; "the raspberry tarts I was making for you, because you like them, and because Dora Bannister was going to make them for you, and I determined that I could do it just as well as she could, and that I would do it and that you would not have to miss her for anything. But it is of no use; I cannot do things as well as she can, and those tarts are not like tarts at all; they are like chimneys."

"I expect they are very good indeed. Now do not drop another tear, and let us go in and eat them."

"No," said Miriam, "they are not good. I know what is the matter with them. I have found out that I have no more idea of making pie crust than I have about the nebulous part of astronomy, and that I never could comprehend. I wanted to make the lightest, puffiest pastry that was possible, and I used some self-raising flour, the kind that has the yeast ground up with it, and when I put those tarts in the oven to bake, they

Frank Richard Stockton

just rose up, and rose up, until I thought they would reach up the chimney. They are perfectly horrid."

Ralph sprang to his feet, and lifted his sister from her seat. "Come along, little one," he cried, "and I shall judge for myself what sort of a pastry-cook you are."

"The pigs shall judge that," said Miriam, who had now dried her eyes, "but fortunately there are other things to eat."

The tarts, indeed, were wonderful things to look at, resembling, as Miriam had said, a plateful of little chimneys, with a sort of swallow's nest of jam at the top, but Ralph did not laugh at them.

"Wait until their turn comes," said Ralph, "and I will give my opinion about them."

When he had finished the substantial part of the meal, he drew the plate of tarts toward him.

"I will show you how to eat the Cobhurst tart. You cut it down from top to bottom: then you lay the two sections on their rounded sides: then you get a lot more of jam, which I see you have on the side table, and you spread the cut surfaces with it: then you put it together as it was before, and slice it along its shorter diameter. Good?" said he; "they are delicious."

Miriam took a piece. "It is good enough," she said, "but it is not a tart. If Dora Bannister had made them, they would have been real tarts."

"It is very well I said nothing about the dog," thought Ralph; and then he said aloud, "It is not Dora Bannister that we have to consider; it is Molly Tooney. She is to save you from the tears and perplexities of flour and yeast, and to make you the happy little lady of the house that you were before the wicked Phoebe went away. But one thing I insist upon: I want the rest of those tarts for my breakfast."

Miriam looked at her brother with a smile that showed her storm was over.

"You are eating those things, dear Ralph," she said, "because I made them, and that is the only good thing about them."

CHAPTER XXI

THE DRANES AND THEIR QUARTERS

In a small room at the back of Dr. Tolbridge's house there sat a young woman by the window, writing. This was Cicely Drane; and although it was not yet ten days since Miss Panney broached her plan of the employment of Miss Drane as the doctor's secretary, or rather copyist, here she was, hard at work, and she had been for two days.

The window opened upon the garden, and in the beds were a great many bright and interesting flowers, but paying no heed to these, Cicely gave her whole attention to her task, which, indeed, was not an easy one. With knitted brows she bent over the manuscript of the "Diagnosis of Sympathy," and having deciphered a line or two, she wrote the words in a fair hand on a broad sheet before her. Then she returned to the study of the doctor's caligraphy, and copied a little more of it, but the proportion of the time she gave to the deciphering of the original manuscript to that occupied in writing the words in her own hand was about as ten is to one. An hour had elapsed since she had begun to write on the page, which she had not yet filled.

Miss Cicely Drane was a small person, nearing her twenty-second year. She had handsome gray eyes, tastefully arranged brown hair, and a vivacious and pleasing face. Her hands were small, her feet were small, and she did not look as if she weighed a hundred pounds, although, in fact, her weight was considerably more than that. Her dress was a simple one, on which a great deal of thought had been employed to make it becoming.

For a longer time than usual she now bent over the doctor's manuscript, endeavoring to resolve a portion of it into comprehensible words. Then she held up the page to the light, replaced it on the table, stood up and looked at it, and finally sat down again, her elbows on the paper, and her tapering fingers in the little brown curls at the sides of her head. Presently she raised her head, with a sigh. "It is of no use," she said. "I must go and ask him what this means; that is, if he is at home."

With the page in her hand, she went to the office door, and knocked.

"Come in," said Dr. Tolbridge.

Miss Drane entered; the doctor was alone, but he had his hat in his hand and was just going out.

"I am glad I caught you," said she, "for there is a part of this page in which I can see no meaning."

"What is it?" said the doctor. "Read it."

Slowly and distinctly she read:—

"'The cropsticks of flamingo bicrastus quack.'"

The doctor frowned, laid his hat on the table, and seating himself took the paper from Cicely Drane.

"This is strange," said he. "It does seem to be 'cropsticks of flamingo,' but what can that mean?"

"That is what I came to ask you," said she. "I have been puzzling over it a good while, and I supposed, of course, you would know what it is."

"But I do not," said the doctor. "It is often very hard for me to read my own writing, and this was written two years ago. You can leave this sheet with me, and this evening I will look over it and try to make something out of it."

Cicely Drane was methodical in her ways; she could not properly go on with the rest of her work without this page, and so she told the doctor.

"Oh, never mind any more work for today," said he. "It is after four o'clock now, and you ought to go out and get a little of this pleasant sunshine. By the way, how do you like this new business?"

"I should like it very well," said Cicely, as she stood by the table, "if I could get on faster with it, but I work so very, very slowly. I made a calculation this morning, that if I work at the same rate that I have been working since I came here, it will take me thirteen years and eleven months to copy your manuscript."

The doctor laughed. "If a child should walk to school," he said, "at the same rate of speed that he takes his first toddling step on the nursery floor, it might take him about thirteen years to get there. That is, if his school were at the average distance. You will get on fast enough when you become acquainted with my writing."

She was on the point of saying that surely he had had time to get acquainted with it, and yet he could not read it; but she considered that she did not yet know the doctor well enough for that.

The doctor rose and took up his hat; then he suddenly turned toward Miss Drane and said, "La Fleur, our cook, came to speak to me this morning about your mother. She says she thinks that you are not well lodged; that the street is in the hottest part of the town, and that Mrs. Drane's health will suffer if you stay there. Does your mother object to your present quarters?"

Cicely, who had been half way to the door, now came back and stood by the table.

"Mother never objects to anything," she said. "She thinks our rooms are very neat and comfortable, and that Mrs. Brinkly is a kind landlady, but she has complained a great deal of the heat. You know our house was very airy."

"I am sorry," said the doctor, "that Mrs. Brinkly's house is not likely to prove pleasant. It is in a closely built portion of the town, but it seemed the only place where we could find suitable accommodations for your mother and you."

"Oh, it is a nice place," exclaimed Cicely, "and I am sure we shall like it, except in hot weather, such as we are having now. I have no doubt we shall get used to it after a little while."

"La Fleur does not think so," said the doctor. "She is very much dissatisfied with the Brinkly establishment. I think I saw signs of mental disturbance in our luncheon to-day."

Cicely laughed. She was a girl who was pleasant to look at when she laughed, for her features accommodated themselves so naturally to mirthful expression.

"It is almost funny," she said, "to see how fond La Fleur is of mother. She lived with us less than a year, and yet one might suppose she had always been a servant of the family. I think one reason for her feeling is that mother never does anything. You know she has never been used to do anything, and of late years she has not been well enough. La Fleur likes all that; she thinks it is a mark of high degree. She told me once that my mother was a lady who was born to be served, and who ought not to be allowed to serve herself."

"She does not seem to object to your working," remarked the doctor.

"I am sure she does not like that, but then she considers it a thing that cannot be helped. You know," continued Cicely, with a smile, "she is not so particular about me, for I have some trade blood. Father's father was a merchant."

"So you are only a grade aristocrat," said the doctor; "but I must go. I will talk to Mrs. Tolbridge about this affair of lodgings."

That evening Mrs. Tolbridge and the doctor held a conference in regard to the quarters of the Dranes.

"I think La Fleur concerns herself entirely too much in the matter," said the lady. "She first came to me, and then she went to you. You have done a good deal for Mrs. Drane in giving her daughter employment, and we cannot be expected to attend to her every need. I do not consider Mrs. Brinkly's house a very pleasant one in hot weather, and I would be glad to do anything I could to establish them more pleasantly, but I know of nothing to do, at least at present; and then you say they have not complained. From what I have seen of Mrs. Drane, I think she is a very sensible woman, and under the circumstances probably expects some discomforts."

"But that is not all that is to be considered," said her husband. "La Fleur's dissatisfaction, which is very evident, must be taken into the question. She has a scheming mind. Before she left this morning she asked me if I thought a little house could be gotten outside the town, for a moderate rent. I believe she would not hesitate to take such a house, and board and lodge the Dranes herself."

"Doctor!" exclaimed Mrs. Tolbridge, "whatever happens, I hope we are not going to be the slaves of a cook."

The doctor laughed.

"Whatever happens," he said, "we are always that. All we can do is to try and be the slaves of a good one."

"I am not altogether sure that that is the right way to look at it," said Mrs. Tolbridge; and then she went on with her sewing, not caring to expatiate on the subject. Her husband appreciated only the advantages of La Fleur, but she knew something of her disadvantages. The work on which she was engaged at that moment would have been done by the maid, had not that young woman's services been so frequently required of late by the autocrat of the kitchen.

The doctor sat silent for a few minutes. He had a kindly feeling for Mrs. Drane, and was willing to do all he could for her, but his thoughts were now principally occupied with plans for the continuance of good living in his own home.

"I suppose it would not be practicable," he said presently, "to invite them to stay with us during the heated term."

Mrs. Tolbridge dropped her work into her lap.

"That is not to be thought of for a moment," she said. "We have no room for them, unless we give up having any more friends this summer; and besides that, you would see La Fleur, with the other servants at her heels, devoting herself to the gratification of every want and notion of Mrs. Drane, and thinking no more of me than if I were a chair in a corner."

"We shall not have that," said the doctor, rising, and placing his hand on his wife's head. "You may be sure we shall not have that. And now I will go and get a bit of my handwriting, and see if you can help me decipher it."

He left the room, but in an instant returned.

"A happy thought has just struck me!" he exclaimed. "I wonder if those young Haverley people would take Mrs. Drane into their house for the rest of the summer? It would be an excellent thing for them, for their household needs the presence of an elderly person, and I am sure that no one could be quieter, or more pleasant, and less troublesome, than Mrs. Drane would be. What do you think of that idea?"

Mrs. Tolbridge looked up approvingly.

"It is not a bad one," she said; "but what would the daughter do? She could not come into town every day to do your work. It is too long a walk for her, and she could not afford a conveyance."

"No," said the doctor, "of course she could not go back and forwards every day, but it would not be necessary. She could take the work out there and do it as well as here, and she could come in now and then, when a chance offered, and ask me about the hard words, for which she could leave blanks. Or, if I happen to be in the neighborhood, I could stop in there and see how she was getting on. I would much rather arrange the business in that way, than have her pop into my office at any moment to ask me about my illegible words."

"I should think the work could be done just as well out of the house as in it," said the doctor's wife, who would be willing to have again the use of the little room that she had cheerfully given up to the copyist of her husband's book, which she, quite as earnestly as Miss Panney, desired to be given to the world.

"The first thing to do," said she, "is to make them acquainted. At first the Haverleys would not be likely to favor the plan. They no doubt consider themselves sufficient company for each other, and although a slight addition to their income would probably be of advantage, I think they are too young and unpractical to care much about that."

"How would it do to have the Dranes and the Haverleys here, and give them a first-class La Fleur dinner?" asked the doctor.

"I do not like that," said his wife. "The intention would be too obvious. The thing should be done more naturally."

"Well," said the doctor, "I wish we had Miss Panney here. She has a great capacity for rearranging and simplifying the circumstances of a complicated case."

Mrs. Tolbridge made no answer, but very intently examined her sewing.

"But if we can think of no deeply ingenious plan," continued the doctor, "we will go about it in a straightforward way. I will see Ralph Haverley, and if I can win him over to the idea I will let him talk to his sister. He can do it better than we can. If they utterly reject the whole scheme, we will wait a week or so, and propose it again, just as if we had never done it before. I have found this plan work very well with persons who, on account of youth, or some other reason, are given to resentment of suggestions and to quick decisions. When a rejected proposition is laid before them a second time, the disposition to resent has lost its force, and they are as likely to accept it as not."

"You are right," said Mrs. Tolbridge, "for I have tried that plan with you."

The doctor looked at her and laughed.

"It is astonishing," he exclaimed, "what coincidences we meet with in this world," and with that he left the room.

As soon as her husband had gone, Mrs. Tolbridge leaned back in her chair and laughed quietly.

"To think of asking Miss Panney to aid in a plan like that!" she said to herself. "Why, when the old lady hears of it she will blaze like fury. To send that pretty Cicely to live in the house for which she herself has selected a mistress, will seem to her like high treason. But the arrangement suits me perfectly, and I can only hope that Miss Panney may not hear of it until everything is settled."

The more Dr. Tolbridge thought of the plan to establish Mrs. and Miss Drane, for a time, at Cobhurst, the better he liked it. Not only did he think the arrangement would be a desirable one on the Drane side, but also on the Haverley side. From the first, he had taken a lively interest in Miriam, and he considered that her life of responsibility and independence in that lonely household was as likely to warp her mind in some directions as it was to expand it in others. Suitable companionship would be a great advantage to her in this regard, and he fancied that Cicely Drane would be as congenial and helpful a chum, and Mrs. Drane as unobjectionable a matronly adviser, as could be found. If the plan suited all concerned, it might perhaps be continued beyond the summer. He would see Ralph as soon as possible.

CHAPTER XXII

A TRESPASS

Having received permission to stop work at four o'clock on a beautiful summer afternoon, Cicely Drane put away her papers and walked rapidly home. She found her mother on Mrs. Brinkly's front piazza, fanning herself vigorously and watching some children, who, on the other side of the narrow street, were feeding a tethered goat with clippings from a newspaper.

After a few words to explain her early return, Cicely went up to her own room, and took from a drawer a little pocketbook, and opening it, examined the money contained therein. Apparently satisfied with the result, she went downstairs, wallet in hand.

"Mother," said she, "you must find it dreadfully hot and stupid here, and as this is a bit of a holiday, I intend we shall take a drive."

Mrs. Drane was about to offer some sort of economic objection, but before she could do so, Cicely was out of the little front yard, and hurrying toward the station, where there were always vehicles to be hired.

She engaged the man who had the best-looking horse, and in a little open phaeton, a good deal the worse for wear, she returned to her mother.

Andy Griffing, the driver, was a grizzled little man with twinkling eyes and a cheery air that seemed to indicate that an afternoon drive was as much a novelty and pleasure to him as it could possibly be to any two ladies; which was odd, considering that for the last forty years Andy had been almost constantly engaged in taking morning, afternoon, evening, and night drives.

The only direction given him by Cicely was to take them along the prettiest country roads that he knew of, and this suited him well, for he not only considered himself a good judge of scenery, but he knew which roads were easiest for his horse.

As they travelled leisurely along, the ladies enjoying the air, the fields, the sweet summer smells, the stretches of woods, the blue and white sky, and everything that goes to make a perfect summer afternoon. Andy endeavored to add to their pleasure by giving them information regarding the inhabitants of the various dwellings they passed.

"That whitish house back there among the trees," said he, "with the green blinds, is called the Witton place. The Wittons themselves are nuthin' out o' the common; but there's an old lady lives there with 'em, who if you ever meet, you'll know agin, if you see her agin. Her name's Panney,—Miss Panney,—and she's a one-er. What she don't know about me, I don't know, and what she won't know about you, three days after she gits acquainted with you, you don't know. That's the kind of a person Miss Panney is. There's a lot of very nice people, some rich and some poor, and some queer and some not quite so queer, that lives in and around Thorbury, and if you like it at Mrs. Brinkly's and conclude to stay there any length of time, I don't doubt you'll git acquainted with a good many of 'em; but take my word for it, you'll never meet anybody who can go ahead of Miss Panney in the way of turnin' up unexpected. I once had a sick hoss, who couldn't do much more than stand up, but I had to drive him one day, 'cause my other one was hired out. 'Now' says I, as I drew out the stable, 'if I can get around town this mornin' without meetin' Miss Panney, I think old Bob can do my work, and to-morrow I'll turn him out to grass.' And as I went around the first corner, there was Miss Panney a drivin' her roan mare. She pulled up when she seed me, and she calls out, 'Andy, what's the matter with that hoss?' I told her he was a little under the weather, but I had to use him that day, 'cause my other hoss was out. Then she got straight out of that phaeton she drives in, and come up to my hoss, and says she, 'Andy, you ought to be ashamed of yourself to make a hoss work when he is in a condition like that. Take him right back to your stable, or I'll have you up before a justice.' 'Now look here, Miss Panney,' says I, 'which is the best, for a hoss to jog a little round town when he ain't feeling quite well, or for a man to sit idle on his front doorstep and see his family starve?' 'Now, Andy,' says she, 'is that the case with you?' and havin' brought up the pint myself, I was obliged to say that it was. 'Very good, then,' said she, and she took her roan mare by the head and led it up to the curbstone. 'Now then,' said she, 'you can take your hoss out of the cab and put this hoss in, and you can drive her till your hoss gets well, and durin' that time I'll walk.'"

"Well, of course I didn't do that, and I took my hoss back to the stable, and my family didn't starve nuther; but I just tell you this to show you what sort of a woman Miss Panney is."

"I should think she was a very estimable person," said Mrs. Drane.

"Oh, there's nothin' the matter with her estimation," said Andy. "That's level enough. I only told you that to show you how you can always expect her to turn up unexpected."

"Mrs. Brinkly spoke of Miss Panney," said Cicely; "she said that she was the first one to come and see her about rooms for us."

"That was certainly very kind," said Mrs. Drane, "considering that she does not know us at all, except through Dr. Tolbridge.

I remember his speaking of her."

"That place over there," said Andy, "you can jest see the tops of the chimneys, that's called Cobhurst; that's where old Matthias Butterwood used to live. It was an awful big house for one man, but he was queer. There's nobody livin' there now but two young people, sort of temporary, I guess, though the place belongs to 'em. I don't think they are any too well off. They don't give us hack-drivers much custom, never havin' any friends comin' or goin', or trunks or anything. He's got no other business, they say, and don't know no more about farmin' than a potato knows about preachin'. There's nothin' on the place that amounts to anything except the barn. There's a wonderful barn there, that old Butterwood spent nobody knows how much money on, and he a bachelor. You can't see the barn from here, but I'll drive you where you can get a good look at it."

In a few minutes, he made a turn, and whipped up his horse to a better speed, and before Mrs. Drane and her daughter could comprehend the state of affairs, they were rolling over a not very well kept private road, and approaching the front of a house.

"Where are you going, driver?" exclaimed Mrs. Drane, leaning forward in astonishment.

Andy turned his beaming countenance upon her, and flourished his whip.

"Oh, I'm just goin' to drive round the side of the house," he said; "at the back there's a little knoll where we can stop, and you can see the whole of the barn with the three ways of gittin' into it, one for each story." At that moment they rolled past the front piazza on which were Miriam and Ralph, gazing at them in surprise. The latter had risen when he had heard the approaching carriage, supposing they were to have visitors. But as the vehicle passed the door he looked at his sister in amazement.

"It can't be," said he, "that those people have come to visit Mike?"

"Or Molly Tooney?" said Miriam.

As for Mrs. Drane and Cicely, they were shocked. They had never been in the habit of driving into private grounds for the sake of seeing what might be there to see, and Mrs. Drane sharply ordered the driver to stop.

"What do you mean," said she, "by bringing us in here?"

"Oh, that's nuthin'," said Andy, with a genial grin; "they won't mind your comin' in to look at the barn. I've druv lots of people in here to look at that barn, though, to be sure, not since these young people has been livin' here, but they won't mind it an eighth of an inch."

"I shall get out and apologize," said Mrs. Drane, "for this shameful intrusion, and then you must drive us out of the grounds immediately. We do not wish to stop to look at anything," and with this she stepped from the little phaeton and walked back to the piazza.

Stopping at the bottom of the steps, she saluted the brother and sister, whose faces showed that they were in need of some sort of explanation of her arrival at their domestic threshold.

In a few words she explained how the carriage had happened to enter the grounds, and hoped that they would consider that the impropriety was due entirely to the driver, and not to any desire on their part to intrude themselves on private property for the sake of sight-seeing. Ralph and Miriam were both pleased with the words and manner of this exceedingly pleasant-looking lady.

"I beg that you will not consider at all that you have intruded," said Ralph. "If there is anything on our place that you would care to look at, I hope that you will do so."

"It was only the barn," said Mrs. Drane, with a smile. "The man told us it was a peculiar building, but I supposed we could see it without entering your place. We will trespass no longer."

Ralph went down the steps, and Miriam followed.

"Oh, you are perfectly welcome to look at the barn as much as you wish to," he said. "In fact, we are rather proud to find that this is anything of a show place. If the other lady will alight, I will be pleased to have you walk into the barn. The door of the upper floor is open, and there is a very fine view from the back."

Mrs. Drane smiled.

"You are very good indeed," she said, "to treat intrusive strangers with such kindness, but I shall be glad to have you know that we are not mere tourists. We are, at present, residents of Thorbury. I am Mrs. Drane, and my daughter is engaged in assisting Dr. Tolbridge in some literary work."

"If you are friends of Dr. Tolbridge," said Ralph, "you are more than welcome to see whatever there is to see on this place. The doctor is one of our best friends. If you like, I will show you the barn, and perhaps my sister will come with us."

Miriam, who for a week or more had been beset by the very unusual desire that she would like to see somebody and speak to somebody who did not live at Cobhurst, willingly agreed to assist in escorting the strangers, and Cicely having joined the group, they all walked toward the barn.

There were no self-introductions, Ralph merely acting as cicerone, and Miriam bringing up the rear in the character of occasional commentator. Mrs. Drane had accepted the young gentleman's invitation because she felt that the most polite thing to do under the circumstances was to gratify his courteous desire to put them at their ease, and, being a lover of fine scenery, she was well rewarded by the view from the great window.

The pride of possession began to glow a little within Ralph as he pointed out the features of this castle-like barn. Mrs. Drane agreed to his proposition to descend to the second floor. But as these two were going down the broad stairway, Cicely drew back, and suddenly turning, addressed Miriam.

"I have been wanting to ask a great many questions," she said, "but I have felt ashamed to do it. I have nearly always lived in the country, but I know hardly anything about barns and cows and stables and hay and all that. Do the hens lay their eggs up there in your hay?"

Miriam smiled gravely.

"It is very hard to find out," she said, "where they do lay their eggs. Some days we do not get any at all, though I suppose they lay them, just the same. There is a henhouse, but they never go in there."

Cicely moved toward the stairway, and then she stopped; she cast her eyes toward the mass of hay in the mow above, and then she gave a little sigh. Miriam looked at her and understood her perfectly, moreover she pitied her.

"How is it," said she as they went down the stairs, "that you lived in the country, and do not know about country things?"

"We lived in suburbs," she said. "I think suburbs are horrible; they are neither one thing nor the other. We had a lawn and shade trees, and a croquet ground, and a tennis court, but we bought our milk and eggs and most of our vegetables. There isn't any real country in all that, you know. I was never in a haymow in my life. All I know about that sort of thing is from books."

When, with many thanks for the courtesies offered them, Mrs.

Drane and her daughter had driven away, Miriam sat by herself on the piazza and thought. She had a good deal of time, now, to think, for Molly Tooney was a far more efficient servant than Phoebe had been, and although her brother gave her as much of his time as he could, she was of necessity left a good deal to herself.

She began by thinking what an exceedingly gentlemanly man her brother was; in his ordinary working clothes he had been as much at his ease with those ladies as though he had been dressed in a city costume, which, however, would not have been nearly so becoming to him as his loose flannel shirt and broad straw hat. She then began to regret that her mind worked so slowly. If it had been quicker to act, she would have asked that young lady to come some day and go up in the haymow with her. It would be a positive charity to give a girl with longings, such as she saw that one had, a chance of knowing what real country life was. It would be pleasant to show things to a girl who really wanted to know about them. From this she began to think of Dora Bannister. Dora was a nice girl, but Miriam could not think of her as one to whom she could show or tell very much; Dora liked to do the showing and telling herself.

"I truly believe," said Miriam to herself, and a slight flush came on her face, "that if she could have done it, she would have liked to stay here a week, and wear the teaberry gown all the time and direct everything,—although, of course, I would never have allowed that." With a little contraction of the brows, she went into the hall, where she heard her brother's step.

CHAPTER XXIII

THE HAVERLEY FINANCES AND MRS. ROBINSON

"It bothers the head off of me," said Molly Tooney to Mike, as she sat eating her supper in the Cobhurst kitchen, "to try to foind out what thim two upstairs is loike, anyway, 'specially her. I've been here nigh onto two weeks, now, and I don't know her no betther than when I fust come. For the life of me I can't make out whether she's a gal woman or a woman gal. Sometimes she's one and sometimes t'other. And then there's he. Why didn't he marry and settle before he took a house to himself? And in the two Sundays I've been here, nather of thim's been to church. If they knowed what was becomin' to thim, they'd behave like Christians, if they are heretics."

Mike sat at a little table in the corner of the kitchen with his back to Molly, eating his supper. He had enough of the Southern negro in him to make him dislike to eat with white people or to turn his face toward anybody while partaking of his meals. But he also had enough of a son of Erin in him to make him willing to talk whenever he had a chance. Turning his head a little, he asked, "Now look a here, Molly; if a man's a heretic, how can he be a Christian?"

"There's two kinds of heretics," said Molly, filling her great tea-cup for the fourth time, and holding the teapot so that the last drop of the strong decoction should trickle into the cup; "Christian heretics and haythen heretics. You're one of the last koind yoursilf, Mike, for you never go nigh a church, except to

Frank Richard Stockton

whitewash the walls of it. And you'll never git no benefit to your own sowl, from Phoebe's boardin' the minister, nather. Take my word for that, Mike."

Mike allowed himself a sort of froggy laugh. "There's nobody gets no good out of that, but him," said he; "but you've got it crooked about their not goin' to church. They did go reg'lar at fust, but the gig's at the wheelwright's gettin' new shaf's."

"Gig, indeed!" ejaculated Molly. "No kirridge, but an auld gig! There's not much quality about thim two. I wouldn't be here working for the likes o' thim, if it was not for me wish to oblige Miss Panney, poor old woman as she's gittin' to be."

Mike shrewdly believed that it was due to Miss Panney's knowledge of some of Molly's misdeeds, and not to any desire to please the old lady, that the commands of the latter were law to the Irishwoman, but he would not say so.

"Kerridge or no kerridge," said he, "they're good 'nough quality for me, and I reckon I knows what quality is. They hain't got much money, that's sure, but there's lots of quality that ain't got money; and he's got sense, and that's better than money. When he fust come here, I jes' goes to him, and ses I, 'How's you goin' to run this farm, sir,—ramshackle or reg'lar?' He looked at me kinder bothered, and then I 'splained. 'Well,' said he, 'reg'lar will cost more money than I've got, and I reckon we'll have to run it ramshackle.' That's what we did, and we're gittin' along fust rate. He works and I work, and what we ain't got no time to do, we let stand jes' thar till we git time to 'tend to it. That's ramshackle. We don't spend no time on fancy fixin's, and not much money on nuthin.'"

"That's jes' what I've been thinkin' mesilf," said Molly. "I don't see no signs of money bein' spint on this place nather for one thing or anuther."

"You don't always have to spend money to get craps," said Mike; "look at our corn and pertaters. They is fust rate, and when we sends our craps to market, there won't be much to take for 'spenses out of what we git."

"Craps!" said Molly, with a sneer. "If you hauls your weeds to market, it'll take more wagons than you can hire in this country, and thim's the only craps my oi has lit on yit."

This made Mike angry. He was, in general, a good-natured man, but he had a high opinion of himself as a farm manager, and on this point his feelings were very sensitive. As was usual with him when he lost his temper, he got up without a word and went out.

"Bedad!" said Molly, looking about her, "I wouldn't have sid that to him if I'd seed there wasn't no kindlin' sphlit."

As Mike walked toward his own house, he was surprised to see, entering a little-used gateway near the barn, a horse and carriage. It was now so dark he could not see who occupied it, and he stood wondering why it should enter that gateway, instead of coming by the main entrance. As he stood there, the equipage came slowly on, and presently stopped in front of his little house. By the time he reached it, Phoebe, his wife, had alighted, and was waiting for him.

"Reckon you is surprised to see me," said she, and then turning to the negro man who drove the shabby hired vehicle, she told him that he might go over to the barn and tie his horse, for she would not be ready to go back for some time. She then entered the house with Mike, and, a candle having been lighted, she explained her unexpected appearance. She had met Miss Dora Bannister, and that young lady had engaged her to go to Cobhurst and take a note to Miss Miriam.

"She tole me," said Phoebe, "that she had wrote two times already to Miss Miriam, and then, havin' suspected somethin', had gone to the pos'-office and found they was still dar. Don't your boss ever sen' to the pos'-office, Mike?"

Frank Richard Stockton

"He went hisself every now an' then, till the gig was broke," said Mike, "but I don't believe he ever got nuthin', and I reckon they thought it was no use botherin' about sendin' me, special, in the wagon."

"Well, they're uncommon queer folks," said Phoebe. "I reckon they've got nobody to write to, or git letters from. Anyway, Miss Dora wanted her letter to git here, and so she says to me that if I'd take it, she'd pay the hire of a hack, and so, as I wanted to see you anyway, Mike, I 'greed quick enough."

Before delivering the letter with which she had been entrusted, Phoebe proceeded to attend to some personal business, which was to ask her husband to lend her five dollars.

"Bless my soul," said Mike, "I ain't got no five dollars. I ain't asked for no wages yit, and don't expect to, till the craps is sold."

"I can't wait for that!" exclaimed Phoebe; "I's got to have money to carry on the house."

"Whar's the money the preacher pays you?" asked her husband.

"Dat's a comin'," said Phoebe, "dat's a comin' all right. Thar's to be a special c'lection next Sunday mornin', and the money's goin' to pay the minister's board. I'm to git every cent what's owin' to me, and I reckon it'll take it all."

"He ain't paid you nuthin' yit, thin?"

"Not yit; there was another special c'lection had to be tuk up fust, but the next one's for me. Can't you go ask your boss for five dollars?"

"Oh, yes," said Mike, "he'll give it to me if I ask him. Look here, Phoebe, we might's well git all the good we kin out of five dollars, and I reckon I'll come to chu'ch next Sunday, and put the five dollars in the c'lection. I'll git the credit of givin' a big lot of money, and that'll set me up a long time wid the congregation, and you git the five dollars all the same."

"Mike," said Phoebe, solemnly, "don't you go and do dat; mind, I tell you, don't you do dat. You give me them five dollars, and jes' let that c'lection alone. No use you wearin' youself out a walkin' to chu'ch, and all the feedin' and milkin' to do besides."

Mike laughed. "I reckon you think five dollars in th' pahm of th' hand is better than a whole c'lection in the bush. I'll see th' boss before you go, and if he's got the money, he'll let me have it."

Satisfied on this point, Phoebe now declared that she must go and deliver her letter; but she first inquired how her husband was getting on, and how he was treated by Molly Tooney.

"I ain't got no use for that woman;" and he proceeded to tell his wife of the insult that had been passed on his crops.

"That's brazen impidence," said Phoebe, "and jes' like her. But look here, Mike, don't you quarrel with the cook. No matter what happens, don't you quarrel with the cook."

"I ain't goin' to quarrel with nobody," said Mike; "but if that Molly 'spects me to grease her wagon wheels for her, she's got hold of the wrong man. If she likes green wood for the kitchen fire, and fotchin' it mos' times for herself, that's her business, not mine."

"If you do that, Mike, she'll leave," said Phoebe.

Mike gave himself a general shrug.

"She can't leave," said he, "till Miss Panney tells her she kin."

Phoebe laughed and rose.

"Reckon I'll go in and see Miss Miriam," she said, "and while I'm doin' that you'd better ask the boss about the money."

Having delivered the letter, and having, with much suavity, inquired into the health and general condition of the Cobhurst family since she had walked off and left it to its own resources, and having given Miriam various points of information in regard to the Bannister and the Tolbridge families, Phoebe gracefully took leave of the young mistress of the house and proceeded to call upon the cook.

"Hi, Phoebe!" cried Molly, who was engaged in washing dishes, "how did you git here at this time o' night?"

"I'd have you know," said the visitor, with lofty dignity, "that my name is Mrs. Robinson, and if you want to know how I got here, I came in a kerridge."

"I didn't hear no kirridge drive up," said Molly.

"Humph!" said Mrs. Robinson, "I reckon I know which gate is proper for my kerridge to come in, and which gate is proper for the Bannister coachman to drive in. I suppose there is cooks that would drive up to the front door if the governor's kerridge was standin' there."

Molly looked at the colored woman, with a grin.

"You're on your high hoss, Mrs. Robinson," said she. "That's what comes o' boardin' the minister. That's lofty business, Mrs. Robinson, an' I expect you're after gittin' rich. Is it the gilt-edged butter you give him for his ash-cakes?"

"A pusson that's pious," said Phoebe, "don't want to get rich onter a minister of the gospel—"

"Which would be wearin' on their hopes if they did," interrupted Molly.

"But I can tell you this," continued Phoebe, more sharply, "that it isn't as if I was a Catholic and boardin' a priest, and had to go on Wednesdays and confess back to him all the money he paid me on Tuesdays."

Molly laughed aloud. "We don't confess money, Mrs. Robinson, we confess sins; but perhaps you think money is a sin, and if that's so, this house is the innocentest place I ever lived in. Sit down, Mrs. Robinson, and be friendly. I want to ax you a question. Has thim two, upstairs, got any money? What made you pop off so sudden? Didn't they pay your wages?"

Phoebe seated herself on the edge of a chair, and sat up very straight. She felt that the answer to this question was a very important one. She herself cared nothing for the Haverleys, but Mike lived with them, and was their head man, and it was not consistent with her position among the members of the congregation and in the various societies to which she belonged, that her husband should be in the employ of poor and consequently unrespected people.

"My wages was paid, every cent," she said, "and as to their money, I can tell you one thing, that I heard him say to his sister with my own ears, that he was goin' to build a town on them meaders, with streets and chu'ches, and stores on the corners of the block, and a libr'y and a bank, and she said she wouldn't object if he left the trees standin' between the house and the meaders, so that they could see the steeples and nothin' else. And more than that, I can tell you," said Phoebe, warming as she spoke, "the Bannister family isn't and never was intimate with needy and no-count families, and nobody could be more sociable and friendly with this family than Miss Dora is, writin' to her four or five times a week, and as I said to Mike, not ten minutes ago, if Mr. Haverley and Miss Dora should git married, her money and his money would make this the finest place in the county, and I tol' him to mind an' play his cards well and stay here as butler or coachman—I didn't care which; and he said he would like coachman best, as he was used to hosses."

Now, considering that the patience of her own coachman must be pretty nearly worn out, and believing that what she had said would inure to her own reputation, and probably to Mike's benefit as well, and that its force might be impaired by any further discussion of the subject, Phoebe arose and took a dignified leave.

Molly stood some moments in reflection.

"Bedad," she said aloud, "to-morrer I'll clane thim lamp-chimbleys and swape the bidrooms."

CHAPTER XXIV

THE DOCTOR'S MISSION

The letter which Phoebe brought was a long and cordial one, in which Dora begged that Miriam would come and make her a visit of a few days. She said, moreover, that her brother was intending to call on Mr. Haverley and urge him to come to their house as frequently as he could during his sister's visit. Dora said that she would enjoy having Miriam with her so very, very much; and although the life at the dear old farm must be always charming, she believed that Miriam would like a little change, and she would do everything that she could to make the days pass pleasantly.

There could not have been a more cordial invitation, but its acceptance was considered soberly and without enthusiasm.

During the past fortnight, there had been no intercourse between the Bannister and Haverley families. Dora, it is true, had written, but her letters had not been called for, and Ralph had not been to her house to inquire about the dog. The reason for this was that, turning over the matter in his mind for a day or two, he thought it well to mention it to Miriam in a casual way, for he perceived that it would be very unwise for him to go to Dora's house without informing his sister and giving her his reasons for the visit. To his surprise, Miriam strenuously opposed his going to the Bannister house on any pretence until Mr. Bannister had called upon him, and showed so much earnest feeling on the subject that he relinquished his

Frank Richard Stockton

intention. He could see for himself that it would not be the proper thing to do; and so he waited, with more impatience on rainy days than others, for Mr. Herbert Bannister to call upon him.

On nearly every morning of the two weeks, Dora asked her brother at breakfast time if he were going that day to call at Cobhurst; and every time she asked him, Herbert answered that he would go that day, if he possibly could; but on each evening he informed her that at the hour he had intended to start for Cobhurst a client or clients had come into the office, or a client or clients had been in the office and had remained there. A very busy man was Mr. Bannister.

Miriam's opinion on the subject had been varied. She frequently felt in her lonely moments that it would be a joy to see Dora Bannister drive in at the gate.

"If only," thought Miriam, with a sigh, "she would content herself to be a visitor to me, just as I would be to her, and not go about contriving things she thinks Ralph would like,—as if it were necessary that any one should come here and do that! As for going to her house, that would leave poor Ralph here all by himself, or else he would be there a good deal, and—"

Here a happy thought struck Miriam.

"I can't go, anyway," she said aloud, "for the gig is broken;" and, her brother coming in at that moment, she informed him, with an air of much relief, how the matter had settled itself.

"But I don't like matters to settle themselves in that way," said Ralph. "The gig should certainly be in order by this time. I will go myself and see the man about it, and if the new shafts are not finished, I can hire a carriage for you. There is no need of your giving up a pleasant visit for the want of means of conveyance."

"But even if the gig were all ready for us to use, you know that you could not go until Mr. Bannister has called," said the cruel-minded sister.

Ralph was of the opinion that there were certain features of social etiquette which ought to be ruthlessly trodden upon, but he could think of nothing suitable to say in regard to the point so frequently brought up by Miriam, and, walking somewhat moodily to the front door, he saw Dr. Tolbridge approaching in his buggy.

The good doctor had come out of his way, and on a very busy morning, to lay before the Haverleys his project concerning Mrs. Drane and her daughter. Having but little time, he went straight to the point, and surprised Miriam and Ralph as much as if he had proposed to them to open a summer hotel. But, without regard to the impression he had made, he boldly proceeded in the statement of his case.

"You couldn't find pleasanter ladies than Mrs. Drane and her daughter," he said. "The latter is copying some manuscript for me, which she could do just as well here as at my house—"

"Are you talking about the two ladies who were here yesterday afternoon?" interrupted Miriam.

"Here, yesterday afternoon!" cried the doctor, and now it was his turn to be surprised.

When he had heard the story of the trespass on private grounds, the doctor laughed heartily.

"Well," said he, "Mistress Fate has been ahead of me. The good lady is in the habit of doing that sort of thing. And now that you know the parties in question, what have you to say?"

Miriam's blood began to glow a little, and as she gazed out of the open door without looking at anything, her eyes grew very bright. In her loneliness, she had been wishing that Dora Bannister would drive in at the gate, and here was a chance to have a very different sort of a girl drive in—a girl to whom she had taken a great fancy, although she had seen her for so short a time.

"Would they want to stay long?" she asked, without turning her head.

The doctor saw his opportunity and embraced it.

"That would be your affair entirely," he said. "If they came for only a week, it would be to you no more than a visit from friends, and to breathe this pure country air, for even that time, would be a great pleasure and advantage to them both."

Miriam turned her bright eyes on her brother.

"What do you say, Ralph?" she asked.

The lord of Cobhurst, who had allowed his sister to tell of the visit of the Dranes, had been thinking what a wonderful piece of good luck it would have been, if, instead of these strangers, Dora Bannister and her family had desired to find quarters in a pleasant country house for a few summer weeks. He did not know her family, nor did he allow himself to consider the point that said family was accustomed to an expensive style of living and accommodation, entirely unlike anything to be found on a ramshackle farm. He only thought how delightful it would be if it were Dora who wanted to come to Cobhurst.

As Ralph looked upon the animated face of his sister, it was easy enough to see that the case as presented by the doctor interested her very much, and that she was awaiting his answer with an eagerness that somewhat surprised him.

"And you, little one, would you like to have these ladies come to us?"

"Yes, I would," said Miriam, and then she stopped. There was much more she could have said, which crowded itself into her mind so fast that she could scarcely help saying it, but it would have been contrary to the inborn spirit of the girl to admit that she ever felt lonely in this dear home, or that, with a brother like Ralph, she ever craved the companionship of a girl. But it was not necessary to say any more.

"If you want them, they shall come," said Ralph, and if it had been the Tolbridges or Miss Panney whose society his sister desired, his assent would have been given just as freely.

In fifteen minutes everything was settled and the doctor was driving away. He was in good spirits over the results of his mission, for that morning La Fleur had waylaid him as he went out and again had spoken to him about the possibility of hiring a little house in the suburbs.

"I am sure this arrangement will suit our good cook," he thought; "but as for its continuance, we must let time and circumstances settle that."

The doctor reached home about eleven o'clock.

"What do you think it would be better to do," he said to his wife, when he had made his report, "to stop at Mrs. Drane's as I go out this afternoon, or to tell Cicely about our Cobhurst scheme, and let her tell her mother?"

"The thing to do," said Mrs. Tolbridge, closing her desk, at which she was writing, "is for me to go and see Mrs. Drane immediately, and for you to send Cicely home and give her a lot of work to do at Cobhurst. They should go there this afternoon."

"Yes," said the doctor; "of course, the sooner the better; but it has struck me perhaps it might be well to mention the matter to Miss Panney before the Dranes actually leave Mrs. Brinkly. You know she was very active in procuring that place for them."

Frank Richard Stockton

Mrs. Tolbridge looked at her husband, gave a little sigh, and then smiled.

"What is your opinion of a bird," she asked, "who, flying to the shelter of the woods, thinks it would be a good idea to stop for a moment and look down the gun-barrel of a sportsman, to see what is there?"

The doctor looked at her for a moment and then, catching her point, gave her a hearty laugh for answer, and walking to his table, took up a sheet of manuscript and carried it to the room where Miss Drane was working.

"The passage which so puzzled you," he said, "has been deciphered by Mrs. Tolbridge and myself, and reads thus: 'The philosophy of physiological contrasts grows.'"

"Why, yes," said Cicely, looking at the paper; "now that you tell me what it is, it is as plain as can be. I will write it in the blank space that I have left, and here are some more words that I would like to ask you about."

"Not now, not now," said the doctor. "I want you to stop work and run home. As soon as I can I will talk with you about what you have written, and give you some more of the manuscript. But no more work for to-day. You must hurry to your mother. You will find Mrs. Tolbridge there, talking to her about a change of quarters."

"Another holiday!" exclaimed Cicely, in surprise.

She was a girl who worked earnestly and conscientiously with the intention of earning every cent of the money which was paid to her, and these successive intermissions of work seemed to her unbusiness-like. But she made no objections, and, putting away her papers, with a sigh, for she had a list of points about which she was ready and anxious to consult the doctor,—she went to join the consultation, which she presumed concerned their removal from one street in Thorbury to another. But when she discovered the heavenly prospect which had opened before her mother and herself, her mind bounded from all thoughts of the manuscript of the "Diagnosis of Sympathy," as if it had been a lark mounting to the sky.

CHAPTER XXV

BOMBSHELLS AND BROMIDE

About noon on the next day, Mrs. Tolbridge sat down at her desk to finish the writing of the letter which had been so abruptly broken off the day before. She had been very busy that afternoon and a part of this morning, assisting Mrs. Drane and her daughter in their removal from a hot street in a little town to the broad freedom and fine air of a spacious country home.

And this change had given so much pleasure to all parties concerned that it was natural that so good a woman as Mrs. Tolbridge should feel a glow of satisfaction in thinking of the part she had taken in it.

She was satisfied in more ways than one: it was agreeable to her to assist in giving pleasure to others, but besides this, she had a little satisfaction which was peculiarly her own; she was pleased that that very pretty and attractive Cicely would now work for the doctor, instead of working so much with him. Of course she was willing to give up the little room if it were needed, but it was a great deal pleasanter not to have it needed.

"It is so seldom," she thought, as she lifted the lid of her desk, "that things can be arranged so as to please everybody."

At this moment she glanced through the open window and saw Miss Panney at the front gate. Closing her desk, Mrs.

Tolbridge pushed back her chair, her glow of satisfaction changing into a little chill.

"Is the doctor at home?" she inquired of the servant who was passing the door, and on receiving the negative reply, the chilly feeling increased.

Miss Panney was in a radiant humor. She seated herself in her favorite rocking-chair; she laid her fan on the table near her and her reticule by it, and she pushed back from her shoulders a little India shawl.

"I am treating myself," she said, "to a regular gala day; in the first place, I intend to stay here to luncheon. People who have a La Fleur must expect to see their friends at their table much oftener than if they had a Biddy in the kitchen. That is one of the penalties of good fortune. I have my cap in my bag, and as soon as I have cooled a little I will take off my bonnet and shawl. This afternoon I am going to see the Bannisters, and after that I intend to call on Mrs. Drane and her daughter. I put off that until the last in order that Miss Drane may be at home. I ought to have called on them before, considering that I did so much in getting them established in Thorbury,—I am sure Mrs. Brinkly would not have taken them if I had not talked her into it,—but one thing and another has prevented my going there. But I have seen Miss Drane; I came to town yesterday in the Witton carriage, and saw her in the street. She is certainly a pretty little thing, and dresses with much taste. We all thought her face was very sweet and attractive. We had a good look at her, for she was waiting for our carriage to pass, in order to cross the street. I told Jim, the driver, to go slowly, for I like to have a good look at people before I know them. And by the way, Kitty, an idea comes into my head," and as she said this, the old lady's eyes twinkled, and a little smile stole over the lower part of her wrinkled face. "Perhaps you may not like the doctor to have such an extremely pretty secretary. Perhaps you may have preferred her to have a stubby nose and a freckled face. How is that, Kitty?"

"Nonsense," said Mrs. Tolbridge. "It makes no manner of difference what sort of a face a secretary has; her handwriting is much more important."

"Oh," said Miss Panney, "I am glad to hear that. And how does she get on?"

"Very well indeed," was the answer; "the doctor seems satisfied with her work."

"That is nice," said Miss Panney, "and how do they like it at Mrs. Brinkly's? I saw their rooms, which are neatly furnished, and Mrs. Brinkly keeps a very good table. I have taken many a meal at her house."

Had there been a column of mercury at Mrs. Tolbridge's back, it would have gone down several degrees, as she prepared to answer Miss Panney's question. She did not exactly hesitate, but she was so slow in beginning to speak, that Miss Panney, who was untying her bonnet-strings, had time to add, reflectively, "Yes, they are sure to find her a good landlady."

"The Dranes are not with Mrs. Brinkly now," said Mrs. Tolbridge. "They left yesterday afternoon, although some of their things were not sent away until this morning."

The old lady's hands dropped from her bonnet-strings to her lap.

"Left Mrs. Brinkly!" she exclaimed. "And where have they gone?"

"To Cobhurst, where they will board for a while, during the hot weather. They found it very close and uncomfortable in that part of the town, with the mercury in the eighties."

Miss Panney sat up tall and straight. Her eyes grew bigger and blacker as with her mental vision she glared upon the situation. Presently she spoke, and her voice sounded as if she were in a great empty cask, with her mouth at the bunghole.

"Who did this?" she asked.

Mrs. Tolbridge was glad to talk; it suited her much better at this time to do the talking than for her companion to do it, and she proceeded quite volubly.

"Oh, we all thought the change would be an excellent thing for them, especially for Mrs. Drane, who is not strong; and as they had seen Cobhurst and were charmed with the place, and as the Haverleys were quite willing to take them for a little while, it seemed an excellent thing all round. It was, however, our cook, La Fleur, who was the chief mover in the matter. She was very much opposed to their staying with Mrs. Brinkly,— you see she had lived with them and has quite an affection for them,—and actually went so far as to talk of taking a house in the country and boarding them herself. And you know, Miss Panney, how bad it would be for the doctor to lose La Fleur."

"Did the doctor have anything to do with this?" asked Miss Panney.

Now Mrs. Tolbridge did hesitate a little.

"Yes," she said, "he spoke to the Haverleys about it; he thought it would be an excellent thing for them."

Miss Panney rose, with her face as hard as granite. She drew her shawl about her shoulders, and took up her fan and bag. Mrs. Tolbridge also rose, much troubled.

"You must not imagine for a minute, Miss Panney," she said, "that the doctor had the slightest idea that this removal would annoy you. In fact, he spoke about consulting you in regard to it, and had he seen you before the affair was settled, I am sure he would have done so. And you must not think, either, that the doctor urged the Haverleys to take these ladies, simply because he wished to keep La Fleur. He values her most highly, but he thought of others than himself. He spoke particularly of the admirable influence Mrs. Drane would have on Miriam."

The old lady turned her flashing eyes on Mrs. Tolbridge, and, slightly lowering her head, she almost screamed these words: "Blow to the top of the sky Mrs. Drane's influence on Miriam! That is not what I care for."

Then she turned and walked out of the parlor, followed by Mrs. Tolbridge. At the front door she stopped and turned her wrathful and inexorable countenance upon the doctor's wife; then she deliberately shook her skirts, stamped her feet, and went out of the door.

When Dr. Tolbridge heard what had happened, he was sorely troubled. "I must go to see her," he said. "I cannot allow her to remain in that state of mind. I think I can explain the affair and make her look at it more as we do, although, I must admit, now that I recall some things she recently said to me, that she may have some grave objections to Cicely's residence at Cobhurst. But I shall see her, and I think I can pacify her."

Mrs. Tolbridge was not so hopeful as her husband; he had not seen Miss Panney at the front door. But she could not bring herself to regret the advice she had given him when he proposed consulting Miss Panney in regard to the Dranes' removal.

"I shall never object to La Fleur," she said to herself. "I will bear all her impositions and queernesses for the sake of his health and pleasure, but I cannot give up my little room to Cicely Drane."

And that very hour she caused to be replaced in the said room the desk and other appurtenances which had been taken out when the room had been arranged for the secretary.

These changes had hardly been made, when Dora Bannister called.

"Miss Panney was at our house to-day," said the girl, "and I cannot imagine what was the matter with her. I never saw anybody in such a state of mind."

"What did she say?" asked Mrs. Tolbridge.

"She said very little, and that was one of the strangest things about her. But she sat and stared and stared and stared at me, as if I were some sort of curiosity on exhibition, and did not answer anything I said to her. I was awfully nervous, though I knew from the few words she had said that she was not angry with me; but she kept on staring and staring and staring, and then she suddenly leaned forward and put her arms around me and kissed me. Then she sat back in her chair again, slapped her two hands upon her knees, and said, speaking to herself, 'It shall be done. I am a fool to have a doubt about it.' And then she went without another word. Now was not that simply amazing? Did she come here, and did she act in that way?"

"She was here," said Mrs. Tolbridge, "but she did not do anything so funny as that."

"Well, I suppose I shall find out some day what she means," said Dora. "And now, Mrs. Tolbridge, I did not come altogether to see you this afternoon. I hope Miss Drane has not gone home yet, for I thought it would be nice to meet her here. Mother and I are going to call on them, but I do not know when that will be; and I have heard so much about the doctor's secretary that I am perishing to see her. They say she is very pretty and bright. I wanted mother to go there to-day, but we have had a long drive this morning, and to-morrow she and I and Herbert are going to call at Cobhurst; and you know mother will never consent to crowd things. And so I thought I would come here this afternoon by myself. It won't be like a call, you know."

"Miss Drane is not here," said Mrs. Tolbridge; "but if you want to see her, you can do it to-morrow, if you go to Cobhurst. She and her mother are now living there, boarding with the Haverleys."

"Living at Cobhurst!" exclaimed Dora; and as she uttered these words, the girl turned pale.

"Heavens!" mentally ejaculated the doctor's wife. "I do nothing this day but explode bombshells."

In a moment Dora recovered nearly all her color, and laughed.

"It is so funny," she said, "that all sorts of things happen in this town without our knowing it. Is she still going to be the doctor's secretary?"

"Yes, she can do her work out there as well as here."

Dora looked out of the window as if she saw something in the garden, and Mrs. Tolbridge charitably took her out to show her some new dahlias.

Early the next morning, Dr. Tolbridge drove into the Witton yard. No matter who waited for him, he would not delay this visit. When he asked for Miss Panney, he had a strong idea that the old lady would refuse to see him. But in an astonishingly short space of time, she marched into the parlor, every war-flag flying, and closed the door behind her.

Without shaking hands or offering the visitor any sort of salutation, she seated herself in a chair in the middle of the room. "Now," said she, "don't lose any time in saying what you have got to say."

Not encouraged by this reception, the doctor could not instantly arrange what he had to say. But he shortly got his ideas into order, and proceeded to lay the case in its most favorable light before the old lady, dwelling particularly on the reasons why she had not been consulted in the affair.

Miss Panney heard him to the end without a change in the

rigidity of her face and attitude. "Very well, then," she said, when he had finished, "I see exactly what you have done. You have thrown me aside for a cook."

"Not at all!" exclaimed the doctor. "I had no idea of throwing you aside. In fact, Miss Panney, I never thought of you in the matter at all."

"Exactly, exactly," said the old lady, with emphatic sharpness; "you never thought of me at all. That is the sum and substance of what you have done. I gave you my confidence. I told you my intentions, my hopes, the plan which was to crown and finish the work of my life. I told you I would make the grandson of the only man I ever loved my heir, and I would do this, because I wished him to marry the daughter of the man who was my best friend on earth. The marriage of these two and the union of the estate of Cobhurst with the wealth of the Bannisters was a project which, as I told you, had grown dear to my heart, and for which I was thinking and dreaming and working. All this you knew, and without a word to me, and if you speak the truth, all for the sake of your wretched stomach, you clap into Cobhurst a girl who will be engaged to Ralph Haverley in less than a month."

The doctor moved impatiently in his chair.

"Nonsense, Miss Panney. Cicely Drane will not harm your plans. She is a sensible, industrious girl, who attends to her own business, and—"

"Precisely," said Miss Panney; "and her own business will be to settle for life at Cobhurst. She may not be courting young Haverley to-day, but she will begin to-morrow. She will do it, and what is more, she would be a fool if she did not. It does not matter what sort of a girl she is;" and now Miss Panney began to speak louder, and stood up; "it does not matter if she had five legs and two heads; you have no right to thrust any intruder into a household which I had taken into my charge, and for which I had my plans, all of which you knew. You are a false friend, Dr. Tolbridge, and at your doorstep I have shaken the dust from my skirts and my feet." And with a quick step and a high head, she marched out of the room.

The doctor took a little book out of his pocket, and on a blank leaf wrote the following:—

> Rx.
> Potass. Bromid.
> 3iij Tr. Dig. Natis.
> m. xxx
> Tr. Lavand. Comp.
> ad 3iij M.S. teaspoonful every three hours. H. D.

Having sent this to Miss Panney by a servant, he went his way. Driving along, his conscience stung him a little when he thought of the fable his wife had told him; but the moral of the fable had made but little impression upon him, and as an antidote to the sting he applied his conviction that match-making was a bad business, and that in love affairs, as well as in many diseases, the very best thing to do was to let nature take its course.

When Miss Panney read the paper which had been sent to her, her eyes flashed, and then she laughed.

"The wretch!" she exclaimed; "it is just like him." And in the afternoon she sent to her apothecary in Thorbury for the medicine prescribed. "If it cools me down," she said to herself, "I shall be able to work better."

CHAPTER XXVI

DORA COMES AND SEES

The call by the Bannisters at Cobhurst was made as planned. Had storm or sudden war prevented Mrs. Bannister and Herbert from going, Dora would have gone by herself. She did not appear to be in her usual state of health that day, and Mrs. Bannister, noticing this, and attributing it to Dora's great fondness for fruit at this season and neglect of more solid food, had suggested that perhaps it might be well for her not to take a long drive that afternoon. But this remark was added to the thousand suggestions made by the elder lady and not accepted by the younger.

Miriam was in the great hall when the Bannister family drove up, and she greeted her visitors with a well-poised affability which rather surprised Mrs. Bannister. Dora instantly noticed that she was better dressed than she had yet seen her.

When they were seated in the parlor, Mrs. Bannister announced that their call was intended to include Mrs. Drane and her daughter, and Herbert hoped that this time he would be able to see Mr. Haverley.

Mrs. Drane was sent for, but Miriam did not know where her brother and Miss Drane should be looked for. She had seen them walk by the back piazza, but did not notice in what direction they had gone. At this moment there ran through Dora a sensation similar to that occasioned by a mild galvanic shock, but as she was looking out of the open door, the rest of the company saw no signs of this.

"Excuse me," said Mrs. Bannister, in a low voice, and speaking rather rapidly, "but I thought that Miss Drane was working for Dr. Tolbridge, copying, or something of that kind."

"She is," answered Miriam, "but she has her regular hours, and stops at five o'clock, just as she did when she was in the doctor's house."

When Mrs. Drane had appeared and the visitors had been presented, Miriam said that she would go herself and look for Ralph and Miss Drane. She thought now that it was very likely they were in the orchard.

"Let me go with, you," exclaimed Dora, springing to her feet, and in a moment she and Miriam had left the house.

"I heard her say," said Miriam, "that she wanted some summer apples, fresh from the tree, and that is the reason why I suppose they are in the orchard. You never knew anybody so wild about country things as Miss Drane is. And she knows so little about them too."

"Do you like her?" asked Dora.

"Ever so much. I think she is as nice as can be. She is a good deal older than I am, but sometimes it seems as if it were the other way. I suppose one reason is that she wants to know so much, and I think I must like to tell people things—nice people, I mean."

Dora's mind was in a state of lively receptivity, and it received an impression from Miriam's words that might be of use hereafter. But now they had reached the orchard, and there, standing on a low branch of a tree, was Ralph, and below was Miss Drane. Her laughing face was turned upward, and she was holding her straw hat to catch an apple, but it was plain that she was not skilled in that sort of exercise, and when the apple dropped, it barely touched the rim of the hat and rolled upon the ground, and then they both laughed as if they had known each other for twenty years.

"What a little thing," said Miss Bannister.

"She is small," answered Miriam, "but isn't she pretty and graceful? And her clothes fit her so beautifully. I am sure you will like her."

Ralph came down from the tree, the straw hat was replaced on the head of Miss Drane, and then came introduction and greeting. Never before had Dora Bannister found it so hard to meet any one as she found it to meet these two. She was only eighteen, and had had no experience in comporting herself in an ordinary way when her every impulse prompted her to do or say something quite extraordinary. But she was a girl who could control herself, and she now controlled herself so well, that had Miss Panney or Mrs. Tolbridge been there they would instantly have suspected what was meant by so much self-control. She greeted Miss Drane with much suavity, and asked her if she liked apples.

As the party started for the house, Dora, who was a quick walker, was not so quick as usual, and Ralph naturally slackened his pace a little. In a few moments Miriam and Miss Drane were hurrying toward the house, considerably in advance of the others.

"It is so nice," said Dora, "for your sister to have ladies in the house with her. I have been wanting to see her ever so much, and was afraid something was the matter with her, especially as you did not come for your dog."

As Ralph was explaining his apparent ungraciousness, Dora's soul was roughly shaken. She was angry with him and wanted to show it, but she saw clearly that this would be unsafe. Her hold upon him was very slight, and a few unwise

　　　Frank Richard Stockton

words now might make him no more than a mere acquaintance. She did not wish to say words that would do that, but if she held him by a cord ever so slender, she would obey the promptings of her soul and endeavor to draw him a little toward her. She would take the risks of that, for if he drifted away from her, the cord would be as likely to break as if she drew upon it.

"Oh yes," she said, "I knew all the time why you and Miriam did not come to make a regular society call, but I did suppose that you would drop in to see about Congo. As soon as I got home, after I promised him to you, I began to educate him to cease to care for me, and to care for you. If you had been there, all this would have been easy enough, but as it was, I had to get Herbert or the coachman to take him out walking at the times I used to take him, and when he was tied up I kept away from his little house altogether, so that he should become accustomed to do without me. I stopped feeding him, and made Herbert do that whenever he had time, and I insisted that he should wear a big straw hat, which he does not like, but which is a good deal like the one you wear, and which I thought might have an influence on the mind of Congo."

This touched Ralph, and he did not wish that Miss Bannister should suppose that he thought so little of a gift of which she thought so much. And in order to entirely remove any suspicion of ungratefulness, he endeavored to make her understand that he had wished very much to go to see the dog, but wished much more to go to see her.

"I hate a great many of these social rules," he said, "and although I did not know any of the rest of your family, I knew you, and felt very much inclined to call on you and let the customs take care of themselves."

"I wish you had!" exclaimed Dora; "I like to see people brave enough to trample on customs."

Her spirits were rising, and she walked still slower. This

tete-a-tete was very delightful to Ralph, but he had no desire to trample on all social customs, and his feelings of courteous hospitality urged him to go as rapidly as possible to greet the special visitor who was waiting for him; but to desert that gentleman's sister, or make her walk quickly when she did not wish to, was equally opposed to his ideas of courtesy, and so it happened that Dora and Ralph entered the parlor so much later than the others that a decided impression was made on the minds of Mrs. and Miss Drane. And this was what Dora wished. She felt that it would be a very good thing in this case to assert some sort of a preemption claim. It could do no harm, and might be of great service.

After the manner of the country gentlemen who in mixed society are apt to prefer their own sex for purposes of converse, Herbert Bannister monopolized Ralph. His sister talked with Cicely Drane, and in spite of her natural courage and the reasons for self-confidence which she had just received, Dora's spirits steadily fell as she conversed with this merry, attractive girl, who knew so well how to make herself entertaining, even to other girls, and who was actually living in Ralph Haverley's house.

Dora made the visit shorter than it otherwise would have been. She had come, she had seen, and she wanted to go home and think about the rest of the business. The drive home was, in a degree, pleasant because Herbert had a great deal to say about Mr. Haverley, whom he had found most agreeable, and because Mrs. Bannister spoke in praise of Ralph's manly beauty, but it would depend upon future circumstances whether or not remarks of this kind could be considered entirely satisfactory.

That evening, in her own room, in a loose dressing-gown, and with her hair hanging over her shoulders, Dora devoted herself to an earnest consideration of her relations with Ralph Haverley. At first sight it seemed odd that there should be any relations at all, for she had known him but a short time, and he had made few or no advances toward her—not half so many or such pronounced ones as other men had made, during her few visits to fashionable resorts. But she settled this part of the question very promptly.

"I like him better than anybody I have ever seen," she said to herself. "In fact, I love him, and now—" and then she went on to consider the rest of the matter, which was not so easy to settle.

Cicely Drane was terribly hard to settle. There was that girl,— all the more dangerous because, being charming and little, a man would be more apt to treat her as a good comrade than if she were charming and tall,—who was with him all the time. And how she would be with him, Dora's imagination readily perceived, because she knew how she herself would be with him under the circumstances. Before breakfast in the dewy grass, gathering apples; during work hours, talking through the open window as he chanced to pass; after five o'clock, walks in the orchard, walks over the farm, in the woods everywhere, and always those two together, because there were four of them. How much worse it was that there were four of them! And the evenings, moonlight, starlight; on the piazza; good-night on the stairs—it was maddening to think of.

But, nevertheless, she thought of it hour after hour, with no other result than to become more and more convinced that she was truly in love with a man who had never given any sign that he loved her, and that there was every reason to believe that when he gave a sign that he loved, it would be to another woman, and not to her.

She rose and looked out of the window. A piece of the moon, far gone in the third quarter, was rising above a mass of evergreens. She had a courageous young soul, and the waning brightness of the lovers' orb did not affect her as a disheartening sign.

"It is not right," she said to herself. "I will not do it. I will not hang like an apple on a tree for any one to pick who chooses, or if nobody chooses, to drop down to the chickens and pigs. A woman has as much right to try to do the best for herself as a man has to try to do the best for himself. I can't really trample on customs as a man can, but I can do it in my mind, and I do it now. I love him, and I will get him if I can."

With this Dora sat down, and left the bit of moon to shed what luminousness it could over the landscape.

Her resolution shed a certain luminousness over Dora's soul. To determine to do a thing is nearly always inspiriting.

"Yes," she thought, "I will do what I can. He has promised to come very soon, and he shall not have Congo the first time he comes. He shall come, and I shall go, and I shall be great friends with Miriam. There will be nothing false in that, for I like her ever so much, and I shall remember to think more of what she likes. No one shall see me break down any customs of society,—especially, he shall not,—but out of my mind they are swept and utterly gone."

Having thus shaped her course, Dora thought she would go to bed. But suddenly an idea struck her, and she stood and pondered.

"I believe," she said, speaking aloud in her earnestness, "I believe that that is what Miss Panney meant. She has spoken so well of him to me; she has heard about that girl, and she said, yes, she certainly did say, 'It shall be done.' She wants it, I truly believe; she wants me to marry him."

For a few minutes she stood gazing at her ring, and then she said,—

"I will go to her; I will tell her everything. It will be a great thing to have Miss Panney on my side. She does not care for customs, and she will never breathe a word to a soul."

Dr. Tolbridge was not mistaken in his estimate of the sort of mind Dora Bannister would have when she should shed her old one.

CHAPTER XXVII

"IT COULDN'T BE BETTER THAN THAT"

The Haverleys could not expect that the people of Thorbury would feel any general and urgent desire to recognize them as neighbors. They did not live in the town, and moreover newcomers, even to the town itself, were usually looked upon as "summer people," until they had proved that they were to be permanent residents, and the leading families of Thorbury made it a rule not to call on summer people.

But the example of the Tolbridges and Bannisters had a certain effect on Thorbury society, and people now began to drive out to Cobhurst; not very many of them, but some of them representative people. Mr. Ames, the rector of Grace Church, came early because the Haverleys had been to his church several times, and Mr. Torry, the Presbyterian minister, came afterwards because the Haverleys had stopped going to Grace Church, and he did not know that it was on account of the gig shafts.

Mr. Hampton, the Methodist, who was a pedestrian, walked out to Cobhurst one day, but as neither the brother or sister could be found, he good-humoredly resolved to postpone a future call until cooler weather.

Lately, when a lady had called, it happened that there had been no one to receive her but Mrs. Drane; and although there could be no doubt that that lady performed the duties of hostess most admirably, Miriam resolved that that thing should never happen again. She did not wish the people to think that there was a regent in rule at Cobhurst, and she now determined to make it a point to be within call during ordinary visiting hours. Or, if she felt strongly moved to a late afternoon ramble, she would invite the other ladies to accompany her. She still wore her hair down her back, and her dresses did not quite touch the tops of her boots, and it was therefore necessary to be careful in regard to her prerogatives as mistress of the house.

Early one afternoon, much sooner than there was reason to expect visitors, a carriage came in at the Cobhurst gate, driven by our friend Andy Griffing. Miriam happened to be at a front window, and regarded with some surprise the shabby equipage. It came with a flourish to the front of the house, and stopped. But instead of alighting, its occupant seemed to be expostulating with the driver. Andy shook his head a great deal, but finally drove round at the back, when an elderly woman got out, and came to the hall door. Miriam, who supposed, of course, that she would be wanted, was there to meet her, and there was no necessity for ringing or knocking.

"My name," said the visitor, "is La Fleur, if you please. I came to see Mrs. Drane and Miss Drane, if you please. Thank you very much, I will come in. I will wait here, or, if you will be so good as to tell me where I can find Mrs. Drane, I will go to her. I used to live with her: I was her cook."

Miriam had been gazing with much interest on the puffy face and shawl-enwrapped body of the old woman who addressed her with a smiling obsequiousness to which she was not at all accustomed.

The thought struck her that with servants like this woman, it would be easy to feel herself a mistress. She had heard from the Dranes a great deal about their famous cook, and she was glad of the opportunity to look upon this learned professor of kitchen lore.

"What would she have said to my tall raspberry tarts?" involuntarily thought the girl.

But it was when La Fleur had gone to Mrs. Drane's room, and Cicely, wildly delighted when informed who had come to see them, had run to meet the dear old woman, that Miriam pondered most seriously upon this visit from a cook. She had not known anything of the ties between families and old family servants. At school, servants had been no more than machines; she was nothing to them, and they were nothing to her; and now she felt that the ignorance of these ties was one of the deprivations of her life. That old woman upstairs had not lived very long with the Dranes, and yet she regarded them with a positive affection. Miriam knew this from what she had heard. If they were in trouble, and needed her, she would come to them and serve them wherever they were. This she had told them often. How different was such a woman from Phoebe or Molly Tooney! How happy would she be if there had been such a one in her mother's family, and were she with her now!

"But I have only Ralph," thought Miriam; "no one else in the world." Ralph was good,—no human being could be better; but he was only one person, and knew nothing of many things she wanted to know, and could not help her in many ways in which she needed to be helped.

With a feeling that from certain points of view she was rather solitary and somewhat forsaken, she went to look for her brother. It would be better to talk to what she had than to think about what she had not.

As she walked toward the barn and pasture fields, Ralph came up from the cornfield by the woods on the other side of the house. As he went in he met Mrs. Drane and La Fleur, who had just come downstairs. Cicely had already retired to her work. At the sight of the gentleman, who, she was informed, was the master of the house, La Fleur bowed her head, cast down her eyes, smiled and courtesied.

Mrs. Drane drew Ralph aside.

"That is La Fleur, who used to be our cook. She is a kind old body, who takes the greatest interest in our welfare. She is greatly pleased to find us in such delightful quarters, but she has queer notions, and now she wants very much to call on your cook. I don't know that this is the right thing, and I have been looking for your sister, to ask her if she objects to it, but I think she is not in the house."

"Oh, bless me!" exclaimed Ralph, "she will not mind in the least. Let the good woman go down and see Molly Tooney, and if she can give her some points about cooking, I am sure we shall all be delighted."

"Oh, she would not do that," said Mrs. Drane. "She is a very considerate person; but I suppose, in any house, her instincts would naturally draw her toward the cook."

When Ralph turned to La Fleur, and assured her that his sister would be glad to have her visit the kitchen, the old woman, who had not taken her eyes from him for an instant, thanked him with great unction, again bowed, courtesied, smiled, and, being shown the way to the kitchen, descended.

Molly Tooney, who was sitting on a low stool, paring potatoes, looked up in amazement at the person who entered her kitchen. It was not an obsequious old woman she saw, but a sedate, dignified, elderly person, with her brows somewhat knitted. Throwing about her a glance, which was not one of admiration, La Fleur remarked,—

"I suppose you are the cook of the house."

"Indade, an' I am," said Molly, still upon the stool, with a knife in one hand, and a potato, with a long paring hanging from it, in the other; "an' the washer-woman, an' the chamber-maid, an' the butler, too, as loike as may be. An' who may you be, an' which do you want to see?"

"I am Madame La Fleur," said the other, with a stateliness that none of her mistresses ever supposed that she possessed. "I came to see Mrs. Drane, in whose service I was formerly engaged, and I wish to know for myself what sort of a person was cooking for the ladies whose meals I used to prepare."

Molly put down her knife and her half-pared potato, and arose. She had heard of La Fleur, whose fame had spread through and about Thorbury.

"Sit down, mum," said she. "This isn't much of a kitchen, for I haven't had time to clane it up, an' as for me, I'm not much of a cook, nather; for when ye have to be iverything, ye can't be anything to no great ixtent."

La Fleur, still standing, looked at her severely.

"How often do you bake?" she asked.

"Three times a week," answered Molly, lying.

"The ladies upstairs," said La Fleur, "have been accustomed to fresh rolls every morning for their breakfast."

"An' afther this, they shall have 'em," said Molly, "Sundays an' weekday, an' sorry I am that I didn't know before that they was used to have 'em."

"How do you make your coffee?" asked La Fleur.

Molly looked at her hesitatingly.

"I am very keerful about that," she said. "I niver let it bile too much—"

"Ugh!" exclaimed La Fleur, raising her hand. "Tell your mistress to get you a French coffee-pot, and if you don't know how to use it, I'll come and teach you. I shall be here off and on as long as Mrs. Drane stops in this house." And then, seating herself, La Fleur proceeded to put Molly through an elementary domestic service examination.

"Well," said the examiner, when she had finished, "I think you must be the worst cook in this part of the country."

"No, mum, I'm not," said Molly. "There was one here afore me, a nager woman named Phoebe, that must have been worse, from what I'm told."

"Where I have lived," said La Fleur, "they have such women to cook for the farm laborers."

"Beggin' your pardon, mum," said Molly, "that's what they are here, or th' same thing. Mr. Haverley, he works on the farm with a pitchfork, jest like the nager man."

"Don't talk to me like that!" exclaimed La Fleur. "Mr. Haverley is a gentleman. I have lived enough among gentlemen to know them when I see them, and they can work and they can play and they can do what they please, and they are gentlemen still. Don't you ever speak that way, again, of your master."

"I thought I had heard, mum," said Molly, "that you looked down on tradespeople and the loike."

"Tradespeople!" said the other, scornfully. "A gentleman farmer is very different from a person in trade; but I can't expect anything better from a woman who boils coffee, and never heard of bouillon. But remember the things I have told you, and thank your stars that a cook as high up in the profession as I am is willing to tell you anything. Are you the only servant in this house?"

"There's a man by the name of Mike," said Molly, "a nager, though you wouldn't think it from his name. He helps me sometimes, an' he helps iverybody else other times."

"Is that the man?" said La Fleur, looking out of the window.

"That's him, mum," said Molly; "he's jest goin' to the woodpile with his axe."

"I wish to speak to him," said La Fleur, and with a very slight nod of the head she left the kitchen by the door that led into the grounds.

Looking after her, Molly exclaimed,—

"Drat you, for a stuck-up, cross-grained, meddlin', bumble-bee-backed old hag of a soup-slopper; to come stickin' yer big nose into other people's kitchens! If there was a rale misthress to the house instead of the little gal upstairs, you'd be rowled down the front steps afore you'd been let come into my kitchen." And with this she returned to her potatoes.

La Fleur stopped at the woodpile, as if in passing she had happened to notice a good man splitting logs. In her blandest voice she accosted Mike and bade him good-day.

"I think you must be Michael," she said. "The cook has been speaking of you to me. My name is La Fleur."

Mike, who had struck his axe into a log, touched his flattened hat.

"Yes, mum," he said; "Mr. Griffing has been tellin' me that. Are you lookin' for any of the folks?"

"Oh no, no," said La Fleur; "I am just walking about to see a little of this beautiful place. You don't mind that, do you, Michael? You keep everything in such nice order. I haven't seen your garden, but I know it is a fine one, because I saw some of the vegetables that came out of it."

Mike grinned. "I reckon it ain't the same kind of a garden that you've been used to, mum. I've heerd that you cooked for

Queen Victoria."

"Oh no, no," said La Fleur, dropping her head on one side so that her smile made a slight angle with the horizon; "I never cooked for the queen, no indeed; but I have lived with high families, lords, ladies, and ambassadors, and I don't remember that any of them had better potatoes than I saw to-day. Is this a large farm, Michael?"

"It's considerable over a hundred acres, though I don't 'xactly know how much. Not what you'd call big, and not what you'd call little."

"But you grow beautiful crops on it, I don't doubt," remarked La Fleur.

"Can't say about that," said Mike, shaking his head a little. "I 'spects we'll git good 'nough craps for what we do for 'em. This ain't the kind of farm your lords and ladies has got. It's ramshackle, you know."

"Ramshackle?" repeated La Fleur. "Is that a sort of sheep farm?"

Mike grinned. "Law, no, we ain't got no sheep, and I'm glad of it. Ramshackle farmin' means takin' things as you find 'em, an' makin' 'em do, an' what you git you've got, but with tother kind of farmin' most times what you git, ye have to pay out, an' then you ain't got nuthin'."

This was more than La Fleur could comprehend, but she inferred in a general way that Mr. Haverley's farm was a profitable one.

"All so pretty, so pretty," she said, looking from side to side; "such a grand barn, and such broad acres. Is it the estate as far as I can see?"

"Yes, mum," said Mike, "an' a good deal furder. The woods

cuts it off down thataway."

"It is a lordly place," said La Fleur, "and it does you honor, Michael, for the cook told me you were Mr. Haverley's head man."

"I reckon she's about right there," said Mike.

"And I am very glad indeed," continued the old woman, "that Mrs. and Miss Drane are living here. And now, Michael, if either of them is ever taken ill, and you're sent for the doctor, I want you to come straight to me, and I'll see that he goes to them. If you knock at the back door of the kitchen, I'll hear you, whether I am awake or asleep. And when you are coming to town, Michael, you must drop in and see me. I can give you a nice bit of a lunch, any day. I daresay you like good things to eat as well as any-body."

Mike stood silent for a moment, and his eyes began to brighten.

"Indeed I do, mum," said he. "If I was to carry in a punkin to you when they're ripe, I wonder if you'd be willin' to make me a punkin pie, same kind as Queen Victoria has in the fall of the year."

La Fleur beamed on him most graciously.

"I will do that gladly, Michael: you may count on me to do that. And I will give you other things that you like. Wait till we see, wait till we see. Good-day, Michael; I must be going now, or the doctor will be kept waiting for his dinner. Where's my cabby?"

"Mr. Griffing has drove round to the front of the house, mum," said Mike.

"Just like the stupid American," muttered the old woman as she hurried away, "as if I'd get in at the front of the house."

Frank Richard Stockton

Andy Griffing talked a good deal on the drive back to Thorbury, but La Fleur heard little and answered less. She was in a state of great mental satisfaction, and during her driver's long descriptions of persons and places, she kept saying to herself, "It couldn't be better than that. It couldn't be better than that."

This mental expression she applied to Mr. Haverley, whom she considered an extraordinarily fine-looking young man; to the broad acres and fine barn; to the fact that the Dranes were living with him; to the probability that he would fall in love with the charming Miss Cicely, and make her mistress of the estate; and to the strong possibility, that should this thing happen, she herself would be the cook of Cobhurst, and help her young mistress put the establishment on the footing that her station demanded.

"It couldn't be better than that," she muttered over and over again as she busied herself about the Tolbridge dinner, and she even repeated the expression two or three times after she went to bed.

CHAPTER XXVIII

THE GAME IS CALLED

In her notions and schemes regarding the person and estate of Ralph Haverley, the good cook, La Fleur, lacked one great advantage possessed by her rival planner and schemer Miss Panney; for she whose cause was espoused by the latter old woman was herself eager for the fray and desirous of victory, whereas Cicely Drane had not yet thought of marrying anybody, and outside of working hours was devoting herself to getting all the pleasure she could out of life, not regarding much whether it was her mother or Miriam or Mr. Haverley who helped her get it. Moreover, the advantages of co-residence, which La Fleur naturally counted upon, were not so great as might have been expected; for Mrs. Drane, having perceived that Ralph was fond of the society of young ladies to a degree which might easily grow beyond her ideas of decorous companionship between a gentleman of the house and a lady boarder, gently interfered with the dual apple gatherings and recreations of that nature. For this, had she been aware of it, Dora Bannister would have been most grateful.

Ralph had gone twice to see Congo, and to talk to Miss Bannister about him, but he had not taken the dog home. Dora said she would take him to Cobhurst the first time she drove over there to see Miriam. Congo would follow her and the carriage anywhere, and this would be so much pleasanter than to have him forced away like a prisoner.

Frank Richard Stockton

The gig shafts had now been repaired, and Ralph urged his sister to go with him to Thorbury and attend to her social duties; but Miriam disliked the little town and loved Cobhurst. As to social duties, she thought they ought to be attended to, of course, but saw no need to be in a hurry about them; so Ralph, one day, having business in Thorbury, prepared to go in again by himself. He had been lately riding Mrs. Browning, who was still his only available horse for family use; but she was not very agreeable under the saddle, and he now proposed to take the gig. He had thought it might be a good idea to take a little drive out of the town, and see if Congo would follow him. Perhaps Miss Bannister would accompany him, for she was very anxious that the dog should become used to Ralph before leaving his present home; and her presence would help very much in teaching the animal to follow.

But although Miriam declined to go with her brother, she took much interest in his expedition, and came out to the barn to see him harness Mrs. Browning.

"Are you going to Dora Bannister's again?" she asked.

"Yes," said Ralph; "at least I think I shall stop in to see the dog. You know the oftener I do that, the better."

"I think it is a shame," said Miriam, "that you should be driving to town alone, when there are other people who wish so much to go, and you have no use at all for that empty seat."

"Who wants to go?" asked Ralph, quickly.

"Cicely Drane does. She has got into trouble over the doctor's manuscript, and says she can't go on properly without seeing him. She has been expecting him here every day, but it seems as if he never intended to come. She asked me this morning how far it was to Thorbury, and I think she intends to walk in, if he does not come to-day."

"Why didn't you tell me this before?" asked Ralph. "I would

have sent her into town or taken her."

"I had not formulated it in my mind," said Miriam. "Will you take her with you to-day? I know that she has made up her mind she cannot wait any longer for the doctor to come."

"Of course I will take her," said Ralph. "Will you ask her to get ready? Tell her I shall be at the door in ten or fifteen minutes."

Ralph's tone was perfectly good-humored, but Miriam fancied that she perceived a trace of disappointment in it. She was sorry for this, for she could not imagine why any man should object to have Cicely Drane as a companion on a drive, unless his mind was entirely occupied by some other girl; and if Ralph's mind was thus occupied, it must be by Dora Bannister, and that did not please her. So she resolutely put aside all Cicely's suggestions that it might be inconvenient for Mr. Haverley to take her with him, and deftly overcame Mrs. Drane's one or two impromptu, and therefore not very well constructed, objections to the acceptance of the invitation; and in the gig Cicely went with Ralph to Thorbury.

After having left the secretary to attend to her business at the doctor's house, Ralph drove to the Bannister's; but Dora would not see him, and technically was not at home. Alas! She had seen him driving past with Miss Drane, and she was angry. This was contrary to the plan of action she had adopted; but her eighteen-year-old spirit rebelled, and she could not help it. A more hideous trap than that old gig could not be imagined, but she had planned a drive in it with Ralph on some of the quiet country roads beyond Cobhurst. They would take Congo with them, and that would be such a capital plan to teach the dog to follow his new master. And now it was the Drane girl who was driving with him in his gig. She could not go down and see him and meet him in the way she liked to meet him.

Miss Panney, on the other side of the street, had been passing the Tolbridge house at the moment when Ralph and Cicely drove up. She stopped for a moment, her feelings absolutely outraged. It was not uncommon for her to pass places at times when people were doing things in those places which she thought they ought not to do; but this was a case which roused her anger in an unusual manner. Whatever else might happen at Cobhurst, she did not believe that that girl would begin so soon to go out driving with him.

She had left her phaeton at a livery stable, and was on her way to the Bannister house to have a talk with Dora on a subject in which they were now both so much interested. She had been very much surprised when the girl had come to her and freely avowed her feelings and hopes, but she had been delighted. She liked a spirit of that sort, and it was a joy to her to work with one who possessed it. But she knew human nature, and she was very much afraid that Dora's purpose might weaken. It was quite natural that a young person, in a moment of excitement and pique, should figuratively raise her sword in air and vow a vow; but it was also quite natural, when the excitement and pique had cooled down, that the young person should experience what might be called a "vow-fright," and feel unable to go through with her part. In a case such as Dora's, this was very possible indeed, and all that Miss Panney had planned to say on her present visit was intended to inspire the girl, if it should be needed, with some of her own matured inflexibility and fixedness of purpose. But if the man were doing this sort of thing already and Dora should know it, she would have a right to be discouraged.

Before the old lady reached the Bannisters' gate, she saw Mr. Haverley, in his gig, drive away. This brightened her up a little.

"He comes here, anyway," she thought; "what a pity Dora is not in."

Nevertheless, she went on to the Bannister house; and when she found Dora was in, she began to scold her.

"This will never do, will never do," she said. "Get angry with him if you choose, but don't show it. If you do that, you may crash him too low or bounce him too high, and, in either case, he may be off before you know it. It is too early in the game to show him that he has made you angry."

"But if he doesn't want me, I don't want him," said Dora, sulkily.

"If you think that way, my dear," said Miss Panney, "you may as well make up your mind to make a bad match, or die an old maid. The right man very seldom comes of his own accord; it is nearly always the wrong one. If you happen to meet the right man, you should help him to know that he ought to come. That is the way to look at it. That young Haverley does not know yet who it is that he cares for. He is just floating along, waiting for some one to thrust out a boat-hook and pull him in."

"I shall marry no floating log," said Dora, stiffly.

The old lady laughed.

"Perhaps that was not a very good figure of speech," she said; "but really, my dear, you must not interfere with your own happiness by showing temper; and if you look at the affair in its proper light, you will see it is not so bad, after all. Ten to one, he brought her to town because she wanted to come with him,—probably on some patched-up errand; but he came here because he wanted to come. There could be no other reason; and, instead of being angry with him, you should have given him an extraordinary welcome. For the very reason that she has so many advantages over you, being so much with him, you should be very careful to make use of the advantages you have over her. And your advantages are that you are ten times better fitted to be his wife than she is; and the great thing necessary to be done is to let him see it. But her chances must come to an end. Those Dranes must be got away from Cobhurst."

"I don't like that way of looking at it," said Dora, leaning back in her chair, with a sigh. "It's the same thing as fishing for a man, though I suppose it might have been well to see him when he came."

Now Miss Panney felt encouraged; her patient was showing good symptoms. Let her keep in that state of mind, and she would see that the lover came. She had made a mistake in speaking so bluntly about getting the Dranes out of Cobhurst. Although she would not say anything more to Dora about that important piece of work, she would do it all the same.

This little visit had been an important one to Miss Panney; it had enabled her to understand Dora's character much better than she had understood it before; and she perceived that in this case of matchmaking she must not only do a great deal of the work herself, but she must do it without Dora's knowing anything about it. She liked this, for she was not much given to consulting with people.

Miss Panney had another call to pay in the neighborhood, and she had intended, for form's sake, to spend a little time with Mrs. Bannister; but she did neither. She went back by the way she had come, wishing to learn all she could about the movements of the Cobhurst gig.

Approaching the Tolbridge house, she saw that vehicle standing before the door, with the sleepy Mrs. Browning tied to a post, and as she drew nearer, she perceived Ralph Haverley sitting alone on the vine-shaded piazza. The old lady would not enter the Tolbridge gate, but she stood on the other side of the street, and beckoned to Ralph, who, as soon as he saw her, ran over to her.

Ralph walked a little way with Miss Panney, and after answering her most friendly inquiries about Miriam, he explained how he happened to be sitting alone on the piazza; the doctor and Miss Drane, whom he had brought to town, were at work at some manuscript, and he had preferred to wait outside instead of indoors.

"I called on Miss Bannister," he said, "but she was not at home, so I came back here."

"It is a pity she was out," said Miss Panney, carelessly, "and now that you have mentioned Miss Bannister, I would like to ask you something; why does not your sister return her visits? I saw Dora not very long ago, and found that her feelings had been a little hurt—not much, perhaps, but a little—by Miriam's apparent indifference to her. Dora is a very sensitive girl, and is slow to make friends among other girls. I never knew any friendship so quick and lively as that she showed for Miriam. You know that Dora is still young; it has not been long since she left school; there is not a girl in Thorbury that she cares anything about, and her life at home must necessarily be a lonely one. Her brother is busy, even in the evenings, and Mrs. Bannister is no companion for a lively young girl."

"I had thought," said Ralph, "that Miss Bannister went a good deal into society."

"Oh, no," answered Miss Panney; "she sometimes visits her relatives, who are society people; but in years and disposition she is too young for that sort of thing. Society women and society men would simply bore her. At heart she is a true country girl, and I think it was because Miriam had country tastes, and loved that sort of life, that Dora's affections went out so quickly to her. I wish your sister had the same feelings toward her."

"Oh, Miriam likes her very much," exclaimed Ralph, "and is always delighted to see her; but my little sister is wonderfully fond of staying at home. I have told her over and over again that she ought to return Miss Bannister's calls."

"Make her do it," said the old lady. "It is her duty, and I assure you, it will be greatly to her advantage. Miriam is a most lovely girl, but her character has not hardened itself into what it is going to be, and association with a thoroughbred girl, such as Dora Bannister, admirably educated, who has seen something of the world, with an intelligence and wit such as I have never known in any one of her age, and more than all with a soul as beautiful as her face, cannot fail to be an inestimable benefit to your sister. What Miriam most needs, at this stage of her life, is proper companionship of her own age and sex."

Ralph assented. "But," said he, "she is not without that, you know. Miss Drane, who with her mother now lives with us, is a most—"

Miss Panney's face grew very hard.

"Excuse me," she interrupted, "I know all about that. Of course the Dranes are very estimable people, and there are many things, especially in the way of housekeeping, which Mrs. Drane could teach Miriam, if she chose to take the trouble. But while I respect the daughter's efforts to support herself and her mother, it must be admitted that she is a working-girl—nothing more or less—and must continue to be such. Her present business, of course, can only last for a little while, and she will have to adopt some regular calling. This life she expects, and is preparing herself for it. But a mind such as hers is, or must speedily become, is not the one from which Miriam's young mind should receive its impressions. The two will move in very different spheres, and neither can be of any benefit to the other. More than that I will not say; but I will say that your sister can never find any friend so eager to love her, and so willing to help and be helped by her in so many ways in which girls can help each other, as my dear Dora. Now bestir yourself, Mr. Haverley, and make Miriam look at this thing as she ought to. I don't pretend to deny that I have spoken to you very much for Dora's sake, for whom I have an almost motherly feeling; but you should act for your sister's sake. And please don't forget what I have said, young man, and give Miriam my best love."

When Ralph walked back to the Tolbridge piazza he found the

working-girl sitting there, waiting for him. His mind was not in an altogether satisfactory condition; some things Miss Panney had said had pleased and even excited him, but there were other things that he resented. If she had not been such an old lady, and if she had not talked so rapidly, he might have shown this resentment. But he had not done so, and now the more he thought about it, the stronger the feeling grew.

As for Cicely Drane, she was a great deal more quiet during the drive home, than she had been when going to Thorbury. Her mind was in an unsatisfactory condition, and this had been occasioned by an interview with La Fleur, who had waylaid her in the hall as she came out of the doctor's office.

The good cook had been in a state of enthusiastic delight, since, looking out of the kitchen window where she had been sitting, with a manuscript book of recipes in her lap, planning the luncheon and dinner, she had seen the lord of Cobhurst drive up to the gate with dear Miss Cicely. It was a joy like that of listening to a party of dinner guests, who were eating her favorite ice. With intense impatience she had awaited the appearance of Cicely from the doctor's office; and, having drawn her to one side, she hastily imparted her sentiments.

"It's a shabby gig, Miss Cicely," she said, "such as the farmers use in the old country, but it's his own, and not hired, and the big house is his own, and all the broad acres. And he's a gentleman from head to heel, living on his own estate, and as fine a built man as ever rode in the Queen's army. Oh, Miss Cicely, your star is at the top of the heavens this time, and I want you to let me know if there is anything you want in the way of hats or wraps or clothes, or anything of that kind. It doesn't make the least difference to me, you know, just now, and we'll settle it all after a while. It is the Christian duty for every young lady to look the smartest, especially at a time like this."

Cicely, her face flushed, drew herself away.

"La Fleur," she said, speaking quickly and in a low voice, "you ought to be ashamed of yourself." And she hurried away, fearing that Mr. Haverley was waiting for her.

La Fleur was not a bit ashamed of herself; she chuckled as she went back to the kitchen.

"She's a young thing of brains and beauty," said she to herself, "and I don't doubt that she had the notion in her own mind. But if it wasn't there, I have put it there, and if it was there, I've dished it and dressed it, and it will be like another thing to her. As for the rest of it, he'll attend to that. I haven't a doubt that he is the curly-headed, brave fellow to do that; and I'll find out from her mother if she needs anything, and not hurt her pride neither."

CHAPTER XXIX

HYPOTHESIS AND INNUENDO

To say that Cicely Drane had not thought of Ralph Haverley as an exceedingly agreeable young man would be an injustice to her young womanly nature, but it would be quite correct to state that she had not thought him a whit more agreeable than Miriam. She was charmed with them both; they had taken her into their home circle as if they had adopted her as a sister. It was not until her mother began to put a gentle pressure upon her in order to prevent her gathering too many apples, and joining in too many other rural recreations with Mr. Haverley, that she thought of him as one who was not to be considered in the light of a brother. There could be no doubt that she would have come to the same conclusion if left to herself, but she would not have reached it so soon.

But the effect that her mother's precautionary disposition had had upon her was nothing compared to that produced by the words of La Fleur. For the first time she looked upon Ralph as one on whom other persons looked as her lover, and to sit by the side of the said young man, immediately after being informed of said fact, was not conducive to a free and tranquil flow of remark.

Her own sentiments on the subject, so far as she had put them into shape,—and it was quite natural that she should imme- diately begin to do this,—were neither embarrassing nor disagreeable. She liked him very much, and there was no reason why she should object to his liking her very much, and if they should ever do more than this, she should not be ashamed of it, and perhaps should be glad of it. But she was sorry that before either of them had thought of this, some one else should have done so.

This might prove to be embarrassing, and the only comfort she could give herself was that La Fleur was such an affectionate old body, always talking of some bit of good fortune for her, that if she had seen her in company with a king or an emperor, she would immediately set herself to find some sort of throne-covering which would suit her hair and complexion.

The definite result of her reflections, made between desultory questions and answers, was that she regarded the young gentleman by her side in a light very different from that in which she had viewed him before she had met La Fleur in the doctor's hall. It was not that she looked upon him as a possible lover—she had sense enough to know that almost any man might be that—he was a hypothetic lover, and in view of the assumption it behooved her to give careful observation to everything in him, herself, or others, which might bear upon the ensuing argument.

As for Ralph, it angered him to look at the young lady by his side, who was as handsome, as well educated and cultured, as tastefully dressed, as intelligent and witty, of as gentle, kind, and winning a disposition, and, judging from what the doctor had told him when he first spoke of the Dranes, of as good blood, family, and position, as any one within the circle of his acquaintance, and then to remember that she had been called a working-girl, and spoken of in a manner that was almost contemptuous.

Ralph always took the side of the man who was down, and, consequently, very often put himself on the wrong side; and although he did not consider that Miss Drane was down, he saw that Miss Panney had tried to put her down, and therefore he became her champion.

"There could not be any one," he said to himself, "better fitted to be the friend and companion of Miriam than Cicely Drane is, and the next time I see that old lady, I shall tell her so. I have nothing to say against Miss Bannister, but I shall stand up for this one."

And now, feeling that it was not polite to treat a young lady with seeming inattention, because he happened to be earnestly thinking about her, he began to talk to Cicely in his liveliest and gayest manner, and she, not wishing him to think that she thought that there was anything out of the way in this, or in his previous preoccupation, responded just as gayly.

Ralph delivered Miss Panney's message to his sister, and Miriam, giving much more weight to the advice and opinion of the old lady, whom she knew very slightly and cared for very little, than to that of her brother, whom she loved dearly, said she would go to see Miss Bannister the next afternoon if it happened to be clear.

It was clear, and she went, and Ralph drove her there in the gig, and Dora was overwhelmed with joy to see her, and scolded Ralph in the most charming way for not bringing her before; Miriam was taken to see Congo, because Dora wanted her to begin to love him, and they were shown into the library, because Dora said that she knew they both loved books, and her father had gathered together so many. In ten minutes, Miriam was in the window seat, dipping, which ended in her swimming, far beyond her depth in Don Quixote, which she had so often read of and never seen, and Dora and Ralph sat, heads together, over a portfolio of photographs of foreign places where the Bannisters had been.

There were very few books at Cobhurst, and Miriam had read all of them she cared for, and consequently it was an absorbing delight to follow the adventures of the Knight of La Mancha.

Ralph had not travelled in Europe, and there were very few pictures at Cobhurst, and he was greatly interested in the photographs, but this interest soon waned in the increasing delight of having Dora seated so close to him, of seeing her fair fingers point out the things he should look at, and listening to her sweet voice, as she talked to him about the scenes and buildings. There was an element of gentle and sympathetic interest in Dora's manner, which reminded him of her visit to Cobhurst, and the good-night on the stairs, and this had a very charming effect upon Ralph, and made him wish that the portfolio were at least double its actual size.

The Haverleys stayed so long that Mrs. Bannister, upstairs, began to be nervous, and wondered if Dora had asked those young people to remain to tea.

On the way home Ralph was in unusually good spirits, and talked much about Dora. She must have seen a great deal of the world, he said, for one so young, and she talked in such an interesting and appreciative way about what she had seen, that he felt almost as if he had been to the places himself.

With this for a text, he dilated upon the subject of Dora and foreign travel, but Miriam was not a responsive hearer.

"I wish you knew Mr. Bannister better," she said in a pause in her brother's remarks. "He must have been everywhere that his sister has been, and probably saw a great deal more."

"No doubt," said Ralph, carelessly, "and probably has forgotten most of it; men generally do that. A girl's mind is not crammed with business and all that sort of stuff, and she can keep it free for things that are worth remembering."

Miriam did not immediately answer, but presently she said, speaking with a certain air of severity:—

"If my soul ached for the company of anybody as Miss Panney told you Dora Bannister's soul ached for my company, I think I should have a little more to say to her when she came to see me, than Dora Bannister had to say to me to-day."

"My dear child!" exclaimed Ralph, "that was because you were so busy with your book. She saw you were completely wrapped up in it, and so let you take your own pleasure in your own way. I think that is one of her good points. She tries to find out what pleases people."

"Bother her good points!" snapped Miriam. "You will make a regular porcupine of her if you keep on. I wish Mr. Bannister had given you the dog."

Ralph was very much disturbed; it was seldom that his sister snapped at him. He could see, now that he considered the matter, that Miriam had been somewhat neglected. She was young and a little touchy, and this ought to be considered. He thought it might be well, the next time he saw Miss Bannister by herself, to explain this to her. He believed he could do it without making it appear a matter of any great importance. It was important, however, for he should very much dislike to see ill will grow up between Miriam and Miss Bannister. What Miss Panney had said about this young lady was very, very true, although, of course, it did not follow that any one else need be disparaged.

Early in the forenoon of the next day, Miss Panney drove to Cobhurst. She had come, she informed Miriam, not only to see her, dear girl, but to make a formal call upon the Dranes.

The call was very formal; Miss Drane left her work to meet the visitor, but having been loftily set aside by that lady during a stiff conversation with her mother about old residents in the neighborhood in which they had lived, she excused herself, after a time, and went back to her table and her manuscripts.

Then Miss Panney changed the conversational scene, and began to talk about Thorbury.

"I do not know, madam," she said, "that you are aware that I was the cause of your coming to this neighborhood."

Mrs. Drane was a quiet lady, and the previous remarks of her visitor had been calculated to render her more quiet, but this roused her.

"I certainly did not," she said. "We came on the invitation and through the kindness of Dr. Tolbridge, my old friend."

"Yes, yes, yes," said Miss Panney, "that is all true enough, but I told him to send for you. In fact, I insisted upon it. I did it, of course, for his sake; for I knew that the arrangement would be of advantage to him in various ways, but I was also glad to be of service to your daughter, of whom I had heard a good report. Furthermore, I interested myself very much in getting you lodgings, and found you a home at Mrs. Brinkly's that I hoped you would like. If I had not done so, I think you would have been obliged to go to the hotel, which is not pleasant and much more expensive than a private house. I do not mention these things, madam, because I wish to be thanked, or anything of that sort; far from it. I did what I did because I thought it was right; but I must admit, if you will excuse my mentioning it, that I was surprised, to say the least, that I was not consulted, in the slightest degree, on the occasion of your leaving the home I had secured for you."

"I am very sorry," said Mrs. Drane, "that I should appear to have been discourteous to one who had done us a service, for which, I assure you, we are both very much obliged, but Dr. and Mrs. Tolbridge managed the whole affair of our removal from Mrs. Brinkly's house, and I did not suppose there was any one, besides them and ourselves, who would take the slightest interest in the matter."

"Oh, I find no fault," said Miss Panney. "It is not an affair of importance, but I think you will agree, madam, that after the interest I had shown in procuring you suitable accommodation, I might have been spared what some people might consider the mortification of being told, when I stated to Mrs. Tolbridge that I intended to call upon you, that you were not then living with the lady whose consent to receive you into her family I had obtained, after a great deal of personal solicitation and several visits."

Upon this presentation of the matter, Mrs. Drane could not help thinking that the old lady had been treated somewhat uncivilly, and expressed her regret in the most suitable terms she could think of, adding that she was sure that Miss Panney would agree that the change had been an excellent one.

"Of course, of course," said Miss Panney. "For a temporary country residence, I suppose you could not have found a better spot, though it must be a long walk for your daughter when she goes to submit her work to Dr. Tolbridge."

"That has not yet been necessary," said Mrs. Drane; "Mr. Haverley is very kind—"

At this point Miss Panney rose. She had said all she wanted to say, and to decline to hear anything about Ralph Haverley's having been seen driving about with a young woman who had been engaged as Dr. Tolbridge's secretary, was much better than speaking of it, and she took her leave with a prim politeness.

Mrs. Drane was left in an uncomfortable state of mind. It was not pleasant to be reminded that this delightful country house was only a temporary home, for that implied a return to Thorbury, a town she disliked; and although she had, of course, expected to go back there, she had not allowed the matter to dwell in her mind at all, putting it into the future, without consideration, as she liked to do with things that were unpleasant.

Moreover, there was something, she could not tell exactly what, about Miss Panney's words and manner, which put an unsatisfactory aspect upon the obvious methods of Cicely's communications with her employer.

Mrs. Drane's mind had already been slightly disturbed on this subject, but Miss Panney had revived and greatly increased the disturbance.

CHAPTER XXX

A CONFIDENTIAL ANNOUNCEMENT

Having finished her visit of ceremony, Miss Panney asked permission of Miriam to see Molly Tooney. That woman was, in a measure, her protege, and she had some little business with her. Declining to have the cook sent for, Miss Panney descended to the kitchen.

She had not talked with Molly more than five minutes, and had not approached the real subject of the interview, which concerned the social relations between the Haverleys and the Dranes, when the Irishwoman lifted up her hands, and opened wide her eyes.

"The Saints an' the Sinners!" she exclaimed, "if here isn't that auld drab of a sausage, that cook of the docther's, a comin' here again to tell me how to cook for them Dranes. Bad luck to them, they don't pay me nothin', an' only give me trouble."

Miss Panney turned quickly, and through the window she saw La Fleur approaching the kitchen door.

"She comes here to tell you how to cook for those people?" said Miss Panney, quickly.

"Indade she does, an' it's none of her business, nather, the meddlin' auld porpoise."

"Molly," said Miss Panney, "go away and leave me here. I want to talk to this woman."

"Which is more than I do," said the cook, and straightway departed to the floor above.

La Fleur had come to see Mrs. Drane, but perceiving Miss Panney's phaeton at the door, she had concluded that there was company in the house, and had consequently betaken herself to the kitchen to make inquiries. When she found there Miss Panney, instead of Molly Tooney, La Fleur was surprised, but pleased, for she remembered the old lady as one who appreciated good cookery and a good cook.

"How do you do, La Fleur," said Miss Panney. "I am glad to see you. I suppose you still keep up your old interest in Mrs. Drane and her daughter. Do you often find time to come out here to see them?"

"Not often, madam, but sometimes. I can always find time for what I really want to do. If I like to be away for an hour or two, I'll sit up late the night before, long after midnight sometimes, planning the meals and the courses for the next day, and when I go away, I leave everything so that I can take it right up, the minute I get back, and lose nothing in time or in any other way."

"It is only a born chef who could do that," said Miss Panney, "and it is very pleasant to see your affection for your former employers. Do you suppose that they will remain here much longer?"

"Remain!" exclaimed La Fleur; "they've never said a word to me, madam, about going away, and I don't believe they have thought of it. I am sure I haven't."

Miss Panney shook her head.

"It's none of my business," she said, "but I've lived a long time in this world, and that gives me a right to speak my mind to people who haven't lived so long. It may have been all very well for the Dranes to have come here for a little vacation of a week or ten days, but to stay on and on is not the proper thing at all, and if you really have a regard for them, La Fleur, I think it is your duty to make them understand this. You might not care to speak plainly, of course, but you can easily make them perceive the situation, without offending them, or saying anything which an old servant might not say, in a case like this."

"But, madam," said La Fleur, "what's to hinder their stopping here? There's no spot on earth that could suit them better, to my way of thinking."

"La Fleur," said Miss Panney, regarding the other with moderate severity, "you ought to know that when people see a young woman like Miss Drane brought to live in a house with a handsome young gentleman, who, to all intents and purposes, is keeping a bachelor's hall,—for that girl upstairs is entirely too young to be considered a mistress of a house,— and when they know that the young lady's mother is a lady in impoverished circumstances, the people are bound to say, when they talk, that that young woman was brought here on purpose to catch the master of the house, and I don't think, La Fleur, that you would like to hear that said of Mrs. Drane."

As she listened, the bodily eyes of La Fleur were contracted until they were almost shut, but her mental eyes opened wider and wider. She suspected that there was something back of Miss Panney's words.

"If I heard anybody say that, madam, meaning it, I don't think they would care to say it to me again. But leaving out all that and looking at the matter with my lights, it does seem to me that if Mr. Haverley wanted a mistress for his house, and felt inclined to marry Miss Cicely Drane, he couldn't make a better choice."

"Choice!" repeated Miss Panney, sarcastically. "He has no choice to make. That is settled, and that is the very reason why people will talk the more and sharper, and nothing you can say, Madam Jane La Fleur, will stop them. Not only does this look like a scheme to marry Mr. Haverley to a girl who can bring him nothing, but to break off a most advantageous match with a lady who, in social position, wealth, and in every way, stands second to no one in this county."

"And who may that be, please?" asked La Fleur.

Miss Panney hesitated. It would be a bold thing to give the answer that was on her tongue, but she was no coward, and this was a crisis of importance. A proper impression made upon this woman might be productive of more good results than if made upon any one else.

"It is Miss Dora Bannister," she said, "and of course you know all about the Bannister family. I tell you this, because I consider that, under the circumstances, you ought to know it, but I expect you to mention it to no one, for the matter has not been formally announced. Now, I am sure that a woman of your sense can easily see what the friends of Mr. Haverley, who know all about the state of affairs, will think and say when they see Mrs. Drane's attempt to get for her daughter what rightfully belongs to another person."

If it had appeared to the mind of La Fleur that it was a dreadful thing to get for one's daughter a lifelong advantage which happened to belong to another, she might have greatly resented this imputation against Mrs. Drane. But as she should not have hesitated to try and obtain said advantage, if there was any chance of doing it, the imputation lost force. She did not, therefore, get angry, but merely asked, wishing to get as deep into the matter as possible, "And then it is all settled that he's to marry Miss Bannister?"

"Everything is not yet arranged, of course," said Miss Panney, speaking rapidly, for she heard approaching footsteps, "and you are not to say anything about all this or mention me in connection with it. I only spoke to you for the sake of the Dranes. It is your duty to get them away from here."

She had scarcely finished speaking when Miriam entered the kitchen. La Fleur had never seen her before, for on her previous visit it had been Ralph who had given her permission to interview Molly Tooney, and she regarded her with great interest. La Fleur's long years of service had given her many opportunities of studying the characters of mistresses, in high life as well as middle life, but never had she seen a mistress like this school-girl, with her hair hanging down her back.

Miriam advanced toward La Fleur.

"My cook told me that you were here, and I came down, thinking that you might want to see me."

"This is Madam La Fleur," interpolated Miss Panney, "the celebrated chef who cooks for Dr. Tolbridge. She came, I think, to see Mrs. Drane."

"Not altogether. Oh, no, indeed," said La Fleur, humbly smiling and bowing, with her eyes downcast and her head on one side. "I wished, very much, also, to pay my respects to Miss Haverley. I am only a cook, and I am much obliged to this good lady—Miss Panic, I think is the name—"

"Panney," sharply interpolated the old lady.

"Beg pardon, I am sure, Miss Panney—for what she has said about me; but when I come to pay my respects to Mrs. Drane, I wish to do the same to the lady of the house."

There was a gravity and sedateness in Miriam's countenance, which was not at all school-girlish, and which pleased La Fleur; in her eyes it gave the girl an air of distinction.

"I am glad to see you," said Miriam, and turned to Miss

Panney, as if wondering at that lady's continued stay in the kitchen. Miss Panney understood the look.

"I am getting points from La Fleur, my dear," she said, "cooking points,—you ought to do that. She can give you the most wonderful information about things you ought to know. Now, La Fleur, as you want to see Mrs. Drane, and it is time I had started for home, it will be well for us to go upstairs and leave the kitchen to Molly Tooney."

Miss Panney was half way up the stairs when La Fleur detained Miriam by a touch on the arm.

"I will give you all the points you want, my dear young lady," she said. "You have brains, and that is the great thing needful in overseeing cooking. And I will come some day on purpose to tell you how the dishes that your brother likes, and you like, ought to be cooked to make them delicious, and you shall be able to tell any one how they should be done, and understand what is the matter with them if they are not done properly. All this the lady of the house ought to know, and I can tell you anything you ask me, for there is nothing about cooking that I do not thoroughly understand; but I will not go upstairs now, and I will not detain you from your visitor. I will take a turn in the grounds, and when the lady has gone, I will ask leave to speak with Mrs. Drane."

With her head on one side, and her smile and her bow, La Fleur left the kitchen by the outer door. She stepped quickly toward the barn, looking right and left as she walked. She wished very much to see Mike, and presently she had that pleasure. He had just come out of the barnyard, and was closing the gate. She hurried toward him, for, although some-what porpoise-built, she was vigorous and could walk fast.

"I am so pleased to see you, Michael," she said. "I have brought you something which I think you will like," and, opening a black bag which she carried on her arm, she produced a package wrapped in brown paper.

"This," she said, opening the wrapping, "is a pie—a veal and 'am pie—such as you would not be likely to find in this country, unless you got me to make it for you. I baked it early this morning, intending to come here, and being sure you would like it; and you needn't have any scruples about taking it. I bought everything in it with my own money. I always do that when I cook little dishes for people I like."

The pie had been brought as a present for Mrs. Drane, but, feeling that it was highly necessary to propitiate the only person on the place who might be of use to her, La Fleur decided to give the pie to Mike.

The face of the colored man beamed with pleasure.

"Veal and ham. Them two things ought to go together fust rate, though I've never eat 'em in that way. An' in a pie, too; that looks mighty good. An' how do ye eat it, Mrs.—'scuse me, ma'am, but I never can rightly git hold of yer name."

"No wonder, no wonder," said the other; "it is a French name. My second husband was a Frenchman. A great cook, Michael, —a Frenchman. But the English of the name is flower, and you can call me Mrs. Flower. You can surely remember that, Michael."

Mike grinned widely.

"Oh, yes indeed, ma'am," said he; "no trouble 'bout that, 'specially when I think what pie crust is made of, an' that you's a cook."

"Oh, it isn't that kind of flower," said La Fleur, laughing; "but it doesn't matter a bit,—it sounds the same. And now, Michael, you must warm this and eat it for your dinner. Have you a fire in your house?"

"I can make one in no time," said Mike. "Then you think I'd better not let the cook warm it for me?"

"You are quite right," said La Fleur. "I don't believe she's half as good a cook as you are, Michael, for I've heard that all colored people have a knack that way; and like as not she'd burn it to a crisp."

Wrapping up the pie and handing it to the delighted negro, La Fleur proceeded to business, for she felt she had no time to lose.

"And how are you getting on, Michael?" said she. "I suppose everybody is very busy preparing for the master's wedding."

"The what!" exclaimed Mike, his eyebrows elevating themselves to such a degree that his hat rose.

"Mr. Haverley's marriage with Miss Dora Bannister. Isn't that to take place very soon, Michael?"

Mike put his pie on the post of the barn gate, took off his hat, and wiped his brow with his shirt-sleeve.

"Bless my evarlastin' soul, Mrs. Flower! who on this earth told you that?"

"Is it then such a great secret? Miss Panney told it to me not twenty minutes ago."

Mike put on his hat; he took his pie from the post, and held it, first in one hand and then in the other. He seemed unable to express what he thought.

"Look a here, Mrs. Flower," he said presently, "she told you that, did she?"

"She really did," was the answer.

"Well, then," said Mike, "the long an' the short of it is, she lies. 'Tain't the fust time that old Miss Panney has done that sort of thing. She comes to me one day, more than six year ago, an' says, 'Mike,' says she, 'why don't you marry Phoebe Moxley?' "'Cause I don't want to marry her, nor nobody else,' says I. 'But you ought to,' said she, 'for she's a good woman an' a nice washer an' ironer, an' you'd do well together.' 'Don't want no washin' nor ironin', nor no Phoebe, neither,' says I. But she didn't mind nothin' what I said, an' goes an' tells everybody that me an' Phoebe was goin' to be married; an' then it was we did git married, jest to stop people talkin' so much about it, an' now look at us. Me never so much as gittin' a bite of corn-bread, an' she a boardin' the minister! Jes' you take my word for it, Mrs. Flower, old Miss Panney wants Miss Dora to marry him, an' she's goin' about tellin' people, thinkin' that after a while they'll do it jes' 'cause everybody 'spects them to."

"But don't you think they intend to marry, Mike?" forgetting to address him by his full name.

Mike was about to strike the pie in his right hand with his left, in order to give emphasis to his words, but he refrained in time.

"Don't believe one cussed word of it," said he. "Mr. Haverley ain't the man to do that sort of thing without makin' some of his 'rangements p'int that way, an' none of his 'rangements do p'int that way. If he'd been goin' to git married, he'd told me, you bet, an' we'd laid out the farm work more suitable for a weddin' than it is laid out. I ain't goin' to believe no word about no weddin' till I git it from somebody better nor Miss Panney. If he was goin' to marry anybody, he'd be more like to marry that purty little Miss Drane. She's right here on the spot, an' she ain't pizen proud like them Bannisters. She's as nice as cake, an' not stuck up a bit. Bless my soul! She don't know one thing about nothin'.'"

"You're very much mistaken, Michael," exclaimed La Fleur. "She is very well educated, and has been sent to the best schools."

Frank Richard Stockton

"Oh, I don't mean school larnin'," said Mike; "I mean 'bout cows an' chickens. She'll come here when I'm milkin', an' ask me things about the critters an' craps that I knowed when I was a baby. I reckon she's the kind of a lady that knows all about what's in her line, an' don't know nothin' 'bout what's not in her line. That's the kind of young lady I like. No spyin' around to see what's been did, an' what's hain't been did. I've lived with them Bannisters."

La Fleur gazed reflectively upon the ground.

"I never thought of it before," she said, "but Miss Cicely would make a very good wife for a gentleman like Mr. Haverley. But that's neither here nor there, and none of our business, Michael. But if you hear anything more about this marriage between Mr. Haverley and Miss Bannister, I wish you'd come and tell me. I've had a deal of curiosity to know if that old lady's been trying to make a fool of me. It isn't of any consequence, but it is natural to have a curiosity about such things, and I shall be very thankful to you if you will bring me any news that you may get. And when you come, Michael, you may be sure that you will not go away hungry, be it daytime or night."

"Oh, I'll come along, you bet," said Mike, "an' I am much obleeged to you, Mrs. Flower, for this here pie."

When the good cook had gone to speak with Mrs. Drane, Mike repaired to the woodshed, where, picking up an axe, he stood for some moments regarding a short, knotty log on end in front of him. His blood flowed angrily.

"Marry that there Bannister girl," he said to himself. "A pretty piece of business if that family was to come here with their money an' their come-up-ence. They'd turn everythin' upside down on this place. No use for ramshackle farmin' they'd have, an' no use for me, nuther, with their top boots an' stovepipe hats."

Mike had been discharged from the Bannisters' service because of his unwillingness to pay any attention to his personal appearance.

"If that durned Miss Panney," he continued, "keeps on tellin' that to the people, things will be a cussed sight worse than me a livin' here without decent vittles, an' Phoebe a boardin' that minister that ain't paid no board yit. Blast them all, I say." And with that he lifted up his axe and brought it down on the end of the upturned log with such force that it split into two jagged portions.

CHAPTER XXXI

THE TEABERRY GOWN IS DONNED

When Miss Panney had driven herself away from Cobhurst and Dr. Tolbridge's cook had finished her conference with Mrs. Drane and had gone out to the barn to look for her carriage, Miriam Haverley was left with an impression upon her mind. This was to the effect that there was a good deal of managing and directing going on in the house with which she had nothing to do.

Miss Panney went into her kitchen to talk to Molly Tooney, and when she did not want to talk to her any more she sent her upstairs, in order that she might talk to Dr. Tolbridge's cook, which latter person had come into her kitchen, as Molly had informed her after La Fleur's departure, for the purpose of finding fault with the family cooking. Whether or not the old woman had felt herself called upon to instruct Mike in regard to his duty, she did not know, but when Miriam went into the orchard for some apples, she had seen her talking to him at the barn gate, and when she came out again, she saw her there still. Even Ralph took a little too much on himself, though of course he did not mean anything by it, but he had told Molly Tooney that she ought to have breakfast sooner in order that Miss Drane and he might get more promptly to their work. While considering her impression, Molly Tooney came to Miriam, her face red.

"What do you think, miss," said she, "that old bundle of a

cook that was here this mornin' has been doin'? She's been bringin' cauld vittles from the docther's kitchen to that nager Mike, as if you an' Mr. Haverley didn't give him enough to eat. I looked in at his winder, a wonderin' what he wanted wid a fire in summer time, an' saw him heatin' the stuff. It's an insult to me an' the family, miss, that's what it is." And the irate woman rested her knuckles on her hips.

Miriam's face turned a little pink.

"I will inquire about that, Molly," she said, and her impression became a conviction.

Toward the close of the afternoon, Miriam went up to her room, and spreading out on the bed the teaberry gown of Judith Pacewalk, she stood looking at it. She intended to put on that gown and wear it. But it did not fit her. It needed all sorts of alterations, and how to make these she did not know; sewing and its kindred arts had not been taught in the schools to which she had been sent. It is true that Miss Panney had promised to cut and fit this gown for her, but Miriam did not wish Miss Panney to have anything to do with it. That old lady seemed entirely too willing to have to do with her affairs.

While Miriam thus cogitated, Cicely Drane passed the open door of her room, and seeing the queer old-fashioned dress upon the bed, she stopped, and asked what it was. Miriam told the whole story of Judith Pacewalk, which greatly interested Cicely, and then she stated her desire to alter the dress so that she could wear it. But she said nothing about her purpose in doing this. She was growing very fond of Cicely, but she did not feel that she knew her well enough to entirely open her heart to her, and tell her of her fears and aspirations in regard to her position in the home so dear to her.

"Wear it, my dear?" exclaimed Cicely. "Why, of course I would. You may not have thought of it, but since you have told me that story, it seems to me that the fitness of things demands that you should wear that gown. As to the fitness of the dress itself, I'll help you about that. I can cut, sew, and do all that sort of thing, and together we will make a lovely gown of it for you. I do not think we ought to change the style and fashion of it, but we can make it smaller without making it anything but the delightful old-timey gown that it is. And then let me tell you another thing, dear Miriam: you must really put up your hair. You will never be treated with proper respect by your cook until you do that. Mother and I have been talking about this, and thought that perhaps we ought to mention it to you, because you would not be likely to think of it yourself, but we thought we had no right to be giving you advice, and so said nothing. But now I have spoken of it, and how angry are you?"

"Not a bit," answered Miriam; "and I shall put up my hair, if you will show me how to do it."

So long as the Dranes admitted that they had no right to give her advice, Miriam was willing that they should give her as much as they pleased.

For several days Cicely and Miriam cut and stitched and fitted and took in and let out, and one morning Miriam came down to breakfast attired in the pink chintz gown, its skirt touching the floor, and with her long brown hair tastefully done up in a knot upon her head.

"What a fine young woman has my little sister grown into!" exclaimed Ralph. "To look at you, Miriam, it seems as if years must have passed since yesterday. That is the pink dress that Dora Bannister wore when she was here, isn't it?"

This remark irritated Miriam a little; Ralph saw the irritation, and was sorry that he had made the remark. It was surprising how easily Miriam was irritated by references to Dora.

"I lent it once," said his sister, as she took her seat at the table, "but I shall not do it again."

That day Mike was interviewed in regard to what might be called his foreign maintenance. The ingenuous negro was amazed. His Irish and his African temperaments struggled together for expression.

"Bless my soul, Miss Miriam," he said; "nobody in this world ever brought me nuthin' to eat, 'cause they know'd I didn't need it, an' gittin' the best of livin' right here in your house, Miss Miriam, an' if they had brought it I wouldn't have took it an' swallowed the family pride; an' what's more, the doctor's cook didn't bring that pie on purpose for me. She just comed down here to ax me how to make real good corn-cakes, knowin' that I was a fust-rate cook, an' could make corn-cakes, an' she wanted to know how to do it. When I tole her jes' how to do it,—ash-cakes, griddle-cakes, batter-cake, every kin' of cake,—she was so mighty obligated that she took a little bit of a pie, made of meat, out of the bag what she'd brought along to eat on the way home, not feelin' hungry at lunch time, an' give it to me. An' not wantin' to hurt her feelin's, I jes' took it, an' when I went to my house I het it an' eat it, an' bless your soul, Miss Miriam, it did taste good; for that there woman in the kitchen don't give me half enough to eat, an' never no corn-bread an' ham fat, which is mighty cheap, Miss Miriam, an' a long sight better for a workin' pusson than crusts of wheat bread a week old an'—"

"You don't mean to say," interrupted Miriam, "that Molly does not give you enough to eat? I'll speak to her about that. She ought to be ashamed of herself."

"Now look here, Miss Miriam," said Mike, speaking more earnestly, "don't you go an' do that. If you tell her that, she'll go an' make me the biggest corn-pone anybody ever seed, an' she'll put pizen into it. Oh, it'd never do to say anythin' like that to Molly Tooney, if she's got me to feed. Jes' let me tell you, Miss Miriam, don't you say nothin' to Molly Tooney 'bout me. I never could sleep at night if I thought she was stirrin' up pizen in my vittles. But I tell you, Miss Miriam, if you was to say Molly, that you an' Mr. Haverley liked corn-cakes an' was always used to 'em before you come here, an' that they 'greed with you, then in course she'd make 'em, an' there'd be a lot left over for me, for I don't 'spect you all could eat the corn-bread she'd make, but I'd eat it, bein' so powerful hungry for corn-meal."

"Mike," said Miriam, "you shall have corn-bread, but that is all nonsense about Molly. I do not see how you could get such a notion into your head."

Mike gave himself a shrug.

"Now look a here, Miss Miriam," he said; "I've heard before of red-headed cooks, an' colored pussons as wasn't satisfied with their victuals, an' nobody knows what they died of, an' the funerals was mighty slim, an' no 'count, the friends an' congregation thinkin' there might be somethin' 'tagious. Them red-headed kind of cooks is mighty dangerous, Miss Miriam, an' lemme tell you, the sooner you git rid of them, the better."

Miriam's previous experiences had brought her very little into contact with negroes, and although she did not care very much about what Mike was saying, it interested her to hear him talk. His intonations and manner of expressing himself pleased her fancy. She could imagine herself in the sunny South, talking to an old family servant. This fancy was novel and pleasant. Mike liked to talk, and was shrewd enough to see that Miriam liked to listen to him. He determined to take advantage of this opportunity to find out something in regard to the doleful news brought to him by La Fleur and which, he feared, might be founded upon fact.

"Now look here, Miss Miriam," said he, lowering his voice a little, but not enough to make him seem disrespectfully confidential, "what you want is a first-class colored cook—not Phoebe, she's no good cook, an' won't live in the country, an' is so mighty stuck up that she don't like nuthin' but wheat bread, an' ain't no 'count anyway. But I got a sister, Miss Miriam. She's a number one, fust-class cook, knows all the northen an' southen an' easten an' westen kind of cookin', an' she's only got two chillun, what could keep in the house all day long an' not trouble nobody, 'side bringin' kindlin' an' runnin' errands; an' the husband, he's dead, an' that's a good sight better, Miss Miriam, than havin' him hangin' round, eatin' his meals here, an' bein' no use, 'cause he had rheumatism all over him, 'cept on his appetite."

This suggestion pleased Miriam; here was a chance for another old family servant.

"I think I should like to have your sister, Mike," she said; "what is her name? Is she working for anybody now?"

"Her name is Seraphina—Seraphina Paddock. Paddock was his name. She's keepin' house now, an' takin' in washin', down to Bridgeport. I reckon she's like to come here an' live, mighty well."

"I wish you'd tell her to come and see me," said Miriam. "I think it would be a very good thing for us to have a colored cook."

"Mighty good thing. There ain't nothin' better than a colored cook; but jus' let me tell you, Miss Miriam, my sister's mighty particular 'bout goin' to places an' takin' her family, an' furniture, an' settin' herself up to live when she don't know whether things is fixed an' settled there, or whether the fust thing she knows is she's got to pull up stakes an' git out agin."

"I am sure everything is fixed and settled here," said Miriam, in surprise.

"Well, now look a here, Miss Miriam," said Mike, "'spose you was clean growed up, an' you're near that now, as anybody can see, an' you was goin' to git married to somebody, or 'spose Mr. Haverley was goin' to git married to somebody, why don' you see you'd go way with your husband, an' your brother he'd come here with his new wife, an' everything would be turned over an' sot upside down, an' then Seraphina, she'd have to git up an' git, for there'd sure to be a new kin' of cook wanted or else none, an' Seraphina, she'd fin' her house down to Bridgeport rented to somebody who had gone way without payin' the rent, an' had been splittin' kindlin' on the front steps an' hacking 'em all up, and white-washin' the kitchen what she papered last winter to hide the grease spots what they made through living like pigs, an' Seraphina, she can't stand nothing like that."

Miriam burst out laughing.

"Mike," she cried, "nobody is going to get married here."

Mike's eyes glistened.

"That so, sure?" he said. "You see, Miss Miriam, you an' your brother is both so 'tractive, that I sort o' 'sposed you might be thinkin' of gittin' married, an' if that was so, I couldn't go to Seraphina, an' git her to come here when things wasn't fixed an' settled."

"If that is all that would keep your sister from coming," said Miriam, "she need not trouble herself."

"Now look a here, Miss Miriam," said Mike, quickly, "of course everything in this world depends on sarcumstances, an' if it happened that Mr. Hav'ley was the one to git married, an' he was to take some lady that was livin' here anyway an' was used to the place, an' the ways of the house, an' didn't want to go anywheres else an' wanted to stay here an' not to chance nothin' an' have the same people workin' as worked before, like Miss Drane, say, with her mother livin' here jes' the same, an' you keepin' house jes' as you is now, an' all goin' on without no upsottin', of course Seraphina, she wouldn't mind that. She'd like mighty well to come, whether your brother was married or not; but supposin' he married a lady like Miss Dora Bannister. Bless my soul, Miss Miriam, everything in this place would be turned heels up an' heads down, an' there wouldn't be no colored pussons wanted in this 'stablishment, Seraphina nor me nuther, an' I reckon you wouldn't know the place in six months, Miss Miriam, with that Miss Dora runnin' it, an' old Miss Panney with her fingers in the pie, an' nobody can't help her doin' that when Miss Dora is concerned, an' you kin see for yourself, Miss Miriam, that Seraphina, an' me, too, is bound to be bounced if it was to come to that."

"I will talk to you again about your sister," said Miriam, and she went away, amused.

Mike was delighted.

"It's all a cussed old lie, jes' as I thought it wuz," said he to himself; "an' that old Miss Panney'll fin' them young uns is harder nuts to crack than me an' Phoebe wuz. I got in some good licks fur dat purty Miss Cicely, too."

Miriam's amusement gradually faded away as she approached the house. At first it had seemed funny to hear any one talk about Ralph or herself getting married, but now it did not appear so funny. On the contrary, that part of Mike's remarks which concerned Ralph and Dora was positively depressing. Suppose such a thing were really to happen; it would be dreadful. She had thought her brother overfond of Dora's society, but the matter had never appeared to her in the serious aspect in which she saw it now.

She had intended to find Ralph, and speak to him about Mike's sister; but now she changed her mind. She was wearing the teaberry gown, and she would attend to her own affairs as mistress of the house. If Ralph could be so cruel as to marry Dora, and put her at the head of everything,—and if she were here at all, she would want to be at the head of everything,— then she, Miriam, would take off the teaberry gown, and lock it up in the old trunk.

"But can it be possible," she asked herself, as a tear or two began to show themselves in her eyes, "that Ralph could be so

Frank Richard Stockton

cruel as that?"

As she reached the door of the house, Cicely Drane was coming out. Involuntarily Miriam threw her arms around her and folded her close to the teaberry gown.

Miriam was not in the habit of giving away to outbursts of this sort, and as she released Cicely she said with a little apologetic blush,—

"It is so nice to have you here. I feel as if you ought not ever to go away."

"I am sure I do not want to go, dear," said Cicely, with the smile of good-fellowship that always went to the heart of Miriam.

CHAPTER XXXII

MISS PANNEY FEELS SHE
MUST CHANGE HER PLANS

Molly Tooney waited with some impatience the result of Miriam's interview with Mike. If the "nager" should be discharged for taking cold victuals like a beggar, Molly would be glad of it; it would suit her much better to have a nice Irish boy in his place.

But when Miriam told her cook that evening that Mike had satisfactorily explained the matter of the pie, and also remarked that in future she would like to have bread or cakes made of corn-meal, and that she couldn't see any reason why Mike, who was accustomed to this sort of food, should not have it always, Molly's soul blazed within her; it would have burst out into fiery speech; but the girl before her, although young, was so quiet and sedate, so suggestive of respect, that Molly, scarcely knowing why she did it, curbed herself; but she instantly gave notice that she wished to quit the place on the next day.

When Ralph heard this, he was very angry, and wanted to go and talk to the woman.

"Don't you do anything of the kind," said Miriam. "It is not your business to talk to cooks. I do that. And I want to go to-morrow to Thorbury and get some one to come to us by the day until the new cook arrives. If I can get her, I am going to engage Seraphina, Mike's sister."

Ralph looked at her and laughed.

"Well, well, Miss Teaberry," he said, "you are getting on bravely. Putting up your hair and letting down your skirts has done wonders. You are the true lady of the house now."

"And what have you to say against that?" asked Miriam.

"Not a word!" he cried. "I like it, I am charmed with it, and I will drive you into Thorbury to-morrow. And as to Mike's sister, you can have all his relations if you like, provided they do not charge too much. If we had a lot of darkies here, that would make us more truly ramshackle and jolly than we are now."

"Ralph," said Miriam, with dignity, "stop pulling my ears. Don't you see Mrs. Drane coming?"

The next day Miriam and Ralph jogged into Thorbury. Miriam, not wearing the teaberry gown, but having its spirit upon her, had planned to inquire of the grocer with whom she dealt, where she might find a woman such as she needed, but Ralph did not favor this.

"Let us first go and see Mrs. Tolbridge," he said. "She is one of our first and best friends, and probably knows every woman in town, and if she doesn't, the doctor does."

This last point had its effect upon Miriam. She wanted to see Dr. Tolbridge to ask if he could not stop in and quiet the mind of Cicely, who really wanted to see him about her work, but who did not like, as Miriam easily conjectured, to ask Ralph to send her to town. Miriam wished to make things as pleasant as possible for Cicely, and Mrs. Tolbridge had not, so far, meddled in the least with her concerns. If, inadvertently, Ralph had proposed a consultation with Mrs. Bannister, there would have been a hubbub in the gig.

The doctor and his wife were both at home, and when the business of the Haverleys had been stated to them, Mrs. Tolbridge clapped her hands.

"Truly," she cried, "this is a piece of rare good fortune; we will lend them La Fleur. Do you know, my dear girl," she said to Miriam, "that the doctor and I are going away? He will attend a medical convention at Barport, and I will visit my mother, to whom he will come, later. It will be a grand vacation for us, for we shall stay away from Thorbury for two weeks, and the only thing which has troubled us is to decide what we shall do with La Fleur while we are gone. We want to shut up the house, and she does not want to go to her friends, and if she should do so, I am afraid we might lose her. I am sure she would be delighted to come to you, especially as the Dranes are with you. Shall I ask her?"

Miriam jumped to her feet, with an expression of alarm on her countenance, which amused the doctor and her brother.

"Oh, please, Mrs. Tolbridge, don't do that!" she exclaimed. "Truly, I could not have a great cook like La Fleur in our kitchen. I should be frightened to death, and she would have nothing to do anything with. You know, Mrs. Tolbridge, that we live in an awfully plain way. We are not in the least bit rich or stylish or anything of the sort. If Cicely had not told me that she and her mother lived in the same way, we could not have taken them. We keep only a man and a woman, you know, and we all do a lot of work ourselves, and Molly Tooney was always growling because there were not enough things to cook with, and what a French cook would do in our kitchen I really do not know. She would drive us crazy!"

"Come now," said the doctor, laughing, "don't frighten yourself in that way, my little lady. If La Fleur consents to go to you for a couple of weeks, she will understand the circumstances, and will be perfectly satisfied with what she finds. She is a woman of sense. You would better let Mrs. Tolbridge go and talk with her."

Miriam sat down in a sort of despair. Here again, her affairs were being managed for her. Would she ever be able to maintain her independence? She had said all she could say, and now she hoped that La Fleur would treat the proposition with contempt.

But the great cook did nothing of the kind. In five minutes, Mrs. Tolbridge returned with the information that La Fleur would be overjoyed to go to Cobhurst for a fortnight. She wanted some country air; she wanted to see the Dranes; she had a great admiration for Miss Haverley, being perfectly able to judge, although she had met her but once, that she was a lady born; she looked upon her brother as a most superior gentleman; and she would be perfectly content with whatever she found in the Cobhurst kitchen.

"She says," added Mrs. Tolbridge, "that if you give her a gridiron, a saucepan, and a fire, she will cook a meal fit for a duke. With brains, she says, one can make up all deficiencies."

Ralph took his sister aside.

"Do go out and see her, Miriam," he said. "If we take her, we shall oblige our friends here, and please everybody. It will only be for a little while, and then you can have your old colored mammy and the pickaninnies, just as you have planned."

When Miriam came back from the kitchen, she found that the doctor had left the house and was going to his buggy at the gate.

"Oh, Ralph!" she exclaimed, "you do not know what a nice woman she is. She is just like an old family nurse." And then she ran out to catch the doctor, and talk to him about Cicely.

"Your sister is a child yet," remarked Mrs. Tolbridge, with a smile.

"Indeed she is," said Ralph; "and she longs for what she never had—old family servants, household ties, and all that sort of thing. And I believe she would prefer a good old Southern mammy to a fine young lover."

"Of course she would," said Mrs. Tolbridge. "That would be natural to any girl of her age, except, perhaps," she added, "one like Dora Bannister. I believe she was in love when she was fifteen."

It seemed strange to Ralph that the mention of a thing of this sort, which must have happened three or four years ago, and to a lady whom he had known a very short time, should send a little pang of jealousy through his heart, but such was the fact.

There were picnic meals at Cobhurst that day; for La Fleur was not to arrive until the morrow, and they were all very jolly.

Mike was in a state of exuberant delight at the idea of having that good Mrs. Flower in the place of Molly Tooney. He worked until nearly twelve o'clock at night to scour and brighten the kitchen and its contents for her reception.

Into this region of bliss there descended, about the middle of the afternoon, a frowning apparition. It was that of Miss Panney, to whom Molly had gone that morning, informing her that she had been discharged without notice by that minx of a girl, who didn't know anything more about housekeeping than she did about blacksmithing, and wanted to put "a dirty, hathen nager" over the head of a first-class Christian cook.

When she heard this news, the old lady was amazed and indignant; and she soundly rated Molly for not coming to her instantly, before she left her place. Had she known of the state of affairs, she was sure she could have pacified Miriam, and arranged for Molly to retain her place. It was very important for Miss Panney, though she did not say so, to have some one in the Cobhurst family who would keep her informed of what was happening there. If possible, Molly must go back; and anyway the old lady determined to go to Cobhurst and look into matters.

Miss Panney was glad to find Miriam alone on the front piazza, training some over-luxuriant vines upon the pillars; and the moment her eyes fell upon the girl, she saw that she was dressed as a woman, and not in the youthful costume in which she had last seen her. This strengthened the old lady's previous impression that Ralph's sister was rapidly becoming the real head of this house, and that it would be necessary to be very careful in her conduct toward her. It might be difficult, even impossible, to carry out her match-making plans if Miriam should rise up in opposition to them.

The old lady was very cordial, and entreated that Miriam should go on with her work, while she sat in an armchair near by. After a little ordinary chat, Miss Panney mentioned that she had heard that Molly Tooney had been discharged. Instantly Miriam's pride arose, and her manner cooled. Here again was somebody meddling with her affairs. In as few words as possible, she stated that the woman had not been discharged, but had left of her own accord without any good reason; that she did not like her, and was glad to get rid of her; that she had an excellent cook in view, and that until this person could come to her, she had engaged, temporarily, a very good woman.

All this she stated without question or remark from Miss Panney; and when she had finished, she began again to tie the vines to their wires. Miss Panney gazed very steadily through her spectacles at the resolute side face of the girl, and said only that she was very glad that Miriam had been able to make such a good arrangement. It was plain enough to her that Molly Tooney must be dropped, but in doing this, Miss Panney would not drop her plans. They would simply be changed to suit circumstances.

Had Miss Panney known who it was who was coming temporarily to the Cobhurst kitchen, it is not likely that she could have glided so quietly from the subject of household service to that of the apple prospect and Miriam's success with hens, and from these to the Dranes.

"Do you expect to have them much longer with you?" she asked. "The work the doctor gave the young lady must be nearly finished. When that is done, I suppose she will go back to town to try to get something to do there."

"Oh, they have not thought of going," said Miriam; "the doctor's book is a very long one, and when I saw him yesterday, he told me that he had ever so much more work for her to do, and he is going to bring it out here before he goes to Barport. I should be very sorry indeed if Cicely had to leave here, and I don't think I should let her do it, work or no work. I like her better and better every day, and it is the greatest comfort and pleasure to have her here. It almost seems as if she were my sister, and Mrs. Drane is just as nice as she can be. She is so good and kind, and never meddles with anything."

Miss Panney listened with great attention. She now saw how she must change her plans. If Ralph were to marry Dora, Miriam must like Dora. As for his own liking, there would be no trouble about that, after the Drane girl should be got rid of. In regard to this riddance, Miss Panney had intended to make an early move and a decided one. Now she saw that this would not do. The Drane girl, that alien intruder, whom Dr. Tolbridge's treachery had thrust into this household, was the great obstacle to the old lady's schemes, but to oust her suddenly would ruin everything. Miriam would rise up in opposition, and at present that would be fatal. Miriam was not a girl whose grief and anger at the loss of one thing could be pacified by the promise of another. Having lost Cicely, she would turn her back upon Dora, and what would be worse, she would undoubtedly turn Ralph's back in that direction.

To this genial young man, his sister was still his chief object on earth. Later, this might not be the case.

When Miriam began to like Dora,—and this must happen, for

Frank Richard Stockton

in Miss Panney's opinion the Bannister girl was in every way ten times more charming than Cicely Drane,—then, cautiously, but with quick vigor, Miss Panney would deliver the blow which would send the Dranes not only from Cobhurst, but back to their old home. In the capacity of an elderly and experienced woman who knew what everybody said and thought, and who was able to make her words go to the very spinal marrow of a sensitive person, she was sure she could do this. And when she had done it, it would cheer her to think that she had not only furthered her plans, but revenged herself on the treacherous doctor.

Now was heard from within, the voice of Cicely, who had come downstairs from her work, and who, not knowing that Miriam had a visitor, was calling to her that it was time to get dinner.

"My dear," said Miss Panney, "go in and attend to your duties, and if you will let me, I shall like ever so much to stay and take dinner with you, and you need not put yourself to the least trouble about me. You ought to have very simple meals now that you are doing your own work. I very much want to become better acquainted with your little friend Cicely and her good mother. Now that I know that you care so much for them, I feel greatly interested in them both, and you know, my dear, there is no way of becoming acquainted with people which is better than sitting at table with them."

Miriam was not altogether pleased, but said the proper things, and went to call Mike to take the roan mare, who was standing asleep between the shafts of her phaeton.

Miss Panney now had her cues; she did not offer to help in any way, and made no suggestions in any direction. At luncheon she made herself agreeable to everybody, and before the meal was over they all thought her a most delightful old lady with a wonderful stock of good stories. On her side Miss Panney was also greatly pleased; she found Ralph even a better fellow than she had thought him. He had not only a sunny temper, but a bright wit, and he knew what was being done in the world. Cicely, too, was satisfactory. She was a most attractive little thing, pretty to a dangerous extent, but in her treatment of Ralph there was not the least sign of flirtation or demureness. She was as free and familiar with him as if she had known him always.

"Men are not apt to marry the girls they have known always," said Miss Panney to herself, "and Dora can do better than this one if she has but the chance; and the chance she must have."

While listening with the most polite attention to a reminiscence related by Mrs. Drane, Miss Panney earnestly considered this subject. She had thought of many plans, some of them vague, but all of the same general character, for bringing Dora and Miriam together and promoting a sisterly affection between them, for her mind had been busy with the subject since Miriam had left her alone on the piazza, but none of the plans suited her. They were clumsy and involved too much action on the part of Dora. Suddenly a satisfying idea shot into the old lady's mind, and she smiled so pleasantly that Mrs. Drane was greatly encouraged, and entered into some details of her reminiscence which she had intended to omit, thinking they might prove tiresome.

"If they only could go away together, somewhere," said Miss Panney to herself, "that would be grand; that would settle everything. It would not be long before Dora and Miriam would be the dearest of chums, and with Ralph's sister away, that Drane girl would have to go. It would all be so natural, so plain, so beautiful."

When Miss Panney drove home, about the middle of the afternoon, she was still smiling complacently at this good idea, and wondering how she might carry it out.

Frank Richard Stockton

CHAPTER XXXIII

LA FLEUR LOOKS FUTUREWARD

According to his promise, Dr. Tolbridge came to Cobhurst on the morning of his intended departure for Barport, bringing with him more of his manuscript and some other copying which he wished Cicely to do. He had never known until now how much he needed a secretary. He saw only the ladies, Ralph having gone off to try to shoot some woodcock. The young man was not in a good humor, for he had no dog, and his discontent was increased by the reflection that a fine setter had been presented to him, and he had not yet come into possession of it. He wanted the dog, Congo, because he thought it was a good dog, and also because Dora Bannister had given it to him, and he was impatient to carry out the plan which Dora had proposed to get the animal to Cobhurst.

But this plan, which included a visit from Dora, in order that the dog might come to his new home without compulsion, and which, as modified by Ralph, included a drive or a walk through the woods with the donor in order that the dog might learn to follow him, needed Miriam's cooeperation. And this cooeperation he could not induce her to give. She seemed to have all sorts of reasons for putting off the invitation for which Miss Bannister was evidently waiting. Of course there was no reason for waiting, but girls are queer. A word from Miriam would bring her, but Miriam was very unresponsive to suggestions concerning said word.

"It is not only ourselves," said the doctor, in reply to some questions from Mrs. Drane in regard to the intended journey, "who are going this afternoon. We take with us Mrs. Bannister and Dora. This is quite a sudden plan, only determined upon last night. They both want a little Barport life before the season closes, and thought it would be pleasant to go with us."

Mrs. Drane and Cicely were not very much interested in the Bannisters, and received this news tranquilly, but Miriam felt a little touch of remorse, and wished she had asked Dora to come out some afternoon and bring her dog, which poor Ralph seemed so anxious to have. She asked the doctor how long he thought the Bannisters would stay away.

"Oh, we shall pick them up as we come back," he said "and that will be in about two weeks." And with this the busy man departed.

Since the beginning of his practice, Dr. Tolbridge had never gone away from Thorbury for an absence of any considerable duration without first calling on Miss Panney to see if she needed any attention from him before he left, and on this occasion he determined not to depart from this custom. It is true, she was very angry with him, but so far as he could help it, he would not allow her anger to interfere with the preservation of a life which he considered valuable.

When the old lady was told that the doctor had called and had asked for her, she stamped her foot and vowed she would not see him. Then her curiosity to know what brought him there triumphed over her resentment, and she went down. Her reception of him was cold and severe, and she answered his questions regarding her health as if he were a census-taker, exhibiting not the slightest gratitude for his concern regarding her physical well-being, nor the slightest hesitation in giving him information which might enable him to further said well-being.

The doctor was as cool as was his patient; and, when he had

finished his professional remarks, informed her that the Bannisters were to go with him to Barport. When Miss Panney heard this she sprang from her chair with the air of an Indian of the Wild West bounding with uplifted tomahawk upon a defenceless foe. The doctor involuntarily pushed back his chair, but before he could make up his mind whether he ought to be frightened or amused, Miss Panney sat down as promptly as she had risen, and a grim smile appeared upon her face.

"How you do make me jump with your sudden announcements," she said. "I am sure I am very glad that Dora is going away. She needed a change, and sea air is better than anything else for her. How long will they stay?"

The slight trace of her old cordiality which showed itself in Miss Panney's demeanor through the few remaining minutes of the interview greatly pleased Dr. Tolbridge.

"She is a good old woman at heart," he said to himself, "and when she gets into one of her bad tempers, the best way to bring her around is to interest her in people she loves, and Dora Bannister is surely one of those."

When the doctor had gone, Miss Panney gave herself up to a half minute of unrestrained laughter, which greatly surprised old Mr. Witton, who happened to be passing the parlor door. Then she sat down to write a letter to Dora Bannister, which she intended that young lady to receive soon after her arrival at Barport.

That afternoon the good La Fleur came to Cobhurst, her soul enlivened by the determination to show what admirable meals could be prepared from the most simple materials, and with the prospect of spending a fortnight with Mrs. Drane and Cicely, and with that noble gentleman, the master of the estate, and to pass these weeks in the country. She was a great lover of things rural: she liked to see, pecking and scratching, the fowls with which she prepared such dainty dishes. In her earlier days, the sight of an old hen wandering near a bed of celery, with a bed of beets in the middle distance, had suggested the salad for which she afterwards became somewhat famous.

She knew a great deal about garden vegetables, and had been heard to remark that brains were as necessary in the culling of fruits and roots and leaves and stems as for their culinary transformation into attractions for the connoisseur's palate. She was glad, too, to have the opportunity of an occasional chat with that intelligent negro Mike, and so far as she could judge, there were no objections to the presence of Miriam in the house.

Ralph did not come back until after La Fleur had arrived, and he returned hungry, and a little more out of humor than when he started away.

"I had hoped," he said to Miriam, "to get enough birds to give the new cook a chance of showing her skill in preparing a dish of game for dinner; but these two, which I may say I accidentally shot, are all I brought. It is impossible to shoot without a dog, and I think I shall go to-morrow morning to see Miss Bannister and ask her to let me take Congo home with me. He will soon learn to know me, and the woodcock season does not last forever."

"But Dora will not be at home," said Miriam; "she goes to Barport to-day with the Tolbridges."

Ralph opened his mouth to speak, and then he shut it again. It was of no use to say anything, and he contented himself with a sigh as he went to the rack to put up his gun. Miriam sighed, too, and as she did so, she hoped that it was the dog and not Dora that Ralph was sighing about.

The next morning there came to Cobhurst a man, bringing a black setter and a verbal message from Miss Bannister to the effect that if Mr. Haverley would tie up the dog and feed him himself for two or three days and be kind to him, she had no doubt Congo would soon know him as his master.

"Now that is the kind of a girl I like," said Ralph to his sister. "She promises to do a thing and she does it, even if the other party is not prompt in stepping forward to attend to his share of the affair."

There was nothing to say against this, and Miriam said nothing, but contented herself with admiring the dog, which was worthy of all the praise she could give him. Congo was tied up, and Mike and Mrs. Drane and Cicely, and finally La Fleur, came to look at him and to speak well of him. When all had gone away but the colored man and the cook, the latter asked why Miss Bannister had been mentioned in connection with this dog.

"'Cause he was her dog," said Mike. "She got him when he was a little puppy no bigger nor a cat, an' you'd a thought, to see her carry him about an' put him in a little bed an' kiver him up o' night an' talk to him like a human bein', that she loved him as much as if he'd been a little baby brother; an' she's thought all the world of him, straight 'long until now, an' she's gone an' give him to Mr. Hav'ley."

La Fleur reflected for a moment.

"Are you sure, Mike," she asked, "that they are not engaged?"

"I'm dead sartain sure of it," he said. "His sister told me so with her own lips. Givin' dogs don't mean nothin', Mrs. Flower. If people married all the people they give dogs to, there'd be an awful mix in this world. Bless my soul, I'd have about eight wives my own self."

La Fleur smiled at Mike's philosophy, and applied his information to the comfort of her mind.

"If his sister says they are not engaged," she thought, "it's like they are not, but it looks to me as if it were time to take the

Bannister pot off the fire."

La Fleur now retired to a seat under a tree near the kitchen door, and applied her intellect to the consideration of the dinner, and the future of the Drane family and herself. The present state of affairs suited her admirably. She could desire no change in it, except that Mr. Haverley should marry Miss Cicely in order to give security to the situation. For herself, this was the place above all others at which she would like to live, and a mistress such as Miss Cicely, who knew little of domestic affairs, but appreciated everything that was well done, was the mistress she would like to serve. She would be sorry to leave the good doctor, for whom, as a man of intellect, she had an earnest sympathy, but he did not live in the country, and the Dranes were nearer and dearer to her than he was. He should not be deserted nor neglected. If she came to spend the rest of her life on this fine old estate, she would engage for him a good young cook, who would be carefully instructed by her in regard to the peculiarities of his diet, and who should always be under her supervision. She would get him one from England; she knew of several there who had been her kitchen maids, and she would guarantee that the one she selected would give satisfaction.

Having settled this part of her plan, she now began to ponder upon that important feature of it which concerned the marriage of Miss Cicely with Ralph Haverley. Why, under the circumstances, this should not take place as a mere matter of course and as the most natural thing in the world, she could not imagine. But in all countries young people are very odd, and must be managed. She had not yet had any good opportunity of judging of the relations between these two; she had noticed that they were on very easy and friendly terms with each other, but this was not enough. It might be a long time before people who were jolly good friends came to look upon each other from a marrying point of view. Things ought to be hurried up; that Miss Bannister would be away for two weeks; she, La Fleur, would be here for two weeks. She must try what she could do; the fire must be brightened,—the draught turned on, ashes raked out, kindling-wood thrust in if necessary, to make things hotter. At all events the dinner-bell must ring at the appointed time, in a fortnight, less one day.

Ralph came striding across the lawn, and noticing La Fleur, approached her.

"I am glad to see you," he said, "for I want to tell you how much I enjoyed your beefsteak this morning. One could not get anything better cooked than that at Delmonico's. The dinner last night was very good, too."

"Oh, don't mention that, sir," said La Fleur, who had risen the moment she saw him, and now stood with her head on one side, her eyes cast down, and a long smile on her face. "That dinner was nothing to what I shall give you when Miss Miriam has sent for some things from the town which I want. And as for the steak, I beg you will not judge me until I have got for myself the cuts I want from the butcher. Then you shall see, sir, what I can do for you. In a beautiful home like this, Mr. Haverley, the cooking should be of the noblest and best."

Ralph laughed.

"So long as you stay with us, La Fleur," he said, "I am sure Cobhurst will have all it deserves in that respect."

"Thank you very much, sir," she said, dropping a little courtesy. Then, raising her eyes, she cast them over the landscape and bent them again with a little sigh.

"You are a gentleman of feeling, Mr. Haverley," she said, "and can understand the feelings of another, even if she be an old woman and a cook, and I know you can comprehend my sentiments when I find myself again serving my most gracious former mistress Mrs. Drane, and her lovely daughter, whose beautiful qualities of mind and soul it does not become me to speak of to you, sir. They were most kind to me when I first came to this country, she and her daughter, two angels, sir, whom I would serve forever. Do not think, sir, that I would not gladly serve you and your lady sister, but they are above all. It was last night, sir, as I sat looking out of my window at the beautiful trees in the moonlight, and I have not seen such trees in the moonlight since I lived in the Isle of Wight at Lord Monkley's country house there; La Fleur was his chef, and I was only there on a visit, because at that time I was attending to the education of my boy, who died a year afterward; and I thought then, sir, looking out at the moonlight, that I would go with the Dranes wherever they might go, and I would live with them wherever they might live; that I would serve them always with the best I could do, and that none could do better. But I beg your pardon, sir, for standing here, and talking in this way, sir," and with a little courtesy and with her head more on one side and more bowed down, she shuffled away.

"Now then," said she to herself, as she entered the kitchen, "if I have given him a notion of a wife with a first-class cook attached, it is a good bit of work to begin with."

Frank Richard Stockton

CHAPTER XXXIV

A PLAN WHICH SEEMS TO SUIT EVERYBODY

Since her drive home from Thorbury with Ralph Haverley, Cicely Drane had not ceased to consider the hypothesis which had been suggested to her that day by La Fleur; but this consideration was accompanied by no plan of action, no defined hopes, no fears, no suspicions, and no change in her manner toward the young man, except that in accordance with her mother's prudential notions, which had been indicated to her in a somewhat general way, she had restricted herself in the matter of tete-a-tetes and dual rambles.

She looked upon the relations between Ralph and herself in the most simple and natural manner possible. She was enjoying life at Cobhurst. It delighted her to see her mother so contented and so well. She was greatly interested in her work, for she was a girl of keen intelligence, and thoroughly appreciated and enjoyed the novel theories and reflections of Dr. Tolbridge. She thought it the jolliest thing in the world to have La Fleur here with them. She was growing extremely fond of Miriam, who, although a good deal younger than herself, appeared to be growing older with wonderful rapidity, and every day to be growing nearer and dearer to her, and she liked Ralph better than any man she had ever met. She knew but little of Dora Bannister and had no reason to suppose that any matrimonial connection between her and Mr. Haverley ever been thought of; in fact, in the sincerity and naturalness of her disposition, she could see no reason why she should not continue to like Mr. Haverley, to like him better and better, if he gave her reason to do so, and more than that, not to forget the hypothesis regarding him.

La Fleur was not capable of comprehending the situation with the sagacity and insight of Miss Panney, but she was a woman of sense, and was now well convinced that it would never do to speak again to Miss Cicely in the way she had spoken to her in Dr. Tolbridge's hall. In her affection and enthusiasm, she had gone too far that time, and she knew that any further suggestions of the sort would be apt to make the girl fly away like a startled bird. Whatever was to be done must be done without the cooeperation of the young lady.

Miss Panney's letter to Dora Bannister contained some mild reproaches for the latter's departure from Thorbury without notice to her oldest friend, but her scolding was not severe, and there was as much pleasant information and inquiry as the writer could think of. Moreover, the epistle contained the suggestion that Dora should invite Miriam Haverley to come down and spend some time with her while she was at the seashore. This suggestion none but a very old friend would be likely to make, but Miss Panney was old enough for anything, in friendship or in any other way.

"My mind was on Miriam Haverley," the old lady wrote, "at the moment I heard that you had gone to Barport, and it struck me that a trip of the sort is exactly what that young person needs. She is shut up in the narrowest place in which a girl can be put, with responsibilities entirely beyond her years, and which help to cramp her mind and her ideas. She should have a total change; she should see how the world, outside of her school and her country home, lives and acts—in fact, she needs exactly what Barport and you and Mrs. Bannister can give her. I do not believe that you can bestow a greater benefit upon a fellow-being than to ask Miriam to pay you a visit while you are at the seaside. Think of this, I beg of you, my dear Dora."

This letter was read and re-read with earnest attention. Dora was fond of Miriam in a way, and would be very glad to give her a glimpse of seaside life. Moreover, Miriam's companionship would be desirable; for although Miss Bannister did not expect to lack acquaintances, there would be times when she could not call upon these, and Miriam could always be called upon.

After a consultation with Mrs. Bannister, who was pleased with the idea of having some one to go about with Dora, when she did not feel like it,—which was almost all the time,—Dora wrote to Miriam, asking her to come and visit her during the rest of her stay at Barport. While writing, Dora was not at all annoyed by the thought which made her stop for a few minutes and look out of the window,—that possibly Miriam might not like to make the journey alone, and that her brother might come with her. She did not, however, mention this contingency, but smiled as she went on writing.

Miriam, attired in her teaberry gown, came up from the Cobhurst kitchen, and walked out toward the garden. She was not in good spirits. She had already found that La Fleur was a woman superior to influences from any power derived from the wearing of Judith Pacewalk's pink chintz dress. She was convinced that at this moment that eminent cook was preparing a dinner for the benefit of the Dranes, without any thought of the tastes or desires of the mistress of the house or its master. And yet she could find nothing to say in opposition to this; consequently, she had walked away unprotesting, and that act was so contrary to her disposition that it saddened her. If she had supposed that a bad meal would be the result of the bland autocracy she had just encountered, she would have been better satisfied; but, as she knew the case would be quite otherwise, her spirits continued to fall. Even the meat, that morning, had been ordered without consultation with her.

As Miriam walked dolefully toward the garden gate, Ralph came riding from Thorbury with the mail-bag, and in it was the letter from Dora.

"Oh, Ralph!" cried Miriam, when, with her young soul glowing in her face, she thrust the open letter into her brother's hand, "may I go? I never saw the sea!"

Of Ralph's decision there could be no question, and the Cobhurst family was instantly in a flurry. Mrs. Drane, Cicely, and Miriam gave all their thoughts and every available moment of time to the work necessary on the simple outfit that was all that Miriam needed or desired; and in two days she was ready for the journey. Ralph was glad to do anything he could to help in the good work, but, as this was little, he was obliged to content himself with encomiums upon the noble character of Dora Bannister. That she should even think of offering such an inexpressible delight and benefit to his sister was sufficient proof of Miss Bannister's solid worth and tender, gracious nature. These remarks made to the ladies in general really did help in the good work, for, while Ralph was talking in this way, Cicely bent more earnestly over her sewing and stitched faster. Until now, she had never thought much about Miss Bannister; but, without intending it, or in the least desiring it, she began to think a good deal about her, even when Ralph was not there.

Miriam herself settled the manner of her journey. She had thought for a moment of Ralph as an escort, but this would cause him trouble and loss of time, which was not at all necessary, and—what was very important—would at least double the expenses of the trip; so she wrote to Miss Pender, the head teacher in her late school, begging that she might come to her and be shipped to Barport. Miss Pender had great skill and experience in the shipping of girls from the school to destinations in all parts of the country. Despatched by Miss Pender, the wildest or the vaguest school-girl would go safely to her home, or to whatever spot she might be sent.

As this was vacation, and she happened to be resting idly at school, Miss Pender gladly undertook the congenial task offered her; and welcomed Miriam, and then shipped her to Barport with even more than her usual success.

When the dear girl had gone, everybody greatly missed her,—even La Fleur, for of certain sweets the child had eaten twice as much as any one else in the house. But all were happy over her great pleasure, including the cook, who hated to have even the nicest girls come into her kitchen.

Thus far Miss Panney's plan worked admirably, but one idea she had in regard to Miriam's departure never came into the mind of any one at Cobhurst. That the Dranes should go away because Miriam, as mistress of the establishment, was gone, was not thought of for an instant. With La Fleur and Mrs. Drane in the house, was there any reason why domestic and all other affairs should not go on as usual during Miriam's brief absence?

Everything did indeed go on pretty much as it had gone on before, although it might have been thought that Ralph was now living with the Dranes. La Fleur expanded herself into all departments of the household, and insisted upon doing many little things that Cicely had been in the habit of doing for herself and her mother; and, with the assistance of Mike, who was always glad to help the good Mrs. Flower whenever she wanted him—which was always—and did it whenever he had a chance—which was often—the household wheels moved smoothly.

In one feature of the life at Cobhurst there was a change. The absence of Miriam threw Cicely and Ralph much more together. For instance, they breakfasted by themselves, for Mrs. Drane had always been late in coming down in the morning, and it was difficult for her to change her habits. Moreover, it now happened frequently that Cicely and Ralph found that each must be the sole companion of the other; and in this regard more than in any other was Miriam missed. But to say that in this regard more than any other her absence was regretted would be inaccurate.

Cicely felt that she ought to regret it, but she did not. To be so much with Ralph was contrary to her own plans of action, and to what she believed to be her mother's notions on the subject; but she could not help it without being rude to the young man, and this she did not intend to be. He was lonely and wanted a companion; and in truth, she was glad to fill the position. If he had not talked to her so much about Dora Bannister's great goodness, she would have been better pleased. But she could nearly always turn this sort of conversation upon Miriam's virtues, and on that subject the two were in perfect accord.

Mrs. Drane intended now to get up sooner in the morning, but she did not do it; and she resolved that she would not drop asleep in her chair early in the evening, as she had felt perfectly free to do when Miriam was with them; but she calmly dozed all the same.

There was another obstacle to Mrs. Drane's good intentions, of which she knew nothing. This was the craft of La Fleur, who frequently made it a point to call upon the good lady for advice or consultation, and who was most apt to do this at times when her interview with Mrs. Drane would leave Ralph and Cicely together. It was wonderful how skilfully this accomplished culinary artist planned some of these situations.

Ralph was surprised to find that he could so well bear the absence of his sister. He would not have believed it had he been told it in advance. He considered it a great piece of luck that Miriam should be able to go to the seashore, but it was also wonderful luck that Miss Drane should happen to be here while Miriam was away. Had both gone, he would have had a doleful time of it. As it was, his time was not at all doleful. All the chickens, hens, cats, calves, and flowers that Miriam had had under her especial care were now attended to most sedulously by Cicely, and in these good works Ralph gave willing and constant assistance. In fact, he found that he could do a great deal more for Cicely than Miriam had been willing he should do for her. This cooeperation was very pleasing to him, for Cicely was a girl who knew little about things rural but wanted to know much, and Ralph was a young fellow who liked to teach such girls as Cicely.

CHAPTER XXXV

MISS PANNEY HAS TEETH ENOUGH
LEFT TO BITE WITH

After her recent quick pull and strong pull, Miss Panney rested placidly on her oars. She knew that Miriam had gone, but she had not yet heard whether the Dranes had returned to their former lodging in Thorbury, or had left the neighborhood altogether. She presumed, however, that they were in the town; for the young woman's work for Dr. Tolbridge was probably not completed. She intended to call on Mrs. Brinkly and find out about this; and she also determined to drop in at Cobhurst, and see how poor Ralph was getting on by himself. But for these things there was no hurry.

But jogging into town one morning, she was amazed to meet Ralph and Mrs. Drane returning to Cobhurst in the gig. Both vehicles stopped, and Ralph immediately began to tell the old lady of Miriam's good fortune. He told, also, of his own good fortune in having Mrs. Drane and her daughter to run the house during Miriam's absence, and was in high good spirits and glad to talk.

Miss Panney listened with rigid attention; but when Ralph had finished, she asked Mrs. Drane if she had left her daughter alone at Cobhurst, while she and Mr. Haverley came to town.

"Oh, yes," answered the other lady; "Cicely is there, and hard at work; but she is not alone. You know our good La Fleur is with us, and will remain as long as the doctor and Mrs. Tolbridge are away."

When Miss Panney received this last bit of information, she gazed intently at Mrs. Drane and then at Ralph, after which she bade them good morning, and drove off.

"The old lady is not in such jolly good humor as when she lunched with us the other day," said Ralph.

"That is true," said Mrs. Drane; "but I have noticed that very elderly people are apt to be moody."

Twice in the course of a year Miss Panney allowed herself to swear, if there happened to be occasion for it. In her young days a lady of fashion would sometimes swear with great effect; and Miss Panney did not entirely give up any old fashion that she liked. Now, there being good reason for it, and no one in sight, she swore, and directed her abjurations against herself. Then her mind, somewhat relieved from the strain upon it, took in the humorous points of the situation, and she laughed outright.

"If the Dranes had hired some sharp-witted rogue to help them carry out their designs, he could not have done it better than I have done it. I have simply put the whole game into their hands; I have given them everything they want."

But before she reached Thorbury, she saw that the situation was not hopeless. There was one thing that might be done, and that successfully accomplished the game would be in her hands. Ralph must be made to go to Barport. A few days with Dora at the seaside, with some astute person there to manage the affair, would settle the fate of Mr. Ralph Haverley. At this thought her eyes sparkled, and she began to feel hungry. At this important moment she did not wish to occupy her mind with prattle and chat, and therefore departed from her usual custom of lunching with a friend or acquaintance. Hitching her roan mare in front of a confectionery shop, she entered for refreshment.

Seated at a little table in the back room, with a cup of tea and some sandwiches before her, Miss Panney took more time over her slight meal than any previous customer had ever occupied in disposing of a similar repast, at least so the girl at the counter believed and averred to the colored man who did outside errands. The girl thought that the old lady's deliberate method of eating proceeded from her want of teeth; but the man who had waited at dinners where Miss Panney was a guest contemptuously repudiated this assumption.

"I've seen her eat," said he, "and she's never behind nobody. She's got all the teeth she wants for bitin'."

"Then why doesn't she get through?" asked the girl. "When is she ever going to leave that table?"

"When she gits ready," answered the man; "that's the time Miss Panney does everything."

Sipping her tea and nibbling her sandwich, Miss Panney considered the situation. It would be, of course, a difficult thing to get that young man to visit his sister at Barport. It would cost money, and there would seem to be no good reason for his going. Of course no such influence could be brought to bear upon him at this end of the line. Whatever inducement was offered, must be offered from Barport. And there was no one there who could do it, at least with the proper effect. The girls would be glad to have him there, but nothing that either of them could, with propriety, be prompted to say, would draw him into such extravagant self-gratification. But if she were at Barport, she knew that she could send him such an invitation, or sound such a call to him, that he would be sure to come.

Accordingly Miss Panney determined to go to Barport without loss of time; and although she did hot know what sort of summons she should issue to Ralph after she got there, she did not in the least doubt that circumstances would indicate the right thing to do. In fact, she would arrange circumstances in such a way that they should so indicate.

Having arrived at this conclusion, Miss Panney finished eating her sandwich with an earnestness and rapidity which convinced the astonished girl at the counter that she had all the teeth she needed to bite with; and then she went forth to convince other people of the same thing. On the sidewalk she met Phoebe.

"How d'ye do, Miss Panney?" said that single-minded colored woman. "I hain't seen you for a long time."

Miss Panney returned the salutation, and stood for a moment in thought.

"Phoebe," said she, "when did you last see Mike?"

"Well, now, really, Miss Panney, I can't say, but it's been a mighty long time. He don't come into town to see me, and I's too busy to go way out thar. I does the minister's wash now, besides boardin' him an' keepin' his clothes mended. An' then it's four or five miles out to that farm. I can't 'ford to hire no carriage, an' Mike ain't no right to expect me to walk that fur."

"Phoebe," said Miss Panney, "you are a lazy woman and an undutiful wife. It is not four miles to Cobhurst, and you walk two or three times that distance every day, gadding about town. You ought to go out there and attend to Mike's clothes, and see that he is comfortable, instead of giving up the little time you do work to that minister, and everybody knows that the reason you have taken him to board is that you want to set yourself up above the rest of the congregation."

"Good laws, Miss Panney!" exclaimed Phoebe, "I don't see as how anybody can think that!"

"Well, I do," replied the old lady, "and plenty of other people besides. But as you won't go out to Cobhurst to attend to your own duty, I want you to go there to attend to something for me. I was going myself, but I start for the seashore to-morrow, and have not time. I want to know how that poor Mr. Ralph is getting along. Molly Tooney has left, and his sister is away, and of course those two Drane women are temporary boarders and take no care of him or his clothes. To be sure, there is a woman there, but she is that English-French creature who gives all her time to fancy dishes, and I suppose never made a bed or washed a shirt in her life."

"That's so, Miss Panney," said Phoebe, eagerly, "an' I reckon it's a lot of slops he has to eat now. 'Tain't like the good wholesome meals I gave him when I cooked thar. An' as fur washin', if there's any of that done, I reckon Mike does it."

"I should not wonder," said the old lady. "And, Phoebe, I want you to go out there this afternoon, and look over Mr. Haverley's linen, and see what ought to be washed or mended, and take general notice of how things are going on. I shall see his sister, and I want to report the state of affairs at her home. For all I know, those Dranes and their cook may pack up and clear out to-morrow if the notion takes them. Then you must meet me at the station at nine o'clock to-morrow morning, and tell me what you find out. If things are going all wrong, Mr. Haverley will never write to his sister to disturb her mind. Start for Cobhurst as soon as you can, and I will pay your carriage hire—no, I will not do that, for I want you to make a good long stay, and it will cost too much to keep a hack waiting. You can walk just as well as not, and it will do you good. And while you are there, Phoebe, you might take notice of Miss Drane. If she has finished the work she was doing for the doctor, and is just sitting about idly or strolling around the place, it is likely they will soon leave, for if the young woman does not work they cannot afford to stay there. And that is a thing Miss Miriam ought to know all about."

"Seems to me, Miss Panney," said the colored woman, "that 'twould be a mighty good thing for Mr. Hav'ley to get married. An' thar's that Miss Drane right thar already."

"What stupid nonsense!" exclaimed Miss Panney. "I thought you had more sense than to imagine such a thing as that. She is not in any way suitable for him. She is a poor little thing who has to earn her own living, and her mother's too. She is not in the least fit to be the mistress of that place."

"Don't see whar he'll get a wife, then," said Phoebe. "He never goes nowhar, and never sees nobody, except p'r'aps Miss Dora Bannister; an' she's too high an' mighty for him."

"Phoebe, you are stupider than I thought you were. No lady is too high and mighty for Mr. Haverley. And if he should happen to fancy Miss Dora, it will be a capital match. What he needs is to marry a woman of position and means. But that is not my business, or yours either, and by the way, Phoebe, since you are here, I will get you to take a letter to the post-office for me. I will go back into this shop and write it. You can take these two cents and buy an envelope and a sheet of paper, and bring them in to me."

With this Miss Panney walked into the shop, and having asked the loan of pen and ink, horrified the girl at the counter by proceeding to the table she had left, which, in a corner favored by all customers, had just been prepared for the next comer, and, having pushed aside a knife and fork and plate, made herself ready to write her letter, which was to a friend in Barport, informing her that the writer intended making her a visit.

"I shall get there," she thought, "about as soon as it does, but it looks better to write."

Before the letter was finished, Phoebe was nearly as angry as the shop-girl; but at last, with exactly two cents with which to buy a stamp, she departed for the post-office.

"The stingy old thing!" she said to herself as she left the shop;

"not a cent for myself, and makes me walk all the way out to that Cobhurst, too! I see what that old woman is up to. She's afraid he'll marry the young lady what's out thar, an' she wants him to marry Miss Dora, an' git a lot of the Bannister money to fix up his old house, an' then she expects to go out thar an' board with 'em, for I reckon she's gittin' mighty tired of the way them Wittons live. She's always patchin' up marriages so she can go an' live with the people when they first begins housekeepin', an' things is bran-new an' fresh. She did that with young Mr. Witton, but their furniture is gittin' pretty old an' worn out now. If she tries it with Mr. Hav'ley an' Dora Bannister, I reckon she'll make as big a botch of it as she did with Mike an' me."

CHAPTER XXXVI

A CRY FROM THE SEA

Miss Panney left Thorbury the next morning, but she had to go without seeing Phoebe, who did not appear at the station. She arrived at Barport in the afternoon, and went directly to the house of the friend to whom she had written, and who, it is to be hoped, was glad to see her. She deferred making her presence known to the Bannister party until the next morning. When she called at their hotel about ten o'clock, she was informed that they had all gone down to the beach; and as they could not be expected to return very soon, Miss Panney betook herself to the ocean's edge to look for them.

She found a wide stretch of sand crowded with bathers and spectators. It had been a long time since she had visited the seashore, and she discovered that seaside customs and costumes had changed very much. She was surprised, amused, and at times indignant; but, as she had come to look for the Bannisters, she confined herself to that business, postponing reflections and judgments.

Her search proved to be a difficult one. She walked up and down the beach until she assured herself that the Bannisters and Miriam were not among those who had come as lookers-on, or merely to breathe the salt air and enjoy the ocean view. When she came to scrutinize the bathers, whether they were disporting themselves in the sea or standing or lying about on the sand, she found it would be almost impossible to recognize anybody in that motley crowd.

"I can scarcely make out," she said to herself, "whether they are men or women, much less whether I know them or not. But if the Bannisters and Miriam are among those water-monkeys, I shall know them when I see their faces, and then I shall take the first chance I get to tell them what I think of them."

It was not long before Miss Panney began to grow tired. She was not used to trudging through soft sand, and she had walked a good deal before she reached the beach. She concluded, therefore, to look for a place where she might sit down and rest, and if her friends did not show themselves in a reasonable time she would go back to their hotel and wait for them there; but she saw no chairs nor benches, and as for imitating the hundreds of well-dressed people who were sitting down in the dirt,—for to Miss Panney sand was as much dirt as any other pulverized portion of the earth's surface,—she had never done such a thing, and she did not intend to.

Approaching a boat which was drawn up high and dry, she seated herself upon, or rather leaned against, its side. The bathing-master, a burly fellow in a bathing-costume, turned to her and informed her courteously but decidedly that she must not sit upon that boat.

"I do not see why," said Miss Panney, sharply, as she rose "for it is not of any use in any other way, lying up here on the sand."

She had scarcely finished speaking when the bathing master sprang to his feet so suddenly that it made Miss Panney jump. For a moment the man stood listening, and then ran rapidly down the beach. Now Miss Panney heard, coming from the sea, a cry of "Help! Help!"

Other people heard it, too, and began hurrying after the bathing master. The cry, which was repeated again and again, came from a group of bathers who were swimming far from shore, opposite a point on the beach a hundred yards or more from where Miss Panney was standing. The spectators now became greatly excited, and crowds of them began to run along the beach, while many people came out of the sea and joined the hurrying throng.

Still the cries came from the ocean, but they were feebler. Those experienced in such matters saw what had happened, a party of four bathers, swimming out beyond the breakers, had been caught in what is called a "seapuss," an eccentric current, too powerful for them to overcome, and they were unable to reach the shore.

As he ran, the bathing master shouted to some men to bring him the lifeline, and this, which was coiled in a box near the boat, was soon seized by two swift runners and carried out to the man.

"Fool!" exclaimed Miss Panney, who, with flushed face, was hurrying after the rest, "why didn't he take it with him?"

When the bathing master reached a point opposite the imperilled swimmers, he was obliged to wait a little for the life-line, but as soon as it reached him he tied one end of it around his waist and plunged into the surf. The men who had brought the line did not uncoil it nor even take it out of the box, and very soon it was seen that the bathing-master was not only making his way bravely through the breakers, but was towing after him the coil of rope, and the box in which it had been entangled. As soon as he perceived this, the man stopped for an instant, jerked the line from his waist and swam away without it.

Meanwhile a party of men had seized the life-boat, and had pushed it over the sand to the water's edge, where they launched it, and with much difficulty kept it from grounding until four young men, all bathers, jumped in and manned the oars. But before the excited oarsmen had begun to pull together, an incoming wave caught the bow of the boat, turned

Frank Richard Stockton

it broadside to the sea, and rolled it over. A dozen men, however, seized the boat and quickly righted her; again the oarsmen sprang in, and having been pushed out until the water reached the necks of the men who ran beside her, she was vigorously pulled beyond the breakers.

The excitement was now intense, not only on the beach, but in the hotels near the spot, and the shore was black with people. The cries had entirely ceased, but now the bathing-master was seen making his way toward the shore, and supporting a helpless form; before he could touch bottom, however, he was relieved of his burden by some of the men who were swimming out after him, and he turned back toward a floating head which could just be seen above the water. He was a powerful swimmer, but without a line by which he and any one he might rescue could be pulled to shore, his task was laborious and dangerous.

The boat had now pulled to the bather who, though farthest out to sea, was the best swimmer, and he, just as his strength was giving way, was hauled on board. The lifeline had been rescued and disentangled, and the shore end of it having been taken into proper charge, a man, with the other end about him, swam to the assistance of the bathing master. Between these two another lifeless helpless body was borne in.

As might have been supposed, Miss Panney was now in a state of intense agitation. Not only did she share in the general excitement, but she was filled with a horrible dread. In ordinary cases of sickness and danger, it had been her custom to offer her services without hesitation, but then she knew who were in trouble and what she must do. Now there was a sickening mystery hanging over what was happening. She was actually afraid to go near the two lifeless figures stretched upon the sand, each surrounded by a crowd of people eager to do something or see something.

But her anxious questioning of the people who were scattered about relieved her, for she found that the two unfortunate persons who had been brought in were men. Nobody knew whether they were alive or not, but everything possible was being done to revive them. Several doctors had made their appearance, and messengers were running to the hotels for brandy, blankets, and other things needed. In obedience to an excited entreaty from a physician, one of the groups surged outward and scattered a little, and Miss Panney saw the form of a strongly built man lying on his back on the sand, with men kneeling around him, some working his arms backward and forward to induce respiration, and others rubbing him vigorously. It was difficult for her to restrain herself from giving help or advice, for she was familiar with, and took a great interest in, all sorts of physical distress, but now she turned away and hurried toward the sea.

She had heard the people say there was another one out there, and her sickening feeling returned. She walked but a little way, and then she stopped and eagerly watched what was going on. The bathing-master had been nearly exhausted when he reached the shore the second time, but he had rallied his strength and had swum out to the boat which was pulling about the place where the unfortunate bathers had been swimming. Suddenly the oarsmen gave a quick pull, they had seen something, a man jumped overboard, there was bustling on the boat, something was pulled in, then the boat was rapidly rowed shoreward, the man in the water holding to the stern until his feet touched ground.

The people crowded to the water's edge so that Miss Panney could scarcely see the boat when it reached shore, but presently the crowd parted, and three men appeared, carrying what seemed to be a very light burden.

"Oh, dear," said a woman standing by, "that one was in the water a long time. I wonder if it is a girl or a boy."

Miss Panney said nothing, but made a few quick steps in the direction of the limp figure which the crowd was following up the beach; then she stopped. Her nature prompted her to go on; her present feelings restrained her. She could not help wondering at this, and said to herself that she must be aging faster than she thought. Her distant vision was excellent, and she knew that the inanimate form which was now being laid on the dry sand was not a boy.

She turned and looked out over the sea, but she could not stand still; she must do something. On occasions like this it was absolutely necessary for Miss Panney to do something. She walked up the beach, but not toward the ring of people that had now formed around the fourth unfortunate. She must quiet herself a little first.

Suddenly the old lady raised her hands and clasped them. It was a usual gesture when she thought of something she ought to do.

"If it is one of them," she said to herself, "he ought to know it instantly! And even if it isn't, he ought to know. They will be in a terrible state; somebody should be here, and Herbert has gone to the mountains. There is no one else." She now began to walk more rapidly. "Yes," she said, speaking aloud in the intensity of her emotion, "he ought to come, anyway. I can't be left here to take any chances. And if he does not know immediately, he cannot get here today."

She now directed her steps toward one of the hotels, where she knew there was a telegraph office.

"No matter what has happened, or what has not happened," she said to herself as she hurried along, "he ought to be here, and he must come!"

The old lady's hand trembled a good deal as she wrote a telegram to Ralph Haverley, but the operator at the window could read it. It ran: "A dreadful disaster here. Come on immediately."

When she had finished this business, Miss Panney stood for a few moments on the broad piazza of the hotel, which was deserted, for almost everybody was on the beach. In spite of her agitation a grim smile came over her face.

"Perhaps that was a little strong," she thought, "but it has gone now. And no matter how he finds things, I can prove to him he is needed. I do not believe he will be too much frightened; men never are, and I will see to it that he has a blessed change in his feelings when he gets here."

Miss Panney was now allowing to enter her mind the conviction, previously denied admittance, that no one of her three friends would be likely to be swimming far from shore with a party of men. And, having thus restored herself to something of her usual composure, she went down to the beach to find out who had been drowned. On the way she met Mrs. Bannister and the two girls, and from them she got her information that two of the persons believed to be beyond any power of resuscitation, and one of these was a young lady from Boston.

CHAPTER XXXVII

LA FLEUR ASSUMES RESPONSIBILITIES

It was toward the middle of the afternoon that the good La Fleur sat upon a bench under a tree by the side of the noble mansion of Cobhurst. She was enjoying the scene and allowing her mind to revel in the future she had planned for herself. She was not even thinking of the dinner. Presently there drove into the grounds a boy in a bowl-shaped trotting-wagon, bringing a telegram for Mr. Haverley. La Fleur went to meet him.

"He is not at home," she said.

"Well," said the boy, "there is seventy-five cents to pay, and perhaps there is an answer."

"Are you sure the message was not prepaid?" asked La Fleur, suspiciously.

"Oh, the seventy-five cents is for delivery," said the boy. "We deliver free in town, but we can't come way out here in the country for nothing. Isn't there somebody here who can 'tend to it?"

La Fleur drew a wallet from her pocket. "I will pay you," she said; "but if there is an answer you should take it back with you. Can't you wait a bit?"

"No," said the boy, "I can't. I shall be away from the office too long as it is."

La Fleur was in a quandary; there was no one at home but herself; a telegram is always important; very likely an immediate answer was required; and here was an opportunity to send one. If the message were from his sister, there might be something which she could answer. At any rate, it was an affair that must not be neglected, and Mr. Haverley had gone off with his fishing-rod, and no one knew when he would get back.

"Wait one minute," she said to the boy, and she hurried into the kitchen with the telegram. She put on her spectacles and looked at it; the envelope was very slightly fastened. No doubt this was something that needed attention, and the boy would not wait. Telegrams were not like private letters, anyway, and she would take the risk. So she opened the envelope without tearing it, and read the message. First she was frightened, and then she was puzzled.

"Well, I can't answer that," she said, "and I suppose he will go as soon as he gets it."

She laid the telegram on the kitchen table and went out to the impatient boy, and told him there was no answer. Whereupon he departed at the top of his pony's speed.

La Fleur returned to the kitchen and reread the telegram. The signature was not very legible, and in her first hasty reading she had not made it out, but now she deciphered it.

"Panney!" she exclaimed, "R. Panney! I believe it is from that tricky old woman!" And with her elbows on the table she gave herself up to the study of the telegram. "I never saw anything like it," she thought. "It looks exactly as if she wanted to frighten him without telling him what has happened. It could not be worse than it is, even if his sister is dead, and if that were so, anybody would telegraph that she was very ill, so as not to let it come on him too sudden. Nothing can be more dreadful than what he'll think when he reads this. One thing is certain: she meant him to go when he got it. Yes, indeed!" And a smile came upon her face as she thought. "She wants him there; that is as plain as daylight."

At this moment a step was heard outside, and the telegram was slipped into the table drawer. La Fleur arose and approached the open door; there she saw Phoebe.

"How d'ye do, ma'am?" said that individual. "Do let me come in an' sit down, for I'm nearly tired to death, an' so cross that I'd like to fight a cat."

"What has happened to you?" asked La Fleur, when she and her visitor had seated themselves.

"Nothin'," replied Phoebe, "except that I've been sent on a fool's errand, an' made to walk all the way from Thorbury, here, an' a longer an' a dirtier an' a rockier road I never went over. I thought two or three times that I should just drop. If I'd knowed how stiff my j'ints would be, I wouldn't 'a' come, no matter what she said."

"She said," repeated La Fleur. "Who?"

"That old Miss Panney!" said Phoebe, with a snap. "She sent me out here to look after Mike, an' was too stingy even to pay my hack fare. She wanted me to come day before yesterday, but I couldn't get away 'til to-day."

"Where is Miss Panney?" asked La Fleur, quickly.

"She's gone to the seashore, where the Bannisters an' Miss Miriam is. She said she'd come here herself if it hadn't been for goin' thar."

"To look after Mike?" asked the other.

"Not 'zactly," said Phoebe, with a grin. "There's other things here she wanted to look after."

"Upon my word!" exclaimed La Fleur, "I can't imagine what there is on this place that Miss Panney need concern herself about."

"There isn't no place," said Phoebe, "where there isn't somethin' that Miss Panney wants to consarn herself in."

La Fleur looked at Phoebe, and then dropped the subject.

"Don't you want a cup of tea?" she asked, a glow of hospitality suddenly appearing on her face. "That will set you up sooner than anything else, and perhaps I can find a piece of one of those meat pies your husband likes so much."

Phoebe was not accustomed to being waited upon by white people, and to have a repast prepared for her by this cook of high degree flattered her vanity and wonderfully pleased her. Her soul warmed toward the good woman who was warming and cheering her body.

"I say it again," remarked La Fleur, "that I cannot think what that old lady should want to look after in this house."

"Now look here, madam," said Phoebe, "it's jes' nothin' at all. It's jes' the most nonsensical thing that ever was. I don't mind tellin' you about it; don't mind it a bit. She wants Mr. Hav'ley to marry Miss Dora Bannister, an' she's on pins an' needles to know if the young woman here is likely to ketch him. That's all there is 'bout it. She don't care two snaps for Mike, an' I reckon he don't want no looking after anyway."

"No, indeed," answered the other; "I take the best of care of him. Miss Panney must be dreadful afraid of our young lady, eh?"

"That's jes' what she is," said Phoebe. "I wonder she didn't take Mr. Hav'ley along with her when she went to the seashore."

La Fleur's eyes sparkled.

"Now come, Phoebe," said she; "what on earth did she want you to do here?"

Phoebe took a long draught of tea, and put down the cup, with a sigh of content.

"Oh, nothin'," said she. "She jes' wanted me to spy round, an' see if Mr. Hav'ley an' Miss Drane was fallin' in love with each other, an' then I was to go an' tell her about it the mornin' before she started. Now I'll have to keep it 'til she comes back, but I reckon thar ain't nothin' to tell about."

La Fleur laughed. "Nothing at all," said she. "You might stay here a week and you wouldn't see any lovemaking between those two. They don't as much as think of such a thing. So you need not put yourself to any trouble about that part of Miss Panney's errand. Here comes your good Michael, and I think you will find that he is doing very well."

About ten minutes after this, when Phoebe and Mike had gone off to talk over their more than semi-detached domestic affairs, La Fleur took the telegram from the drawer, replaced it in its envelope, which she closed and fastened so neatly that no one would have supposed that it had been opened. Then she took from a shelf a railroad time-table, which lay in company with her cookbook and a few other well-worn volumes; for the good cook cared for reading very much as she cared for her own mayonnaise dressing; she wanted but little at a time, but she liked it.

"The last train to the city seems to be seven-ten," she said to herself. "No other train after that stops at Thorbury. If he had been at home he would have taken an early afternoon train, which was what she expected, I suppose. It will be a great pity for him to have to go tonight, and for no other reason than for that old trickster's telegram. If anything has really happened, he'll get news of it in some sensible shape."

At all events, there was nothing now to be done with the telegram, so she put it on the shelf, and set about her preparations for dinner, which had been very much delayed.

Ralph had gone off fishing; but, before starting, he had put Mrs. Browning to the gig and had told Cicely that as soon as her work was finished, she must take her mother for a drive. The girl had been delighted, and the two had gone off for a long jog through the country lanes.

It was late in the afternoon when Ralph came striding homeward across the fields. He was still a mile from Cobhurst, and on a bit of rising ground when, on the road below him, he saw Mrs. Browning and the gig, and to his surprise the good old mare was demurely trotting away from Cobhurst.

"Can it be possible," he exclaimed, "that they have just started!" And he hurried down toward the road. He now saw that there was only one person in the gig, and very soon he was near enough to perceive that this was Cicely.

"I expect you are wondering what I am doing here by myself, and where I am going," she said, when she stopped and he stood by the gig. "I shall tell you the exact truth, because I know you will not mind. We started out a long time ago, but mother had a headache, and the motion of the gig made it worse. She was trying to bear it so that I might have a drive, but I insisted upon turning back. I took her as far as the orchard, where I left her, and since then I have been driving about by myself and having an awfully good time. Mother did not mind that, as I promised not to go far away. But I think I have now gone far enough along this road. I like driving ever so much! Don't you want me to drive you home?"

"Indeed I do!" said Ralph, and in he jumped.

"I expect Miriam must be enjoying this lovely evening," she said. "And she will see the sun set from the beach, for Barport faces westward, and I never saw a girl enjoy sunsets as she does. At this moment I expect her face is as bright as the sky."

"And wouldn't you like to be standing by her?" asked Ralph.

Cicely shook her head. "No," she said. "To speak truly, I should rather be here. We used to go a good deal to the seashore, but this is the first time that I ever really lived in the country, and it is so charming I would not lose a day of it, and there cannot be very many more days of it, anyway."

"Why not?" asked Ralph.

"I am now copying chapter twenty-seventh of the doctor's book, and there are only thirty-one in all. And as to his other work, that will not occupy me very long."

Ralph was about to ask a question, but, instead, he involuntarily grasped one of the little gloved hands that held the reins.

"Pull that," he said quickly. "You must always turn to the right when you meet a vehicle."

Cicely obeyed, but when they had passed a wagon, drawn by a team of oxen, she said, "But there was more room on the other side."

"That may be," replied Ralph, with a laugh, "but when you are driving, you must not rely too much on your reason, but must follow rules and tradition."

"If I knew as much about driving as I like it," said she, "I should be a famous whip. Before we go, I am going to ask Miriam to take me out with her, two or three times, and give me lessons in driving. She told me that you had taught her a great deal."

"So you would be willing to take your tuition secondhand," said Ralph. "I am a much better teacher than Miriam is."

"Would you like to make up a class?" she asked. "But I do not know how the teacher and the two pupils could ride in this gig. Oh, I see. Miriam and I could sit here, and you could walk by our side and instruct us, and when the one who happened to be driving should make a mistake, she would give up her seat and the reins, and go to the foot of her class."

"Class indeed!" exclaimed Ralph; "I'll have none of it. I will take you out tomorrow and give you a lesson."

So they went gayly on till they came to a grassy hill which shut out the western view.

"Do you think I could go through that gate," asked Cicely, "and drive Mrs. Browning up that hill? There is going to be a grand sunset, and we should get a fine view of it up there."

"No," said Ralph, "let us get out and walk up, and as Mrs. Browning can see the barn, we will not worry her soul by tying her to the fence. I shall let her go home by herself, and you will see how beautifully she will do it."

So they got out, and Ralph having fastened the reins to the dashboard, clicked to the old mare, who walked away by herself. Cicely was greatly interested, and the two stood and watched the sober-minded animal as she made her way home as quietly and properly as if she had been driven. When she entered the gate of the barnyard, and stopped at the stable door, Ralph remarked that she would stand there until Mike came out, and then the two went into the field and walked up the hill.

"I once had a scolding from Miriam for doing that sort of thing," said Ralph; "but you do not seem to object."

"I do not know enough yet," cried Cicely, who had begun to

run up the hill; "wait until I have had my lessons."

They stood together at the top of the little eminence.

"I wonder," said Cicely, "if Miriam ever comes upon this hill at sunset. Perhaps she has never thought of it."

Ralph did not know; but the mention of Miriam's name caused him to think how little he had missed his sister, who had seemed to live in his life as he had lived in hers. It was strange, and he could not believe that he would so easily adapt himself to the changed circumstances of his home life. There was another thing of which he did not think, and that was that he had not missed Dora Bannister. It is true that he had never seen much of that young lady; but he had thought so much about her, and made so many plans in regard to her, and had so often hoped that he might see her drive up to the Cobhurst door, and had had such charming recollections of the hours she had spent in his home, and of the travels they had taken together by photograph, her blue eyes lifted to his as if in truth she leaned upon his arm as they walked through palace and park, that it was wonderful that he did not notice that for days his thoughts had not dwelt upon her.

When the gorgeous color began to fade out of the sky, Cicely said her mother would be wondering what had become of her, and together they went down the hill, and along the roadside, where they stopped to pick some tall sprays of goldenrod, and through the orchard, and around by the barnyard, where Mike was milking, and where Ralph stopped while Cicely went on to the house.

Phoebe was standing down by the entrance gate. She was waiting for an oxcart, whose driver had promised to take her with him on his return to Thorbury. She had arranged with a neighbor to prepare the minister's supper, but she must be on hand to give him his breakfast. As there was nothing to interest her at Cobhurst, and nothing to report, she was glad to go, and considered this oxcart a godsend, for her plan of getting Mike to drive her over in the spring cart had not been met with favor.

Waiting at the gateway, she had seen Ralph and Cicely walk up the hill, and watched them standing together, ever and ever so long, looking at the sky, and she had kept her eyes on them as they came down the hill, stopped to pick flowers which he gave to her, and until they had disappeared among the trees of the orchard.

"Upon my word an' honor!" ejaculated Mrs. Robinson, "if that old French slop-cook hasn't lied to me, wus than Satan could do hisself! If them two ain't lovers, there never was none, an' that old heathen sinner thought she could clap a coffee bag over my head so that I couldn't see nothin' nor tell nothin'. She might as well a' slapped me in the face, the sarpent!"

And unable, by reason of her indignation, to stand still any longer, she walked up the road to meet the returning oxcart, whose wheels could be heard rumbling in the distance.

La Fleur had seen the couple standing together on the little hill, but she had thought it a pity to disturb their tete-a-tete.

CHAPTER XXXVIII

CICELY READS BY MOONLIGHT

Just before Cicely reached the back piazza, La Fleur came out of the kitchen door with the telegram in her hand.

"Do you know," she said, "if Mr. Haverley has come home, and where I can find him? Here is a message for him, and I have been looking for him, high and low."

"A telegram!" exclaimed Cicely. "He is at the barn. I will take it to him. I can get there sooner than you can, La Fleur," and without further word, she took the yellow missive and ran with it toward the barn. She met Ralph half way, and stood by him while he read the message.

"I hope," she cried as she looked into his pale face, "that nothing has happened to Miriam."

"Read that," he said, his voice trembling. "Do you suppose—" but he could not utter the words that were in his mind.

Cicely seized the telegram and eagerly read it. She was on the point of screaming, but checked herself.

"How terrible!" she exclaimed. "But what can it mean? It is from Miss Panney. Oh! I think it is wicked to send a message like that, which does not tell you what has happened."

"It must be Miriam," cried Ralph. "I must go instantly," and at the top of his voice he shouted for Mike. The man soon appeared, running.

"Mike!" exclaimed Ralph, "there has been an accident, something has happened to Miss Miriam. I must go instantly to Barport. I must take the next train from Thorbury. Put the horse to the gig as quickly as you can. You must go with me."

With a face expressing the deepest concern, Mike stood looking at the young man.

"Don't stop for a minute," cried Ralph, in great excitement. "Drop everything. Take the horse, no matter what he has been doing; he can go faster than the mare. I shall be ready in five minutes!"

"Mr. Hav'ley," said Mike, "there ain't no down train stops at Thorbury after the seven-ten, and it's past seven now. That train'll be gone before I can git hitched up."

"No train tonight!" Ralph almost yelled, "that cannot be. I do not believe it."

"Now look here, Mr. Hav'ley," said Mike, "I wouldn't tell you nothin' that wasn't so, 'specially at a time like this. But I've been driving to Thorbury trains an' from 'em, for years and years. There's a late train 'bout ten o'clock, but it's a through express and don't stop."

"I must take that train," cried Ralph, "what is the nearest station where it does stop?"

"There ain't none nearer than the Junction, and that's sixteen miles up, an' a dreadful road. I once druv there in the daytime, an' it tuk me four hours, an' if you went to-night you couldn't get there afore daylight."

"Why don't you go to Thorbury and telegraph?" asked Cicely,

who was now almost as pale as Ralph. "Then you could find out exactly what has happened."

"Oh, I must go, I must go," said Ralph; "but I shall telegraph. I shall go to Thorbury instantly, and get on as soon as I can."

Mike stood looking on the ground.

"Mr. Hav'ley," he said, as the young man was about to hurry to the house, "tain't no use, the telegraph office is shet up, right after that down train passes."

"It is barbarous!" exclaimed Ralph. "I will go anyway. I will find the operator."

"Mr. Hav'ley," said Mike, "don't you go an' do that. You is tremblin' like a asp. You'll be struck down sick if you go on so. There's a train a quarter of six in the mornin', an' I'll git you over to that. If you goes to Thorbury, you won't be fit to travel in the mornin', an' you won't be no good when you gits there."

Tears were now on Cicely's cheeks, in spite of her efforts to restrain herself.

"He is right, Mr. Ralph," she said. "I think it will be dreadful for you to be in Thorbury all night, and most likely for no good. It will be a great deal better to leave here early in the morning and go straight to Barport. But let us go into the house and talk to mother. After all, it may not be Miriam. You cannot tell what it is. It is a cruel message."

Mrs. Drane was greatly shocked, but she agreed with her daughter that it would not be wise for Ralph to go to Thorbury until he could start for Barport. La Fleur was somewhat frightened when she found that her wilful delay of the telegram might occasion Mr. Haverley an harassing and anxious night in Thorbury, and was urgent in her endeavors to quiet him and persuade him to remain at home until morning.

But it was not until Cicely had put in her last plea that the young man consented to give up his intention of going in search of the telegraph operator.

"Mr. Ralph," said she, "don't you think it would be awful if you were to send a message and get a bad answer to it, and have to stay there by yourself until the morning? I cannot bear to think of it; and telegraphic messages are always so hard and cruel. If I were you, I would rather go straight on and find out everything for myself."

Ralph looked down at her and at the tears upon her cheeks.

"I will do that," he said, and taking her hand, he pressed it thankfully.

Every preparation and arrangement was made for an early start, and Ralph wandered in and out of the house, impatient as a wild beast to break away and be gone. Cicely, whose soul was full of his sorrow, went out to him on the piazza, where he stood, looking at the late moon rising above the treetops.

"What a different man I should be," he said, "if I could think that Miriam was standing on the seashore and looking at that moon."

Cicely longed to comfort him, but she could not say anything which would seem to have reason in it. She had tried to think that it might be possible that the despatch might not concern Miriam, but she could not do it. If it had been necessary to send a despatch and Miriam had been alive and well, it would have been from her that the despatch would have come. Cicely's soul was sick with sorrow and with dread, not only for the brother, but for herself, for she and Miriam were now fast friends. But she controlled herself, and looking up with a smile, said, "What time is it?"

Ralph took out his watch and held the face of it toward the moon, which was but little past the full.

"It is a quarter to nine," he said.

"Well, then," said she, "I will ask Miriam, when I see her, if she was looking at the moon at this time."

"Do you believe," exclaimed Ralph, turning suddenly so that they stood face to face, "do you truly believe that we shall ever see her again?"

The question was so abrupt that Cicely was taken unawares. She raised her face toward the eager eyes bent upon her, but the courageous words she wished to utter would not come, and she drooped her head. With a swift movement, Ralph put his two hands upon her cheeks and gently raised her face. He need not have looked at her, for the warm tears ran down upon his hands.

"You do not," he said; and as he gazed down upon her, her face became dim. For the first time since his boyhood, tears filled his eyes.

At a quick sound of hoofs and wheels, both started; and the next moment the telegraph boy drove up close to the railing and held up a yellow envelope.

"One dollar for delivery," said he; "that's night rates. This come jest as the office was shetting up, and Mr. Martin said I'd got to deliver it to-night; but I couldn't come till the moon was up."

Cicely, who was nearer, seized the telegram before Ralph could get it.

"Drive round to the back of the house," she said to the boy, "and I will bring you the money."

She held the telegram, though Ralph had seized it.

"Don't be too quick," she said, "don't be too quick. There,

you will tear it in half. Let me open it for you."

She deftly drew the envelope from his hand, and spread the telegram on the broad rail of the piazza, on which the moon shone full. Instantly their heads were close together.

"I cannot read it," groaned Ralph; "my eyes are—"

"I can," interrupted Cicely, and she read aloud the message, which ran thus,—

"Fear news of accident may trouble you. We are all well. Have written. Miriam Haverley."

Ralph started back and stood upright, as if some one had shouted to him from the sky. He said not one word, but Cicely gave a cry of joy. Ralph turned toward her, and as he saw her face, irradiated by the moonlight and her sudden happiness, he looked down upon her for one moment, and then his arms were outstretched toward her; but, quick as was his motion, her thought was quicker, and before he could touch her, she had darted back with the telegram in her hand.

"I will show this to mother," she cried, and was in the house in an instant.

La Fleur was in the hall, where for some time she had been quietly standing, looking out upon the moonlight. From her position, which was not a conspicuous one, at the door of the enclosed stairway, she had been able to keep her eyes upon Ralph and Cicely; and held herself ready, should she hear Mrs. Drane coming down the stairs, to go up and engage her in a consultation in regard to domestic arrangements. She had known of the arrival of the telegraph boy, had seen what followed, and now listened with rapt delight to Cicely's almost breathless announcement of the joyful news.

After the girl went upstairs, La Fleur walked away; there was no need for her to stand guard any longer.

"It isn't only the telegram," she said to herself, "that makes her face shine and her voice quiver like that." Then she went out to congratulate Mr. Haverley on the news from his sister. But the young man was not there; his soul was too full for the restraints of a house or a roof, and he had gone out, bareheaded, into the moonlight to be alone with his happiness and to try to understand it.

When Mrs. Drane returned to her room, having gone down at her daughter's request to pay the telegraph messenger, she found her daughter lying on a couch, her face wet with tears. But in ten minutes Cicely was sitting up and chattering gayly. The good lady was rejoiced to know that there was no foundation for the evils they had feared, but she could not understand why her daughter, usually a cool-headed little thing and used to self-control, should be so affected by the news. And in the morning she was positively frightened when Cicely informed her that she had not slept a wink all night.

Mrs. Drane had not seen Ralph's face when he stretched out his arms toward her daughter.

CHAPTER XXXIX

UNDISTURBED LETTUCE

When Ralph Haverley came in from his long moonlight ramble, he was so happy that he went to bed and slept as sound as rock. But before he closed his eyes he said to himself,—

"I will do that to-morrow; the very first thing to-morrow."

But people do not always do what they intend to do the very first thing in the morning, and this was the case with Ralph. La Fleur, who knew that a letter was expected, sent Mike early to the post-office, and soon after breakfast Ralph had a letter from Miriam. It was a long one; it gave a full account of the drowning accident and of some of her own experiences, but it said not one word of the message sent by Miss Panney, to whom Miriam alluded very slightly. It gave, however, the important information that Mrs. Bannister had been so affected by the dreadful scene on the beach that she declared she could not go into the ocean again, nor even bear the sight of it, and that, therefore, they were all coming home on the morrow.

"She will be here to-night," said Ralph, who knew the trains from Barport.

As soon as he had read the letter Ralph went to look for Cicely. She had come down late to breakfast, and he had been

Frank Richard Stockton

surprised at her soberness of manner. On the other hand, Mrs. Drane had been surprised at Ralph's soberness of manner, and she found herself in the unusual position of the liveliest person at the breakfast table.

"People who have heard such good news ought to be very happy," she thought, but she made no remark on the subject.

It was Cicely's custom to spend the brief time she allowed herself between breakfast and work, upon the lawn, or somewhere out of doors, but to-day Ralph searched in vain for her. He met La Fleur, however, and that conscientious cook, in her most respectful manner, asked him, if he happened to meet Miss Cicely, would he be so good as to give her a message?

"But I don't know where she is," said Ralph. "I have a letter to show her."

La Fleur wished very much to know what was in the letter, which, she supposed, explained the mystery of the telegrams, but at a moment like this she would not ask.

"She is in the garden, sir," she said. "I asked her to gather me some lettuce for luncheon. She does it so much more nicely than I could do it, or Mike. She selects the crispest and most tender leaves of that crimped and curled lettuce you all like so much, and I thought I would ask you, sir, if you met her, to be so very kind as to tell her that I would like a few sprigs of parsley, just a very few. I would go myself, sir, but there is something cooking which I cannot leave, and I beg your pardon for troubling you and will thank you, sir, very much if you—"

It was not worth while for her to finish her sentence, for Ralph had gone.

He found Cicely just as she stooped over the lettuce bed. She rose with a face like a peach blossom.

"I have a letter from Miriam," he said, "I will give it to you presently, and you may read the whole of it, but I must first tell you that she, with Mrs. Bannister and Dora, are coming home to-day. They will reach Thorbury late this afternoon. Isn't that glorious?"

All the delicate hues of the peach blossom went out of Cicely's face. That everlasting person had come up again, and now he called her Dora, and it was glorious to have her back! She did not have to say anything, for Ralph went rapidly on.

"But before they leave Barport," he said, "I want to send Miriam a telegram. If Mike takes it immediately to Thorbury, she will get it before her train leaves."

"A telegram!" exclaimed Cicely, but she did not look up at him.

"Yes," said he; "I want to telegraph to Miriam that you and I are engaged to be married. I want her to know it before she gets here. Shall I send it?"

She raised to him a face more brightly hued than any peach blossom—rich with the color of the ripe fruit. Ten minutes after this, two wood doves, sitting in a tree to the east of the lettuce bed, and looking westward, turned around on their twig and looked toward the east. They were sunny-minded little creatures, and did not like to be cast into the shade.

As they went out of the garden gate, Cicely said, "You have always been a very independent person and accustomed to doing very much as you please, haven't you?"

"It has been something like that," answered Ralph; "but why?"

"Only this," she said; "would you begin already to chafe and rebel if I were to ask you not to send that telegram? It would be so much nicer to tell her after she gets back."

"Chafe!" exclaimed Ralph, "I should think not. I will do exactly as you wish."

"You are awfully good," said Cicely, "but you must agree with me more prudently now that we are out here, and I will not tell mother until Miriam knows."

A gray old chanticleer, who was leading his hens across the yard, stopped at this moment and looked at Ralph, but it is not certain that he sniffed.

Ralph knew very well when people, coming from Barport, should arrive in Thorbury, but his mind was so occupied that when he went to the barn, he forgot so many things he should have done at the house, and he ran backward and forward so often, and waited so long for an opportunity to say something he had just thought of, to somebody who did not happen to be ready to listen at the precise moment he wished to speak, that he had just stepped into the gig to go to the station for his sister, when Miriam arrived alone in the Bannister carriage. Not finding anybody at the station to meet her, they had sent her on.

Mrs. Drane was not the liveliest person at the dinner table, and she wondered much how Ralph and Cicely, who had been so extremely sober at breakfast time, should now be so hilarious. The arrival of Miriam seemed hardly reason enough for such intemperate gayety.

As for Miriam, she overflowed with delight. The ocean was grand, but Cobhurst was Cobhurst. "There was nothing better about my trip than the opportunity it gave me of coming back to my home. I never did that before, you know, my children."

This she said loftily from her seat at the head of the table. Dinner was late and lasted long, and Ralph had gone into the room on the lower floor, in which he kept his cigars, and which he called his office, when Miriam followed him. There was no unencumbered chair, and she seated herself on the edge of the table.

"Ralph," said she, "I want to say something to you, now, while it is fresh in my mind. I think we can sometimes understand our affairs better when we go away from them and are not mixed up in them. I have been thinking a great deal since I have been at Barport about our affairs here, not only as they are but as they may be, and most likely will be, and I have come to the conclusion that some of these days, Ralph, you will want to be married."

"Do you mean me?" cried Ralph. "You amaze me!"

"Oh, you are only a man, and you need not be amazed," said his sister. "This is the way I have been thinking of it: if you ever do want to get married, I hope you will not marry Dora Bannister. I used sometimes to think that that might be a good thing to do, though I changed my mind very often about it, but I do not think so, now, at all. Dora is an awfully nice girl in ever so many ways, but since I have been at Barport with her, I am positive that I do not want you to marry her."

Ralph heaved a long sigh and put his hands in his pockets.

"Bless my soul!" he exclaimed, "this is very discouraging; if I do not marry Dora, who is there that I can marry?"

"You goose," said his sister, "there is a girl here, under your very nose, ever so much nicer and more suitable for you than Dora. If you marry anybody, marry Cicely Drane. I have been thinking ever and ever so much about her and about you, and I made up my mind to speak to you of this as soon as I got home, so that you might have a chance to think about it before you should see Dora. Don't you remember what you used to tell me about the time when you were obliged to travel so much, and how, when you had a seat to yourself in a car, and a crowd of people were coming in, you used to make room for the first nice person you saw, because you knew you would have to have somebody sitting alongside of you, and you liked to choose for yourself? Now that is the way I feel about your getting married; if you marry Cicely Drane, I shall feel safe for the rest of my life."

"Miriam!" exclaimed Ralph, "you astonish me by the force of your statements. Wait here one moment," and he ran into the hall through which he had seen Cicely passing, and presently reappeared with her.

"Miss Drane," said he, "do you know that my sister thinks that I ought to marry you?"

In an instant Miriam had slipped from the table to the floor.

"Good gracious, Ralph!" she cried. "What do you mean?"

"I am merely stating your advice," he answered; "and now, Miss Drane, how does it strike you?"

"Well," said Cicely, demurely, "if your sister really thinks we should marry, I suppose—I suppose we ought to do it."

Miriam's eyes flashed from one to the other, then there were two girlish cries and a manly laugh, and in a moment Miriam and Cicely were in each other's arms, while Ralph's arms were around them both.

"Now," said Cicely, when this group had separated itself into its several parts, "I must run up and tell mother." And very soon Mrs. Drane understood why there had been sobriety at breakfast and hilarity at dinner. She was surprised, but felt she ought not to be; she was a little depressed, but knew she would get over that.

La Fleur did not hear the news that night, but it was not necessary; she had seen Ralph and Cicely coming through the garden gate without a leaf of lettuce or a single sprig of parsley.

CHAPTER XL

ANGRY WAVES

The ocean rolled angrily on the beach, and Miss Panney walked angrily on the beach, a little higher up, however, than the line to which the ocean rolled.

The old lady was angrier than the ocean, and it was much more than mere wind that made her storm waves roll. Her indignation was directed first against Mrs. Bannister, that silly woman, who, by cutting short her stay at the seashore, had ruined Miss Panney's plans, and also against Ralph, who had not come to Barport as soon as he had received the telegram. If he had arrived, the party might have stayed a little longer for his sake. Why he had not come she knew no more than she knew what she was going to say to him in explanation of her message, and she cared as little for the one as for the other.

Her own visit to Barport had been utterly useless. She had spent money and time, she had tired herself, had been frightened and disgusted,—all for nothing. She did not remember any of her plans that had failed so utterly.

Meeting the bathing-master, she rolled in upon him some ireful waves, because he did not keep a boat outside the breakers to pick up people who might be exhausted and in danger of drowning. In vain the man protested that ten thousand people had said that to him, before, and that the thing could not be done, because so many swimmers would make for the boat and hang on to its sides, just to rest themselves until they were ready to go back. It would simply be a temptation to people to swim beyond the breakers. She went on, in a voice that the noise of the surf could not drown, to tell him that she hoped ten thousand more people would say the same thing to him, and to declare that he ought to have several boats outside during bathing hours, so that people could cling to some of them, and so, perhaps, save themselves from exhaustion on their return, and so that one, at least, could be kept free to succor the distressed. At last the poor man vowed that he acted under orders, and that, if she wanted to pitch into anybody, she ought to pitch into the proprietors of the hotel who employed him, and who told him what he must do.

Miss Panney accepted this advice; and if the sea had broken into the private office of that hotel, the owners and managers could not have had a worse time than they had during the old lady's visit. It may be stated that for the remainder of the season two or three boats might always be seen outside the breakers during bathing hours at the Barport beach.

For the sake of appearances, Miss Panney did not leave Barport immediately; for she did not wish her friends to think that she was a woman who would run after the Bannisters wherever they might please to go. But in a reasonable time she found herself in the Witton household, and the maid who had charge of her room had some lively minutes after the arrival of the old lady therein.

The next day she went to Thorbury to see what had happened, and chanced to spy Phoebe resting herself on a bench at the edge of the public green. Instantly the colored woman sprang to her feet, and began to explain to Miss Panney why she had not made her report before the latter set out on her journey.

"You see, ma'am, I hadn't no shoes as was fit for that long walk out in the country, an' I had to take my best ones to the shoemaker; and though I did my best to make him hurry, it took him a whole day, an' so I had to put off going to Cobhurst, an' I've never got over my walk out thar yit. My j'ints has creaked ever sense."

"If you used them more, they would creak less," snapped Miss Panney. "How are things going on at Cobhurst? What did you see there?"

"I seed a lot, an' I heard a lot," the colored woman answered. "Mike's purty nigh starved, an' does his own washin'. An' things are in that state in the house that would make you sick, Miss Panney, if you could see them. What the rain doesn't wash goes dirty; an' as for that old cook they've got, if she isn't drunk all the time, her mind's givin' way, an' I expect she'll end by pizenin' all of them. The vittles she gave me to eat, bein' nearly tired to death when I got thar, was sich that they give me pains that I hain't got over yit. And what would have happened if I'd eat a full meal, nobody knows."

"Get out with you," cried Miss Panney. "I don't want any more of your jealousy and spite. If that woman gave you anything to eat, I expect it was the only decently cooked thing you ever put into your mouth. Did you see Mr. Haverley? Were the Drane women still there? How were they all getting on together?"

Phoebe's eyes sparkled, and her voice took in a little shrillness.

"I was goin' to git the minister to write you a letter 'bout that, Miss Panney," said she; "but you didn't tell me whar you was goin', nor give me no money for stamps nor nothin'. But I kin say to you now that that woman, which some people may call a cook, but I don't, she told me, without my askin' a word 'bout nothin', that Mr. Hav'ley an' that little Miss Drane was to be married in the fall, an' that they was goin' away, all of them, to the wife's mother's to live, bein' that that old farm out thar didn't pay to run, an' never would. I reckoned they'd git sick of it afore this, which I always said."

"Phoebe!" exclaimed Miss Panney, "I do not believe a word of all that! How dare you tell me such a lot of lies?"

Phoebe was getting very angry, though she did not dare to show it; but instead of taking back anything she had said, she put on more lie-power.

"You may believe me, Miss Panney, or you needn't; that's just as you choose," she said "but I can tell you more than I have told you, and that is, that from what I've seen and heard, I believe Mr. Hav'ley an' Miss Drane is married already, an' that they was only waitin' for the Tolbridges to come home to send out the cards."

Miss Panney glared at the woman. "I tell you what I believe, and that is that you never went to Cobhurst at all. You must tell me something, and you are making up the biggest story you can," and with this she marched away.

"I reckon the next time she sends me on an arrand," thought Phoebe, whose face would have been very red if her natural color had not interfered with the exhibition of such a hue, "she'll send me in a hack, and pay me somethin' for my time. I was bound to tell her 'zactly what she didn't want to hear, an' I reckon I done it, an' more'n that if she gets her back up 'bout this, an' goes out to Cobhurst, that old cook'll find herself in hot water. It was mighty plain that she was dreadful skeered for fear anybody would think thar was somethin' goin' on 'twixt them two."

If Phoebe had been more moderate in her doubleheaded treachery, Miss Panney might have been much disturbed by her news, but the story she had heard was so preposterous that she really believed that the lazy colored woman had not gone to Cobhurst, and by the time she reached the Bannister house her mind was cleared for the reception of fresh impressions.

She was fortunate enough to find Dora alone, and as soon as it was prudent she asked her what news she had heard from

Cobhurst. Dora was looking her loveliest in an early autumn costume, and answered that she had heard nothing at all, which surprised Miss Panney very much, for she had expected that Miriam would have been to see Dora before this time.

"Common politeness would dictate that," said Miss Panney, "but I expect that that child is so elated and excited by getting back to the head of her household that everything else has slipped out of her mind. But if you two are such close friends, I don't think you ought to mind that sort of thing. If I were you, I would go out and see her. Eccentric people must be humored."

"They needn't expect that from me," said Dora, a little sharply. "If Miriam lived there by herself, I might go; but as it is, I shall not. It is their duty to come here, and I shall not go there until they do."

Miss Panney drummed upon the table, but otherwise did not show her impatience.

"We can never live the life we ought in this world, my dear," she said, "if we allow our sensitive fancies to interfere with the advancement of our interests."

"Miss Panney," cried Dora, sitting upright in her chair, "do you mean that I ought to go out there, and try to catch Ralph Haverley, no matter how they treat me?"

"Yes," said Miss Panney, leaning back in her chair, "that is exactly what I mean. There is no use of our mincing matters, and as I hold that it is the duty of every young woman to get herself well married, I think it is your duty to marry Mr. Haverley if you can. You will never meet a man better suited to you, and who can use your money with as much advantage to yourself. I do not mean that you should go and make love to him, or anything of that sort. I simply mean that you should allow him to expose himself to your influences."

"I shall do nothing of the kind!" cried Dora, her face in a flush; "if he wants that sort of exposure, let him come here. I don't know whether I want him to come or not. I am too young to be thinking of marrying anybody, and though I don't want to be disrespectful to you, Miss Panney, I will say that I am getting dreadfully tired of your continual harping about Ralph Haverley, and trying to make me push myself in front of him so that his lordship may look at me. If he had been at Barport, or there had been any chance of his coming there, I should have suspected that you went there for the express purpose of keeping us up to the work of becoming attached to each other. And I say plainly that I shall have no more to do with exerting influence on him, through his sister or in any other way. There are thousands of other men just as good as he is, and if I have not met any of them yet, I have no doubt I shall do so."

"Dora," said Miss Panney, speaking very gently, "you are wrong when you say that there was no chance of Ralph's coming to Barport. If some things had not gone wrong, I have reason to believe he would have been there before you left, and I am quite sure that if you had stayed there until now, you would have been walking on the sands with him at this minute."

Dora looked at her in surprise, and the flush on her face subsided a little.

"What do you mean?" she asked. "You do not think he would have gone there on my account?"

"Yes, I do," said Miss Panney. "That is exactly what I mean, and now, my dear Dora, do not let—"

At this moment Mrs. Bannister walked into the room, and was very glad to see Miss Panney, and to know that she had returned in safety from the seashore.

When Dora went up to her room, after the visitor had gone, she shut the door and sat down to think.

"After all," she said to herself, "I do not believe much in the thousand other men. Not one of them is here, and none may ever come, and if Ralph really did intend to come to me at the seashore, I wish we had stayed there. It is such a good place to find out just how people feel."

In this frame of mind she sat and thought and thought, until a servant, who had been to the post office, came up and brought her a note from Miriam Haverley.

The next morning Dora Bannister, in an open carriage, drawn by the family bays, appeared at the door of the Witton mansion. Miss Panney, with overshoes on and a little shawl about her, for the mornings were beginning to be cool, was walking up and down between two rows of old-fashioned boxwood bushes. She hurried forward, for she knew very well that Dora had not come to call on the Wittons.

"Miss Panney," said the young lady, "I am on my way to Cobhurst, and I thought you might like to go there, and so if you choose, I shall be glad to take you with me."

"Now, my dear girl," said Miss Panney, "you are a trump. I always thought you were, but I will not say anything more about that. I shall be delighted to go with you, and we can talk on the way. If you will come in or take a seat on the piazza, I shall be ready in five minutes."

As Miss Panney busied herself preparing for the drive and the call, her mind was a great deal more active than her rapid fingers. She had been intending to go to Cobhurst, but did not wish to do so until she had decided what she should say to Ralph about the telegram she had sent him. Until that morning, this had given her very little concern, but as the time approached when it would be absolutely necessary to speak upon the subject, she found that she was a good deal concerned about it. She saw that it was very important that nothing should be said to rouse Ralph into opposition.

But now everything seemed bright and clear before her. After Dora, looking perfectly lovely, as she did this morning, had shone upon Ralph for half an hour, or even less, the old lady felt that if the young man asked her any questions about her telegram she would not in the least mind telling him how she came to send it, giving him, of course, a version of her motive which would make him understand her anxious solicitude, in case anything had happened to any one dear to him, that his arrival should not be delayed an instant, as well as the sympathetic delight she would have felt in witnessing the joy his presence in Barport would cause to the dear ones, alive and well.

This somewhat complicated explanation might need policy and alteration, but Miss Panney now felt quite ready for anything Ralph might ask about the telegram. If any one else asked any questions, she would answer as happened to please her.

As they drove away Miss Panney immediately began to congratulate Dora on her return to her senses. She was in high good humor, "You ought to know, my dear, that if the loveliest woman in the world found herself stuck in a quagmire, it would be quite foolish for her to expect that the right sort of man would come and pull her out. In all probability it would be precisely the wrong sort of man who would do it. Consequently, it would be wise in her if she saw the right sort of man going by, not only to let him know that she was there, but to let him understand that she was worth pulling out. All women are born in a quagmire, and some are so anxious to get out that they take the first hand that is stretched toward them, and some, I am sorry to say, never get out at all. But they are the wise ones who do not leave it to chance, who shall be their liberators. Number yourself, my dear, among this happy class. I am so glad it is cool enough this morning for you to wear that lovely costume. It is as likely as not that by tomorrow it will be too warm. All these little things tell, my child, and I am glad to know that even the thermometer is your friend."

"I had a letter from Miriam yesterday afternoon," said Dora, "in which she told me that her brother Ralph is engaged to Miss Drane."

Miss Panney turned around like a weather vane struck by a squall. She seized the girl's arm with her bony fingers.

"What!" she exclaimed.

Ordinarily, the pain of the old lady's grasp would have made Dora wince, but she did not seem to feel it. Without the slightest sign of emotion in her face, she answered,—

"It is so. It happened while I was at Barport."

"Stop!" cried Miss Panney, in a voice that made the driver pull up his horses with a jerk. In a moment she had stepped from the low carriage to the ground, and with quick strides was walking back to the Witton house. Dora turned in the seat, looked after her, and laughed. It was a sudden, bitter laugh, which the circumstances made derisive.

Never before had Miss Panney's soul been so stung, burned, and lacerated, all at once, as by this laugh. But the sound had scarcely left Dora Bannister's lips when she bounded out of the carriage and ran after the old lady. Throwing her arms around her neck, she kissed her on the cheek.

"I am awfully sorry I did that," she said, "and I beg your pardon. I don't mind the thing a bit, and won't you let me take you home in the carriage?"

Dora might as well have embraced a milestone and talked to it, for the moment she could release herself, Miss Panney stalked away without a word.

When she was again driving toward Cobhurst, Dora took from the front of the carriage a little hand mirror, and carefully arranged her hat, her feathers, her laces and ribbons. Then having satisfied herself that her features were in perfect order, she put back her glass.

"I am not going to let any of them see," she said, "that I mind it in the least."

CHAPTER XLI

PANNEYOPATHY AND THE ASH-HOLE

Neither Ralph nor his sister nor either of the Drane ladies had the least reason to believe that Dora minded the news contained in Miriam's note, except that it had given her a heartfelt delight and joy, and that it had made her unable to wait a single moment longer than was necessary to come and tell them all how earnestly she congratulated them, and what a capital good thing she thought it was. She caught Ralph by himself and spoke to him so much like a sympathetic sister that he was a little, just the least little bit in the world, pained.

As Cicely had never had any objection to Miss Bannister, excepting her frequent appearances in Ralph's conversation, she received Dora's felicitations with the same cordiality that she saw in her lovely eyes and on her lips. And Mrs. Drane thought that if this girl were a sample of the Haverleys' friends and neighbors, her daughter's lot would be even more pleasant than she had supposed it would be. As for Miriam, she and Dora walked together, their arms around each other's waists, up and down in the garden, and back and forward in the orchard, until the Bannister coachman went to sleep on his box.

During this long interview, the younger girl became impressed, not only with the fact that Dora thought so well of the match, that, if she had been looking for a wife for Ralph, she certainly would have selected Miss Drane, but with the stability of Miss

Frank Richard Stockton

Bannister's affection for her, which did not seem to be affected in the least by the changes which would take place in the composition of the Cobhurst household. Dora had said, indeed, that she had no doubt that she and Miriam would be more intimate than ever, because Mr. Haverley would be so monopolized by his wife.

This was all very pleasant to Miriam, but it did not in the least cause her to regret Ralph's choice. Dora was a lovely girl, but it was now plainer than ever that she was also a very superior one, whereas Cicely was just like other people and did not pretend to be anything more, and, moreover, she would not have wished her brother to marry anyone whose idea of matrimony was the monopoly of her husband, and she knew that Cicely had no such idea. But Dora was the dearest of good friends, Miriam was very sure of that.

The Bannister carriage had scarcely left the Cobhurst gates when the dog, Congo, came bounding after it. Dora looked at him as his great brown eyes were turned up towards her, and his tail was wagging with the joy of following her once more, she knew that his training was so good that she had only to tell him to go back and he would obey her, sorrowfully, with his tail hanging down. He was Ralph's dog now, and she ought to send him back, but would she? She looked at him for a few moments, considering the question, and then she said,—

"Come, Congo" and with a bound he was in the carriage and at her feet. "You were not an out and out gift, poor fellow," she said, stroking his head. "I expected you to be partly my dog, all the same, and now we will see if she will let him claim you."

The dog heard all this, but Dora spoke so low, the coachman could not hear it, and she did not intend that any one else should know it unless the dog told.

Ralph did not miss Congo until the next morning, and then, having become convinced that the dog must have followed the

Bannister carriage, he expressed, in the presence of Cicely, his uncertainty as to whether it would be better for him to go after the dog himself, or to send Mike.

"If I were you," said Miss Cicely, "I would not send for him at all. If Miss Bannister really wants to get rid of him, and does not know anybody else who would take him, she may send him back herself. But it seems to me that a setter is not the best sort of a dog for a farm like this. I should think you ought to have a big mastiff, or something of that sort."

"It is a great pity," said Ralph, musingly, "that he happened to be unchained."

"The more I think about it," said Cicely, "the less I like setters. They are so intimately connected with the death of the beautiful. Did you ever think of that?"

Ralph never had, and as a man now came up to talk to him about hay, the dog and everything connected with it passed out of his mind.

When Miss Panney reached home after her abrupt parting from Dora Bannister, she took a dose of the last medicine that Dr. Tolbridge had prescribed for her. It was against her rules to use internal medicines, but she made exceptions on important occasions, and as this was a remedy for the effects of anger, she had taken it before and she took it now. Then she went to bed and there she stayed until three o'clock the next afternoon. This greatly disturbed the Wittons, for they had always believed that this hearty old lady would not be carried off by any disease, but when her time had come would simply take to her bed and die there, after the manner of elderly animals.

About the middle of the afternoon Mrs. Witton came up into her room. She did not do this often, for the old lady had always made everybody in the house understand that this room was her castle, and when any one was wanted there, he or she would be summoned.

"You must be feeling very badly," said the meek and anxious Mrs. Witton "don't you think it would be better to send for a doctor?"

"There is no doctor," said Miss Panney, shortly.

"Oh yes," said the other, "there are several excellent doctors in Thorbury, and Dr. Parker takes all of Dr. Tolbridge's practice while he is away."

"Stuff!" remarked Miss Panney. "I spanked Dr. Parker, when he wore little frocks, for running his tin wheelbarrow against me so that I nearly fell over it."

"But he has learned a great deal since then," pleaded Mrs. Witton "and if you do not want any new doctors, isn't there something I can do for you? If you will tell me how you feel, it may be that some sort of herb tea—or a mustard plaster—"

"Gammon and spinach!" cried Miss Panney, throwing off the bedclothes as if she were about to spring into the middle of the floor. "I want no teas nor plasters. I have had as much sleep as I care for, and now I am going to get up. So trot downstairs, if you please, and tell Margaret to bring me up some hot water."

For an hour or two before supper time, Miss Panney occupied herself in clearing out her medicine closet. Every bottle, jar, vial, box, or package it contained was placed upon a large table and divided into two collections. One consisted of the lotions and medicines prescribed for her by Dr. Tolbridge, and the other of those she herself, in the course of many years, had ordered or compounded,—not only for her own use, but for that of others. She had long prided herself on her skill in this sort of thing, and was always willing to prepare almost any sort of medicine for ailing people, asking nothing in payment but the pleasure of seeing them take it.

When everything had been examined and placed on its appropriate end of the table, Miss Panney called for an empty coalscuttle, into which she tumbled, without regard to spilling or breakage, the whole mass of medicaments which had been prepared or prescribed by herself, and she then requested the servant to deposit the contents of the scuttle in the ash-hole.

"After this," she said to herself, "I will get somebody else to do my concocting," and she carefully replaced her physician's medicines on the shelves.

It was three days later when Miss Panney was told that Dr. Tolbridge was in the parlor and wished to see her.

"Well," said the old lady, as she entered the parlor, "I supposed that after your last call here, you would not come again."

"Oh, bless my soul!" said the doctor, "I haven't any time to consider what has happened, I must give my whole attention to what is happening or may happen. How are you? and how have you been during my absence?"

"Oh, I had medicines enough" said she, "if I had needed them, but I didn't."

"Well, I wanted to see for myself, and, besides, I was obliged to come," said the doctor; "I want to know what has happened since we left. We got home late last night, and I have not seen anybody who knows anything."

"And so," said the old lady, "you will swallow an insult in order to gratify your curiosity."

"Insult, indeed!" said he. "I have a regular rule about insults. When anybody under thirty insults me, I give her a piece of my mind if she is a woman, and a taste of my horsewhip if he is a man. But between thirty and fifty, I am very careful about my resentments, because people are then very likely to be cracked or damaged in some way or other, either in body or mind, and unless I am very cautious, I may do more injury than I intend. But toward folks over fifty, especially when they are old friends, I have no resentments at all. I simply button up my coat and turn up my collar, and let the storm pelt; and when it is fine weather again, I generally find that I have forgotten that it ever rained."

"And when a person is in the neighborhood of seventy-five, I suppose you thank her kindly for a good slap in the face."

The doctor laughed heartily.

"Precisely," said he. "And now tell me what has happened. You are all right, I see. How are the Cobhurst people getting on?"

"Oh, well enough," said Miss Panney. "The young man and that Cicely Drane of yours have agreed to marry each other, and I suppose the old lady will live with them, and Miriam will have to get down from her high horse and agree to play second fiddle, or go to school again. She is too young for anything else."

The doctor stared. "You amaze me!" he cried.

"Oh, you needn't be amazed," said Miss Panney; "I did it!"

"You?" said the doctor, "I thought you wanted him to marry Dora."

"If you thought that," said Miss Panney, flashing her black eyes upon him, "why did you lend yourself to such an underhanded piece of business as the sending of that Drane girl there?"

"Oh, bless my soul!" exclaimed the doctor, "I did not lend myself to anything. I did not send her there to be married. Let us drop that, and tell me how you came to change your mind."

"I have a rule about dropping things," said the old lady, "and with people of vigorous intellect, I never do it, but when any one is getting on in years and a little soft-minded, so that he does what he is told to do without being able to see the consequences of it, I pity him and drop the subject which worries his conscience. I have not changed my mind in the least. I still think that Dora would be the best wife young Haverley could have, and after I found that you had added to your treacheries or stupidities, or whatever they were, by carrying her off to Barport, I intended to take advantage of the situation, so I got Dora to invite Miriam there, feeling sure that the Drane women would have sense enough to know that they then ought to leave Cobhurst; but they had not sense enough, and they stayed there. Then I saw that the situation was critical, and went to Barport myself, and sent the young man a telegram that would have aroused the heart of a feather-bed and made it be with me in three hours, but it did not rouse him and he did not come; and before that silly Mrs. Bannister got back with the two girls, the mischief was done, and that little Drane had taken advantage of the opportunity I had given her to trap Mr. Ralph. Oh, she is a sharp one! and with you and me to help her, she could do almost anything. You take off her rival, and I send away the interfering sister; and all she has to do is to snap up the young man, while her mother and that illustrious cook of yours stand by and clap their hands. But I do not give you much credit. You are merely an inconsiderate blunderer, to say no more. You did not plan anything; I did that, and when my plans don't work one way, they do in another. This one was like a boomerang that did not hit what it was aimed at, but came banging and clattering back all the same. And now I will remark that I have given up that sort of thing. I can throw as well as ever, but I am too old to stand the back-cracks."

"You are not too old for anything," said the doctor, "and you and I will do a lot of planning yet. But tell me one thing; do you think that this Haverley-Drane combination is going to deprive me of La Fleur?"

"Upon my word!" cried the old lady, springing to her feet,

"never did I see a man so steeped in selfishness. Not a word of sympathy for me! In all this unfortunate affair, you think of nothing but the danger of losing your cook! Well, I am happy to say you are going to lose her. That will be your punishment, and well you deserve it. She will no more think of staying with you, after the Dranes set up housekeeping at Cobhurst, than I would think of coming to cook for you. And so you may go back to your soggy bread, and your greasy fries, and your dishwater coffee, and get yellow and green in the face, thin in the legs, and weak in the stomach, and have good reason to say to yourself that if you had let Miss Panney alone, and let her work out that excellent plan she had confided to you, you would have lived to a healthy old age, with the best cook in this part of the country making you happy three times a day, and satisfied with the world between meals."

"Deal gently with the erring," said the doctor. "Don't crush me. I want to go to Cobhurst this morning, to see them all, and find out my fate. Wouldn't you like to go with me? I have a visit to make, two or three miles above here, but I shall be back soon, and will drive you over. What do you say?"

"Very good," said Miss Panney. "I have been thinking of calling on the happy family."

As soon as the doctor had departed Miss Panney ordered her phaeton.

"I intended going to Cobhurst to-day," she said to herself, "but I do not propose to go with him. I shall get there first and see how the land lies, before he comes to muddle up things with his sordid anxieties about his future victuals and drink."

CHAPTER XLII

AN INTERVIEWER

The roan mare travelled well that morning, and Miss Panney was at Cobhurst before the doctor reached his patient's house. To her regret she found that Mrs. Drane and Miriam had driven to Thorbury. Miss Drane was upstairs at her work, and Mr. Haverley was somewhere on the place, but could easily be found. All this she learned from Mike, whom she saw outside.

"And where is the cook?"

"She's in the kitchen," said Mike.

"A good place for her," replied the old lady; "let her stay there. I will see Mr. Haverley, and I will see him out here. Go and find him and tell him I am sitting under that tree."

Ralph arrived, bright-eyed.

"Well, sir," cried the old lady, "and so you have decided to take a wife to yourself, eh?"

"Indeed I have," said he, with the air of one who had conquered a continent, and giving Miss Panney's outstretched hand a hearty shake.

"Sit down here," said she, "and tell me all about it. I suppose your soul is hungering for congratulations."

"Oh yes," he said, laughing; "they are the collateral delights which are next best to the main happiness."

"Now," said Miss Panney, "I suppose you feel quite certain that Miss Drane is a young woman who will suit your temperament and your general intellectual needs?"

"Indeed I do," cried Ralph. "She suits me in every possible way."

"And you have thoroughly investigated her character, and know that she has the well-balanced mind which will be very much wanted here, and that she has cut off and swept away all remnants of former attachments to other young men?"

Ralph twisted himself around impatiently.

"One moment," said Miss Panney, raising her hand. "And you are quite positive that she would have been willing to marry you if you had not owned this big farm; and that if you had had a dozen other girls to choose from, you still would have chosen her; and that you really think such a small person will appear well by the side of a tall fellow like you; and you are entirely convinced that you will never look around on other men's wives and wish that your wife was more like this one or that one; and that—"

"Miss Panney!" cried Ralph, "do you suppose there was ever a man in the world who thought about all those things when he really loved a woman?"

"No," said she, "I do not suppose there ever was one, and it was in the hope that such a one had at last appeared on earth that I put my questions to you."

"Well, I can answer them all in a bunch," said he; "she is exactly the wife I want, and nobody in the world would suit me as well. And if there is any one who does not think so—"

"Stop!" exclaimed Miss Panney; "your face is getting red. Never jump over a wall when there is a bottomless ditch on the other side. You might miss the ditch, but it is not likely. You are in love, and when people are that way, the straight back of a saw is parallel to every line of its teeth. Don't quarrel, and I will go on with my congratulations."

"Very queer ones they are so far, I am sure," replied Ralph, his face still flushed a little.

"Oh yes," said Miss Panney, rising, "there are a lot of queer things in this world, and I may be one of them. Now I will go and see your young lady. I do not know her very well yet, and I must make her better acquaintance."

"Miss Panney," said Ralph, quickly, "if you are going to stir her up with questions such as you put to me, I beg you will not see her."

"Boy, boy," said the old lady, "don't bubble and boil. I have a great regard for you, and care a great deal more for you than I do for her, and it is only people that I care a great deal for that I stir up. Go back to your grindstone, or whatever you were at work at, and do not worry your mind about your little Cicely. It may be that I shall like her enough to wish that I had made the match."

When Cicely accidentally met Ralph in the garden, a few hours later, she said to him that she could not have imagined that Miss Panney was such a dear old lady.

"Why, Ralph," said the girl, looking up at him with moistened eyes, "she talked to me so sweetly and gave me such good advice that I actually cried. And never before, dear Ralph, did good advice make me feel so happy that I had to cry."

And at this point the two wood doves, who had become regular detectives, actually pecked at each other in their despair of emulation.

Miss Panney's interview with Cicely had not been very long, because the old lady was anxious to see La Fleur before the doctor got there, and she went down into the kitchen, where, although she did not know it, the cook was expecting her. La Fleur's soul was in a state of turbulent triumph, but her expression was as soft as a dish of jelly.

Miss Panney sat down on the chair offered her, while the cook remained standing.

"I came down to ask you," said the old lady, "if you have heard whether Dr. Tolbridge and his wife have returned. I suppose you will be going back to them immediately."

"Oh no," said La Fleur, her eyes humbly directed toward the floor as she spoke, "at least not for a permanency. I shall get the doctor a good cook. I shall make it my business to see that she is a person fully capable of filling the position. I have my eyes on such a one. As for me, I shall stay here with my dear Miss Cicely."

"Good heavens, woman!" exclaimed Miss Panney, "your Miss Cicely isn't head of this house. What do you mean by talking in that way? Miss Haverley is mistress of this establishment. Haven't you sense enough to know that you are in her service, and that Miss Drane and her mother are merely boarders?"

Not a quiver or a shake was seen on the surface of the gentle jelly.

"Oh, of course," said La Fleur, with her head on one side, and her smile at its angle of humility, "I meant that I would come to her when she is settled here as Mrs. Haverley, and her dear mother is living with her, and when Miss Miriam has gone to finish her education at whatever seminary is decided on. Then this house will seem like my true home, and begging your pardon, madam, you cannot imagine how happy I am going to be."

"You!" exclaimed Miss Panney. "What earthly difference does it make to anybody whether you are happy or not?"

The jelly seemed to grow softer and more transparent.

"I am only a cook," said La Fleur, "but I can be as happy as persons of the highest quality, and I understand their natures very well, having lived with them. And words cannot tell you, madam, how it gladdens my old heart to think that I had so much to do myself with the good fortunes of us all, for the Dranes and me are a happy family now, and I hope may long be so, and hold together. I am sure I did everything that my humble mind could conceive, to give those two every chance of being together, and to keep other people away by discussing household matters whenever needed; for I had made up my mind that Miss Cicely and Mr. Haverley were born for each other, and if I could help them get each other, I would do it. When your telegram came, madam, it disturbed me, for I saw that it might spoil everything, by taking him away just at the time when they had nobody but each other for company, and when he was beginning to forget that he had ever been engaged to Miss Bannister, as you told me he was, madam, though I think you must have been a little mistaken, as we are all apt to be through thinking that things are as we want them to be. But I couldn't help feeling thankful that nobody but me was home when the telegram was brought without any envelope on it, and I had no chance to give it to him until it was too late to take a train that night; for the trouble the poor gentleman was in on account of his sister, being sure, of course, that something had happened to her, put him into such a doleful way that Miss Cicely gave herself up, heart and soul, to comfort him. And when a beautiful young woman does that for a young man, their hearts are sure to run together, like two eggs broken into one bowl. Now that's exactly what theirs did that night, for being so anxious about them I watched them and kept Mrs. Drane away. The very next morning when I asked her to go into the garden and pick some lettuce, and then told him where she was, he offered himself and was accepted. So you see, madam, that without boasting, or exalting myself above others, I may really claim that I made this match that I set my heart on. Although, to be sure—for I don't take away rightful credit from anybody—some of the credit is yours for having softened up their hearts with your telegram, just at the very moment when that sort of softening could be of the most use."

Miss Panney sat up very cold and severe.

"La Fleur," said she, "I thought you were a cook who prided herself on attending to her business. Since I have been sitting here, listening to your twaddle, the cat has been making herself comfortable in that pan of bread dough that you set by the fire to rise."

La Fleur turned around; her impulse was to seize a poker and rush at the cat. But she stood where she was and infused more benignity into her smile.

"Poor thing," said she, "she doesn't do any harm. There's a thick towel over the pan, and I should be ashamed of my yeast if it couldn't lift a cat."

When Miss Panney went upstairs she laughed. She did not want to laugh, but she could not help it. She had scarcely driven out of the gate when she met Dr. Tolbridge.

"A pretty trick you have played me!" he cried.

"Yes, indeed, a very pretty one," replied the old lady, pulling up her mare. "I thought you knew me better than to think that I would come here to look into this engagement business with you or anybody else. Or that I would let you get ahead of me, either. Well, I have got all the points I want, and more too, and now you can go along, and Mr. Ralph will tell you that he is the happiest man in the world, and your secretary will tell you that she is the happiest young woman, and the cook you are going to lose will vow that she is the happiest old woman, and if you stay until Mrs. Drane and Miriam come back, the one will tell you that she is the happiest middle-aged woman, and the other that she is the happiest girl, and if you give Mike a half dollar, he will tell you that he is the happiest negro in the world. Click!"

The doctor went on to Cobhurst, where Mrs. Drane and Miriam soon arrived, and he heard everything that Miss Panney told him he would hear.

CHAPTER XLIII

THE SIREN AND THE IRON

The summer, the Dranes, La Fleur, and Miriam had all left Cobhurst. The summer had gone south for an eight months' stay; the Dranes had gone to their old Pennsylvania home to settle up their affairs, and prepare for the marriage of the younger lady, which was to take place early in the coming spring; La Fleur had returned to the Tolbridges' to remain until the new Cobhurst household should be organized; and Miriam, whose association with Dora and Cicely had aroused her somewhat dormant aspirations in an educational direction, had gone to Mrs. Stone's school for the winter term.

November had come to Cobhurst, and there Ralph remained to get his farm ready for the winter, and his house in order for the bride who would come with the first young leaves. He did not regret this period of solitary bachelorhood, for not having very much money, he required a good deal of time to do what was to be done.

He had planned a good deal of refitting for the house, although not so much as to deprive it of any of those characteristics which made it dear old Cobhurst. And there were endless things to do on the farm, the most important of which, in his eyes, was the breaking of the pair of colts, which task he intended to take into his own hands. Mrs. Browning and the gig were very well in their places, but something more would be needed when the green leaves came.

Seraphina, Mike's sister, now ruled in the kitchen, but Ralph's thoughts had acquired such a habit of leaving the subject on which he was engaged and flying southward, that even when he took a meal with the Tolbridges, which happened not infrequently, he scarcely noticed the difference between their table and his own. Nothing stronger than this could be said regarding his present power of abstracting his mind from surrounding circumstances.

His income was a limited one, although it had been a good deal helped by the products of his farm, and he had to do a great deal of calculating with his pencil before he dared to order work which would oblige him to draw a check with his pen. But by thus giving two dollars' worth of thought to every dollar of expenditure, he made his money go a long way, and the lively and personal interest he took in every little improvement, made a garden fence to him of as much importance and satisfaction as a new post-office would have been to the people of Thorbury.

One day he went into a hardware store of the town to buy some nails, and there he met Miss Panney, who had just purchased a corkscrew.

"A thing you will not want for some time," she said, "for you do not look as if you needed anything to cheer your soul. Now tell me, young man, is it really the engagement rapture that has lasted all this time?"

"Oh, yes," said Ralph, laughing, "and besides that I have had all sorts of good fortune. For instance, one of my hens, setting unbeknown to anybody in a warm corner of the barn, has hatched out a dozen little chicks. Think of that at this season! I have put them in a warm room, and by the time we begin housekeeping we shall have spring chickens to eat before anybody else. And then there is that black colt, Dom Pedro. I had great doubts about him, because he showed such decided symptoms of free will, but now he is behaving beautifully. He has become thoroughly reconciled to a haycart. I have driven him in a light wagon with his sister, and he is just as good as she is, and yesterday I drove him single, and find that he has made up his mind to learn everything I can teach him. Now isn't that a fine thing?"

"Oh, yes," said Miss Panney, "it must be such things as those that make your eyes sparkle! But of course it warms your heart to give her delicate eating when she first comes to you, and to have a fine pair of horses for her to drive behind. If your face beams as it does now while she is away, it will serve as an electric light when she comes back. Good fortune! Oh, yes, of course, you consider that you have it in full measure. But we are sometimes apt to look on our friends' good fortune in an odd way. Now, if I had wanted you to go to Boston to get rich, and instead of that you had insisted on going to Nantucket, and had become rich there, I suppose that I should have been satisfied as long as you were prosperous, but I do not believe I would have been; at least, not entirely so. In this world we do want people to do what we think they ought to do."

"Yes," said Ralph, knowingly, "I see. But now, Miss Panney, don't you really think that Boston would have been too rich a place for me? That it would have expected too much of me, and that perhaps it would have done too much for me? Boston is a good enough place, but if you only knew how much lovelier Nantucket is—"

"Stop, stop, boy!" said the old lady. "I am getting so old now, that I am obliged to stop happy people and disappointed people from talking to me. If I listened to all they had to say, I should have no time for anything else. By the way, have you heard any news from the Bannister family? That sedate Herbert is going to be married, and he intends to live with his wife in the Bannister mansion."

"And how will his sister like that?" asked Ralph.

"She won't like it at all. She has told me she is going away."

"I am sorry for that," he said. "That is too bad."

"Not at all. She could not do better. A girl like that in a town such as Thorbury, with nobody to marry her but the rector, is as much out of place as a canary bird in a poultry yard. I have advised her to visit her relatives in town, and go with them to Europe, where I hope she will marry a prince. Good conscience! Look at her! Imagine that girl in a sweeping velvet robe with one great diamond blazing on her breast."

Ralph turned quickly, and as his eyes fell upon Dora, as she entered the store, it struck him that no royal gowns could make her more beautiful than she was at that moment.

"Now, my dear," said Miss Panney, "what did you come here for? Do you want a saw or a pitchfork?"

"I came," said Dora, with her most charming smile, "because I saw you two in here, and I wanted to speak to you. It is a funny place for this sort of thing, but I do not see either of you very often, now, and I thought I would like to tell you, before you heard it from any one else, of my engagement."

"To whom?" cried Miss Panney, in a voice that made the ox-chains rattle.

Dora looked around anxiously, but there was no one in the front part of the store.

"To Mr. Ames," she replied.

"The rector!" exclaimed Ralph.

"Yes," said Dora; "I want to write to Miriam about it, and do you know I have lost her address."

"Dora Bannister," interrupted Miss Panney, "it may be a little early to make bridal presents, but I want to give you this corkscrew. It is a very good one, and I think that after a while you will have need of it. Good morning."

When the old lady had abruptly departed, the two young people laughed, and Ralph offered his congratulations.

"I do not know Mr. Ames very well," he said, "but I have heard no end of good of him. But this is very surprising. It seems—"

"Seems what?" asked Dora.

"Well, since you ask me," Ralph answered, hesitating a little, "it seems odd, not, perhaps, that you should marry the rector, but that you should marry anybody. You appear to me too young to marry."

"Oh, indeed!" said Dora; "you think that?"

"I do not know that you understand me," said Ralph, "but I mean that you are so full of youth—and all that, and enjoy life so much, that it is a pity that you should not have more of youthful enjoyment before you begin any other kind."

Dora laughed.

"Truly," said she, "I never looked at the matter in that light. Perhaps I ought to have done so. You think me too young, and if you had had a chance, perhaps you would have warned me! You are so kind and so considerate, but don't you think you ought to speak to Mr. Ames about it? He does not know you very well, but he has heard no end of good of you, and perhaps what you say might make him reflect."

As she spoke she looked at him with her eyes not quite so wide open as usual. Ralph returned her gaze steadfastly.

"I know what you are thinking of," he said. "You are thinking of a fable with an animal in it and some fruit, and the animal was a small one, and the fruit was on a high trellis."

"Oh, dear," said Dora. "It must be very nice to have read as much as you have, and to know fables and all sorts of things to refer to. But my life hasn't been long enough for all that."

The more Ralph's mind dwelt upon the matter, the more dissatisfied did he feel that this beautiful young creature should marry the rector. If, in truth, she applied the fable to him, this was all the more reason why he should feel sorry for her. If anything of all this showed itself in his eyes, he did not know it, but Dora's eyes opened to their full width, and grew softer.

"I expect I surprise you," she said, "by talking to you of these things, but I have so few friends to confide in. Herbert is wrapped up in his own engagement, and Mrs. Bannister is entirely apart from me. Almost ever since I have known you two, I have felt that Miriam and you were friends with whom I could talk freely, and I am now going to tell you, and I know you will never mention it, that I do not believe I shall ever marry Mr. Ames."

"What!" exclaimed Ralph. "Didn't you say you were engaged to him?"

"Of course I said so; and I am, and I was very glad to be able to say it to Miss Panney, for she is always bothering me about such things; but the engagement is a peculiar one. Mr. Ames has been coming to see me for a long time, and I think it was because he heard that I was planning to go away that he decided to declare himself at once, before he lost his opportunity. I told him that I had never thought of anything of the sort; but he was very insistent, and at last I consented, provided the engagement should be a long one, and that, if after I had seen more of the world and knew myself better, I should decide to change my mind, I must be allowed to do so. He fought terribly against this, but there was nothing for him to do but agree, and so now we are engaged on approbation, as it were. This is a great relief to me in various ways, because I feel as if I were safely anchored, and not drifting about whichever way the wind blows, while other people are sailing where they want to; and yet, whenever I please, I can loosen my anchor, and spread my sails, and skim away over the beautiful sea."

It is seldom that a siren, leaning lightly against a bright new hay-cutter, with a background of iron rakes and hoes and spades, sings her soft song. But it was so now, and Dora, her heart beating quickly, looked from under her long lashes to note the effect of her words.

"If he will drop the little Drane," she said to herself, "I will drop the rector."

But Ralph stood looking past her. It was as plain as could be that he was not approaching the rocks; that he did not like the song; and that he was thinking what he should say about it.

"Oh, dear," said Dora, suddenly starting. "I have ever so much to do this morning, and it must be nearly noon. I wonder what made that queer Miss Panney think of giving me this corkscrew."

Ralph knew very well that the old lady meant the little implement as a figurative auxiliary of consolation, but he merely remarked that Miss Panney did and gave very queer things. He opened the door for her, and she bade him good-by and went out.

She crossed the street, and when on the opposite sidewalk, she turned her luminous eyes back upon the glass doors she had passed through.

But there was no one looking out after her. Ralph was standing at the counter, buying nails.

CHAPTER XLIV

LA FLEUR'S SOUL REVELS, AND MISS PANNEY PREPARES TO MAKE A FIRE

Cobhurst never looked more lovely than in the early June of the following year. With the beauty of the trees, the grass, the flowers, the vines, and all things natural, it possessed the added attractiveness of a certain personal equation. To all the happy dwellers therein, the dear old house appeared like one in which good people had always lived. Although they used to think that it was as charming as could be, they now perceived that the old mansion and all its surroundings had shown strong evidences of that system of management which Mike called ramshackle. No one said a word against any of the changes that Ralph had made, for in spite of them Cobhurst was still Cobhurst.

On a bench under a tree by the side of the house sat La Fleur, shelling some early spring peas, a tin basin of which she held in her lap. Mrs. Drane, in a rustic chair near by, was sewing, and Miriam, who had come laden with blossoms from the orchard, had stopped in the pleasant shade. Mike, absolutely picture-sque in a broad new straw hat, was out in the sunshine raking some grass he had cut, and Seraphina, who remained in the household as general assistant, could be seen through the open window of the kitchen.

"As I told you before, madam," said La Fleur, "I don't think you need feel the least fear about the young horses. Their master has a steady hand, and they know his voice, and as for Mrs. Haverley, she's no more afraid of them than if they were two sheep. As they drove off this afternoon, I had a feeling as if I were living with some of those great families in the old country in whose service I have been. For, said I to myself, 'Here is the young master of the house, actually going to drive out with his handsome wife and his spirited horses, and that in the very middle of the working day, and without the prospect of making a penny of profit.' You don't see that often in this country, except, perhaps, among the very, very rich who don't have to work. But it is a good sign when a gentleman like Mr. Haverley sets such an upper-toned example to his fellow young men.

"I spoke of that to Dr. Tolbridge once. 'Begging your pardon, sir,' said I, 'it seems to me that you never drive out except when you have to.' 'Which is true,' said he, 'because I have to do it so much.' 'You will excuse me, sir, for saying so,' said I, 'but if you did things for pleasure sometimes, your mind would be rested, and you would feel more like comprehending the deliciousness of some of my special dishes, which I notice you now and again say nothing about, because you are so hungry when you eat them, you don't notice their savoriness.'"

"La Fleur," said Mrs. Drane, "I am surprised that you should have spoken to the doctor in that way."

"Oh, I have a mind," said La Fleur, "and I must speak it. My mind is like a young horse—if I don't use it, it gets out of condition; and I don't fear to speak to the doctor. He has brains, and he knows I have brains, and he understands me. He said something like that when I left him, and I am sure I never could have had a night's rest since if I hadn't put a good woman there in my place. With what Mary Woodyard knows already, and with me to pop in on her whenever I can coax Michael to drive me to town, the doctor should never have need for any of his own medicines, so far as digestion goes."

"Don't you think," interpolated Miriam, "that there is a great deal more said and done about eating than the subject is worth?"

Mrs. Drane looked a little anxiously at La Fleur, but the cook did not in the least resent the remark.

"You are young yet, Miss Miriam," she said; "but when you are older, you will think more of the higher branches of education, the very topmost of which is cookery. But it's not only young people, but a good many older ones, and some of them of high station, too, who think that cooking is not a fit matter for the intellect to work on. When I lived with Lady Hartleberry, she said over and over to my lord, and me too, that she objected to the art works I sent up to the table, because she said that the human soul ought to have something better to do than to give itself up to the preparation of dishes that were no better to sustain the body than if they had been as plain as a pike-staff. But I didn't mind her; and everything that Tolati or La Fleur ever taught me, and everything I invented for myself, I did in that house. My lady was an awfully serious woman, and very particular about public worship: and on Sunday morning she used to send the butler around to every servant with a little book, and in that he put down what church each one was going to, and at what time of day they would go. But when he came to me, I always said, 'La Fleur goes to church when she likes and where she chooses.' And the butler, being a man of brains, set down any church and time that happened to suit his fancy, and my lady was never the wiser; and if I felt like going to church, I went, and if I didn't, I didn't. But when the family went to their seat in Scotland, they did not take their butler with them, and the piper was sent round on Sunday morning to find out about the servants going to church. And when he came to me, I said the same thing I had always said, and do you know that pink-headed Scotchman put it down in the book and carried it to my lady. And when she read it, she was in a great rage, to be sure, and sent for me and wanted to know what I meant by such a message. Then I told her I meant no offence by it, and that I didn't think the idiot would put it down, but that I was too old to change my ways, and that if her ladyship wasn't willing that I should keep on in them, she would have to dismiss me. And then I curtsied and left her; and my lord, when he heard of it, got a new piper. 'For,' said he, 'a fool's a dangerous thing to have in the house,' and I stayed on two years. So you see, Miss Miriam, that we are getting to the point,—even my strait-laced lady made her opinions about church-going give way before high art in her cook. For, as much as she might say against my creations and compositions, she had gotten so used to 'em, she couldn't do without 'em."

"Well," said Miriam, "I suppose when the time comes I do not like everything as I do now, I shall care more for some things. But I mustn't sit here; I must go up to my sewing."

"Miriam!" exclaimed Mrs. Drane, "what on earth are you working at? Shutting yourself up, day after day, in your room, and at hours, too, when everything is so pleasant outside. Cannot you bring out here what you are doing?"

"No," said Miriam, "because it is a secret; but it is nearly finished, and as I shall have to tell you about it very soon, I may as well do it now: I have been altering Judith Pacewalk's teaberry gown for Cicely. It was altered once for me, and that makes it all the harder to make it fit her now. I am not very good at that sort of thing, and so it has taken me a long time. I expected to have it ready for her when she came back from the wedding trip, but I could not do it. I shall finish it to-day, however, and to-morrow I am going to invest her with it. She is now the head of the house, and it is she who should wear the teaberry gown. Don't tell her, please, until to-morrow; I thought it would be nice to have a little ceremony about it, and in that case I shall have to have some one to help me."

"It is very good of you, my dear," said Mrs. Drane, "to think of such a thing, and Cicely and your brother will be delighted, I know, to find out what you think of this change of administration. Ralph said to me the other day that he was afraid you were not altogether happy in yielding your place to another. He had noticed that you had gotten into the habit of going off by yourself."

Miriam laughed.

"Just wait until he hears the beautiful speech I am going to make to-morrow, and then he will see what a wise fellow he is."

"Mrs. Drane! Miss Miriam!" exclaimed La Fleur, her face beginning to glow with emotion; "let me help to make this a grand occasion. Let me get up a beautiful lunch. There isn't much time, it is true, but I can do it. I'll make Michael drive me to town early in the morning, and I'll have everything ready in time. A dinner would be all very well, but a luncheon gives so much better chance to the imagination and the intellect. There're some things you have to have at a dinner, but at a lunch there is nothing you are obliged to have, and nothing you may not have if you want it. And if you don't mind, I'd like you to ask old Miss Panney. I've been a good deal at odds with her since I have known her, but I'm satisfied now, and if there is anything I can do to make her satisfied, I'm more than ready. Besides, when I do get up anything extraordinary in the way of a meal, I like to have people at the table who can appreciate it. And as for that, I haven't met anybody in this country who is as well grounded in good eating as that old lady is."

Her proposition gladly agreed to, La Fleur rose to a high heaven of excited delight. She had had no chance to show her skill in a wedding breakfast, for the young couple had been married very quietly in Pennsylvania, and she was now elated with the idea of exhibiting her highest abilities in an Investiture Luncheon.

She handed the basin of peas through the open window to Seraphina, and retired to her room, to study, to plan, and to revel in flights of epicurean fancy.

"Mike," said Seraphina to her brother, who was now raking the grass near the kitchen window, "did you hear dat ar ole cook a talkin' jes' now?"

"No," said Mike, "I hain't got no time to harken to people talkin', 'cept they're talkin' to me, an' it 'pends on who they is whether I listens then or not."

"That fool thinks she made this world," said Seraphina. "I've been thinkin' she had some notion like dat. She do put on such a'rs."

"Git out," said Mike. "You never heard her say nothing like that."

"I didn't hear all she said," replied the colored woman, "but I heard more'n 'nough, an' I heard her talkin' about her creation. Her creation indeed! I'll let her know one thing; she didn't make me."

"Now look a here, Seraphiny," said Mike; "the more you shet up now, now you's in the prime of life, the gooder you'll feel when you gits old. An' so long as Mrs. Flower makes them thar three-inch-deep pies for me, I don't care who she thinks she made, an' who she thinks she didn't make. Thar now, that's my opinion."

* * * * *

The Investiture Luncheon, at which the Tolbridges and Miss Panney were present, was truly a grand and beautiful affair, to which Dora would certainly have been invited had she not been absent on her bridal trip with Mr. Ames. Seldom had La Fleur or either of her husbands prepared for prince, ambassador, or titled gourmand a meal which better satisfied the loftiest outreaches of the soul in the truest interests of the palate.

Cicely appeared in the teaberry gown, and if the spirit of

Judith Pacewalk hovered o'er the scene, and allowed its gaze to wander from the charming bride, over the happy faces of the rest of the company, to the half-open door of the dining-room, where shone the radiant face of the proudest cook in the world, it must have been as well satisfied with the fate of the pink garment as it could possibly expect to be.

It was late in the afternoon when the luncheon party broke up, and although Miss Panney was the last guest to leave, she did not go home, but drove herself to Thorbury, and tied her roan mare in front of the office of Mr. Herbert Bannister. When the young lawyer looked up and perceived his visitor, he heaved a sigh, for he had expected in a few moments to lock up his desk, and stop, on his way home, at the house of his lady love. But the presence of Miss Panney at his office meant business, and business with her meant a protracted session. Miss Panney did not notice the sigh, and if she had, it would not have affected her. Her soul had been satisfied this day, and no trifle could disturb her serenity.

"Now what I want," said she, after a good deal of prefatory remark, "is for you to give me my will. I want to alter it."

"But, madam," said young Bannister, when he had heard the alterations desired by Miss Panney, "is not this a little quixotic? Excuse me for saying so. Mr. Haverley is not even related to you, and you are bestowing upon him—"

"Herbert Bannister," said the old lady, "if you were your father instead of yourself, you would know that this young man ought to have been my grandson. He isn't; but I choose to consider him as such, and as such I shall leave him what will make him a worthy lord of Cobhurst. Bring me the new will as soon as it is ready and bring also the old one, with all the papers I have given you, from time to time, regarding the disposition of my property. I shall burn them, every one, and although it may set the Wittons' chimney on fire the conflagration will make me happy."

Choose from Thousands of 1stWorldLibrary Classics By

A. M. Barnard
Ada Leverson
Adolphus William Ward
Aesop
Agatha Christie
Alexander Aaronsohn
Alexander Kielland
Alexandre Dumas
Alfred Gatty
Alfred Ollivant
Alice Duer Miller
Alice Turner Curtis
Alice Dunbar
Allen Chapman
Alleyne Ireland
Ambrose Bierce
Amelia E. Barr
Amory H. Bradford
Andrew Lang
Andrew McFarland Davis
Andy Adams
Angela Brazil
Anna Alice Chapin
Anna Sewell
Annie Besant
Annie Hamilton Donnell
Annie Payson Call
Annie Roe Carr
Annonaymous
Anton Chekhov
Archibald Lee Fletcher
Arnold Bennett
Arthur C. Benson
Arthur Conan Doyle
Arthur M. Winfield
Arthur Ransome
Arthur Schnitzler
Arthur Train
Atticus
B.H. Baden-Powell
B. M. Bower
B. C. Chatterjee
Baroness Emmuska Orczy
Baroness Orczy
Basil King
Bayard Taylor
Ben Macomber
Bertha Muzzy Bower
Bjornstjerne Bjornson

Booth Tarkington
Boyd Cable
Bram Stoker
C. Collodi
C. E. Orr
C. M. Ingleby
Carolyn Wells
Catherine Parr Traill
Charles A. Eastman
Charles Amory Beach
Charles Dickens
Charles Dudley Warner
Charles Farrar Browne
Charles Ives
Charles Kingsley
Charles Klein
Charles Hanson Towne
Charles Lathrop Pack
Charles Romyn Dake
Charles Whibley
Charles Willing Beale
Charlotte M. Braeme
Charlotte M. Yonge
Charlotte Perkins Stetson
Clair W. Hayes
Clarence Day Jr.
Clarence E. Mulford
Clemence Housman
Confucius
Coningsby Dawson
Cornelis DeWitt Wilcox
Cyril Burleigh
D. H. Lawrence
Daniel Defoe
David Garnett
Dinah Craik
Don Carlos Janes
Donald Keyhoe
Dorothy Kilner
Dougan Clark
Douglas Fairbanks
E. Nesbit
E. P. Roe
E. Phillips Oppenheim
E. S. Brooks
Earl Barnes
Edgar Rice Burroughs
Edith Van Dyne
Edith Wharton

Edward Everett Hale
Edward J. O'Biren
Edward S. Ellis
Edwin L. Arnold
Eleanor Atkins
Eleanor Hallowell Abbott
Eliot Gregory
Elizabeth Gaskell
Elizabeth McCracken
Elizabeth Von Arnim
Ellem Key
Emerson Hough
Emilie F. Carlen
Emily Bronte
Emily Dickinson
Enid Bagnold
Enilor Macartney Lane
Erasmus W. Jones
Ernie Howard Pie
Ethel May Dell
Ethel Turner
Ethel Watts Mumford
Eugene Sue
Eugenie Foa
Eugene Wood
Eustace Hale Ball
Evelyn Everett-green
Everard Cotes
F. H. Cheley
F. J. Cross
F. Marion Crawford
Fannie E. Newberry
Federick Austin Ogg
Ferdinand Ossendowski
Fergus Hume
Florence A. Kilpatrick
Fremont B. Deering
Francis Bacon
Francis Darwin
Frances Hodgson Burnett
Frances Parkinson Keyes
Frank Gee Patchin
Frank Harris
Frank Jewett Mather
Frank L. Packard
Frank V. Webster
Frederic Stewart Isham
Frederick Trevor Hill
Frederick Winslow Taylor

Friedrich Kerst
Friedrich Nietzsche
Fyodor Dostoyevsky
G.A. Henty
G.K. Chesterton
Gabrielle E. Jackson
Garrett P. Serviss
Gaston Leroux
George A. Warren
George Ade
Geroge Bernard Shaw
George Cary Eggleston
George Durston
George Ebers
George Eliot
George Gissing
George MacDonald
George Meredith
George Orwell
George Sylvester Viereck
George Tucker
George W. Cable
George Wharton James
Gertrude Atherton
Gordon Casserly
Grace E. King
Grace Gallatin
Grace Greenwood
Grant Allen
Guillermo A. Sherwell
Gulielma Zollinger
Gustav Flaubert
H. A. Cody
H. B. Irving
H.C. Bailey
H. G. Wells
H. H. Munro
H. Irving Hancock
H. R. Naylor
H. Rider Haggard
H. W. C. Davis
Haldeman Julius
Hall Caine
Hamilton Wright Mabie
Hans Christian Andersen
Harold Avery
Harold McGrath
Harriet Beecher Stowe
Harry Castlemon
Harry Coghill
Harry Houidini

Hayden Carruth
Helent Hunt Jackson
Helen Nicolay
Hendrik Conscience
Hendy David Thoreau
Henri Barbusse
Henrik Ibsen
Henry Adams
Henry Ford
Henry Frost
Henry James
Henry Jones Ford
Henry Seton Merriman
Henry W Longfellow
Herbert A. Giles
Herbert Carter
Herbert N. Casson
Herman Hesse
Hildegard G. Frey
Homer
Honore De Balzac
Horace B. Day
Horace Walpole
Horatio Alger Jr.
Howard Pyle
Howard R. Garis
Hugh Lofting
Hugh Walpole
Humphry Ward
Ian Maclaren
Inez Haynes Gillmore
Irving Bacheller
Isabel Cecilia Williams
Isabel Hornibrook
Israel Abrahams
Ivan Turgenev
J.G.Austin
J. Henri Fabre
J. M. Barrie
J. M. Walsh
J. Macdonald Oxley
J. R. Miller
J. S. Fletcher
J. S. Knowles
J. Storer Clouston
J. W. Duffield
Jack London
Jacob Abbott
James Allen
James Andrews
James Baldwin

James Branch Cabell
James DeMille
James Joyce
James Lane Allen
James Lane Allen
James Oliver Curwood
James Oppenheim
James Otis
James R. Driscoll
Jane Abbott
Jane Austen
Jane L. Stewart
Janet Aldridge
Jens Peter Jacobsen
Jerome K. Jerome
Jessie Graham Flower
John Buchan
John Burroughs
John Cournos
John F. Kennedy
John Gay
John Glasworthy
John Habberton
John Joy Bell
John Kendrick Bangs
John Milton
John Philip Sousa
John Taintor Foote
Jonas Lauritz Idemil Lie
Jonathan Swift
Joseph A. Altsheler
Joseph Carey
Joseph Conrad
Joseph E. Badger Jr
Joseph Hergesheimer
Joseph Jacobs
Jules Vernes
Julian Hawthrone
Julie A Lippmann
Justin Huntly McCarthy
Kakuzo Okakura
Karle Wilson Baker
Kate Chopin
Kenneth Grahame
Kenneth McGaffey
Kate Langley Bosher
Kate Langley Bosher
Katherine Cecil Thurston
Katherine Stokes
L. A. Abbot
L. T. Meade

L. Frank Baum
Latta Griswold
Laura Dent Crane
Laura Lee Hope
Laurence Housman
Lawrence Beasley
Leo Tolstoy
Leonid Andreyev
Lewis Carroll
Lewis Sperry Chafer
Lilian Bell
Lloyd Osbourne
Louis Hughes
Louis Joseph Vance
Louis Tracy
Louisa May Alcott
Lucy Fitch Perkins
Lucy Maud Montgomery
Luther Benson
Lydia Miller Middleton
Lyndon Orr
M. Corvus
M. H. Adams
Margaret E. Sangster
Margret Howth
Margaret Vandercook
Margaret W. Hungerford
Margret Penrose
Maria Edgeworth
Maria Thompson Daviess
Mariano Azuela
Marion Polk Angellotti
Mark Overton
Mark Twain
Mary Austin
Mary Catherine Crowley
Mary Cole
Mary Hastings Bradley
Mary Roberts Rinehart
Mary Rowlandson
M. Wollstonecraft Shelley
Maud Lindsay
Max Beerbohm
Myra Kelly
Nathaniel Hawthrone
Nicolo Machiavelli
O. F. Walton
Oscar Wilde

Owen Johnson
P.G. Wodehouse
Paul and Mabel Thorne
Paul G. Tomlinson
Paul Severing
Percy Brebner
Percy Keese Fitzhugh
Peter B. Kyne
Plato
Quincy Allen
R. Derby Holmes
R. L. Stevenson
R. S. Ball
Rabindranath Tagore
Rahul Alvares
Ralph Bonehill
Ralph Henry Barbour
Ralph Victor
Ralph Waldo Emmerson
Rene Descartes
Ray Cummings
Rex Beach
Rex E. Beach
Richard Harding Davis
Richard Jefferies
Richard Le Gallienne
Robert Barr
Robert Frost
Robert Gordon Anderson
Robert L. Drake
Robert Lansing
Robert Lynd
Robert Michael Ballantyne
Robert W. Chambers
Rosa Nouchette Carey
Rudyard Kipling
Saint Augustine
Samuel B. Allison
Samuel Hopkins Adams
Sarah Bernhardt
Sarah C. Hallowell
Selma Lagerlof
Sherwood Anderson
Sigmund Freud
Standish O'Grady
Stanley Weyman
Stella Benson
Stella M. Francis

Stephen Crane
Stewart Edward White
Stijn Streuvels
Swami Abhedananda
Swami Parmananda
T. S. Ackland
T. S. Arthur
The Princess Der Ling
Thomas A. Janvier
Thomas A Kempis
Thomas Anderton
Thomas Bailey Aldrich
Thomas Bulfinch
Thomas De Quincey
Thomas Dixon
Thomas H. Huxley
Thomas Hardy
Thomas More
Thornton W. Burgess
U. S. Grant
Upton Sinclair
Valentine Williams
Various Authors
Vaughan Kester
Victor Appleton
Victor G. Durham
Victoria Cross
Virginia Woolf
Wadsworth Camp
Walter Camp
Walter Scott
Washington Irving
Wilbur Lawton
Wilkie Collins
Willa Cather
Willard F. Baker
William Dean Howells
William le Queux
W. Makepeace Thackeray
William W. Walter
William Shakespeare
Winston Churchill
Yei Theodora Ozaki
Yogi Ramacharaka
Young E. Allison
Zane Grey

www.ingramcontent.com/pod-product-compliance
Lightning Source LLC
Chambersburg PA
CBHW020258030726
47499CB00001B/252